DW

Patricia Scanlan was born in Dublin, where she still lives. Her books have sold worldwide and have been translated into many languages. Patricia is the series editor and a contributing author to the *Open Door* series. She also teaches creative writing to second-level students and is involved in Adult Literacy.

Find out more by visiting Patricia Scanlan on Facebook.

Also by Patricia Scanlan

Apartment 3B
Finishing Touches
Foreign Affairs
Promises, Promises
Mirror Mirror
Francesca's Party
Two for Joy
Double Wedding
Divided Loyalties
Coming Home

Trilogies

City Girl
City Lives
City Woman

Forgive and Forget
Happy Ever After
Love and Marriage
With All My Love
A Time for Friends

Patricia
SCANLAN

City Lives

SIMON &
SCHUSTER

London · New York · Sydney · Toronto · New Delhi

A CBS COMPANY

First published in Ireland by Poolbeg Press, 1999
This paperback edition published by Simon & Schuster UK Ltd, 2015
A CBS COMPANY

1 3 5 7 9 10 8 6 4 2

Simon & Schuster UK Ltd
1st Floor
222 Gray's Inn Road
London WC1X 8HB

www.simonandschuster.co.uk

Simon & Schuster Australia, Sydney
Simon & Schuster India, New Delhi

A CIP catalogue record for this book
is available from the British Library

PB ISBN: 978-1-47116-321-0
EBOOK ISBN: 978-1-47114-116-4

Printed and bound by CPI Group (UK) Ltd, Croydon, CR0 4YY

ACKNOWLEDGEMENTS

May your love be upon us O Lord,
as we place all our hope in you. (Psalm 33).

Thank you, Lord for the love that surrounds me.

There were many joyful and loving moments during the writing of this book, especially when the final chapter was completed. I am so blessed with the love and friendship of such wonderful family and friends, I could write a *book* of acknowledgements!
Special thanks:
To my mother and father who give such love and support.
To Mary and Henry and Yvonne and Donald who kept me going right through and who fed and watered me in Wicklow and wouldn't let me do any washing-up either, so as not to keep me from the computer!
To Dermot who's always getting me out of fixes, and to Catherine who never minds.
To Paul and Lucy and Hugh and Rose, always supportive and encouraging.
To Fiona, Caitriona, Patrick, Laura, Rebecca, and Tara and to Miss Rachel Bellew who has all of us wrapped around her little finger. I'm so lucky to have such beautiful nieces and a very special nephew.
To Maureen, a very dear godmother.

🍎🍎🍎

To the friends who are always there.
To Breda Purdue . . . what giggles we've had. And loads more to come. Everyone should have a Breda in their life. Dear Breda, thanks for everything.
To Sarah Lutyens, Felicity Rubinstein, and Susannah Godman, my three adopted sisters. The good times came, and we're having fun. For all the love and encouragement you send winging my way a million thanks. I'm really looking forward to our next 'posh' lunch.
To Francesca Liversidge, a *wonderful* editor. It's been a joy to work with you and an even greater joy to know that you're a real friend. I'm so lucky. I bet it's not every author who has editing sessions in Fortnum & Mason!! Here's to the next one.
To Annette Tallon . . . a very honest, courageous and special lady.
To Deirdre Purcell . . . a super talented woman who gives so much to everyone and not enough to herself.
To Anne Schulman, thanks for all the encouragement and especially for the lovely letter that came at just the right time.
To Geraldine Crowley and Helen and Brenda for coming to my rescue. It was the best photocopied manuscript, ever.

To Margaret Daly. We still have to have our 'elbows on the table' lunch!

To Jo O'Donoghue my first editor who was with me for *City Girl* and *City Woman*. For all that you taught me, Jo, and for being a great editor. Thanks.

To Debbie Sheehy. I want an acknowledgement in *your* book. Keep writing!!!

To Anne Jensen who helped more than she will ever know. Dear Anne may your life be full of joy.

To Catherine MacLiam. A great art teacher and a very talented artist. Thanks for all the happy hours and for all the scrumptious lunches.

To Sheila O'Flanagan. Hang in there, Sheila, good times are coming and what a celebration we will have!!

To Chris Green. Thanks for the hug, just when I needed it most.

To Gareth O'Callaghan, Cathy Kelly, Marian Keyes, Lia Mills, Louise Cooper, Anne Wiley and Aoibhinn Hogan, for all the Keep-in-Touch phonecalls.

🍎🍎🍎

To the Shy Man who won't let me write his name. You're a joy and a blessing in my life.

To Alil O Shaughnessy . . . it was a *terrific* prescription! You're a pal.

To Tony Kavanagh who gets told everything whether he likes it or not. Thanks for being a great mate.

To Kieran Connolly . . . Now I have seen . . . What can I say? I'm speechless!! It was awesome!!!!!

To Dr Frankie Fine. We have great laughs. You're the best!

To Peter Orford. For a great kindness during a difficult time.

To the *very* busy Michael McLoughlin for deigning to ring now and again.

🍎🍎🍎

To all in Transworld, I'd love to thank everyone by name. But you all know how much I appreciate and value your kindness. It's a pleasure and fun to be part of the 'family'.

To all my friends in the book trade. You know who you are. Thanks for all the support.

To Nikki, Jean, Pauline, Louise, and Laura, in Nikki's Hair Studio. Thanks for all the kindness.

To all in Mac's Gym who *try* and keep me on my toes.

To Eileen and Carmel in Kilbride Post Office for being so helpful.

To Catherine, John, Jennifer, Anthony, Alison, Gillian, Emma, Lorna, and Ryan . . . the Wicklow gang.

To my friends in Massey butchers in Ballygall who want to call my next novel 'Strip Loin'. 'Himself' loved the steak!

To everyone who buys and enjoys my novels. Thank you.

To my Anam Cara,
who gave me the most Perfect Day of my life.
I would never have written this book
without him.

Never stop trying to succeed. It's always the last key that opens the lock.

Nancy Woods

One

DEVLIN

Devlin Delaney's hands shook as she took the slim wand from its packet. In a few minutes she'd know if her dearest wish was to be granted. To be pregnant with Luke's baby would make her happy beyond belief.

Her blue eyes darkened in sadness. How different this was from when she'd first thought she was pregnant all those years ago. How frightened she'd been. So young and naïve and single. Deluding herself that her boss and seducer, the eminent and respected gynaecologist Colin Cantrell-King, loved her and would stand by her. That had been a forlorn wish. Colin had packed her off to an abortion clinic in England.

Devlin shivered as she remembered her desperation and fear in that place, all the doubts and anxieties that had beset her. She'd felt as though she was swimming in the darkest, thickest fog . . . alone. And then the morning she was due to have the termination she'd simply packed her bags and walked out of the clinic and never looked back.

Her baby, Lynn, the greatest joy of her life, had changed her from a spoilt, rather selfish young woman to one who took responsibility for her actions and in the process became caring, strong and motivated.

Devlin swallowed and tears blurred her eyes. Her baby's death in a car crash had quenched her spirit so completely that she'd thought she'd never climb out of the darkness.

But then Luke had come into her life, sent to her like a guardian angel. They'd gone into business, created the luxurious City Girl health and leisure complex, and, in the process, fallen in love and married. Luke was her rock. The greatest blessing in her life. And he was waiting anxiously in the bedroom to know if he was going to be a father.

She wiped her eyes and did the test. It wasn't fair to dawdle. She slipped the wand into her dressing-gown pocket. He was standing by the bedroom window looking out towards the twinkling lights of Howth when she padded in to him and slipped an arm around his waist.

He dropped an arm around her shoulder and smiled down at her.

'How long do we have to wait?'

'Just another minute or so. My heart's thumping so fast I can almost hear it.'

'Mine too.'

'Are you sure this is what you want, Luke?' Devlin stared up into her husband's amber eyes, searching for reassurance.

'Of course it's what I want, Devlin. More than anything. As long as you're happy about it.'

'Oh Luke, I want your baby so much. I've always hoped this day would come. I can't believe it. It's a bit like a dream.'

'It's no dream. You keep seducing me against my

will. You're a nymphomaniac. I'm not safe anywhere. It was bound to happen.'

'Stop it, you. Be serious.' Devlin giggled.

'I *am* serious,' he protested. 'Very serious. I mean, Devlin, jumping me in the lift . . . if your public saw you. And what about the time we went for a walk down in Wicklow and you—'

'Stop it. You're as bad. Remember the time at the airport?'

They smiled and wrapped their arms around each other, happier than they'd ever been.

'But we'll have to decide where we're going to live. London or Dublin. And I'd like a house with a garden. Apartments are no places to raise children.' Devlin's brow furrowed.

Luke laughed. 'Will you stop panicking, Delaney. You're an awful woman for jumping the gun. We don't even know if you *are* pregnant yet. Let me see that thing.'

Devlin took the wand from her pocket. They glanced down at it together.

'Oh my God!' he exclaimed. 'It's blue! It's blue! Devlin, we're pregnant! We're pregnant!'

'Oh Luke, you idiot.' Devlin was half laughing, half crying as he swept her up in his arms and hugged the daylights out of her again.

'I think I'll do another one just to be sure,' she murmured, rubbing her nose against his.

'I've a better idea,' Luke grinned as he carried her over to the bed. 'Let's make sure, sure.'

'I forgot I'd married a genius . . . and you call *me* a nymphomaniac.'

'Well, you couldn't call *me* one,' Luke teased and Devlin burst out laughing.

13

'I love you. I really, really love you,' she whispered.

'I love you too, Devlin, with all my heart.'

Devlin drew him down to her and kissed her husband soundly.

Afterwards, drowsy, replete, and utterly content, Devlin lay cradled in Luke's arms. 'It just gets better and better,' she murmured.

'Yeah!' Luke smiled down at her.

'What would you prefer, boy or girl?' Devlin snuggled closer.

'I don't mind. I just can't believe that I'm going to be a father. Let's not ask when you go for your scan. Let's have a surprise.' He gently stroked the softness of her still-flat belly. 'Are you all right about the baby, Devlin? I mean I'm sure it's going to bring back memories of Lynn. Promise me you won't keep it all bottled in. Share it all with me, won't you?'

'I had a little cry in the loo, when I was doing the test,' she confessed. 'I was just thinking how joyful this is and how devastated I was when I discovered I was pregnant with Lynn. And then how happy I was when she was born. She was a beautiful baby, Luke.'

'I know she was. How could she not be with you as her mother,' Luke said gently. 'And this baby isn't a replacement for Lynn. No-one will ever replace that precious little child for you. So if you get a bit down, please don't hide it from me. Promise.'

'I promise, Luke. But I want this to be a good time for you.' Devlin took his face in her hands and smiled at him.

'All my times with you are good times,' Luke said

huskily as he lowered his head and kissed her passionately.

Later, Luke made tea and toasted-cheese sandwiches and they sat snuggled up in front of the fire eating their supper.

'Will you still think I'm sexy when I'm waddling around with a big bump?' Devlin asked.

'I'll always think you're sexy,' Luke assured her. 'I even think you're sexy with a big dribble of butter and melted cheese running down your chin. Here.' He handed her a napkin.

'You're such a brat, Luke Reilly.' Devlin wiped her chin. 'I'm looking for reassurance here. When I was pregnant with Lynn I was like an elephant.'

'Does this mean I'm in danger of being *squashed* if you jump on me in lifts, or wrestle me to the ground under oak trees in the country? Is my life in danger?' Luke stared at her in pretend horror.

'Oh Luke!' Devlin laughed.

'Devlin, honestly I don't care what you look like. I love you. I'm delighted you're pregnant. I'll go to classes and decorate nurseries and do whatever you want. I just want to be with you and share every moment of this with you and I want it to be the happiest time of your life.' Luke reached over to her and took her face between his hands.

Devlin promptly burst into tears.

Luke looked horrified. 'For God's sake, what's wrong?'

'I'm just so happy,' she sniffed. 'Don't mind me, it's my hormones.'

'Oh God! I'd forgotten about *The Hormones*.' Luke smote his forehead. 'Are pregnancy hormones worse than PMT ones?'

'A hundred times worse,' Devlin assured him, half laughing, half crying.

'Interesting times ahead, so.' Luke raised an eyebrow. 'But don't worry, I'll cope. I'm made of stern stuff. Do you want another sanger, now that you're eating for two?'

'Oh yeah, I'm ravenous,' Devlin declared.

'OK, sit there and put your feet up. One Reilly special coming up.' Luke kissed the top of her head and departed to the kitchen.

Devlin sat in the fire's dancing shadows and watched the flames flickering up the chimney. Scented candles cast a gentle glow around the room. Enya, soft and soothing, sang in the background. Peace enveloped her. How lucky she was. When this baby was born her life would be perfect. She'd have everything she'd ever wanted. Was it possible to experience perfect happiness? Right now Devlin knew she'd never been as happy in all her life. She was so happy she was almost afraid. The griefs and sorrows of her past were a constant reminder that what was given could also be taken away.

Don't think like that, she chided herself silently. Live in the now, wasn't that what it was all about? One of the beauty therapists at City Girl, who specialized in aromatherapy and reflexology, had a little poster in her room that always comforted Devlin.

The past is gone, to be no more
Tomorrow may never come
Enjoy today and be at peace
And you and God are one.

'Enjoy today and be at peace,' she whispered to herself as she rubbed her hand gently over her tummy, longing for the moment when she would feel the first faint flutterings of life.

Two

CAROLINE

It would probably be one of the last public functions they would appear at together, Caroline reflected somewhat sadly as she lightly tipped a mascara brush to her eyelashes. She'd be giving up her envied status as wife to one of Dublin's most successful lawyers.

Big brown eyes stared back at her from the mirror. She could see the fear in them. Divorce was very final. She was, as she had always feared, going to be on her own. It wasn't as if Richard was even going to be living in Dublin. He was moving to Boston, bag and baggage.

Even though in the last few years they'd lived together in the apartment like flatmates, not husband and wife, she'd miss the companionship. She'd miss knowing there was someone to come home to.

Caroline squeezed a little gel onto her fingers and ran them through her short inky-black hair. How ironic to think that she had a better marriage now than she'd had all those years ago when Richard had battered her black and blue, and made her feel completely worthless and utterly unattractive. It was only when she'd found out that he was gay, and she had dragged herself up from the pits of alcoholism, that they had become friends. Those years had been a nightmare she thought she'd never survive. But she had. She'd grown strong and more self-reliant

Why, then, did the knowledge that he was going cause those feared, fluttery panicky little butterflies to dance tangos in her stomach? Would that fear ever leave her? The fear of aloneness. Why was she so terrified that she couldn't hack it? She'd gone off to Abu Dhabi on her own to work for six months. She'd lived in an apartment on her own for another four until Richard had begged her to come back home, because he was so lonely after his mentor and lover Charles Stokes had died.

Soft-hearted as always, Caroline had done as he'd asked. And they'd lived together since then. It had been a mistake, she reflected ruefully as she sprayed White Linen on her neck and wrists. She'd got used to being with someone once more. She was going to have to face being alone, yet again. It was a daunting prospect. Life alone didn't seem so bad in your twenties. In your mid-thirties it was little short of scary.

'Caro, will you fix this damned dickey bow for me.' Richard knocked perfunctorily on her bedroom door and strode in, the offending article dangling from his fingers.

'You'd think one of the hundred most influential men in Ireland would surely be able to tie his own bow-tie,' Caroline said dryly. Her husband had made the much coveted placing in *Icon*, Ireland's glossiest of glossy, trendiest of trendy, monthly magazine. A cocktail party was being held in the Clarence in celebration and already there was fierce controversy – among those who took such things seriously – about the inclusions and exclusions. Subscriptions to *Icon*

19

had already suffered a loss from very miffed personages who had expected to feature and hadn't. Outraged wives and mistresses had gone batting for excluded spouses and lovers. The feathers were flying among the jet set of the city.

Richard was very pleased at his inclusion. He'd never lost his vanity in such matters. What would everyone think when he put his hugely successful practice on the market? The gossips would have a field day, especially when news of the divorce leaked out. Caroline dreaded it. It had been bad enough when they'd separated the first time. The social columnists had had a ball. She deftly arranged the black silky material into a perfectly shaped bow at Richard's throat. 'There. It's fine.'

'You know we don't have to get a divorce if you don't want to, Caroline.' Richard took her hand. 'We can just say we're separating. I won't be getting married again,' he added with a wry smile.

'I can't be tied to your apron strings for ever, Richard. It's better this way. We can both make a fresh start. It's something I really want to do.'

'Has it been so awful?' he asked a little defensively.

'It's not ideal, Richard. It's not a real life. You'll have your life in Boston. I'll have my life here and at least we'll always be friends. Now let's put our best foot forward and get on with it.'

'If you say so.' Richard sighed.

'I do,' Caroline said, very firmly.

He held her coat for her and they walked out of the apartment in silence, lost in their own thoughts.

Three

MAGGIE

Maggie Ryan cursed long and loudly as the pot of mushy peas boiled over on the hob. Pressing the save key, she jumped up from her laptop and hurried over to wipe up the offensive green frothy mess.

'Blast Terry and his mushy peas,' she muttered crossly as she burned the tip of her finger.

The phone rang. In the background she could hear the children squabbling upstairs. Her head was beginning to pound.

'Hello?' Her tone held a trace of impatience.

Her mother's agitated voice came down the line. 'Maggie, do you think you could come tomorrow? The parish harvest fête is on and your father's got gout. I need someone to give him his dinner and tea because I'll be gone all day.'

Maggie's jaw dropped. Go to Wicklow for the day? She'd planned to finish chapter ten tomorrow, and besides, the children had swimming in the morning.

'It's not really very convenient, Mam. Couldn't you make any other arrangements?' she asked, trying to hide her irritation.

'Don't you think I would have, if I could. And then I wouldn't have had to *bother* you,' her mother snapped.

Oh no, don't let her get into a huff. Maggie gave a silent groan. Nelsie's huffs were legendary.

'I should have known, of course. You're always up to your eyes these days now that you're a *famous author*.' The last was said with dripping sarcasm. 'But I thought you might be able to oblige me. It's not much I ask of you, God knows.' Nelsie gave a martyred sniff.

Maggie's fingers curled in her palms. Were all mothers like this or just hers?

'Well if you can't come down I'll just have to miss the fête and that's the end of it. I'll go, Maggie, and not take up any more of your time.'

'Hold on, Mother,' Maggie ordered. 'Look, I'll give Terry a ring just to make sure he's got nothing on tomorrow, and I'll phone you back and make the arrangements.'

'Sure what would he be doing tomorrow, it's Saturday? Call me as soon as you can – I need to let Brona Kelly know what time I can do a stall at. Oh and if you're coming down would you be able to get me a couple of those sponges out of the bakery in Superquinn. They're very tasty and I could bring them with me for our cup of tea. Thanks, Maggie. I have to go. I see Mrs Keegan coming up the drive. Bye bye.'

Maggie heard the click of the receiver and shook her head as she stared at the phone. Her mother was really something else. The thoughts of going to Superquinn again when she'd only done a big shop there this morning made her want to scream. Superquinn on Friday night was not for the faint-hearted.

Maggie knew full well why her mother wanted

22

Superquinn sponges. They were so tasty, she was going to pass them off as her own. She'd been doing it for years. Every time she came to visit Maggie or Maggie went to visit her, Nelsie always made sure to get a couple of sponges. There was no Superquinn in Wicklow so the Ladies' Club never knew the difference. And all were agreed that Nelsie McNamara had a very light touch with the sponges, even though she didn't make them that often.

Maggie dialled her husband's mobile. It was handier than ringing the office and being put through by his secretary. Maybe going to Wicklow wasn't as bad as it seemed. Thinking about it, if she brought her laptop with her she could get some work done in peace and quiet. The trip to Wicklow might turn out to be a blessing in disguise after all. The traffic shouldn't be too bad, she'd be there in little over an hour. She could spend four or five hours writing with no children demanding attention. Her father would be content to watch sport on TV.

'Where are you?' she muttered. The phone was ringing away. It would go into divert soon.

'Yep?' Terry sounded crusty.

'Hi, it's me. I've just had a call from Ma. She needs me to go down to Wicklow tomorrow. Dad's sick and she has to go to the harvest fête. Can you bring the kids swimming in the morning? I'll cook a lasagne tonight so that all you'll have to do then is pop it in the microwave tomorrow.'

'Maggie, I've arranged to play golf with John Dolan, he's a big client. It's important. And I'll be taking him to lunch. You'll have to bring the kids with you.'

'This is the third Saturday in a row that you've

been out playing golf all day. It's not fair, Terry. I'm trying to get a novel written. I have the kids all week and the least you could do is be here at the weekends,' Maggie protested. If she had to bring her three children to Wicklow with her she'd get nothing done. And she'd be delayed leaving. That would mean Nelsie would have to wait in for her.

'Do you think I enjoy going around a golf course listening to John Dolan wittering in my ear?' Terry asked irascibly. 'It's not a day out for me, Maggie. It's work.'

Maggie had heard that one before.

'Yeah, yeah,' she snapped. 'I'll see you later. Bye.' She slammed the phone down. Typical of Terry. She should have known better. How she wished they'd never got back together again after his affair with Ria Kirby. Her husband was a constant source of disappointment to her.

They'd reunited for the sake of the children and initially he'd made an effort, but gradually he'd slipped back into his old selfish ways and Maggie had lost heart.

Was it so much to ask? A bit of support. A sharing of the domestic workload. Taking responsibility for being a parent. Why was it all left to her? Why did Terry not see her as an equal? Why was his career and his well-being more important than hers? Why could he not be more like Luke Reilly?

Maggie sighed. A deep, depressed, weary sigh that came from her core. Watching Devlin and Luke together was a constant reminder of how lacking her own marriage was. She knew she shouldn't be comparing. Luke and Devlin were still in the early years of their marriage, but from the start of her own she'd always had to suffer Terry putting himself first. Luke always put Devlin first. He treated her as an equal. She was his business partner, not his housekeeper. Maggie felt a surge of anger. That's all she was to Terry when it boiled right down to it.

She was sick of it, heartily sick of it, but what could she do? The children came first. That's what being a parent was all about, wasn't it?

She slumped down onto the chair at the kitchen table. She'd ring her mother in a little while. She wanted to finish the page she'd been working on. The cursor blinked, awaiting her attention. Maggie ran her eye over what she'd just written. Her new novel was called *Betrayal*. It was written from the heart and from bitter personal experience. It was her third book and she knew without question that it was her best.

The phone shrilled again.

'Oh for God's sake!!!' she exclaimed.

'Hello?' This time she knew she sounded downright ratty. She didn't care. She was half expecting it to be her mother. Checking.

'Maggie, sorry for disturbing you.' Marcy Elliot's crisp tone at the other end of the phone came as a surprise. It was almost five p.m. Why was her editor phoning her so late on a Friday evening?

'Hi, Marcy. What's up? You sound as harassed as I feel.'

'Maggie, you should know that I'm leaving Enterprise Publishing. I've handed in my notice, but I'll be around to tie up loose ends for a week or two. I wanted to tell you myself. I didn't want you to hear it from anyone else. I'm up to my eyes. I can't talk to you now. I'll phone early on Monday to arrange a meeting.'

'But Marcy, what's happened? Why?' Maggie asked aghast.

'Look Maggie, I really can't talk. I've a few other authors to call. I promise I'll ring first thing on Monday. We'll talk then. Bye.'

Maggie stood rooted to the spot and stared at the phone in disbelief. Was she dreaming? Had her editor – one of the most highly regarded in the publishing trade – just told her that she was leaving? It wasn't possible. It couldn't be true. How would she ever write a book without her? Marcy was her guide, her mentor, her teacher. Had she been head-hunted? That wouldn't be surprising. She was the best. But Maggie had never for a minute considered that Marcy would leave Enterprise. She was a director, a share-holder. She had enormous clout.

Maggie felt a vague stirring of apprehension. Things didn't sound too good. Typical of her luck. Just when she needed all the support she could get.

Four

'Have you booked my flight to Galway on Monday, Liz?' Devlin asked her PA as she breezed into her office as happy as a lark.

The stylish young woman seated at her computer leaned back in her chair and stretched.

'I have. You're on the late afternoon flight. There's no early morning flight unfortunately so you can't do it all in the one day, so I've booked you into the Great Southern Hotel for the night. A car will meet you at the airport to bring you there, collect you in the morning and drop you down to City Girl. I've booked you on the last flight home the following afternoon. The meetings have been arranged to suit your flight schedule.'

'Great, Liz. Anything I should know about?'

'Not much going on here. We've got a party of twenty coming for the All Day Make-over next Thursday. It's a corporate thing. That side of business has really taken off,' Liz remarked.

'I wish we had rooms for residential nights in Dublin. I'm really looking forward to seeing how it takes off in Galway.' Devlin flicked through the itinerary for her Galway visit. It was crammed. Architects, builders, landscape gardeners. All with plans for phase two of the Galway City Girl.

Liz pressed a button on her computer. 'I'm just sending a copy of your itinerary to Anne in Galway. She'll have everything organized for you. It will be a whole new ball game, Devlin. The first City Girl health farm.'

'I know. I can't wait. What a stroke of luck that we got the site next door. Sites are like gold-dust in that part of Galway. There's apartments going up everywhere. We had to pay through the nose, of course. Luke did a bit of humming and hawing.' Devlin smiled. 'But then he had to admit that Galway was doing so well, expansion on that scale was justified.'

'Just as well you've a new accountant on board, too. Poor old Scrooge would never have been able to cope with the amount you're spending,' Liz laughed, referring to their former accountant who had left to go to a less stressful position in a knitwear factory.

'Don't be nasty,' Devlin admonished with a grin. 'Dealing with my accounts takes a real man. Wimps are out. Fortunately Andrew seems to have a bit of get up and go in him. Hopefully he can see the bigger picture.'

'Just as well,' murmured Liz wickedly.

Devlin laughed as she strode into her elegant office. She'd had it redecorated recently and she loved its warm tones of honey gold and pale blue. Lightly patterned cream and blue curtains drew the eye to the long sash windows. The pattern, taken up in the luxurious sofa and chairs, gave the impression of an informal sitting-room. Devlin much preferred informality. And as relaxation was what City Girl was all about, she felt strongly that business meetings should be held in a relaxed environment. Vases of fresh flowers, soft pastel silk paintings, and scented candles added to the calming atmosphere.

She pressed a button on a panel on her desk and tranquil and soothing strains of piano and strings filled the room as Philip Chapman's *Keeper of Dreams* played softly on her CD.

Devlin sat in her cream leather chair and swivelled until she was facing the long narrow windows that faced out onto St Stephen's Green. An autumnal squall hurled droplets of rain against the window-panes and the red-gold leaves of the great oak trees swept in great flurries along the green railings.

Devlin loved looking out on St Stephen's Green. She enjoyed watching the hustle and bustle of city life beneath her windows. She saw a black, sleek, stretch limo draw up outside the Shelbourne and watched a woman wearing huge dark glasses emerge and hurry inside its portals. Whoever it was would probably grace City Girl with her presence. They'd had many movers and shakers since opening several years ago.

Devlin still found it hard to credit how her idea of placing the most up-market and classy health and leisure centre right in the heart of the city had taken off so successfully. Belfast had worked even better than they'd hoped and there was a waiting list as long as your arm for membership. And now Galway's expansion was a whole new challenge. Devlin loved a challenge. She was fiercely proud of City Girl. If she hadn't had it to drive and push her after Lynn's death she would have sunk into a pit of darkness and depression and might never have emerged.

Her hand dropped to her stomach. Another baby

snuggled in her womb now. Luke's baby. This pregnancy was going to be so different . . . so joyful for both of them. Having a partner made an immense difference. No fears about coping, no worries about providing. No great big cloud of worry wrapped around her. She was going to enjoy every second of this pregnancy, Devlin promised herself.

Her hand hovered over the phone. She was dying to tell Caroline and Maggie. They'd be immensely delighted for her. The thought warmed her. They'd shared so much down the years. It was going to be great to give them this wonderful piece of news. But it wasn't the same telling them over the phone. She wanted to see the look on their faces and hear the shrieks of delight and have the daylights hugged out of her. Reluctantly she dropped her hand.

But she was dying to tell someone. Devlin tapped her fingers in a drumbeat on the desk. She knew she should tell her mother and father. But memories of the day Lydia Delaney had discovered that her daughter was pregnant outside of marriage still haunted her. That was the day she'd discovered that she was adopted, and Lydia was in fact her aunt. They'd been estranged for years after that. They'd made their peace, thankfully, and had become friends as Lydia had battled alcoholism and won. But still, even now the thought of telling her mother that she was pregnant made her stomach lurch. It was crazy, she knew that, but the residue of that traumatic time still lingered in her psyche and today wasn't the day for informing her mother she was going to be a grandmother for the second time.

Devlin sighed. She'd wait another while before giving her parents the news. It would have to be a phone call. Lydia and Gerry Delaney were in Brussels for a year. Her father's promotion in the bank had been on the cards. He was one of their most senior and experienced managers. Now he was part of the team co-ordinating their organization's strategy for the Euro currency. It had necessitated a move to Belgium for at least a year. Her parents were hugely enjoying living abroad.

Devlin and Luke had been to visit them just weeks ago and it did her heart good to see how much they were enjoying the experience. All the years of worry Gerry had endured because of Lydia's drinking had gone, and her beloved father looked twenty years younger. Lydia too had a serenity about her that was so different from the brittle, agitated air she always used to have. To see them enjoying life and each other was a great comfort to Devlin, who'd worried herself sick over them when things were at their worst.

Sometimes she resented Lydia for robbing her of her childhood and teenage years and making her grow up before she was ready. Shouldering the burden of an alcoholic parent had left its scars, Devlin reflected. Only the children of alcoholics could understand that gut-wrenching, stomach-knotting fear, dread and apprehension that was part and parcel of her daily life. Always waiting . . . always hoping that this time would be the last . . . always wishing for normality like the rest of her friends enjoyed.

Her child would never know those fears . . . ever . . . she vowed. 'Thank you, God for Luke.' She murmured the heartfelt prayer as she often did, knowing how lucky she was. Of the three of them, Caroline, Maggie and herself, Devlin knew that in Luke she had a diamond compared to her friends' spouses. Richard had beaten Caroline black and blue in their marriage before she'd found out he was gay. And Terry . . . Devlin frowned. Terry, who'd fooled them all with his boyish charm and devil-may-care ways. Terry in his true colours was every woman's nightmare and Maggie's in particular. Selfish, immature, lying, irresponsible, a womanizer. It was difficult sometimes to keep her mouth shut when she saw how unsupportive he was of her friend. Didn't he realize how lucky he was to have a wife like Maggie? *And* three beautiful children. He was always bragging about how he'd filled a pram three times. Devlin felt like crowning him. Helping with homework, making time to play, being there for birthday parties were not high on Terry's agenda any more. That was all left to Maggie. Terry might be the children's biological father, but a father in any other sense he was not these days. Ever since Maggie'd had her first book published Terry had withdrawn his support. It was almost as though he was jealous of her, Devlin thought grimly. She was worried about Maggie and the stress she was under these days.

A girls' night out was definitely on the cards. She'd ring Maggie and Caroline over the weekend and arrange it. Caroline was her very able administrator and Human Resources manager and normally Devlin would see her every day, but she was on a few days' leave and wasn't due back in work until Monday. They all hadn't had a good long natter in ages. And she'd be able to tell them her news. Devlin's eyes sparkled. Instead of dressing up and going out, she'd have them over to the apartment for a cosy night in. It would be like old times. And they'd have loads of news to catch up on, they always had.

She glanced at her diary. She had a budget meeting in fifteen minutes. At least they weren't nightmares anymore. Andrew Dawson, the new accountant, could see the logic of spending money on expansion and development.

She was going to suggest some refurbishing of the Dublin City Girl. So many new therapies were being practised nowadays. Reiki healing, soma therapy, bio energy, kinesiology, homeopathy, they were all in the mainstream now. City Girl had its own acupuncturist who also taught t'ai chi classes. They were always booked out. The reflexologist was excellent. Devlin had had many soothing treatments at her hands.

She sat back in her chair, thinking, planning. For a long time now one of her projects for City Girl had been a small meditation room. The factor most common to the majority of clients who used City Girl was stress. Women had immensely stressful lives these days, she reflected. She glanced out at the street below her as a taxi beeped loudly and aggressively at another driver who had cut in. The traffic was brutal. Gridlock was all that people ever talked about. City Girl opened at six a.m. for the benefit of women who wanted to be in town earlier to miss the morning traffic jams.

Athough City Girl had plush comfortable lounging areas and a well stocked reading-room and library, a meditation room would be perfect for anyone who just wanted a little time out to be still and silent. Candles, chimes, crystals, meditation music, very soft lighting, cushions on the floor . . . it could be beautiful. She was definitely going to have one built in the new Galway premises.

Times were different. The hard combative buzz of the early Nineties when she'd opened City Girl had changed. True, she conceded, the workout classes and the gym were always full, but women were looking for more and she had to keep pace with clients' requirements.

Devlin picked up her phone. 'Liz, after I get back from Galway I want you to schedule a meeting for me with the managers, I want to throw a few ideas around and see where they land. And would you get me a copy of the *Irish Guide to Complementary Alternative Therapies*, Caroline recommended it. I'd like to have a look at it. Thanks.'

'Sure, Devlin,' her PA responded cheerfully and Devlin grinned. Nothing ever fazed Liz. Devlin could guarantee that the book would be on her desk before the day was out.

She glanced at her watch: she still had ten minutes to go before her meeting. There were calls she should return, Liz had given her a list, but she decided to wait. Something else needed her attention.

Devlin walked over to the low coffee-table which held a selection of the day's papers and several up-to-date magazines. She picked up the property supplement of the morning's paper and settled back on the plush sofa with anticipation.

Now that she was pregnant they were going to have to make a decision about where to live. London or Dublin. They'd been commuting for the past few years. Luke had a penthouse overlooking the Thames. A very elegant, spacious penthouse. But it wasn't the place to rear a child. Nor was her own luxury apartment ideal.

Devlin sighed. When she'd had Lynn and they

were living in the Ballymun flats, the thing she had longed for most was a garden. She wanted to have a garden for this new baby. And she wanted a home that was hers and Luke's. One that they would plan and decorate and choose furnishings for, together. It wasn't that she didn't feel at home in his place in London, or he in her apartment – Devlin knew that once he was with her it didn't matter where they were. When she was with Luke she always felt she was in the place that was home to her mind, body and soul. But it would be nice for them to have some-where that they had chosen together.

In her heart of hearts she would prefer to stay in Dublin. She'd been glad to come back home with Lynn after her years of living in London. But Luke was a property developer and a very successful one. His base was London. Would it be easier all round for them to live in London and for her to commute to Dublin for two or three days a week to look after City Girl? Whatever happened, she was going to be up to her eyes. After the Galway expansion there were long-term plans to open City Girls in Cork, Wexford, and Limerick.

Still, there was no need to get into a tizzy about all that now, Devlin decided as she cast her eye over the property supplement. Her priority decisions were where to live and what to buy. She and Luke would discuss it over the weekend, but in the meantime it was no harm to have a few places in mind for viewing, just in case Luke thought staying in Dublin was their best option.

Five

Luke Reilly handed his hard hat to his site manager and shook hands with him. 'Excellent progress, Ronan. These babies will be onstream soon. I'm off to look at a site in North County Dublin, the land's up for rezoning so I reckon we could be building some houses in the near future.' He grinned.

'OK boss, suits me.' Ronan Williams smiled back.

'Right so, keep in touch, you have the numbers if you need me,' Luke said briskly as he strode over to where he'd parked his Volvo.

He swung out of the docklands building site and headed up towards The Point. A flurry of rain, driven by a strong easterly wind, spattered the window and he switched on the wipers. The Liffey looked choppy, small white-crested waves eddying around the buoys. He wouldn't mind heading down-river in a twenty-thousand-tonner, carrying cargo to Africa or the States. He sighed nostalgically, remembering his days as a seaman when he'd traversed the world.

How he'd love to bring Devlin on a voyage. To show her the sights that he'd seen. Sunsets and sunrises that would take your breath away. Seas that were smooth as glass one day, bubbling cauldrons, storm-tossed and angry, the next. The ports of Africa and the Far East, the unforgettable skyline of New York, he'd seen them all and sometimes he hankered for those days of freedom and adventure. Devlin and he were always so busy. They always had been ever since they met: he commuting from London, Devlin immersed in her business. A sea voyage would be perfect. He'd have her all to himself. Wouldn't have to share her with City Girl. Luke smiled as he turned left off the Port roundabout and drove towards the Alfie Byrne Road. Trying to get Devlin to go to sea with him was pure pie in the sky, but it was a nice fantasy.

The tide was in, when he turned right for Clontarf. Gulls circled and screeched, skimming the choppy water. Clontarf was a nice place to live, he mused. He liked looking out at the sea from Devlin's apartment. He liked the fact that less than an hour's drive from any point in the city led to the sea or the countryside.

Now that Devlin was expecting a baby they were going to have to decide where to have a family home.

He could always promote one of his managers to look after his English business. His most trusted manager, Joe Kinsella, was well capable of the job. Luke could concentrate on building up his Irish property portfolio. It was something he'd put on the back burner until he'd met Devlin. Now, with a booming property market, Dublin was the place to be. In a funny sort of way it looked as though it was all working itself out and the decision was being made for him.

This field he was off to inspect sounded like a good prospect for development. A couple of miles from the airport, ten from the city centre. An ideal spot.

Fifteen minutes later he drove under the M50 onto

the North Road. The rain was easing off and the sun was doing its best to make an appearance. He was in the country now. Luke loved it. The nearest he got to the country when he was in London was Primrose Hill, he thought wryly, as he took a left turn and drove down a narrow country road. Halfway along he found the entrance to the field. He could see tractors driving up and down in the distance. Luke parked, opened the boot, and took out his wellies.

Spatters of rain wet his face. He inhaled the air, sweet and fresh, with pleasure. He walked into the field, squelching into the muck. It was a fine field. Fourteen acres. At his feet red rooster potatoes stuck out of the mud. A field of spuds. A shame to think that by the time he was finished with it, it would hold over a hundred or more houses. Still, if he didn't buy it someone else would. That was progress.

Luke walked the boundary, listening to the birds chirruping and the sounds of the tractors in the distance. He thought of his father. How much he would have enjoyed coming out to view the field with him. Even now the memory of his much loved father could make him sad. After a while he got back in the car and drove back towards the city but when he reached the slipway for the M50, impulsively he swung left and headed up to join the fast-flowing stream of traffic that travelled eastwards along the motorway. Twenty minutes later he pulled up outside Sutton cemetery where his mother and father were buried.

Ever since Devlin had told him that she was pregnant his parents had been on his mind. If only they'd been here to share his joy and his apprehension. They would have been so happy for him and they would have made wonderful grandparents.

'Please God, let Devlin be all right,' he murmured in prayer as he strode along the pathway towards his parents' grave. He felt bad that he'd come empty-handed, but the flowers he and Devlin had placed on the grave a week ago still bloomed healthily.

Luke stood, head bowed. The rain was battering down again, sleety, needle-sharp cold. He didn't care.

'Help me to be a good father. As good as you were to me, Dad. Help Devlin, Mam. Let everything go well for her. And look after our baby.' His prayer was carried on the wind as he stood at his parents grave in the grey autumn dusk, his happiness tinged with sadness that they would never see this longed-for child.

Six

'Congratulations!! You made the list! I'm just about to kiss one of the most influential men in the country. What a THRILL!!! Caroline, darling, you look stunning. Richard, be still my beating heart. I envy this woman *sooo* much.' Antonia Dunwoody, dramatic in crimson, swooped down on Caroline and Richard like a great flapping cockatoo, air-kissed them both and stood back to discreetly observe, in the huge bevelled mirrors of the restaurant, who was looking at her. Caroline's heart sank. They'd left the cocktail party after several hours of boring social chit-chat, to dine quietly together. Antonia Dunwoody was the last person she wanted to see. Antonia enjoyed the limelight, being – in her own mind at least – one of Dublin's most glamorous and influential socialites. Richard stood up politely. 'Antonia, a delight as always. You look marvellous, as ever.'

'Just back from Milan, darling. Spent a fortune. But then that's what fortunes are for!' She gave a tinkling laugh. She'd deliberately pitched her tone just a *little* higher so everyone in the restaurant would know she'd gone shopping, and, more importantly, that she had the money to do so. Some of the exquisitely dressed women dining tonight didn't have two pennies to rub together unless they were given to them by their husbands, or, more often than not, their lovers.

One matron, at the table opposite, liked to think she was impressing the set and had such a who-but-me air. But they all knew she'd put more men through her hands than she'd had hot dinners. She was practically a tart, and a mutton-dressed-as-lamb tart at that, Antonia reflected cattily. She turned her attention to Caroline.

'That's a divine creation you're wearing – where on earth did you get it?'

Caroline smiled sweetly. 'I do like to support our own designers. I had it made up by a very talented young woman just out of college. She's Charles Stokes's niece.'

'Oh . . . Oh . . . I see. It was tragic the way he died of cancer. A lovely man.' Just who did Caroline Yates think she was? Snooty little cat. *Supporting our own*, indeed . . . Richard probably wouldn't give her the money to go to Milan . . . or even Paris. He was a notorious tightwad when he was presenting bills. No such thing as friendship getting in the way of business. Discounts didn't feature in his vocabulary. She shouldn't have bothered to stop and draw attention to them.

'Well, darlings, must dash. Have to make an appearance at Will Reid's bash. You know how miffed he gets at no-shows. Obviously you weren't invited. Pity. His parties, when they take off, are to die for. See you.'

Antonia glided through the restaurant, throwing greetings right and left as she went.

'Silly bitch. Well, I won't miss that carry-on,' Richard growled.

'She's something else.' Caroline picked at her succulent scallop.

'How are you going to deal with all the crap when I'm in Boston and the divorce comes through?' Richard put his fork down and stared across the table at his wife.

Caroline took a sip of her Ballygowan. 'Richard, they won't want to know me. The only reason they invite me to functions is because I'm your wife. And the only reason I go to them is to oblige you. If I never saw any of that lot again it wouldn't bother me in the slightest.'

'But it will probably be in the gossip columns. We're a high-profile couple. Remember the carry-on when we separated. Remember what that awful woman did to Devlin a few years back? That was scurrilous,' Richard added glumly, reminding Caroline of a dreadful article that had been written about Devlin.

'Well I can always bring them to court and you can fly home and defend me,' joked his wife.

'No, seriously though.'

Caroline groaned. 'Look, Richard, if I start thinking like that and if I start thinking about all the problems that are going to surface, I'm going to lose my nerve and probably not go through with it. I just want to deal with it one day at a time, the way they taught us in AA.'

'I'm telling you, Caro, we don't have to divorce,' Richard said earnestly.

Caroline stared at her husband with exasperated affection. 'Look, Richard, we've discussed all this. We've agreed it. Why are you doing this? Why are you backtracking?'

'I'm not, I'm not. I'm just thinking of you. I'm concerned about you,' he muttered defensively.

Caroline took a deep breath. 'Richard, stop it. This isn't about me. It's about you, isn't it? You're thinking that if you go to Boston and you don't like it and it doesn't work out you can come back to me and go on the way we are. Don't you see, neither of us will ever have the guts to move on if we hang onto each other as a safety net.'

'You're very brave, Caroline. You always were. I do want to go to America. I was very comfortable being gay there. If they ever found out about it here I'd be pilloried. In Boston no-one knew who I was. I had no image to maintain. Charles and I were very happy the few months before he died.' He swallowed hard.

'I know you were.' Caroline reached out a comforting hand. 'And I wish he hadn't died. I miss him too. But he's dead and you have to pick up the pieces. I wanted to die when my mother died. I used to go to bed at night and pray to die in my sleep. When I'd wake up in the morning I'd be so angry and so sorry that I was still here. But you have to get on with it. You have no choice. There's no point in saying otherwise.'

'I suppose I'm afraid of facing the unknown. I've always had you . . . Charles . . . my mother. Over there I've no-one.'

'Well, it might not always be like that,' Caroline comforted. 'You might meet someone very nice. Anyway, there's a freedom in having to answer to no-one. That has its own advantages. You might enjoy it. Talking of mothers,' she arched an eyebrow at him. 'When are you telling your mother?'

Richard took a gulp of white wine. 'I'll have to do

43

it at the weekend. The practice is going up for sale on Monday. She'll freak. I don't know what will be the worst, telling her about the divorce or that I'm emigrating. It will probably kill her.'

Caroline frowned. 'Your mother's the toughest nut I know. She'll get over it.'

'Well, you know how she depends on me—'

'Now, Richard,' Caroline cut in sharply, 'we've been over that before. Your mother's a controller. She's never let you live the life you wanted. This is your chance to make the break. She's loaded. She has a housekeeper now who can drive her wherever she needs to go. She's in the best of health. Seventy isn't that old. She has another ten years at least, if not more.'

'I know, I know, it's just she's going to give me such an ear-bashing about the Church and mortal sins. You know the way she is.'

Sarah Yates was a staunch Catholic. In her eyes divorce was worse than a cardinal sin. Divorce was the devil's invention. She wouldn't entertain the idea that her son was gay. Homosexuality was even worse than divorce, in her opinion. It was nonsense for him to think that he was homosexual. *She* hadn't given birth to one of those dreadful creatures, she'd assured him when he'd finally told her of his sexual orientation. He only *thought* he was a homosexual because he wasn't having satisfactory relations with his wife. And that was all Caroline's fault, she'd informed Richard. And, in an angry phone call that evening, had said the same thing to Caroline.

She might be a staunch Roman Catholic but she was no Christian, Caroline thought wrathfully. Sarah hadn't an ounce of compassion. She was an interfering, controlling, cold, rigid woman and she'd wreaked havoc on her son's psyche. She was an expert at emotional blackmail. If Richard didn't jump when Sarah said jump she made him feel very guilty. She niggled and nagged and exerted subtle but insidious pressure until she got her way. Caroline loathed her.

Richard interrupted her musings. 'Are you sure you wouldn't come with me when I'm telling her we're divorcing?' he urged.

'Absolutely not. Remember that phone call when she said it was my fault that you thought you were gay? Remember when we told her we were separating when you went to Boston and I went to Abu Dhabi? She wiped the floor with me. Remember the scene when she told me I was common and that if I'd been a proper wife all this would never have happened? No, Richard, I'm not going near that woman. I might say something I'd regret. You have to do this on your own. You have to stick up for yourself at least this once. Just keep saying to yourself, "This is my life and I'll live it my way." She's lived hers.'

'I know. I'd prefer to face the toughest judge in the law courts than her,' Richard admitted.

'That's because you're doing something for yourself. It's always much harder to do something for yourself than for someone else.'

The waiter arrived to clear away after their first course. Caroline and Richard sat back in their chairs and smiled at each other. The rippling hum of laughter and talk eddied and flowed around them. It was an elegant restaurant, luxuriously but tastefully decorated. The tables were well spaced, giving privacy. Rich gold damask curtains with crimson tassels hung at long narrow floor-to-ceiling windows, giving a cosy old-fashioned air. Candles flickered on all the tables. Discreet up-lighting threw shadows on the crimson and gold flock paper that adorned the walls. Touches of crimson in the lampshades and tiebacks picked up the colour in the wallpaper. It reminded Caroline of a salon in a stately home, but the nice touches, like the real log fire and the fresh cut flowers, lent a homely air. She had dined in all the top restaurants in the city, some of them so pretentious she'd dreaded going to them. This was one of her favourites. She was glad they'd had their last meal here before announcing the divorce.

When the silent, efficient young man had glided away, Richard remarked quizzically, 'You know, you're so different from the shy quiet mouse that I married. You're much more assertive and assured now, aren't you? You wouldn't say boo to a goose then.'

Caroline grimaced. 'I know. I was a disaster. I was terrified. But I've been through a lot. It leaves its mark and makes you stronger. I hope I'll never go back to the way I was. But there are still times that I have those scary, fluttery, panicky fears. I want to let go of fear. The only way you can do that is by walking up to the thing you fear most and facing it. And for me that's the fear of being on my own.' She sighed. 'That's one of the reasons I want the divorce, Richard.'

'You might meet someone,' Richard said diffidently, fiddling with his soup spoon.

'I'm not going looking. If it happens it happens, if it doesn't . . .' She shrugged her shoulders. 'I was too needy with you, that's why I married you. I don't want to make the same mistake again.'

Richard didn't reply.

They sat in silence for a while, awaiting their next course. 'Have you told Devlin and Maggie that we're divorcing?' he asked. Caroline shook her head.

'Not yet. I just wanted to get used to the idea myself first.'

'I'm sure they'll be delighted.' Richard's tone was caustic.

'That's not fair, Richard! Don't be like that,' Caroline retorted.

'Sorry!' His apology was half-hearted.

'The girls were very kind to me when you were putting me through hell. They've always been there for me.' Her voice held a note of anger.

'I said I'm sorry. Don't go on about it. It's all water under the bridge now,' Richard muttered uncomfortably. He hated it when she brought up the subject of his past treatment of her.

'OK. Just don't be nasty about my friends,' Caroline said shortly. 'I wonder who'll buy the practice?' she pondered, changing the subject.

Richard gave a dismissive shrug. 'I don't care as long as I get plenty of cash. It's worth a quid or two.'

Caroline looked at her husband, so handsome, so successful, and so empty, and felt sad for him. He'd built up his practice to be one of the most lucrative in the country. Driven by the will to succeed. Pushed by his mother into a career he'd never wanted, so that he'd follow his father's illustrious trail in the legal field. When she'd first met him, he'd been so ambitious. Now it meant nothing to him. Maybe it was good that way, she thought. That was why he could walk away from it so easily. His heart wasn't in it any more.

'I hope you get a fortune. You deserve it,' she said warmly as the waiter arrived with consommé for her husband and potato and leek soup for Caroline.

They ate in silence for a while, lost in their own thoughts, each wondering what the future held.

Caroline squeezed some cleansing lotion into the palm of her hand and gently patted it onto her face in light circular motions. She'd been so tempted just to get into bed and bury her head under the pillows, but that way lay disaster, not to mention streaks of make-up and mascara on her pillowcases. The fine web of lines around her eyes was a clear indication that skin-care was now a must, she thought ruefully. Once you were over thirty you couldn't get away with slapping on the odd bit of cleanser and toner now and again. Men were so bloody lucky, she thought resentfully. Richard's black hair had traces of grey and the lines around his eyes and mouth were deepening quite noticeably, but on him it looked attractive. Made him look mature and seasoned.

Caroline felt suddenly depressed. Here she was, in her mid-thirties, and what had she to show for it? She was an alcoholic. She was childless. Her marriage was and always had been a sham and now she was getting divorced. Was she always going to be alone? Was this what was in the map of her life? Aloneness? How she hated the solitude of this bedroom, repository of so many memories of misery and pain. She should never have come back to the apartment. It had been a huge backward step. Why couldn't she be more like her friends. They'd taken what was thrown at them and turned it around. She had run away, as usual.

There was Devlin, successful beyond dreams, married to the most beautiful man a woman could wish for, although Caroline admitted that her best friend's life had not been easy and she'd overcome a lot of suffering to get to where she was. Still, she'd done it.

And Maggie, OK, she might be married to a toad but she had three beautiful children and a successful career as writer. She had *achieved*.

What had *she* achieved? Caroline asked herself as she slathered more cleanser on her face. Bugger all!

'Stop that!' she said irritably to her reflection. 'You stopped drinking. You made a career for yourself.'

Big deal! You drank because you were a coward and you made a career on Devlin's coat-tails. That's nothing to be particularly proud of. Now you're going to be on the shelf again. You've come around full circle, that's exactly where you've got to in life, Caroline Yates, that hated inner voice taunted.

Caroline scowled at her reflection. She'd done very well giving Richard advice. What advice should she give herself, seeing as she was so smart? She should read some of her self-help books and try and lift her spirits and get into a meditative state of mind before going to sleep. She couldn't summon up the right attitude. It was much easier to wallow in negativity. It always was.

'Oh . . . Oh *deal* with it,' she gritted, before snapping off the light and getting into bed where she curled up in a ball and tried to ignore the rage and fear and disappointment and resentment that battled within her.

Seven

Richard tossed and turned, desperate for sleep, desperate to try and forget the ordeal that lay ahead of him the following day. How could he, one of the most successful legal eagles in the country, a grown man in his thirties, possibly be apprehensive about telling his aged mother that he was taking a step towards a future that he hoped would bring him happiness? It was ridiculous, he told himself over and over, his thoughts chasing each other like whirling dervishes.

He was doing the right thing, he assured himself, as he pummelled his pillow into a more comfortable shape.

When Charles had died he'd lost heart. Charles had always been his rock. Encouraging, listening, advising. Richard would have spent his life with him and been content. He'd always been peaceful with Charles.

When his best friend and lover had been diagnosed with cancer, Richard, for the first time in his life, had put his own needs and career aside and gone to Boston to live out Charles's last weeks. The bond had deepened, strengthened and he had his first experience of living an openly gay life.

America had been a revelation to him. Watching gay men holding hands and being openly affectionate towards each other had been a discovery of delight for him. For once he'd felt free to be himself. To be who and what he truly was.

After Charles's death he had come home to his practice but the buzz wasn't there any more. The drive, the ambition to be bigger, more successful than his peers had gone. He was working on autopilot and he didn't care. His life was an empty shell. He'd gone back to Boston for a week, six months later, and knew America was the place where he wanted to be. He'd got in touch with some old friends who'd been very supportive when Charles was dying. One of them, Martin, also a lawyer and an Irishman, had half jokingly suggested that he become a partner in his law firm.

'There's lots of Irish people here that need advice about buying property and suchlike at home. Wills are always being contested. You know, the few acres that were left behind, and that kind of thing. It would be good to have an Irish slant on things.'

'Everything's moved on a lot these days. We're a booming nation,' Richard reminded the younger man.

'All the more reason we should have you on board. You're up to date. Think about it, Richard,' Martin urged, and Richard knew that his interest was more than professional.

Richard had felt alive for the first time in a long, long time. His mind started ticking. Pros and cons were examined, rationalized.

You'd be running away.
You'd be living the life you want on your own terms.
Mother would freak.

51

Let her freak! You'd be thousands of miles away from her. You'd never have to be at her beck and call again.

You'd have to give Caroline a divorce. It wouldn't be fair not to.

You should give her a divorce anyway, whether you're in Dublin or Boston.

Back and forth went the internal dialogue. But the push in him was strong. It was time to change his life and Richard knew it. If he didn't do it now he never would. It was all a question of guts. Did he have the guts to do it?

He'd come home and tentatively told Caroline. She had been taken aback at first. She couldn't believe that he'd consider selling the firm and emigrating. It was such a radical step for him. But she'd encouraged him to go for it and had agreed that divorce was their most realistic option. They had talked about divorce before but had always put it on the long finger. Now that the reality was looming both of them were apprehensive.

As he lay in the dark, alone and unable to sleep, Richard conceded that it was more than apprehension he was feeling. It was almost terror. Now that he was putting his law practice on the market he would be taking a leap into the unknown. He'd never done that before. He'd always known from day to day, hour to hour exactly what he was doing. And on top of all that he had to break the news to his mother.

Richard groaned. It wasn't too late. He could still change his mind. But if he did, he'd never be able to look himself in the eye again without seeing the coward he knew was there.

At ten thirty the following morning it was a weary

Richard who stood outside his mother's big red-brick Clontarf home and felt like a guilty seven-year-old. His palms were sweaty as he took a deep breath and put his key in the lock.

'Good heavens, Richard! You're very early. I'm just arranging my flowers. I went out in the garden to cut some roses and the state of it! Leaves everywhere. I shall be having a word with Nolan when he comes,' Sarah Yates grumbled as she took a spray of greenery from her basket and arranged it artistically in a vase of peach roses.

'But Mother, it *is* autumn,' Richard pointed out, feeling sorry for poor old Mick Nolan, who'd been doing Sarah's garden for donkey's years and who was stiff and arthritic and long past it.

'That's no excuse.' Sarah sniffed. 'Come into the parlour. Shall I tell Mrs Gleeson to bring you tea?'

'No, no, thank you, Mother. I'm fine,' Richard assured her. 'I . . . ah . . . well . . . that is—'

'Oh for heaven's sake, Richard! Spit it out. You're always the same when you've got something to tell me. And don't tell me you haven't. You wouldn't be here at this hour of a Saturday morning otherwise.' Sarah sat back in her hard wing-backed armchair and clasped her hands together.

Richard looked at his mother. Ramrod straight. She might be seventy but she was as fit and sprightly as she'd been twenty years ago. Rake-thin and small-boned, she looked as if a puff of smoke would knock her over. But Sarah Yates was as tough as old boots despite her delicate air and ladylike ways. Bright blue eyes lasered in on him.

'Well?'

Richard's heart galloped. 'I'm putting the practice

on the market. I'm emigrating.' The words came out faster than he meant them to. He decided he'd leave news of the divorce until last.

Sarah's eyes registered shock but her gaze never flinched. 'Don't be ridiculous, Richard.' Her tone was sharp. 'Sell up, and you one of the most successful lawyers in the country! I never heard such nonsense.'

'Nonsense or not, Mother. I'm going. I've had enough here. I'm going to Boston,' Richard said steadily.

'And whose idea is this? The drunk's?' Sarah's nostrils flared disdainfully.

'Mother!' Richard jumped to his feet. 'That's very unfair. Caroline hasn't had a drink in years and you know it.'

'Huh! The woman's unstable, Richard. And always has been. Remember our Christmas shopping trip to London. She got so drunk she couldn't get out of bed the next day. I'll never forget it. And why else would she go off to the back of beyond – which isn't even a Christian country - for six months and then go and live in a flat on her own until you took her back out of the goodness of your heart. I bet she's behind this notion. The day you married her was a sorry day indeed. You married beneath you.' Sarah twisted and untwisted her fingers in her lap. She was getting more agitated by the minute.

'That's enough, Mother!' Richard said heatedly. 'And anyway you won't ever have to have anything to do with her again. We're getting a divorce.' There! It was said. Out in the open.

Sarah's jaw dropped and the pale tight parchment skin of her cheeks flushed bright red.

54

'*Divorced*!! Under no circumstances. I'll not permit it, Richard. Do you hear me? You will not disgrace the family name with a divorce. I'll cut you out of the will again. You'll be excommunicated. I've never heard such . . . such sacrilege.' Sarah was livid.

'Mother, I've all the money I need. I don't need yours. And as for being excommunicated, I don't believe in any of that bullshit. I don't even go to Mass any more. I don't know if I even believe in God any more,' he retorted defiantly. Now that he'd told her his plans, it was as if a weight had lifted from his shoulders.

The sharp stinging slap of her hand on his jaw shocked him.

'How dare you! How dare a son of mine use such language to me and dare to deny the existence of God. How dare you come into this house in a state of mortal sin,' Sarah raged.

Richard rubbed his jaw. He had a crazy, reckless urge to laugh. She was so angry she looked as if she might drop dead of a seizure.

What a relief that would be. The greatest favour she could ever do him. The thought came unbidden.

'You'd better come and talk to Father Redmond.' Sarah paced backwards and forwards. 'It must be living with that . . . with . . . *her* . . . that's caused you to become like this. Father Redmond will put you on the straight and narrow. It's just a phase you're going through.'

'Mother, for God's sake! A phase is what teen-agers go through. I'm in my thirties, for crying out loud.' Richard was so exasperated he wanted to shake Sarah. 'I'm saying it once more. I'm selling up and emigrating. And Caroline and I are divorcing.' He glared at his mother.

'After all I did for you? I reared you single-handedly. I sent you to college. I gave you the money to set you up. You're an ingrate, Richard. A selfish uncaring son, ready to drag our good name through the gutter. What will the relations think? What will the neighbours say? What will all your father's respected friends think? And how will I manage when you've . . . *emigrated*? I'm an elderly woman . . . alone.' Sarah was incandescent.

Something snapped in Richard. For years she'd made him feel guilty, throwing it up in his face that she'd reared him on her own. She was a wealthy woman. Her husband had left her well provided for. And the money for setting him up in a practice had come from his own inheritance, something his mother always conveniently forgot. All his life he'd had to put up with her emotional blackmail. No more!

He walked over to the door, turned and stared coldly at his mother.

'You can keep your money. I don't need it. And as for what you're going to do when I'm gone, I don't give a tuppenny damn.'

'Where are you going? Come back here. I'm not finished with you yet, Richard. Don't you dare walk out on me.'

'I'm going into town to buy myself another suit-case. I'll need it for all I'm bringing with me to America. Because I won't be coming back!'

He slammed the door so hard Sarah's collection of Aynsley fine bone china rattled from the vibration.

Richard walked out of his mother's house and felt

exuberant. The worm had turned. He felt strong. He'd faced down his mother for the first time in his life. He hadn't had to bite back the words and suffer agonies of resentment and frustration. He'd said what he wanted to say. It was better than winning his first case. He wasn't her pawn any more. He wasn't tied to her apron strings. He was separate. Free. Her equal. She had no power over him. The feeling was indescribable. It was the best day of his life.

'My God. My God. My Lord and my God help me in my hour of need,' Sarah prayed fervently, her fingers trembling as she pressed them to her lips.

This was a nightmare. What had become of her well-mannered, cultured, obedient son? It was *her*! Sarah knew it. That daughter-in-law was a curse on the Yates family. She had done this to Richard.

Sarah sat bolt upright. She was going to see Madame Caroline. By the time she was finished with her, she'd be a very sorry young woman. And over Sarah's dead body would Richard sell his firm and emigrate to America.

Eight

'Mrs Gleeson?' Sarah tried to keep the tremor out of her voice as she called to her housekeeper, who was upstairs. So Richard was going into town. That meant that Madame Caroline would be at home alone. That was if she wasn't out gadding somewhere. Or *drinking*! Sarah's nostrils flared.

'Yes Mrs Yates?' Hannah Gleeson bustled into the room with a bottle of Pledge in one hand and a duster in the other.

'I need you to drive me somewhere. Leave that and get your coat,' Sarah ordered imperiously.

'Oh now, Mrs Yates, I'll be leaving at one sharp, today. You know I always have to leave on time on Saturdays. I go to my daughter's for lunch and—'

'Yes, yes, I know all that,' Sarah snapped. 'I'm not going far, just down to my son's penthouse on the sea front. We'll be back within the hour or sooner.'

'Very well, ma'am,' Mrs Gleeson muttered with bad grace. She had planned to get the upstairs rooms polished this morning. She didn't like it when her routine was upset. Especially her Saturday morning routine.

Sarah dismissed her with a bossy wave and hurried upstairs to prepare herself for the meeting with her daughter-in-law. That girl was as common as muck and always had been. Sarah had known from the start that she wasn't right for Richard. He'd needed someone from his own social milieu. Someone who could hold her own in company. Someone who could command respect in society. He could have had the cream of the crop. Mothers had done novenas that her Richard might marry their daughters. Sarah could think of half a dozen perfectly suitable young women who'd all wanted to marry him. Barristers' daughters. Bankers' daughters. Consultants' daughters. But no, he'd chosen that little gold-digger from Marino. Her father was a maths teacher. He knew his sums all right, Sarah thought sourly. He could see dollar signs as far as Richard was concerned. Sarah was no fool. She knew.

She'd warned Richard. But would he listen?

Well, he was sorry now that he hadn't taken his mother's advice. All this nonsense about being a homosexual was just that . . . *nonsense*. If he had a proper wife there'd be none of that. How could he want to have marital relations with a woman who was a hardened drinker? It was quite understandable that he'd be repulsed. A drunken woman was a deeply revolting sight. Sarah gave a little shudder. And even if she'd stopped drinking as she'd claimed to, the damage was done.

But it was too late to be crying over spilt milk. He'd made his bed and he could lie on it. They'd have to get on with it. That was the trouble with young people today. They gave up far too easily. This divorce business was all *her* idea. Sarah knew it. Whatever hold she had over Richard, he jumped to her every whim. Well, this was one whim where Caroline Yates was not getting her own way, Sarah decided as she dabbed Max Factor's *Twilight Glow* over her reddened cheeks.

Caroline had a hold over Richard all right. And Sarah was going to use that to her own advantage. She snapped shut her compact, dabbed some *L'Air du Temps* on her wrists, traced some Coral Rose across her thin lips, ran her mother-of-pearl-handled comb through her fine white hair and nodded at her reflection in the mirror. She was a lady to her fingertips. Something Madame Caroline would never be. Today was a day for her fur, she decided. There was nothing as intimidating as fur to little hussies who came from nowhere and thought they were someone.

'Mrs Gleeson?' she called. 'Get my fur and my Chanel handbag, quickly if you please. I'm ready to leave.'

'*Oh are ye, yer ladyship, yer Royal Highness,*' the housekeeper muttered *sotto voce* down in the kitchen as she shook a fist skywards and made a face. It would be a happy day when she could tell the old bat to stuff her job but the money was good, higher than the odds, probably because Sarah Yates was such a briar to work for. Hannah shook her head sorrowfully. Her daughter's husband had left her with a small baby, to shack up with a slag with margarine legs and Hannah needed all the money she could get right now to help out. But the day would come and she'd let rip on Sarah Yates before she went.

'Coming, Mrs Yates,' she said in her best-butter-wouldn't-melt voice as she hurried to do as she was bid.

'I'd love a girls' night, Devlin. I've loads to tell you. If you're off to Galway on Monday I won't see much of you at work, so tomorrow night's fine. Is it OK for Maggie?' Caroline doodled on a pad as she spoke to her best friend.

'I'm trying to get her. The answering machine's on at home and I keep getting divert on her mobile. Anyway even if she can't come, you come and we'll have a good natter. Luke's flying to London tomorrow evening because he's got to be in Brighton early on Monday so he won't be able to slag us about our gossiping.' Devlin laughed.

Caroline smiled. Luke was always teasing them about their capacity for gossip. He was so different from Richard. So secure in himself. So loving to Devlin. Would she ever find a man like that? A man who would love her completely. Depression hovered. 'Well, I have some news for you that will give the gossips a field day,' she said, keeping her tone light.

'Oohh . . . don't keep me waiting. Tell me,' Devlin reproached.

'It will keep. See you tomorrow then.'

'That's cruelty. I'll see you around seven. Bye Caroline,' Devlin hung up.

Caroline replaced the phone gently in the cradle. Devlin sounded so bubbly and happy. She envied her deeply. Not in a nasty way. She loved Devlin. It was just that her friend's happiness and joy in her marriage showed such a lack in her own life. She'd married Richard so she wouldn't be left on the shelf. She'd made do. And it had been a disaster. Since she'd come home from Abu Dhabi she'd made do again. Settling for safety and security and half a life. Well, she was sick of it. Sick of being a coward. Sick of being alone. Sick of no sex life, sick of knowing that she was in her mid-thirties and childless.

But was it all too late now? All the men of her own age, should she ever find one, would be married. The separated ones would have lots of baggage . . . like she had. Her sell-by date was gone, she thought mournfully as depression invaded every pore.

'What's *wrong* with you? Don't be such a bloody drip. Stop whinging and feeling sorry for yourself.' Caroline raged aloud at herself. She was such a wimp she drove herself mad. Where was all the positive stuff? All the I-Can-Survive stuff. All the We-Need-To-Make-A-Clean-Break stuff. Why had all her optimism deserted her just when she needed it most? She was a fine one to be lecturing Richard. Hadn't she even said to him that she wasn't looking for a man? And half believed it. She'd read so many self-help and spiritual books recommended by counsellors and other alcoholics at her AA meetings. The message was always the same. Peace and happiness comes from within. Entering relationships for the 'wrong' reasons – out of neediness like she had – to end loneliness, to recover from a previous relationship, to have a sex life, would never bring fulfilment. There'd always be searching and wanting, just like she was searching and wanting now.

But how did you find that longed-for 'peace within'? Caroline mused. Would she ever not be needy? How did you change a lifetime pattern? When she read the self-help and spiritual books she was always fired with good intentions and would find herself practising positive thinking for a while. But then, when times got tough, like now, she'd slip back into her old ways of negativity and fear.

'Come on, you've come a long way, stop being so hard on yourself,' she murmured as she walked into the bathroom. It was only to be expected that the decision to divorce would make her feel down. She still had to tell her father and brothers, although she knew that they wouldn't take it half as badly as her mother-in-law. No doubt Richard had by now told his mother about the divorce. Sarah Yates was one person she'd be glad to see the back of. She was a bitter old pill. She was probably freaking to think that the family name was going to be disgraced by a divorce. Good enough for her, Caroline thought uncharitably. She hoped to God that Richard hadn't lost his nerve. The woman had to be told one way or another. The sooner this was all over the better.

He was going into town to get another suitcase and he'd told her that he'd have lunch in Temple Bar, so she was at a bit of a loose end. Maybe she'd go for a walk down on the Bull Wall. She liked that walk. It always calmed her. She'd have a shower, get dressed, and clear her head with a walk. She had just slipped out of her towelling robe when the doorbell chimed.

She wasn't expecting callers. It could hardly be Devlin, who lived in the apartment block opposite. She'd just spoken to her on the phone. Caroline pulled on her robe again and hurried out to the video intercom. Her eyes nearly popped out of her head when she saw her mother-in-law standing on the steps.

'Oh shit!' she muttered.

'I know you're there, Caroline, I can see your car. Open up and let me in,' Sara snapped into the intercom.

Caroline, who hadn't lifted the handset, couldn't hear her, but could just see Sarah's lips moving furiously. She dithered. It would be so easy not to answer the door. Not to have to deal with the confrontation that was inevitable. But she'd have to face the woman sometime. Sarah would never let it go. She'd be like a dog with a bone until she'd had her say. She might as well get it over and done with. Caroline took a deep breath.

'Good morning, Mrs Yates. I'll send the lift down to you,' she said calmly into the handset.

'Be quick about it. I'm not used to being left standing on doorsteps,' her mother-in-law hissed.

'Oh, Lord!' Caroline groaned as she pressed the button that would send the penthouse lift gliding silently downwards. She wished she was dressed. A towelling dressing-gown was not the thing to wear when one was going to have a confrontation with a perfectly groomed and turned-out mother-in-law.

Her mouth was dry so she rushed into the kitchen and took a big gulp of water before going to the front door. The gates of the lift were just swishing open as Caroline opened her door.

'I want a word with you,' Sarah stalked past her, wasting no time on social greetings.

Caroline closed the door quietly and turned to face her.

'Do sit down, Mrs Yates. Can I get you some tea?' she said politely, determined not to be ruffled.

'Indeed and I don't want tea, thank you. My son arrived at my house not more than half an hour ago to inform me that you and he are to divorce and that he's emigrating to America. Well I'm here to inform you, madam, that the Yates name will not be sullied by divorce. And I will not allow my son to ruin his life and his career and give up everything he's worked for just because *you* want out. You are going to talk him out of this madness before it goes any further. I always knew you weren't right for Richard. He married you against my wishes. You got what you wanted. Marriage is for life. And I don't care how you do it, but you had better talk Richard out of this reckless foolishness immediately. Do you hear me, Caroline?' Sarah demanded. Her voice shook with anger. Her cheeks were an ugly mottled red.

Caroline felt sick. She wasn't good at confrontation. And Sarah Yates was a very intimidating woman. A master of manipulation, a controlling emotional blackmailer. The very worst sort of bully. The only way to deal with bullies was to face up to them. She took a deep breath.

'And if I don't do as you say, Mrs Yates?' Her voice was admirably calm, giving no clue to the tightly coiled knots in her stomach or the sweatiness of her palms.

'I beg your pardon?' Sarah was taken aback at the quietly issued challenge.

'If I don't do as you . . . order . . . what are you going to do?'

'Now you listen to me, my girl. If you go ahead with this course of action, Richard will be ruined. He'll end up penniless. I'll cut him out of my will. Do you want that on your conscience? Can you live with the knowledge that you, and you alone, are responsible for wrecking a man's life?' Sarah's eyes were like flints.

She really was a cold, malicious bitch, Caroline thought, horrified. To think that she'd cut her only child out of her will. Anger ripped through her. She wasn't taking all Sarah Yates's crap on board. She'd enough problems to deal with in her own life.

'You listen to me, you horrible, selfish, despicable woman, don't you *dare* speak to me about my conscience. You should look at your own . . . if you can . . . and get down on your knees and apologize to Richard for what you've done to him. You've fucked up his head so badly he doesn't know who he is. How *dare* you come to my home and speak to me the way you just have? I'm entitled to respect. Any human being is and you've shown none to me or Richard. We'll deal with our marriage and our lives as we see fit and not because of anything you say or do. Now get out, Mrs Yates, and don't you ever come near me again.'

'Oh . . . Oh . . . I . . . I've never heard . . . Well . . . I . . . such language . . .' Sarah stuttered.

'There's a lot more where that came from, believe me. Out . . . now!' Caroline marched over to the door and flung it open.

Sarah couldn't believe her ears or her eyes.

'I wouldn't stay here to be insulted by the likes of you,' she managed to sputter, drawing her fur coat around her as she tried to regain her dignity. 'You're a little slut. Look at you . . . not even *dressed* at this hour of the morning,' was her quavering parting shot.

Caroline watched her mother-in-law step into the lift. 'Goodbye and good riddance,' she gritted as the doors closed and it began its descent. She felt utterly drained but at the same time a sense of elation began to bubble within. She'd spoken her piece. She hadn't submitted to bullying. She'd faced down her mother-in-law. She'd turned the situation around and taken control of it and Sarah was the one who was left floundering. Best of all . . . she'd never have to see the old wagon again. Whatever doubts she had about the divorce, one thing was certain. Sarah had just put the iron in Caroline's soul. This was one battle that malignant, appalling woman was not going to win. With a determined jut to her jaw, Caroline went back into the bathroom and stood under the steaming jets of water. She felt she was washing Sarah Yates's dark vicious energy down the plug-hole and out of her life.

'Drive me home,' Sarah ordered as she got into the car. She was incandescent with rage. How dare that cheap, slutty, ill-mannered hussy speak to her like that? She had never been spoken to like that in all her life. It was shocking.

Sarah trembled in the front seat of the car. Things had not gone at all to plan. A cold fear gripped her heart. What would she do if Richard left for America? And if they got divorced, it would be in the papers. Richard was very high-profile. The family name would be disgraced. All the neighbours and relations would know. She'd never be able to hold her head up.

A sensation in her chest, like a vice getting tighter and tighter, made her gasp. Blackness enveloped her. Sarah gave a little moan and slumped forward.

'Holy God! The old bat's snuffed it!' Hannah Gleeson squawked in terror as she came to a screeching halt amidst a cacophony of beeping horns.

Nine

Caroline breathed deeply the salty tangy fresh air as she strode briskly down the woodenworks of the Bull Wall. It was cold and windy. She didn't care. It was just what she needed to clear her head of the lethargy and depression that had invaded her. She'd had a leisurely shower and a cup of coffee and croissants before she'd left, and that had perked her up.

In front of her, a couple, their two young children and a frisky little cocker spaniel were having fun as they skimmed stones on top of the waves.

'Mammy, Mammy look,' the younger child cried as the dog barked encouragement when she threw a stone as far as she could. The man gave his wife a hug as she stood cheering.

Caroline walked past them and tried not to feel envious. That little tableau made her feel that her own life was very empty. When she'd married Richard she'd always imagined that they'd have children. A happy family life had been her dream. Maybe hers was to be a life without children, and if that was the case she just had to put up with it. Perhaps it was a blessing anyway that she'd never conceived a child with Richard. The poor child wouldn't have grown up in a very happy environment. Perhaps when she and Richard finally went their separate ways there'd be a relationship there for her. Who knew what would happen? Optimism surged. She could go to a fortune-teller. She hadn't been to one in ages.

Caroline smiled to herself as she walked along past the golf club. At least she was rid of Mrs Yates. She was very proud of the way she'd stood up to her mother-in-law. The old Caroline wouldn't have done that. And she was proud of Richard for having the guts to tell her that he was going to live his own life.

She was definitely going to find somewhere new to live. A total break with the past was called for. It would be nice to have a place of her own. A place she could decorate as she pleased. It wasn't the best time to be buying property. Prices were horrendous but she had a good salary and some savings behind her, she wouldn't have any trouble getting a mortgage. If Richard wanted to sell the penthouse, that was his business. It was his, lock stock and barrel, and always had been. She wouldn't be making any claims against him for it. If he wanted to keep it as a place of his own, that was up to him. If America didn't work out and he came home it would still be there for him, but she wouldn't be living in it.

She knew that he wouldn't like the idea of selling the penthouse. Caroline knew that in the back of his mind he'd like her to keep living there so that he could always come back. But that wasn't on the cards.

Closure! Wasn't that what the Americans called it? Well, closure was what she wanted and today had been the start of it for her.

She watched a plane descending slowly out of the clouds, gliding low across the sea, and then over the suburbs on its final approach to Dublin airport. She felt energized looking at it. There was nothing to stop her taking a trip to London or Paris some weekend if the fancy took her. She'd be a free agent. She could come and go as she pleased. In time she could even go and visit Richard in Boston if she wished. The joy of it. If *she* wished. It was all going to be about her now. For the first time in her life. She smiled broadly. An elderly man coming in the opposite direction smiled back at her. Caroline felt almost giddy. Today was the start of the rest of her life and it was going to be a good life, she promised herself. She felt ravenous. There was a little café opposite the entrance to the Bull Wall, she'd buy herself the paper and have lunch and a relaxing read. That was a very laid-back, Single-Woman-About-Town kind of thing to do, Caroline assured herself. After all, she'd spent this type of day before when she and Richard had separated the first time and it hadn't been too lonely.

She got back home about an hour and a half later, well pleased with herself. The light on the answering machine flashed impatiently. Obviously Richard wasn't home. Caroline pressed the play button and shrugged herself out of her coat.

'Mother's had a heart attack, Caroline. It's serious. She might not survive. What in the name of God did you say to her? And why don't you carry your mobile with you? What's the point in having one if you don't use it?' Richard's frantic voice punctuated the silence of the penthouse.

Caroline's hand flew to her mouth in horror. This wasn't happening. It was a nightmare. When Mrs Yates had stalked out in high dudgeon she'd looked

70

perfectly healthy, if somewhat flushed. How could Richard now be saying that she might be going to die? And worse, that it was *her* fault.

'The bitch, the old bitch,' she muttered as tears welled up in her eyes. What a typically spiteful thing for her to go and do. And how disloyal of Richard to blame it on her. It was true what they said about blood being thicker than water, Caroline thought despairingly. His mother and her opinions and feelings had always meant far more to Richard than she ever had. He simply couldn't see how controlled he was by her. She could see it clearly, but then she'd had the benefit of counselling and therapy. She'd read many books about dependency and co-dependency, but Richard never wanted to know when she tried to talk to him about it.

That was why she'd been so excited for him when he'd decided to sell up and go and create a new life in Boston. She'd felt that she'd finally got through. He'd started to take responsibility for his own life and let go of his false sense of duty and obligation to his mother. But having heard him on the answering machine Caroline had the utterly disheartening feeling that he wasn't interested in changing, even though he paid it lip-service.

Might it not dawn on her thoroughly selfish and immature husband that *he* might have caused his mother's heart attack? But Richard would never take responsibility for that. He'd be far more inclined to let her shoulder the blame . . . and the guilt. That was quite obvious from the message on the answering machine. The sooner she was divorced the better, Caroline thought bitterly.

She walked into the kitchen and switched on the

kettle. It was crazy even to think that one or other of them had caused Sarah's heart attack, she thought glumly. That was wrong thinking. Guilt stuff. She should ring Richard, she supposed. Find out what hospital Mrs Yates was in. See if she needed a case packed.

Reluctantly she dialled Richard's mobile number. It went straight into divert. Caroline took a deep breath.

'Hi, Richard, it's me. I'm at home. Do you want me to get any night clothes and toiletries for your mother? Call me when you can.'

She hung up, heavy-hearted. He must be in the coronary care unit if his phone was turned off. Was Mrs Yates alive or dead? It would solve a lot of problems if she were dead. Caroline couldn't help the callous thought that sprang to mind. There'd be no more hassle about the divorce.

If she survived, she'd milk it for the rest of her days. Would Richard be strong enough to stick to his guns? Caroline didn't dare to think about it. All she was sure of was that the next few days were going to be hell.

There was no word from him within the next two hours. Caroline knew that he must have checked his messages. How mean of him to keep her hanging on. It wouldn't have taken five minutes to call her. He was obviously very angry with her. Had Mrs Yates regained consciousness and regaled him with a whole pack of lies? Knowing her mother-in-law, Caroline wouldn't put it past her, she thought agitatedly as she paced the lounge for the umpteenth time.

Unable to wait another minute, she dialled Richard's number again. Again it went into divert.

'Richard, please call.' Her message was terse.

Ten minutes later he rang.

'Why did it take you so long to call me back, Richard? I phoned two hours ago,' Caroline snapped, fraught. 'Is your mother all right?'

'I was in the CCU. You're not allowed to have your phone on there. She's stable at the moment. The next seventy-two hours are critical,' Richard said testily.

'What hospital is she in?'

'The Mater.'

'Do you want me to pack a case and bring in night-dresses and toiletries?'

'No. I can collect them tomorrow. She doesn't need them yet.' His tone was anything but friendly.

'Do you want me to come in?' Caroline asked.

There was silence for a moment. Then Richard said coldly, 'No Caroline. I don't think that's a good idea.'

'I don't have to go in and see your mother. I just thought you might like some support.' Caroline tried to keep the edge of irritation out of her voice.

'I'm fine, thank you. I'll see you when I see you. Bye.' Richard clicked off.

Caroline stood staring at the dead receiver. Hurt. After all they'd been through. After all she'd forgiven him for, and he could still treat her like this. She knew what was wrong with him. If his mother lived he was going to back out of everything. He wasn't going to sell the firm. Divorce was out and he was going to try and lay the blame at her feet. Well, fuck him! She wasn't putting up with it. She was going and he could do what he liked and go to hell.

Frustration engulfed her. For a moment she thought of the vodka in the drinks cabinet. One lovely sharp cold vodka and tonic. Would one make such a difference? How many times had she asked herself the same old question. It was too big a risk to take. Caroline walked out of the room, away from temptation. She went into her bedroom and took a well-thumbed little yellow book from her bedside locker. It was called *The Game of Life* and in its pages she'd found inspiration and solace every time she opened it. She lit a scented candle, put on some soft music and tried to find calmness and peace in the depths of her being. She knew that she was going to need all her inner strength and resources to face what lay ahead.

Richard sat looking at his waxen-faced mother. In the hospital bed attached to monitors and hooked up to drips she looked very frail and small. Shrivelled, almost. Her face, without her false teeth, was pinched and puckered like a walnut shell. It was hard to believe that this was the same woman who had taken him to task so sternly that morning.

She'd been fine when he'd left her, just hours ago. Angry, certainly. But there'd been nothing wrong with her physically, he assured himself.

Whatever had happened to her had happened when she'd gone to see Caroline. Mrs Gleeson had phoned him, panic-stricken, to say that she'd collapsed in the car on the way home from visiting his wife and had been taken into the Mater in an ambulance. When he'd quizzed her about why she'd gone to see Caroline, the housekeeper had informed him that she hadn't a clue but that she'd been very agitated before she went and twice as agitated when she got back in the car after the visit.

It was a bad heart attack. If she had another one within the next seventy-two hours she wouldn't survive it. The doctor seemed to have no doubts on that score. If she made it through the next few days she'd need bypass surgery. However, her constitution was strong, she was fit and thin and that was in her favour, the doctor had informed him kindly.

He couldn't go and put the firm up for sale on Monday now. Not the way things were. Unless, of course, she died. She wouldn't give a damn then. Or would she come back and haunt him?

Richard buried his head in his hands. Only this morning he'd wished death on her and now it was hovering, ready to take her. He felt deeply, deeply guilty. Why did she have to have a bloody heart attack? He never had any luck, he thought sorrowfully. If she died he'd feel guilty for the rest of his life. If she didn't, he was stuck here. There was no way he could take off to America if she was going to have a bypass. Even if she recovered from that he wouldn't be able to leave. The fear of her having another attack would always be there. Damn Caroline for whatever she'd said. She must have caused a hell of a scene to get Sarah so worked up. It was all this weird New Age codology that Caroline was into now. All those strangely titled books. *Feel the Fear and Do It Anyway; Men Are from Mars, Women Are from Venus; Anatomy of the Spirit.* She always had her nose stuck in a book these days and she was getting very peculiar ideas.

God knows what she'd said to his mother. Caroline wouldn't be at all happy when she heard that he was putting off selling the firm. He knew she was anxious to have things settled between them. But what could he do? He was stuck between a rock and a hard place. Surely Caroline would be able to see his dilemma. She'd just have to have patience. Everything hinged on whether his mother lived or died. It was out of his hands now.

Caroline heard the ping of the lift bell and knew Richard was in the foyer waiting for the lift to descend. It was twelve thirty p.m. She'd been lying in bed unable to sleep, waiting for him to come home. Would he knock on her door and come in to her? She'd deliberately left the door ajar so that he could see that the light was still on. Would he be confrontational and abusive, or cold and sulky? Or by some miracle would he have calmed down and seen sense?

Her fingers curled tightly in her palms in an unconscious act of tension. She almost held her breath as she heard Richard open the front door. She listened as he locked the door behind him and walked into the kitchen. She heard him open the fridge door and a cupboard. Moments later he switched off the light and she heard him walking down the hall. Her heart sank as he marched past her bedroom and into his own.

So . . . it was to be the cold huffy silence. The freeze-out that could last for weeks. He wouldn't tell her what was going on. She wouldn't know whether he was staying or going. He wouldn't discuss Sarah's illness. If she died, he'd hold it against her and somehow, as usual, in his eyes, everything would be all her fault. He'd accept responsibility for nothing.

How long would she have to put up with it? If this went on for months what was she expected to do?

How could she make plans? She bit her lip. Should she go in and ask him how Sarah was? Or would he reef her out of it and once again accuse her of causing his mother's heart attack?

Caroline lay back against her pillows. She was weary. She'd already had one draining confrontation with Sarah, she didn't want another with Richard. Maybe it was better to sleep on it and see what the morning brought.

She slept fitfully and was awake around seven. She lay quietly in the snug little hollow of her bed. Richard was always an early riser, today she wanted to be up before him so that he couldn't sneak off without speaking to her.

When she heard the sound of his shower running she slipped out of bed and wrapped her dressing-gown around her. She went down to the kitchen, filled the kettle, and began to prepare the breakfast.

Twenty minutes later Richard appeared, showered and dressed.

'Morning,' Caroline said easily.

'Morning.' His tone was cool.

'How's your mother?' The question hung in the air between them. Richard didn't answer. He picked up the glass of orange juice she had poured for him and gulped it down. Then he began to butter a croissant.

'Richard, I asked how's your mother?' Caroline repeated, trying not to get angry.

Richard put his knife back on the plate and stared at her. 'Do you really care, Caroline? What did you say to her yesterday that sent her out of here in such a state? Mrs Gleeson said she was trembling.'

'Richard that's not fair! And don't do this to me. Did you ask *me* what did she say to upset *me*? Your

77

mother treated me with total disrespect yesterday ... and, may I add ... you too. I even stood up for you. I shouldn't have wasted my breath. You know I hope I never see your mother again, but I wouldn't wish harm on her. That's why I asked how she was.'

'Well she's not very good, actually. And you probably *will* never see her again,' Richard said sulkily. 'So that will be a wish come true, won't it,' he added nastily.

'Grow up, Richard,' Caroline snapped. 'Are you putting the business up for sale tomorrow?'

Richard stared at her in disgust. 'How crass, Caroline. This isn't the time to think of things like that. My mother is *dying*!'

'And if she recovers?' Caroline asked tartly. She knew she was being bitchy but she couldn't help herself.

'Look, I have to postpone things for a while, to see what way it goes. I'm not that selfish. Surely even *you* can understand that.'

'Listen, Richard, I understand that you have to postpone your plans for a while. I just hope for your sake as well as for mine that you're not going to change your mind about going to America. But if you do, and if you decide to stay here, I think it's only fair to tell you that I'm going for the divorce even if you decide to chicken out.'

'Thanks for that! Just what I needed today. Your timing as usual is impeccable. You're as self-centred as ever. You haven't one ounce of sympathy towards my mother.' Richard glared at her, bristling with hostility.

'I just want you to remember that I'm in this equation too ... that's all, Richard.' Caroline turned on her heel and walked out of the kitchen. Her lower lip trembled.

'Don't you dare cry,' she muttered as she hurried towards her bedroom. She was angry, frustrated and pissed off. This was not all about Richard and his precious mother. Why could Richard never see that? How come her needs and feelings were judged of no importance? And always had been in their marriage.

This was about her, too. Why should she feel bad about that? She had every right to put her feelings forward for consideration. But because she had, Richard had accused her of being self-centred and unsympathetic. If he'd been approachable and civil when she'd asked about his mother, she wouldn't have brought up the subject of his plans or postponement of them until he had broached it. But he'd been cold and huffy and she knew from bitter past experience that that was his favourite ploy when he wanted to be evasive and avoid difficult decisions. It was a way he used to undermine her and keep her off balance until he was ready to make choices and decisions.

Caroline breathed deeply and tried not to feel like an insensitive bitch. Maybe she'd gone in a bit too strong. When *was* the right time to stand up for yourself? This carry-on could continue for weeks, months, if Sarah recovered. Her mother-in-law was pulling all the strings as usual, even on her sickbed, Caroline thought bitterly.

She had the feeling that Richard was half glad of the excuse to postpone selling up. He was too afraid to make his leap of faith and move on, she recognized sadly. If she wasn't careful, his fear would hold her back and she'd never get on with her life. This wasn't all about Richard. This was about her, too. But it looked like she was going to have to make the break on her own.

Caroline's stomach tightened in knots. All her optimism of yesterday was well and truly gone. She'd be taking this step on her own. Right now she didn't think she was going to make it.

Ten

'Mammy, I don't want to get out of the pool. Why do we have to go to Wicklow? I want to keep swimming.' Mimi, Maggie's elder daughter, pouted petulantly.

'I've told you why we have to go to Wicklow, Mimi, now don't give me a hard time,' Maggie warned, as she swam to the side of the pool.

'But it's not fair—'

'Mimi Ryan, Grandad McNamara is sick and we have to go and look after him. Stop being so selfish this minute and get out of the pool and go and have your shower.' Maggie's patience was dwindling fast. Mimi always pushed as far as she could go. Today Maggie was not in the mood to humour her.

With bad grace, Mimi climbed the ladder and flounced towards the showers, dripping indignation.

'Mammy. Mammy look I can swim underwater. Watch me.' Shona, her youngest child, took a deep breath, stuck her head underwater and managed a half-dozen ungainly strokes before she surfaced red-faced, gasping and proud.

'Oh you're great. A brilliant swimmer,' Maggie praised. 'Now run in and have your shower with Mimi, and I'll be in to you, OK.'

'OK, Mam,' Shona responded obediently as she swam to the ladder and pulled herself up. Maggie smiled at her. Shona was such a peaceful little soul. Mimi was much more strong-willed and argumentative. They were like chalk and cheese.

'Michael, time to go,' she called down the pool to where her son, Mimi's twin, was swimming with some friends. She heard them teasing him. He laughed back and her heart lightened. Michael was a happy-go-lucky little chap these days – it was a joy to watch him having fun and living life to the full. He'd been devastated when Terry had gone to live with Ria Kirby. He'd started bedwetting and had become introverted and clingy. His reaction to their separation was the main reason Maggie had decided to get back with Terry. Her son was swimming towards her now, good strong strokes. He was fearless in the water.

'Mam can I go to the pictures with Owen and Raymond tomorrow? Owen's mam is going to bring us.' He brushed the water from his hair and she had to resist a fierce urge to smother him in kisses. He'd have died of mortification if she'd disgraced him in front of his friends by kissing him.

'Sure,' Maggie agreed. 'Hurry on and have your shower now, and don't forget to dry between your toes. And don't talk to strangers.'

'I won't,' he said cheerfully as he eschewed the namby-pamby ladder and hauled himself out onto the side of the pool. Maggie watched him going into the men's shower room. She wished Terry was going with him. It was terrible to have to worry about children in this way, but there was so much abuse these days, it was a fact of life.

She sighed. How did you balance it? How did you try to instil discernment in children? Michael was such an open boy. He'd talk to the man in the moon.

A friend had told her recently that she'd got a letter from the school saying that there was a child molester in the area. Parents were to be extra vigilant. Two children had been approached to get into a blue car. Another young girl had been physically assaulted. It was downright worrying.

When she was growing up she'd roamed the Wicklow countryside on her bicycle with never a worry. Her children wouldn't have that freedom.

She squeezed the water out of her hair and climbed out of the pool. Mimi was already stripped and soaping herself in the shower. Shona was struggling with her wet togs.

'Well at least we didn't have to wait until a shower was free,' Maggie remarked as she eased off Shona's swimsuit. Mimi stayed stubbornly silent. She was as bad as her grandmother for getting into huffs.

She turned on the water and enjoyed the feel of the hot jets of spray that cascaded down over them. Nelsie no doubt would be like a cat on a hot tin roof until they got to Wicklow. She'd been none too pleased to hear that Maggie was not going to be down at the crack of dawn.

Maggie frowned as she shampooed Shona's hair. She'd much more to be worrying about right now than Nelsie's bad humour. Marcy Elliot's news had left her feeling very vulnerable. Why was she leaving? What was the new editor going to be like? Would she, or he, be as good as Marcy? As professional and conscientious?

She'd once heard another writer describe the relationship between editor and author as like a marriage. You really had to trust your editor so much, Maggie mused as she shampooed her own hair. You were at your most vulnerable with an editor. Taking well-meant criticism on board was never easy unless you had the proper perspective. You had to remind yourself that your editor had your best interests at heart and that she shared your vision for your book. Maggie had always been able to do that with Marcy. Her editing sessions with her focused, clear-thinking editor always left her feeling invigorated and mentally stimulated. Marcy challenged everything. She let nothing go. Maggie was always on her toes with her.

She dreaded meeting the new person who was going to have such an impact on her writing career. Would it be a man or a woman? Somehow Maggie wasn't sure whether she'd be able to achieve the same rapport with a man.

'Mammy can we collect the eggs when we get to Wicklow?' Shona piped up as she lathered half a bottle of Oil of Ulay onto her puff.

'Go easy with that!' exclaimed Maggie as frothy bubbles engulfed her daughter.

'It's very foamy,' Shona declared happily, covering herself with a coating of white suds. 'Can we collect the eggs?'

'Yes of course you can, so hurry up and let's get dressed and get going.'

'I don't want to collect eggs. That's just for babies,' Mimi announced with immense disdain.

'Fine,' Maggie responded lightly, knowing full well that Mimi would be as engrossed as Shona in looking for eggs when they got to the farm.

'I'm nearly nine you know. That's too old for silly old eggs.'

'Eggs aren't silly. An' I'm not a baby either, Miss Mimi. I'm going to big school,' Shona retorted indignantly between mouthfuls of water as Maggie hosed her down.

'So?' scoffed Mimi.

'Mimi, I told you not to say that. It's rude.' Maggie said irately.

'So?' was Mimi's latest. And it could sound very cheeky.

'Get a life,' Mimi muttered.

'What did you say?' Maggie demanded. 'How *dare* you! How dare you speak to your mother like that! How dare you speak to any adult like that! *"Get a life."* Who do you think you are, Madam? I'm telling you, Mimi Ryan, any more impudence like that and you're grounded for the week.'

Mother and daughter glowered at each other.

'Apologize immediately.'

Stubborn silence.

'*Immediately!*'

'Sorry,' Mimi muttered.

'Right, let's forget it. And I don't want to hear any more smart-alec talk like that again. Now go and get fifty pence from my purse and dry your hair please,' Maggie instructed crisply.

Mimi wrapped her towel around her and stalked out of the shower cubicle.

'I don't think she really meant it, Mammy,' Shona said anxiously. She hated confrontations.

'Maybe not. But it's not nice to be cheeky,' Maggie was firm. 'Now come on, we have to hurry.'

Michael was waiting for them outside the ladies' changing-room.

'Hi Mam,' he greeted her cheerfully, his cheeks glowing from the swim and the shower.

'That was quick, Michael, good boy,' Maggie praised. 'Did you have the shower room to yourself?' She posed the question lightly.

'Yep. No-one else is out of the pool yet and no-one came in,' Michael replied airily, quite unaware of her reasons for asking the question. Only last week a teenager had exposed himself to children playing in the school yard. Fortunately Michael had been at the other end of the playground, but how did you explain these things to children without frightening them, Maggie wondered glumly as she ushered her three out to the car park.

The traffic was light enough, for which she was immensely grateful. The sun was shining and, as they drove along the Strand Road half an hour later, her bad humour evaporated. The sea sparkled. A ferry glided towards Dun Laoghaire and a DART train sped past the Merrion Gates, causing great excitement in the back seat.

'You said you'd bring us on the DART out to Bray, Mam,' Michael reminded her.

'I know . . . I know. I will. I promise.'

'Soon,' persisted her son.

'Soon,' she echoed.

Guilt set in. She really should spend more time with her children doing fun things with them. She was always making excuses lately. It wasn't fair on them. Her writing was going to have to take a back seat for a while. It was so bloody hard juggling all the balls in the air. She got stuck behind a Merc turning into the Blackrock Clinic and drummed her fingers impatiently on the steering-wheel. Bad move staying in the outside lane. But he hadn't turned on his indicator until the last minute. Bloody-Fat-Cat-Big-Noise, too arrogant to think of other drivers, she fumed silently, wondering if he was a consultant. Maybe she'd worked with him when she'd been nursing all those years ago, before her marriage. That seemed like another lifetime ago, she thought regretfully.

She'd been happy then. Living in the flat in Sandymount with Devlin and Caroline, full of hopes and dreams. Now she was a disappointed woman living a life of discontent. Nothing had gone as she planned. Her marriage was a sham. It gave her nothing and she had nothing left to give it. If it wasn't for the children she'd walk away from Terry and start afresh.

Maggie sighed from the depths of her being.

'Mammy, are you sad?' Shona, always intuitive in her own little way, asked from the back.

'Why did you say that?' Maggie asked, startled.

'It was just when you did that . . .' She imitated the sigh.

'No, love, I'm not.' She glanced in the rear-view mirror and saw Michael's face tense up. He was always watching her and Terry now. Maggie knew in her heart that the fear of his parents separating again was the one great cloud in his otherwise happy young life.

'I just sighed because I was stuck behind that car. He should have indicated long ago,' she added reassuringly. 'I was just thinking, if we have time in the afternoon after we've given Grandad his lunch we could go for a walk on Brittas beach.'

'YES!' Michael shot a triumphant hand in the air.

'Goody.' Shona beamed.

Mimi remained stony-faced.

'Are you going to come with us, Mimi? We might even go into the Old Forge for hot chocolate on the way back.' Maggie offered the olive branch. Hot chocolate was the ultimate treat for her elder daughter.

'Oh . . . OK.' Mimi brightened.

Thank God, Maggie thought, stilling the thought that she'd won over her daughter with bribery. Mimi's sulks could be wearing. Now that she had the children with her for the day she wanted to give them a treat and have some fun with them. A walk on Brittas would be perfect. Blow the cobwebs from her brain and maybe inspire her for her next chapter.

She was blessed with a run of green lights from Blackrock to Deansgrange and before long they were swinging left opposite Cornelscourt onto the N11.

'I can see the Sugar Loaf . . . I can see the Sugar Loaf,' sang Shona a while later and Maggie's heart lifted at the sight of the familiar and much loved peak, so much a part of her childhood.

If only she was rich enough she'd buy a cottage in Wicklow and spend the summers there with her children in her haven. When they were reared she'd up sticks and leave Dublin and to hell with Terry.

Someday, she promised herself, *someday*.

Eleven

'Morning Nicola.' Terry gave the statuesque blonde his most charming smile. He'd been hoping Nicola Cassidy would be playing golf this morning. He liked her. She had style. Glamorous, well groomed, with curves in all the right places, oozing confidence . . . she was his type of woman.

Maggie had been like that once, he thought ruefully. Now she was heading for forty, stuck in a rut, and he wasn't the number one priority in her life any more, that was for sure. Terry scowled. Sometimes he felt that she'd only asked him to come back home for the children's sake. If it wasn't for them he wasn't at all sure if she'd want him in her life. It wasn't good for a man's ego. Didn't women realize that men's egos were just as easily bruised as theirs?

OK, he'd had a fling with Ria Kirby, and Maggie had made him pay for that. But she'd had her fling too with that Adam bloke, so they were all square. Why couldn't she let bygones be bygones? Why couldn't she just make more of an effort, for a start? She didn't dress up for him any more. The only time she ever dressed up now was if she was going to some function to do with her writing. She'd given up entertaining his clients at home, telling him that he could take them to restaurants. She didn't have time to cook, she said. Maggie and he had given great dinner parties in the early years of their marriage. That was all changed now. It was this bloody writing. It took all her time. She was either writing or doing publicity. And he was sadly neglected.

'Nice day for a round,' he remarked as Nicola strolled past him.

'Ya, I'm in a threeball at eleven. How about you?' Nicola's green eyes reminded him of a cat's.

'I'm just playing a round with a client.' Terry glanced at his watch. 'I've twenty minutes before he arrives. Fancy a coffee? It's a bit early for a drink.'

'Coffee's fine,' Nicola purred.

You haven't lost it, boy. Terry silently congratulated himself as they strolled to the clubhouse.

'How are things going with you? You were telling me about the big conference you were setting up for your European colleagues,' Terry asked as he held open the heavy swing doors that led to the clubhouse. Nicola was a development manager in a big international insurance corporation.

'It's going fine. I've booked Ashford Castle. That was the easy part. The worst thing is arranging the table seating. You know, inter-office rivalries and all that.'

'Tell me about it.' Terry pulled a face.

'You know what it's like, Terry.' Nicola eased her long limbs into a red velvet banquette. He wouldn't mind her wrapping those long legs around him, he thought longingly.

'I know exactly what it's like, believe me. But I bet a woman like you could handle ... *anything*.' He gave her a knowing look. He knew what he'd like her to

90

handle. She'd be magnificent at sex. He had no doubts on that score.

Nicola stared back unabashed. 'Some things aren't worth the effort,' she drawled.

Was he mistaken or was there contempt in those green eyes?

'Can I get you a cake or biscuits with the coffee? Did you have breakfast?' He changed direction rapidly.

'Oh ya, I've done an hour's workout in City Girl earlier. I ate breakfast there.'

'Oh! My wife's best friend owns City Girl,' Terry boasted.

'Ya?' Nicola arched a perfectly shaped eyebrow. 'That's Devlin Delaney, isn't it? I admire her. Does your wife work out there?'

Idiot. Terry cursed himself. What kind of a fool was he at all to bring Maggie into the conversation.

'Sometimes. She's very busy these days.'

'Ya, she's a writer isn't she? And successful too. I must confess I don't read much popular fiction so I haven't read any of hers. I prefer more meaty stuff. I've just finished John Banville's *The Book of Evidence*. An excellent book. Now I'm into Annie Proulx, *The Shipping News*. Have you read it? I find Quoyle a fascinating character.'

'Haven't read it myself, I don't get much time. I did enjoy Roddy Doyle's Booker Prizewinner,' he spoofed. For the life of him he couldn't remember the name of the book. He just knew Roddy Doyle had won the Booker Prize. Terry hadn't read a book since he'd left school, he was far too busy. But he had to save face.

'Now that Maggie's up to her eyes I try and spend

as much time as I can with the kids so that they don't feel too neglected.' Terry gave a poor-me sigh. 'If it wasn't for the fact that I'm playing a round with my client I wouldn't have come today. I would have gone swimming with them.'

'That's very nice, Terry. And rare. Believe me, I work with men who are so ambitious and so driven their kids never get a look-in,' Nicola replied.

'Look, I'll go get the coffee. And a cake?'

'Why not.'

Five minutes later they sipped their coffee and Terry watched as Nicola licked the sticky icing of her coffee slice from her fingers. He was having such dirty thoughts if he wasn't careful he'd get a hard-on.

'Do you have children yourself?' he ventured, crossing his legs.

'No . . . I made a conscious decision that I wanted to be successful in my career. Marriage and children would only hold me back.'

'Don't you find it lonely?' Terry asked curiously.

'Not really. I was in a relationship for seven years but he just couldn't cope with the fact that I became more successful than he was. I was earning more than him in the end. He couldn't hack that at all. He was a bit of a prat like that really.' Nicola took a sip of coffee, crossed her legs, sat back and studied Terry coolly.

I bet you liked to rub his nose in it too, Terry thought but he just said smoothly, 'He doesn't sound as if he was too secure in himself.'

'Correct,' drawled his companion. 'Are you secure in yourself, Terry?'

He laughed. This was ridiculous.

'Is anyone really secure in themselves? There's

always a need or a want to be fulfilled. I'd like to say that I was, but that would be bull. I need to be as successful as the next man.' *And I need to know I can still pull a bird*, he admitted silently, knowing deep down that he wasn't secure at all. And knowing that if he was living with a ball-breaker like Nicola Cassidy he'd have left too, even if she *had* legs that went up to her armpits.

He drained his cup and stood up. 'Nice having coffee with you, but please excuse me. I want to keep an eye out for my client, he hasn't played at this club before. See you, Nicola. Enjoy your round.'

'Bye, Terry. Enjoy yours.' Nicola smiled at him but her tone was dry and he had the strangest sense that she was laughing at him. He made his way to the front door and stood outside, glad to breathe in the crisp autumnal air after the cloying scent of her perfume.

Women! They weren't worth it, he thought irritably. Just who did she think she was? All that bullshitting about being secure. And letting him know that she looked down her nose at Maggie's sort of book. Sure wasn't one book the same as another? He scowled. Maybe men-only golf clubs were a good idea, at least the members wouldn't have to listen to that sort of pretentious crap from the likes of Nicola Cassidy. She wasn't that fantastic, now that he thought of it. She had thin lips.

Terry was as mad as hell, and he wasn't sure why. But the interlude with Nicola had left him agitated. It was as if *she* had been in control of the whole thing, not him. Anyway he wouldn't waste his time flirting with her again. She wasn't his type after all, he decided as he composed his face into a smile of welcome to greet John Dolan, who had just driven up in a brand-new Jag.

Nicola Cassidy watched Terry make his way out of the coffee dock and smirked to herself. What did he think she was? Some sort of a blonde *bimbo*? She knew an attempted pick-up when she saw one. He'd been sniffing around her for weeks. Did he think that she was just going to fall into his arms because he'd bought her a cup of coffee? Because he was a successful broker who entertained his clients to a round of golf? Was she supposed to be *impressed*? She'd dealt with too many Terry Ryans on her hard slog up the ladder to be impressed with his type. What was it with these guys that they couldn't handle a successful woman? And his childish innuendoes weren't worthy of a schoolboy. *I bet you could handle anything.* His best was probably pathetic.

I bet I could beat him at golf too, she thought dismissively as she sat back in her seat and ordered another cup of coffee.

Three hours later Terry and John Dolan sat in the bar having a drink before they headed off for lunch. Terry had let the older man win the game. He needed his business.

'See the blonde bird coming towards the clubhouse?' He pointed Nicola out as she strode across the links. 'She has a thing for me. We had coffee this morning and if I pushed it I could get places. What do you think?'

'Great ass,' his companion said appreciatively. 'Are you going to go for it?'

'Maybe.' Terry shrugged. But as he watched Nicola undulating into the clubhouse he knew one thing was for sure. He was pissed off at home. He was pissed off with Maggie, and from now on it was open season with women. He only had one life. He was going to live it and have some fun living it. He'd have his affairs, only this time he'd make damn sure not to get caught.

Twelve

'I thought you'd be down much earlier than this, Maggie,' Nelsie said crossly as Maggie stepped out of the car.

'Mam, I told you I'd be a bit late because of the swimming,' Maggie explained patiently as she opened the car door for the children. 'How's Dad?'

'Ach, he's whinging and moaning in there. You think it was my fault he had gout. Honest to God, Maggie, but he's a terrible patient. Did you bring the sponges for me? I'll take them with me for our tea break.'

'I have them here.' Maggie handed her the Superquinn bakery bag.

Nelsie took them from her with satisfaction. Never a word of thanks or a 'I hope I didn't put you to any trouble', Maggie thought resentfully.

'Hello, Mimi. Hello Michael. And how's my little angel?' Nelsie turned her attention to her grandchildren.

'Hi, Gran, can we collect the eggs?'

'Gran can we have brown bread and sugar?'

'Gran can I make lavender perfume like I did the last time?'

Nelsie laughed at the barrage of questions.

'Michael, say can I have brown bread and sugar, *please*. Shona, can I collect eggs, *please*. Mimi, can I make lavender perfume, *please*.' Maggie reproved.

'*Please*, Gran,' they chorused impatiently.

'Of course you can. Come on now, because I have to be getting along. Come in and say hello to Grandad. He's looking forward to seeing you.' Nelsie led the way into the farmhouse.

She was looking well, Maggie reflected as she followed her mother. Small and wiry, Nelsie McNamara was blessed with abundant energy. In her late sixties, she often left Maggie feeling totally inadequate as she buzzed around attending to the farm, taking part in all the parish activities and always with several projects on the go, such as quilting, crochet or a piece of embroidery, perfectly stitched. She played cards two nights a week and Maggie often thought in amusement that her mother had a better social life than she had. Today she was wearing her best dress. A lovely wine and green Paisley print with a V-neck to show off her treasured amethyst pendant, a gift from her husband on their wedding day. She wore a wine-coloured cardigan to keep out the autumnal chill. She looked extremely smart and Maggie, despite her earlier irritation, felt a surge of pride for her mother.

'You look great, Mam!' she said as Nelsie ushered the children into the house in front of her.

'Well thank you, Maggie. I try and look my best for these occasions and thank God I'm in the full of my health,' Nelsie responded cheerfully. 'You look a little peaky yourself.'

'Ah, I'm a bit tired. I'm trying to get a book finished and it's hard going.'

'Would you not give it up until the children are a

97

bit older,' her mother urged as they walked into the kitchen.

'We'll see,' Maggie murmured noncommittally. Her father was sitting beside the fire in his armchair, one foot resting on a small pouffe.

'Hello, Dad.' She leaned down and kissed her father's cheek. 'How are you feeling?'

'Hello, Maggs, I'm browned off to be honest with you. This old dose has me rightly stuck.' Behind him, Nelsie threw her eyes up to heaven as she took the sponges out of the supermarket bags and placed them in two cake tins to bring with her.

'Hi, Grandad,' Shona threw herself into his arms. 'Will we look for eggs?'

'I can't unfortunately, pet, Mammy will have to go looking with you today.'

'Aw Grandad, that's not the same.' Shona made a face.

'Thanks!' Maggie said dryly.

'Ah, Mammy . . . it's just that Grandad does great adventures,' Shona explained earnestly. 'I like going with you too.'

'I know,' Maggie soothed, understanding Shona's disappointment. Her father doted on his grand-children and went out of his way to entertain them when they came to visit. Harrison Ford's search for the Holy Grail paled into insignificance compared to Grandad McNamara's and his trusted assistants' search for the speckled and brown eggs of the seven hens.

'Get the egg basket in the scullery and start look-ing in the hen shed and I'll be out soon,' Maggie instructed as she took off her jacket. The children needed no second urging.

'Maggie, I've cooked a big pot of beef and kidney stew, just heat it up. There's a rice pudding ready to go in the oven and there's home-made blackberry and apple tart. If your father had been able to put weight on his foot he'd have been grand, but he can't and that's why I had to call on you. But I have it all ready for you, so you won't have to do too much.' Nelsie stood at the mirror in the hall, gave her hair a final brush, and retouched her lipstick.

'I'd have got it all ready, Mam. You didn't have to go to such trouble,' Maggie protested. She felt a bit of a heel for making such a fuss about coming down.

'No trouble. I did it while I was waiting for you to arrive. It was better than twiddling my thumbs all morning,' Nelsie responded tartly.

'I did have to bring the children swimming,' Maggie pointed out defensively.

'I'm sure missing it once in a blue moon wouldn't be a tragedy.' Nelsie sniffed. 'Anyway, you're here now and I'm off. I'll be home around seven, if that's all right with you.'

'Seven's fine,' Maggie said irritably but her acerbity was wasted on her mother, who was putting on her good tweed coat and jaunty green beret.

'There's a quiche in the fridge for tea,' she called out and then she was gone, her small sprightly figure hurrying across the gravel to the car with her two cake tins swinging in a string bag.

'You've no business being late on fête day,' Harry McNamara said drolly from his chair beside the fire, 'swimming or no.'

Maggie laughed. 'Mother's something else.'

'Mind, you haven't been down in a while, you'd think you lived at the other end of the country

99

instead of an hour's drive away,' her father remonstrated. 'Stick the kettle on there and make us a cup of tea, like a good girl.' He settled himself more comfortably in his chair and picked up the paper.

Silently Maggie went to the sink and filled the kettle. What did her parents think, that she lolled around every morning painting her nails? She had three children of school age, a husband who did not pull his weight and a career that would be rapidly going down the tubes now that her editor was leaving.

No-one understood the pressure she was under. Was her mother right? Should she leave aside her writing career until her children were older? What had started out as a joy and a release was rapidly becoming a burden. The pressure of a deadline was intense. But she knew better than anyone how important it was to build up her name as a writer. Her first two novels had sold well, maybe her third, *Betrayal*, would be her breakthrough. If she could just have some money at her back to become more independent of Terry it would be worth the slog. It was good having her own money. Her royalty cheques were on the rise. She was due one any day now. That would lift her spirits, she comforted herself as she waited for the kettle to boil.

She glanced around the homely farmhouse kitchen with its great pine dresser full of crockery, nestled in the alcove beside the fire. The big square pine table and chairs had been there in the centre of the room since she'd been a child. The fireplace, with its gleaming brass fender, had two small red-cushioned seats at either side of the chimney-breast. Her parents' armchairs stood at either side of the fire, old and worn but more comfortable than the grandest suite. The perfect place to curl up for a snooze.

On Sundays Nelsie lit the fire in the front parlour, but, apart from Sundays, life was mostly lived in the snug, warm, aroma-filled kitchen that had hardly changed from her childhood.

She'd like a kitchen like this in her dream cottage, Maggie decided as she cut two thick slices of tea brack and smeared them with butter. She might as well join her father in a cup of tea before going out on the hunt for eggs. After lunch, while her father had a snooze, she'd take the kids for a long walk on Brittas and inhale some good healthy sea air. When she'd finished her tea she buttoned up her jacket and went out to the children.

'Mammy we found three eggs,' Shona shrieked excitedly as the hens squawked, running here and there across the farmyard. Maggie smiled and relaxed. Searching for eggs always brought back happy memories of her childhood. She was here now with her children, her computer was at home, it was their time.

'Great, let's see if we can find any more. Look over there in the old nest by the gate,' Maggie urged and laughed as the three children broke into a gallop.

They got a good haul by the time they'd finished their search. Two speckled eggs, three brown eggs and one white one.

'Do you think Gran will give us some to take home?' Michael asked as he carried the egg basket carefully into the kitchen.

'I'm sure she will.'

'I'm having the white one 'cos I found it,' Shona announced.

'That's not fair. The names should go into a hat,' Mimi shot back immediately.

'I think we should give it to Grandad because he's sick,' Michael said firmly.

'A very good idea. And a very thoughtful one, Michael,' Maggie concurred, relieved that an argument had been averted. 'Now go upstairs to the bathroom and wash your hands, all of you, and come down for your lunch. After that how about a walk on the beach?'

'Cool.' Michael's eyes lit up.

'I've to collect shells for nature study,' Mimi said self-importantly.

'Me too,' Shona echoed as she scampered upstairs.

'Don't always be copying me,' Mimi said crossly. 'You don't *do* nature study.'

'Yes we do! We have a nature table and teacher told us to collect shells *and* leaves, Mimi Ryan.'

Maggie left them arguing and threw her eyes up to heaven. If they were like this now, what were they going to be like when they were teenagers?

They devoured their lunch. Maggie, too, enjoyed every morsel. The taste of succulent organic meat, vegetables, and roosters freshly dug out of the ground, and then to round it off a creamy rice pudding topped with blackberry jam, was indescribable. Maggie silently saluted her mother's prowess as a cook. Nelsie had never served frozen food or processed meals in her life.

An hour later, as her father snoozed contentedly in front of the fire, waking now and again to listen to the racing on the wireless, Maggie and her children walked along the beach, revelling in the fresh air and watching the waves, wild and thunderous, tossing spray among the rocks. They searched happily for crabs and periwinkles and pearly shells for the nature table.

It was so peaceful, Maggie reflected. The wind blew her thick auburn hair back from her face as she stood looking at the green and gold fields in the distance, and the long green rippling swathe of marram grass that grew along miles of fine white sand dunes as far as the eye could see. The sea, blue-green, capped with frothy foam, surged and ebbed in rhythmic flow, the sound and sight immensely soothing to her hassled spirit.

Maybe Nelsie was right. After this book she might take a break for a year and take some time out for herself and her children. The royalty cheque that she was expecting should be fairly substantial, going on the sales figures she'd been given. One thing was for sure, she couldn't keep going at this pace for much longer. She was flying on fumes at this stage. And Terry would have to start pulling his weight. Maggie's lips tightened. He'd been getting away with murder for far too long.

Terry pulled the tab on a can of Harp, took a slug, ate a handful of peanuts and switched on Sky Sports. The house was satisfyingly peaceful. He stretched out on the sofa and prepared to spend a long lazy afternoon. He'd had lunch in the clubhouse with John Dolan and they'd concluded a very successful deal. He deserved some R&R.

The shrill burr of the phone intruded.

'Piss off,' he swore grumpily. He'd switched off the answering machine. That had been a mistake, he decided, as he lumbered up off the sofa. It was going back on after he'd taken this call.

'Yep?' he barked testily, half expecting it to be Maggie.

'Terry?' An accented voice came down the line.

'Sulaiman! Sulaiman, my old buddy!' Terry instantly recognized his old friend from his Saudi days. Sulaiman Al Shariff was a Pakistani kidney specialist. His wife Alma was a radiologist from Cork. They'd worked in the same hospital as Maggie when they'd been in Saudi and had kept in touch. Alma was a sexy bird, Terry thought admiringly, remembering the curvy, sensual blonde who liked to tease and flirt.

'Terry, how are you? We haven't heard from you in a while. How about that trip to Dubai that you're always promising to take? You know we could meet up and have some fun while you and Maggie have a holiday.'

'One of these days, Sulaiman. One of these days. How about you? You didn't come home this summer. What's happening?'

'Aw, nothing much.' Sulaiman gave his little laugh. 'Now that Alma's parents are dead she doesn't like to go back to Cork. It's too sad for her. And of course she was an only child so there is no close family.'

'That's understandable,' Terry agreed. 'How are the kids?'

'Fine, fine. And yours?'

'Thriving. Big and bold.'

'The thing is,' Sulaiman cleared his throat. 'Ramadan falls during Christmas this year and we were thinking of going to the States for a month. I'll be attending a medical conference there. I'm due some leave, also. As you know, I've a brother in

Washington, we were hoping to have a holiday with him. The thing is, it's a very long journey for the kids and we wondered if we could fly via London and Dublin and have a stopover with you for a day or two? It would be lovely to see you. We'd be travelling about twelve days or there abouts before Christmas. I haven't the exact date yet.'

'Day or two, my hat,' Terry said expansively, 'spend a week with us. Maggie would be delighted to see you.'

'A week? Are you sure? We'd get a lot of drinking in, old buddy. We could make home-made brew.' Sulaiman chuckled.

'No drinks for you. It's Ramadan.' Terry grinned.

'And we all know how devout I am.' Sulaiman guffawed. 'Look, I'll finalize the details at this end and get back to you. If you're sure. Do you want to check with Maggie?'

'No need. Not at all. It will be fine, Sulaiman, we'll be delighted to have you. Maggie'll be thrilled. The more the merrier at Christmas time. We'll paint the town red.'

'Will we what?' Sulaiman agreed happily. 'I'll get back to you soon.'

'Great stuff, great stuff.' Terry rubbed his hands. 'Talk to you soon.'

A visit from Sulaiman and Alma would be fun. Maggie would really enjoy their company. Terry beamed as he hung up and switched on the answering machine. It would be just like old times.

'You did what?' shrieked Maggie.

'I asked them to stay for a week.'

'You asked the Al Shariffs to stay for a week at

Christmas?' Maggie couldn't believe her ears.

'It's no big deal, Maggie. What's got into you?' Terry rasped.

'I've got a book to finish. That's what's got into me. I don't need two adults and two kids foisted on me at Christmas. I'll have enough on my hands, for God's sake. What made you do it? The least you could have done was to discuss it with me, Terry.'

'You weren't here for fuck's sake. He asked me straight out.'

In view of her mood, Terry omitted to tell Maggie that Sulaiman had asked only to stay for a day or two.

'What could I say? They were always very hospitable to us when we were in Saudi.'

'It's easy to be hospitable in Saudi when you've got two housemen and a chef, Terry,' Maggie raged. 'Where are we going to put them all? They'll have their maid with them as well.'

'Naw they won't,' Terry blustered.

'Don't be ridiculous, Terry! Alma Al Shariff is not going to go anywhere without her maid. The maid always travels with the family. Otherwise Alma'd have to mind the kids and can you see her doing *that*?' Maggie demanded sarcastically.

'Oh! Oh I suppose not,' Terry muttered.

'I can't believe this.' Maggie put her head in her hands. Five people landed in on top of her. Christmas was mad enough as it was. She'd never get her book finished. She'd have to bring Alma shopping. She'd have to cook morning noon and night. How could Terry have done this to her?

'You can bloody well take a week's holiday. I'm not looking after them by myself for the whole time they're here,' she said truculently.

'I can't do that, Maggie.' Terry was aghast. 'I can take a half-day here and there.'

'You can take a goddamn week, buster, and that's the end of it. This has nothing to do with me. You issued the invitation. You take responsibility for it. I'm not dealing with it all by myself. I'm telling you that right now.' Maggie marched out of the sitting-room and slammed the door behind her.

As if her life wasn't hectic enough, she fumed, as she thundered upstairs and flung herself on her bed. What kind of a total idiot was she married to? Typical Terry to issue an invitation to the Al Shariffs and to leave her to look after them.

And it wasn't as if they were the easiest house guests in the world. They'd stayed with Terry and Maggie for a week a couple of years ago, and they'd expected to be entertained. Life in the Al Shariff lane was frantic and frenetic. Sulaiman was like a blue-arsed fly. Fidgety and restless, he couldn't sit down for a minute but always had to be on the go. They weren't the types who could curl up with a book and relax for an hour or two. And the kids were as bad. A boy and a girl, seven and four respectively, Maggie hadn't seen them for a year. Hopefully a year had made a difference, she thought glumly, because they'd been spoilt rotten the last time she'd encountered the darlings.

A day or two she could have coped with. But a *week*!! This was a nightmare.

Michael would have to go into the girls' bedroom. The maid and the kids could have his room. And Sulaiman and Alma would have the guest-room.

She'd have to get two fold-up beds. She'd have to get all her Christmas shopping done early, so that she wouldn't be stuck with that. And she'd have to try and do a big cook-up and freeze some meals so that she wouldn't be spending all her time in the kitchen. Maggie lay on the bed, her thoughts racing. She was tired after her day in Wicklow, although Nelsie had been appreciative. She'd enjoyed her day immensely, she'd told Maggie. It was as good as a holiday, she'd announced.

It had been after nine when they got home. The kids went straight to bed, flaked out after all the fresh air. She'd made herself a cup of coffee and was just about to settle down and watch *Kenny Live* when Terry'd made his proclamation. She could *throttle* him, she thought savagely. Stupid, thick, gobshite. Well, he could take that week off at Christmas or she'd make his life hell. And he could bloody well stay at home and mind the kids tomorrow night. She was going over to Devlin's come hell or high water. Devlin had left a message on the mobile and when she'd called back her best friend had invited her over for dinner and a girls' night out.

A girls' night out was just what she needed, because if she didn't unburden to someone she'd burst. Thank God for friends like Devlin and Caroline. They kept her sane, she reflected, as she slid off the bed and started to undress. She was going to have an early night and if Terry had any sense he'd sleep on the sofa if he wanted to keep his goolies intact, because a good hard kick to them would give her a great deal of satisfaction right this minute.

Thirteen

'Take care of yourself, Devlin, I'll see you soon. Good luck in Galway. Have fun tonight. I'll ring later.' Luke hugged Devlin tighily at the departure gate. Then he was gone, his broad-shouldered figure disappearing into the security area, leaving Devlin with a pang of loneliness that was always there when he flew to London without her. Today she felt particularly lonely. Probably because she was pregnant and her hormones were up in a heap, she decided, as she walked forlornly back along the concourse.

Luke hadn't wanted her to come to the airport, but she hated the idea of him getting a taxi when she could so easily drive him and spend a few more precious minutes in his company. Besides, it was Sunday and the traffic was light, so it had only taken fifteen minutes to get there.

She brightened up as she drove out of the car park. The girls were coming for dinner. They'd been delighted with her invitation. Caroline had news for her. She was dying to hear it. And Maggie was going to bring the latest batch of pages from her new novel. It was a great read so far.

She was doing a salmon and pasta dish for the main course. That would only take twenty minutes to prepare, and she'd serve it with a Caesar salad. She had spare ribs in plum sauce for starters. Pecan pie smothered in cream and ice-cream would slide down gently for afters, Devlin thought with satisfaction as she got into lane to pay the parking fee.

An hour later she had all her preparations made. The ribs were ready to pop in the oven, the salmon flaked, to be added to the cream sauce. The dill was chopped for garnish. Wine was chilling although she wouldn't be drinking any of it, she thought regretfully. A glass of chilled wine would go down a treat but she'd wait until her three months were up before indulging in the odd glass. She'd share a bottle of Amé with Caroline.

She put the finishing touches to the table and decided to read the Sunday supplements in a nice, frothy, warm, scented bath. Devlin spent a lazy hour relaxing in a lavender-and-rose-oil-perfumed bath that left her pleasantly lethargic.

She dressed in a pair of black palazzo pants and a cream silk shirt and having brushed her blond bob and traced Wild Rose lipstick over her mouth, she padded out to the kitchen in her bare feet. She loved being barefoot. It always made her feel as though she was off duty.

She was just finishing the sauce for the pasta when the doorbell rang and she hurried to press the intercom to let the girls into the foyer. Moments later Maggie and Caroline stood at her door, grinning.

'I collected Caroline *en route*,' Maggie said as she enveloped Devlin in a hug. 'You look stunning! What are you up to?' She stood back and stared at her friend.

'Me? Nothing.' Devlin feigned innocence. 'Hi,

Caroline. Come in and tell me what your news is before I burst. This brat told me on the phone that she had news that would put the cat among the pigeons and then she hung up without telling me what it was. Was that cruel or what?' Devlin asked Maggie as she took their coats.

'Spill the beans, Caro,' Maggie ordered as they trooped into the lounge.

'It's a bit of a damp squib at this stage,' Caroline sighed as she dropped into a big soft luxurious armchair and kicked off her shoes. 'Richard was going to sell the firm, he was putting it up for sale tomorrow. He was going to move to Boston and we were going to get a divorce and start afresh but Ma Yates went ballistic when he told her and she came haring over to have a go at me. I lost my cool and gave her a piece of my mind and ordered her out of the apartment and the old biddy went and had a massive heart attack ten minutes later. And now Richard's blaming me and everything's on hold and the gossip columnists will have to wait for their field day.' She pulled a face.

'Well, the old bitch,' Maggie declared. 'Isn't that just typical of her?'

'That's terrible,' Devlin exclaimed. 'What are her chances?'

'She's still in the danger period and another heart attack could kill her—'

'Would you be so lucky?' Maggie interrupted.

'Believe me, Maggie, I've had that thought myself,' Caroline said grimly. 'Anyway, if she survives she has to have a bypass and Richard says he won't do anything until she's OK. Which, knowing my mother-in-law, will be never. She'll milk this until the day she dies. She'll use it to bind Richard even tighter

111

and she'll fill him with so much guilt he'll never take the risk of upsetting her again. And in the meantime, I'm in limbo. I'll never get a divorce from him while she's alive. And she'll live until she's a hundred just to spite us.'

'Go for the divorce yourself,' Devlin suggested as she handed her a glass of Amé and handed Maggie a glass of chilled white wine.

'Yeah I know, but he might contest it and it will take ages, whereas before Mrs Yates had the heart attack we'd agreed to go ahead – it would have gone through in a few months. I just needed this like I need a hole in the head.'

'Caroline, as you're always saying to me . . . rise above it,' Maggie said dryly.

'Am I always saying that to you, Maggie?' Caroline grinned.

'Yeah! And don't forget, Mrs Yates is a spiritual being, and you have lessons to learn from her. *No man is my friend. No man is my enemy. Every man is my teacher.* Isn't that right?' Maggie had a wicked twinkle in her eye.

'Are you hoisting me by my own petard, by any chance?' Caroline arched an eyebrow.

'I sure am, honey. Now you see why I find it hard to understand when you come out with that kind of stuff. How can you possibly think anything other than that your mother-in-law is the greatest wagon going?'

'Because, Maggie, whether I like it or not, she was created by The Divine. She has the spark of The Divine in her the same as you and I. In the eyes of God she is your equal and my equal and she is perfect,' Caroline explained earnestly, forgetting for a

112

moment that just a while back she'd wished Sarah dead.

'Bullshit, Caroline, she's an interfering, manipulative old woman who is thoroughly selfish and you've said that yourself many times. You can't have your cake and eat it. She can't be perfect and selfish and manipulative at the same time. And what's more I object strongly to being considered her equal—'

'Now girls, don't fight!' Devlin murmured. She'd listened to many such arguments in the past and always enjoyed them.

'We're not fighting, Devlin, we're discussing spirituality,' Caroline said calmly. 'And OK, Maggie, yes I've called her names and thought badly of her but that's not a reflection on her, that's a reflection on me. That's me being judgemental. The worst thing you can possibly be. It's something I'm trying to change. With great difficulty, I hasten to add.'

'But Caroline, no-one could live like that. It's totally impossible to live in this world and not judge people. What do you do, let her walk all over you?'

'No, you always have to respect yourself and your own dignity, Maggie, but for me to think of Mrs Yates as a spiritual being helps me to detach a little from her actions. Something I haven't been doing this weekend. Thank you for reminding me. I'll try and "rise above it".' Caroline smiled at her friend.

'I give up, Caro.' Maggie took a slug of her wine. 'I don't understand any of it. At the moment if I were to rise above my little problems I'd need a couple of dozen mega-sized helium balloons at least.'

'Why, what's bugging you?' Devlin stretched out on the sofa.

113

'What's bugging me!' Maggie exclaimed theatrically. 'Do you know what that thick idiot of a husband of mine did yesterday?'

'What?' Devlin and Caroline asked simultaneously.

'He invited Alma and Sulaiman Al Shariff, their two obnoxious kids and their maid to stay with us for a week at Christmas.'

'Crikey!' exclaimed Devlin. 'What possessed him?'

'Possessed him is right. And I suppose he's a great spirit too.' She threw a glance at Caroline, who giggled.

'He says that Sulaiman phoned and asked could they stay *en route* to the States. They're not staying in Saudi for Christmas because it's Ramadan. He could have said that we were going away or that we were having other guests, but you know Terry. He thinks it's a great idea. I mean I've only got a book to finish,' Maggie complained mournfully. 'And on top of all that, my editor, Marcy Elliot, phoned me to tell me that she's leaving Enterprise Publishing and I think she's got some news for me that I'm not going to like. I'm meeting her next week. Caroline, my life is a shambles, "rising above it" is not an option.'

'Well, Maggs, that all depends on how you look at it. All I can say is that during the worst times in my life there was some help available to me, even though I didn't know it at the time. It's only when I look back I see how much I was helped. Maybe your new editor will be a stepping-stone to greater things. Who knows? Maybe the Al Shariffs' visit will give you reams of material for a new book. You could call it *Entertaining Old Friends*,' she teased.

'Remember the party you had for them the last time they stayed and Alma got into a rip-roaring row with Adrian McNulty about politics?' Devlin grinned.

'Oh God!' Maggie groaned. 'Don't remind me. I had a week of political lectures from the pair of them. They don't discuss politics with you, they harangue you. It's very wearing and mighty rude. Oh Lordy, I'd forgotten what it was like, thanks for reminding me. And if you dare tell me that they're great spirits with something to teach me, Caroline Yates, *I'll* teach *you* a lesson you'll never forget.'

'Ah stay calm, Maggie,' Caroline soothed. 'If there's anything I can do to help just let me know.'

'Me too,' Devlin put in.

'Thanks. I'll be on the phone every night getting it off my chest.'

'Bring Alma into City Girl for a few treatments,' Devlin suggested.

'Good idea,' Maggie brightened up. 'That would suit her down to the ground. Thanks, Dev, I'll do that.'

'You could come up to my office and get a couple of pages written while she's having her massages and whatever.'

'Hey, Dev, that would be brilliant. I could leave Terry and Sulaiman to mind the kids, have a couple of hours of peace to write while she's having her beauty bits done and still feel I'm entertaining her. Delaney, you're a genius!' She held up her glass in toast to her friend.

Devlin raised hers. 'See! Caroline was right. There's always someone there to help in your hour of need.'

'Don't *you* start,' Maggie warned. 'Do you want another glass of wine?'

115

'Er . . . no. I'm going to serve. Come on out to the kitchen,' Devlin said hastily. She'd been drinking Amé, Maggie hadn't noticed.

'It smells delicious. I'm starving.' Maggie sniffed appreciatively.

'Me too,' echoed Caroline as she uncoiled herself from her chair.

'Light the candles, Caroline, and plonk your ass. Maggie, fill your glass,' Devlin instructed as she took the succulent juicy ribs from the oven.

'They look scrumptious,' Maggie enthused as she topped up her glass. 'Here, let me fill yours.'

'I'm fine,' Devlin murmured as she served out the ribs. Now that they were here she was waiting for an appropriate moment to tell them that she was pregnant.

'Devlin Delaney, I've never heard you refuse a glass of wine bef—' Maggie stopped in mid-sentence and stared at her friend.

'I knew it. I knew there was something different about you. You're pregnant, aren't you?'

Devlin blushed to her roots and started to laugh. Caroline jumped up from her chair and hugged Devlin tightly.

'Devlin! Devlin, I'm so happy for you.'

'Oh Devlin—' Maggie couldn't say any more. Tears welled in her eyes as she stood beside her friend.

'Oh don't start me off,' Devlin pleaded, as a lump the size of a melon formed in her throat.

'Sorry,' sniffled Maggie, who was as soft as butter. 'I'm so glad. Is Luke over the moon?'

Devlin nodded. She couldn't speak as she stood encircled in the arms of her two best friends.

'Oh look at us!' Maggie laughed and cried at the same time.

'When's the baby due?' Caroline asked.

'May. I'm only a few weeks gone.' Devlin wiped her eyes. 'You're the first to know. I was dying to tell you. But I'm not saying anything at work. I want to wait until the three months are up.'

'May is a lovely time to have a baby. It will be nice and hardy and in a routine by the time winter comes. Trust me, I know these things.' Maggie carried the plates to the table. 'Sit down and let's tuck in. The joy of sitting down to a meal that I haven't cooked.'

Devlin toyed with a piece of lettuce.

'Don't say you're queasy,' Maggie said sympathetically as she forked some meat and ate it with relish.

'No . . . no. It's not that. It's just . . . oh girls, I'm scared.' She put her fork down.

'Of what, Dev?' Caroline reached over and took her hand.

'You've been pregnant before, Dev. You know what it's like,' Maggie soothed.

'No, it's not that. I'm just afraid something will happen. I suppose it's because Lynn died on me. I'm afraid to be happy. I don't want to say it to Luke. He's so chuffed I don't want to spoil it for him. It's crazy, isn't it.'

'No it's not, Devlin. It's very understandable,' Maggie commiserated.

'It's human nature, Devlin. When bad things have happened to you, being happy again is almost a scary concept. You think, this is too good to be true, it's not going to last.' Caroline grimaced.

'And yet look at you, Devlin. Of all of us, you've

ended up the happiest and most fulfilled,' Maggie remarked.

'Oh don't say that,' murmured Devlin.

'Well, you are. You're successful. You've a great marriage. Luke's a real man. He's decent, honest, kind and dead sexy. Which is a hell of a lot more than what me and Caroline have. What I'm saying is you're happy now and you're coping with it. The baby'll just be the icing on the cake.'

'I suppose I am, but you know what I mean, Maggie.' Devlin sighed.

'Yeah, I know.'

'You're successful too, and you've got three lovely children, Maggs,' Caroline pointed out. 'You're doing better in the happy stakes than me.'

'I'm not happy, Caro,' Maggie said morosely. 'I'd leave Terry in the morning if it wasn't for the kids. And writing novels is too hard when you've got young children. I'm thinking of taking a year off after this one.'

'Are you?' Devlin was surprised. 'That's a shame, Maggie.'

'I know. If Terry were more supportive it would be different. But he resents my writing. The kids hate to see me stuck at the computer. They're not good conditions for someone who's trying to be creative. I keep having to turn down publicity opportunities because a lot of them are overnighters and Terry gives me such a hard time it's not worth it to do it.'

'Are things no better between you?' Caroline asked.

'We live under the same roof, we share the same bed, we occasionally have sex which does nothing for me. Do you know what I'd love? I'd love a good shag.' Maggie took a gulp of her wine and grinned.

'Me too,' Caroline said fervently. 'It's been so long since I had sex I'd need to be told the facts of life again to know what to do.'

'Well, now that you've made the decision to divorce, even if it doesn't come off for a while, there's nothing to stop you going out on the hunt,' Devlin said firmly.

'Devlin, at my age they're either going to be married, or separated like me, which means baggage. Is it worth it?'

'Do you hear, Methuselah?' jeered Devlin. 'They're only excuses, Caroline, and you know it.'

'If it happens, it happens.' Caroline shrugged.

'Oh for God's sake don't be so passive. Get out there and strut your stuff!'

'Yes, Mammy,' Caroline said meekly

'I mean it.'

'At least you're not tied. You're more or less a free agent,' Maggie interjected. 'If you were like me you'd be really stuck.'

'Have another affair, why don't you?' Caroline suggested.

'With who, for God's sake? The man in the moon?' Maggie laughed at the idea.

'Haven't you met anyone on your publicity jaunts or at the posh do's you go to?' Caroline started to fill Maggie's glass.

'Go easy or I'll be pissed. And I'll have to get a taxi home.'

'Get pissed, Maggie. Go on, do it for us, the Alcho and the Mother-To-Be-On-The-Dry,' Caroline urged.

'Yeah go on, Maggie, have one for me.' Devlin

cleared away the plates and brought the steaming pasta dish to the table.

'Oh well, all right so, I deserve a night out.'

'That's the Maggie we know and love.' Caroline filled the glass to the brim. 'Now you haven't answered my question. Isn't there anyone that would set you tingling?'

'I wish. Nope, not a sinner. Sad, isn't it. I'll be a dried-up old prune before I know it, and it will be too late.'

'Don't be daft. I was talking to Lorna MacNeal in the gym the other day. She looks fantastic. Have you seen her lately?' Devlin queried as she dished out the meal.

'She does look great,' Caroline agreed.

'I haven't seen her for a while.' Maggie helped herself to a slice of garlic bread. 'What's Lorna MacNeal got to do with me being a dried-up old prune?'

'Just listen and I'll tell you.' Devlin sat down and picked up her fork. 'Remember she was in a relationship with that bastard James Conway, and we just couldn't figure out what she saw in him?'

'He was scum, the lowest of the low,' Maggie said. 'He and Terry used to drink together. And two-time. He couldn't be faithful if he tried. They're not together any more, sure they're not? Didn't he go off with her cousin?'

'That's right and she got what she deserved too. They're perfect for each other. No, Lorna's finished with him a couple of years now. There's someone else in her life and she's crazy about him and he's crazy about her. And she said it's taken her until she was forty-two to fall in love with a really good man. She's glowing, Maggie. She's happy, she's serene and they're never out of bed. That could be you and you're not nearly forty-two.'

'Devlin, if it happens, I swear you'll be the first to know.'

'Good shags come to all who wait,' Devlin laughed. 'I've every faith in the pair of you.'

'It's really nice to have dinner together. It's been ages,' Caroline reflected.

'Yeah, too long. We really shouldn't let it go so long,' Maggie agreed.

'I'd love a girls' weekend away. We haven't done that in a long long time, either. What do you think? Will we try and arrange something?' Devlin's eyes lit up at the idea.

'That would be a real treat, Dev. I could do with a weekend away,' Caroline enthused.

'Me too.' Maggie's tone was heartfelt. 'How could I get around Terry?' She nibbled on a pasta swirl. She sat up straight. 'Hey! What am I saying? Why should I have to get around Terry. He owes me big time and especially now that he's issuing invitations right left and centre. I'm in, girls, and that's the be-all and end-all of it,' she said firmly.

'Good woman,' applauded Devlin gleefully.

'Where will we go?' Caroline beamed.

'Kilkenny,' volunteered Maggie.

'Let's go somewhere that we haven't been before,' Caroline suggested.

'How about something completely different,' Devlin said slowly. 'You know the way we're turning Galway into a residential health farm? How about if we go down to Powerscourt Springs in Wicklow, have a load of treatments and see how they run it. A kind of busman's holiday for me and Caroline.'

'Oh bliss!' Maggie sighed deeply. 'I've heard it's fabulous.'

'Hmm, Crona Ryan goes down there regularly and she swears by it. The food is supposed to be out of this world. And the scenery's gorgeous. It's set in magnificent grounds, Crona says. You can walk to the Powerscourt waterfall. Brainwave, Dev.' Caroline beamed.

'Let's do it then.'

'When?'

'As soon as possible. The next couple of weeks?'

'OK with me,' Caroline nodded.

'Me too.' Maggie took a long satisfying slug of her wine. 'Fill me up, Caroline. I mean business. I'm drinking for three!'

'Right then. I'll check it out during the week and off we go,' Devlin said with satisfaction. 'You sort it out with Terry, Maggs. We better give him a couple of weeks' notice, just to get him used to the idea.'

'If he doesn't like it, tough!' Maggie scowled.

'Let's hope Ma Yates will be ten foot under or on the mend,' Devlin added casually.

'Devlin, you're desperate,' Caroline giggled.

'Well, I don't want her mucking up my girls' weekend away. I'll have to make the most of it for the next couple of months before I turn into a whale,' Devlin retorted as she speared a piece of salmon and ate it with relish.

'You won't be able to go into the Jacuzzi,' Maggie interjected.

'Oh drat! Won't I? Why not? I know I can't go into a sauna. I didn't know about the Jacuzzi.'

'It's not recommended for pregnant women. It's the same theory as the sauna – raising body temperature. And don't have very hot baths either. And of course you know not to eat pâté and cream cheeses and the like.'

'I know that. At least I can swim, though. There's a pool down there. I'll sit on the edge of the Jacuzzi and dangle my feet in,' Devlin said cheerfully.

'To a weekend of pure and unadulterated pleasure.' Maggie held up her glass.

'You bet,' agreed Caroline fervently as the trio clinked glasses happily.

'We deserve it,' Devlin said firmly, thrilled that her suggestion had been met with such enthusiasm. 'We all need some fun, badly.' She raised her glass. 'Here's to our girls' weekend away. Here's to fun!'

Fourteen

Devlin stifled a yawn as she strapped the seat-belt across her and settled into her seat, waiting for the small Aer Lingus commuter plane to roll off the tarmac and head for the runway. It was a nuisance that there wasn't an early morning flight to Galway. She was taking the last flight out of Dublin and overnighting in the Great Southern in Eyre Square. She would have preferred to commute all in the one day, but that would have meant two long train journeys. That wasn't an option.

She yawned again. It was ridiculous to be this tired so late in the afternoon. It must be her pregnancy. She had a long day ahead of her tomorrow, she'd have an early night so that she'd be fresh and alert. Devlin was looking forward to the meetings the following day. There was always a sense of excitement and anticipation when a new project was getting off the ground.

A residential centre was a major challenge. She wanted to get everything just right. She didn't want a Champneys or Forest Mere. Too big. Too grand. A little impersonal. Small, intimate and luxurious was Devlin's goal for Galway City Girl. Twenty *en suite* bedrooms. State-of-the-art treatment rooms.

Sumptuous, relaxing lounges. She loved the idea of it.

Devlin sat back in her seat as the plane moved backwards and swung left. The air stewardess went through her routine and Devlin turned to listen, hoping to discourage the man beside her from any more small talk. She had replied to him out of politeness, although her mind was racing and she longed for the flight to start so that she could review the questions she had for the architect and builders. She had typed up a list of her requirements and gone over it with Luke, Andrew and Caroline. They had added to the list and she was satisfied that it was as comprehensive as could be. Caroline had pointed out that they needed provision for a separate staff-room in the new block and had asked several pertinent questions in relation to staff requirements that Devlin had overlooked. She had been too busy concentrating on the client side of things.

Caroline was an excellent office manager, Devlin reflected. She was very lucky to have her on the staff. It was a pity things had taken such a bad turn between her and Richard. Just when it looked as if life was giving her friend a break and things were going her way, Ma Yates had to cock it up. Caroline was such a good person, she deserved a hell of a lot more than she'd been given, Devlin mused. And so did Maggie. It was awful to see Maggie being worn down. She had been such a vibrant, sexy woman, full of fun and full of life. Now, when she should be blooming, thanks to the success she richly deserved, she was tired and stressed and her marriage was a shambles.

Devlin felt a pang of sadness. The Ryans' wedding had been the best she'd ever attended. Who would have ever thought that it would end like this. Caroline and Richard had been doomed from the start. They should never have married. It was no surprise that the marriage had failed. They should have divorced long ago. Devlin scowled. There was no love lost between her and Richard and never had been. As far as she was concerned he was an insincere shit who had always put himself first, no matter what the consequences to Caroline. She'd seen that from the very beginning, but trying to warn Caroline had been like banging her head off a brick wall. Her flatmate and friend just hadn't wanted to know. Now she was paying the price.

Devlin sighed deeply. So many friends' and acquaintances' marriages were breaking up, it was frightening. She couldn't imagine life without Luke. He was her best friend, her lover, her guide and rock. Would she still feel the same way about him in twenty years' time? Would he still love her and want to be with her because he loved her deeply, and not out of a sense of duty, obligation, or routine, because nothing better had come his way? Who knew what toil the stresses and strains of life would take on their relationship? One thing Devlin was sure of. You could never be smug and take a relationship for granted, the nurturing and cherishing of the early years shouldn't be allowed to slip away . . . ever.

The captain's voice came over the Tannoy giving details of their flight and instructing the crew to take their seats for take-off. Then they were racing down the runway and up into the gun-metal sky, bumping slightly as they cut through the clouds. Devlin felt a sudden queasiness as her stomach gave a little lurch. Her heart sank. This wasn't the ideal moment to experience her first morning, or even late afternoon, sickness. This certainly wasn't on the agenda. She fished in her handbag and found a packet of Polo mints and slipped one into her mouth. The man beside her looked at her sympathetically.

'Ears popping?' he asked.

Devlin nodded. She wasn't sure for a minute if that was all that would be popping. She felt a cold sweat break across her forehead and decided she'd better make a move for the loo before her lunch came up over the man beside her. As suddenly as the nausea swept over her, it passed, and she took a deep breath of relief.

'Do you not like flying?' The man asked chattily. His eyes roved all over her. He had been throwing glances at her, lingering on her legs and the part of her thigh that wasn't covered by her skirt. Devlin's heart sank. He was a florid heavyset man in a pinstriped suit, obviously ready to engage her in conversation all the way to Galway. Her earlier effort obviously hadn't worked. Stronger measures were called for.

'I don't mind flying at all,' she murmured. 'I just have some all-day morning sickness. I hope I won't have to use the sick bag. Let's hope it's not a bumpy ride.'

A look of horror crossed his face. Devlin almost laughed at his expression.

'Oh dear. I hope not too,' he muttered before retreating behind his in-flight magazine.

Put that in your pipe and smoke it, Devlin thought silently, more than satisfied with his reaction. Morning sickness and sexy legs didn't quite gel, obviously.

Pillock! She let the plastic tray down, took her questions out of her briefcase and perused them slowly but found it hard to concentrate. The man had annoyed her. What was she supposed to do? Wear a skirt down to her ankles? Her skirt came to about an inch or two above the knee. It was perfectly respectable. She was no Ally McBeal for God's sake! Some men were such prats.

A while later, she caught him glancing in her direction again.

'You're a businesswoman, obviously? What line are you in?' He lowered his magazine. Devlin couldn't believe it. He was gearing up for another chat and his eyes were now copper-fastened to her camisole.

'Health and leisure. You must excuse me. I have a report to read before I get to my meeting.' Her tone was polite but her eyes were cold.

'Health and leisure. Interesting. I thought you might be in the beauty trade all right. I'm in computers myself.'

Devlin nodded and reached into her briefcase. She had just told the imbecile beside her that she had a report to read and he had ignored it completely. She pulled out Maggie's manuscript.

'Big report,' the Obnoxious One commented cheerily, still leering. They hit an air pocket and the plane shuddered. Devlin took her sick bag out of the pocket of the seat in front of her and opened it. Panic replaced the Obnoxious One's leer.

'The toilet is vacant,' he said hastily.

'I'm not sure standing up would be such a good idea,' Devlin replied, putting her hand to her mouth.

'Oh!' He retreated behind his magazine again and Devlin could sense his tension. She fiddled with the sick bag for a few moments before laying it down and picking up Maggie's pages. She was untroubled for the rest of the flight and escaped into Maggie's novel with pleasure. It was a cracking read and Devlin was sorry to come to the end of the latest chunk. She was dying for more.

Their descent into Galway was extremely turbulent and again nausea overtook her. This time she thought she really might have to use the sick bag. It would be good enough for her, she thought wryly as she sucked frantically on a Polo mint. The Obnoxious One's hands were clenched with tension and Devlin wasn't sure if it was because of the rough descent or the fear that she might puke.

It was a huge relief when the aircraft finally taxied to a halt. She breathed deeply, trying to regain her equilibrium. It was wonderful to be pregnant but the nausea had to be the pits, she thought glumly as she unfastened her seat-belt, took her bag and briefcase and walked down the aisle without a backward glance. She hoped that horrible man wouldn't be on her return flight tomorrow.

Her car was waiting for her and she sank gratefully into the leather seat and settled back for the short drive to Galway city. The sun had come out by the time they reached Eyre Square, the heavy dark clouds dissipating to reveal a welcome blue sky. She'd take a little stroll around the square as soon as she had checked in, she decided. It would be good to stretch her legs and clear her head. The reception was busy. A coachload of Japanese had just arrived and she noticed a lot of elderly couples sitting in the foyer, obviously taking advantage of the off-peak special packages. Galway city was the perfect place for elderly visitors. The shops were all within walking distance of the hotel and for those who didn't fancy walking too far the magnificent Eyre Square Centre was right across the street from the hotel. There was a huge variety of shops and restaurants to suit all tastes. Devlin grinned, remembering her first visit, when she and Caroline had shopped till they dropped and had come back to Dublin laden down with goodies.

It was a pity Caroline wasn't with her today, she thought regretfully as she filled out her registration form. They could have spent a nice evening together, especially as her friend could do with some cheering-up.

Her room overlooked the square and in the late evening sunshine it looked very picturesque. It had turned much milder and young couples sat snuggled together on the benches in Kennedy Park, laughing and chatting. Devlin kicked off her shoes, changed into a track suit and loafers, slipped her jacket on and locked her door behind her. She handed the big old-fashioned key into reception and hurried outside into the fresh air. She could smell the salt tang of the sea breeze but decided against the walk down to the sea front and City Girl. She wanted to have a swim in the hotel pool before dinner and she didn't want to eat late.

She crossed the road at the pedestrian crossing, marvelling again at the courtesy of Galway's drivers. Every time she visited Galway she was struck by how pedestrian-friendly the city was. In Dublin you took your life in your hands trying to cross a busy road . . . even at a pedestrian crossing. She walked briskly through Kennedy Park, past The Cannons that had been brought to Galway after the Crimean War. She couldn't help but wonder how many lives they'd taken, how many bodies they'd maimed and bloodied. She shivered at the gruesome thought, pushed it away impatiently, annoyed with herself for her morbidity. What on earth was wrong with her? Her emotions were very close to the surface this past week or so. Was it because of the massive hormonal changes taking place in her body as it adjusted to the physical and emotional demands of pregnancy?

Oh stop being so dramatic! she chided herself silently as she crossed the square again and headed for Hollands Newsagents where she treated herself to *Hello!*, *Vanity Fair* and a Twix bar for which she had a terrible weakness. The streets were alive with people and buskers and street entertainers. Strains of music wafted down William Street. Laughter and chat and the foreign accents of tourists permeated the air. Devlin thought back with nostalgia to the times she and Caroline and Maggie used to be out on the town with not a care in the world except worrying about whether they'd shift a man.

It seemed a long time ago. Fifteen years *was* a long time, and a lot of water had flowed under the bridge since then. Galway was such a youthful city, it made her feel a little past it, she thought wryly as she watched a stunning redhead saunter along the street in a short black mini, thigh-high patent leather boots and a cream Aran sweater. If the Obnoxious One had been sitting beside *her* on the flight, his eyes would have been out on stalks, Devlin thought as she cast an envious glance at the young woman. Such confidence, such nonchalant chic, such *youth*. Devlin felt vaguely depressed. She'd never have that again. She

131

might have success and wealth and style but she was no longer what was considered young. Early thirties was practically middle-aged. Early thirties, married and pregnant . . . forget it, she thought glumly as she turned and headed back to the hotel.

It must be tiredness that had made her feel ancient, it had to be, she decided as she changed into her swimsuit and studied her appearance in the mirror. It was too early for her pregnancy to show. She still looked supple and toned from her workouts. Her bobbed hair added definition to her cheekbones. Her blue eyes were wide and bright under dark lashes and she didn't look anywhere *near* a thirty-something, she decided defiantly, as she pulled her track suit on over her swimsuit and hurried up to the pool.

The views from the floor-to-ceiling windows that ran the length of the pool were magnificent and she was just in time to see the sun, a huge pale orange-red orb, sinking behind the hills. The sunsets in the West of Ireland were awe-inspiring, she'd viewed many from the dining-room in City Girl and never failed to appreciate their unique beauty. There were only two other people in the large heated pool, a middle-aged woman and an elderly man who stayed up in the shallow end so she was able to slice through the water with ease as she swam steady laps. Three-quarters of an hour later, refreshed and invigorated, she swam to the ladder and climbed out. A sauna would have gone down well, she thought longing, as she dried herself off in the changing-room, preferring to have a bath in her own room.

Too relaxed even to think of dressing up for dinner, she had a long leisurely soak with *Hello!* before wrapping her pale blue silk dressing-gown around her and ordering a light meal from room service.

She watched the news and weather as she ate, stretched out on the double bed, and at ten, as promised, Luke rang and she regaled him with the day's happenings. She was fast asleep by eleven, her arms wrapped around a pillow in lieu of Luke's strong comforting body.

The following morning Devlin had eaten breakfast and checked out by eight thirty. Her car had arrived to take her the short drive to City Girl and she felt ready for anything.

The manageress, Ciara Hanlon, was waiting for her as she walked into the marble- and wood-finished foyer.

'Devlin, great to see you. I hope you had a good night in the Great Southern. I have everything set up. You have three meetings scheduled. Two this morning and one in the afternoon,' she announced briskly.

Devlin smiled at the tall, thin young woman in front of her. Ciara Hanlon was one of the most efficient people she had ever encountered. She had started out as a therapist in Dublin's City Girl and had proved herself so capable that she had quickly been promoted to salon manager, before becoming assistant manager in Belfast. Ciara was ambitious and hungry. When Galway had come onstream she had been by far the best candidate at interview and Devlin had felt very confident that she would do a good job as manager of Galway City Girl.

She'd certainly proved herself, Devlin admitted, as she cast an eye around the foyer and reception area. The place was spick and span. Mirrors and chandeliers gleamed. The wooden floor, with its scattering of luxurious deep-pile rugs, shone. The reception desk was neat and tidy. The receptionists in their royal blue suits looked smart and well groomed. Trailing pot plants dotted around bloomed healthily and vases of freshly cut flowers were arranged artistically here and there. Current editions of glossy magazines lay in neat piles on small coffee-tables in front of several luxurious two-seater sofas. Soothing music played in the background. Although it was relatively early, guests wandered around in white towelling robes and an aerobics class was at full swing in the well-equipped gym.

'We have twenty minutes before your first meeting, if you'd like tea or coffee,' Ciara suggested. 'We can have it in my office.'

'Fine,' Devlin agreed. 'A cup of tea, milk no sugar, I'll be up to the office in a few minutes. I'd just like to say hello to the girls.'

'Some of them will be doing treatments,' Ciara said smoothly. 'You should relax for a little while before the meetings.'

'Don't worry, I will. I'll be along in a minute. You go ahead and organize the tea, Ciara,' Devlin said lightly. She always liked, and made it a point, to talk to the staff when she was visiting Belfast or Galway. She walked down the bright French-windowed corridor that overlooked the panorama of gardens and the bay and thought how lucky they'd been to get such a marvellous site for the Galway centre. Gulls screamed and dived into the choppy white-capped waves, late roses swayed in the gusts of wind that swirled the leaves beneath the trees like dervishes doing their wild crazy dancing. The windswept, sea-lashed, autumnal landscape seemed cold and uninviting viewed from the snug, warm, serene interior of

City Girl, and Devlin envied the two towelling-robed women she noticed relaxing in the huge deep arm-chairs in the lounge overlooking the bay. How nice it would be to change out of her business suit into one of those big soft robes and snuggle into an armchair to snooze while waiting to be called for a facial or body massage or some such delightful treatment.

She walked on past the swimming-pool where several energetic swimmers cut through the warm azure water. A group sat laughing and chatting in the Jacuzzi, utterly relaxed.

Devlin smiled. That was what she liked to see.

She popped into the airy dining-room and greeted Margaret, the supervisor, warmly.

'How are things, Margaret? Are you keeping well? How's your little boy after his operation?'

'Ah, Devlin! Come in. He's fine. I'm fine. Are you staying or is it a flying visit?' The attractive grey-haired woman's face creased in a welcoming smile.

'It's just a flying visit this time. But I'll probably spend a lot more time down here when things get under way.' Devlin smiled. They chatted for a minute or so, then she slipped into the kitchen to say hello to the chef and the kitchen staff before hurrying down to the treatment rooms to have a chat with the thera-pists, who were poring over the timetable with their appointments indicated in black marker.

There was great excitement about the proposed new residential unit and Devlin was delighted with their enthusiasm.

'If you've any suggestions, I'll be happy to take them on board. After all, you all know better than I do what works and what doesn't, and what's needed and what isn't. I'm going to come over some day next month and we'll have a staff meeting with everyone and see what comes up. So anything that you think might work or any changes you feel we could make, please feel free to discuss them with me. We'll get Chef to do a buffet breakfast and enjoy one of his nosh-ups while we're at it,' she suggested. 'I'll tell Ciara to schedule all treatments for ten a.m. so that we can have a good hour and a half for our session.'

Her proposal was greeted with much approval and Devlin hurried back to Ciara's office well pleased with her morning's work. It was important to include all the staff in discussions relating to their work and the changes that were going to take place. It made for a good working atmosphere. Luke, who had been in business for a long time before he met her, had taught her that if the company employees weren't happy and fulfilled in their jobs, their dissatisfaction would permeate every level of the business with very negative results. From the start, Devlin had paid over the odds in wages and given her staff a very attractive employment package. Her highly motivated workforce was one of the most important contributing factors to City Girl's phenomenal success. Devlin intended to keep it that way.

Fifteen

Ciara was tapping her fingers on the desk when Devlin arrived. Devlin ignored her manageress's impatience.

'The place is humming, the girls seem happy, you're doing a great job, Ciara. Thank you,' she said warmly as she poured tea for both of them from the silver pot that rested on a silver tray on Ciara's desk.

'I'd have done that,' Ciara protested.

'Sit down and relax.' Devlin grinned. 'By the time today's over it's more than tea you'll be needing. By the way, I'm going to come down some day next month and have a general staff meeting. I'll get Liz to arrange it with Anne. They can check our diaries and see what day suits both of us. We'll get Chef to do a buffet breakfast and we can all have a chat over it. Don't schedule any appointments until 10 a.m. I'd like to hear what everyone has to say about the new proposals. I want you to put the plans on display on the notice-board in the staff-room when the architects have drawn them up, to see what the staff think. All suggestions welcome. OK?'

'Sure. No problem,' Ciara agreed enthusiastically. 'Great idea to get everyone so involved.'

'It makes for good working relations and that's

what makes things tick over nicely. I intend to keep it like that. Obviously we're going to have to employ a lot of new staff. Housekeeping, dining-room, and of course new therapists. There'll be promotions, naturally. I'd like to promote from inhouse as much as possible. But we'll discuss that at a later meeting,' Devlin said crisply. Now that she was in gear the adrenaline was flowing and she was raring to go. A moment later a call came from reception to say that the architect had arrived. Shortly afterwards the first meeting of the day got underway.

It was a very satisfying meeting. The architect, Brendan Quinn, was young and enthusiastic. Devlin knew she was in good hands when she brought up her suggestion for a meditation room and he'd latched onto it eagerly.

'That's a humdinger of an idea, Devlin. I like your style.' He rubbed his hands in anticipation. 'Serenity is the key. It will be one of the most important rooms in the building so it definitely has to have a sea view. A nice big bay window. Just think, all that light pouring in, reflecting off crystals and wind chimes. And I think lots of wood. Maple is very warm. The site here is so good we have to make the most of the view and the light. Do you agree?'

'Oh yes.' Devlin was excited about his suggestions. She was very pleased that he understood immediately the ambience she was trying to create. His suggestion of a semicircular lounge interspersed with bay windows, with the treatment rooms radiating off the circle so that clients wouldn't have far to walk, met with uniform approval.

By the time the builder arrived, Devlin was ready to burst with excitement. This truly was going to be a health and leisure centre *par excellence*, she promised herself.

The builder, a giant of a Connemara man by the name of John Joseph Connolly, was a man of few words, but he had built the original Galway City Girl on time and within budget and his standards were superb. Luke and he went back a long way. Devlin was very glad when he'd agreed to take on the new project. He didn't see any major obstacles as he and Brendan discussed briefly the overall plan. He'd have more to say when he saw the plans drawn up, he told Devlin in his slow, calm way.

She took Ciara to lunch in K.C. Blake's brasserie, one of her favourite restaurants in Galway's Latin Quarter. They sat in a window-seat watching the world go by as they waited to be served and Devlin, who loved the buzz and energy of the place, decided that she was going to bring Luke with her the next time she came to Galway. They could take a few days off and shop and walk, and dine out and relax and pretend that they were on a second honeymoon.

'Do you miss Dublin at all, Ciara?' Devlin asked between mouthfuls of the most delicious potato and leek soup she had ever tasted.

'Not at all. I've a great social life here. Being manageress of City Girl helps enormously, of course. Membership is very "in" over in this neck of the woods. I get invited to all the best parties. It wasn't like that in Dublin. Well, unless you were you, that is.' She laughed.

'If that's what you like, good for you. I'm not really into posh parties myself. I much prefer to have an elbows on the table, gossip all night, sort of dinner with close friends at home,' Devlin confessed.

'God no! I much prefer to be out and about. I hate being stuck at home.' Ciara wrinkled her pert little nose in distaste at the idea.

'To each his own,' Devlin murmured, amused by the younger woman's response. She'd been very like her once, until a few of life's hard knocks had taken the stuffing out of her and she'd picked herself up, got her priorities sorted, and grown up. Ciara was utterly confident, focused and ambitious but there was a hardness about her sometimes that was surprising in one so young. Nevertheless she was excellent at her job and Devlin was very pleased with the way City Girl had taken off in Galway.

A meeting with the landscape gardener concluded her day. This, however, did not run as smoothly as the two earlier ones. Matthew Moran was a man who knew his own mind. He reminded Devlin of Luke in some ways, although he was older. Mid-forties at least. Tall, fit, as lean as a panther, he had a craggy, tanned face that was intense and serious in repose. When he smiled, his eyes crinkled up and he lost ten years. He had the bluest eyes Devlin had ever seen.

He gazed at her in horror when she informed him blithely that she wanted dozens of pink roses, cherry blossoms, flowering almond trees, lots of heathers and some pyracantha for winter colour. His eyebrows shot up to his hairline at the mention of pyracantha. 'And some nice voluptuous fuchsias. You know, the double flowering ones,' she added for good measure, ignoring his reaction.

'My dear good woman,' he said slowly in that delicious western accent that rolled off the tongue so silkily. 'This is the West of Ireland and your site is extremely exposed to the elements. If you take my advice you'll let me plant escallonia, cotoneaster, lavender, hebes, ulex, Spanish gorse, rock roses, cordyline and New Zealand flax. I'll get pictures of them for you,' he added helpfully.

'That would be great,' she enthused. Devlin knew some of the shrubs that he referred to and they were beautiful. But she knew what she wanted herself and she wasn't going to be dictated to, even if he was an expert. 'But couldn't I have those *and* heathers, fucshia and pink roses? And I'm sure pyracantha are extremely hardy—'

'And thorny,' he interjected. 'They have no aesthetic value whatsoever.'

'But they're beautiful in the winter. The berries are so vibrant. I don't agree with that at all,' Devlin exclaimed. He was somewhat taken aback at her vehemence.

'Vibrant berries, voluptuous fuchsia . . . ummm. Miss Delaney, we'd better get real here,' Matthew Moran said slowly.

'Call me, Devlin, Matthew,' Devlin smiled sweetly. 'Think of the challenge of it. I can visualize it just standing here looking out. I'm sure you could come up with some design to incorporate your ideas with mine.'

'We do aim to give our clients what they want, of course, Devlin,' she could see he was trying his best to hide his irritation, 'but realism has to play some part and you are paying me for my advice. It's rather a waste of money not to take it.'

Blue eyes met blue eyes and locked.

He's kind of dishy, Devlin thought. If she wasn't a happily married woman she'd definitely be interested.

'Tell you what, Matthew, live dangerously, you

come up with a design that suits both of us. I'm sure you'll rise to the occasion.'

'Are you now?' he drawled, as he shoved his hands into his jeans pockets and stared at her. 'What's so special about pink roses? Why pink? Why not red or orange or yellow? Just as a matter of curiosity?'

'Don't you know? And you're a gardener. Pink is the colour of love. The love of my life always gives me pink roses.'

Matthew looked frankly astonished at this piece of information. 'Is that so. Well, I suppose that goes some way towards explaining your propensity for pink. I always thought red roses did the trick in that department.'

'Oh no, I wouldn't thank you for a red rose. Maybe in romantic terms red is considered *the* colour but a friend of mine who knows all about these things says that, spiritually, pink is the colour of love and my centre here is going to be serene and spiritual and a place of cherishing. And besides, pink is much more subtle and pleasing to the eye,' Devlin explained.

Matthew Moran stared at her for a long moment. 'I see,' he said quietly after a while. 'In that case as well as making the most of the panorama, perhaps you'd like me to develop some secluded little nooks and crannies where clients can go and sit and be alone to read or just to sit and think?'

Devlin's eyes lit up. 'Oh Matthew that's a lovely idea! I love it,' she said warmly.

'Do you?' He smiled then, pleased at her reaction, and she was struck by the kindness in his eyes when they weren't guarded and remote. 'Well then, we'd better see what we can do. I'll get the plans from Brendan Quinn and then I'll be in touch. Good day to you, and to you, Miss Hanlon.' He nodded courteously in Ciara's direction. Then he strode out the door and the office felt strangely empty when he was gone.

'Were you winding him up, Devlin?' Ciara giggled.

'Well, I was in the beginning,' Devlin admitted.

'All that stuff about pink being the colour of love. That was a put-on, wasn't it? Did you see his face? I think he thinks you're for the birds. You know these culchies . . . haven't a clue.' Ciara prattled on.

'Actually, pink *is* the colour of love, Ciara, and in the end I think he understood where I was coming from,' Devlin said coolly. 'And he might be a culchie, but he was a sexy culchie in a very masculine sort of way, don't you think?'

'God no, you're joking! I like suave men in suits.' Ciara made a face at the notion that she could be attracted to a countryman who wore jeans and a jumper and spoke with an accent.

'You would,' Devlin thought.

'You know a lot about flowers,' Ciara remarked. 'I'd just about know a daisy from a dandelion.'

'I don't really. My parents are keen gardeners, I spent a lot of time in the garden with them when I was a child. Matthew is right though, some of my suggestions aren't practical for the site and climate here. Not that I'd admit it, yet,' Devlin explained as she gathered her papers together. 'Right, Ciara. I'm off to catch my flight. A great day's work all round. We'll be in touch. Thanks for everything.' She held out her hand and gave Ciara a firm handshake.

The younger woman returned it limply. It was a real wet-fish handshake. So at odds with Ciara's forceful personality, Devlin always felt.

Her car was waiting in the drive and she sank back into the leather seat with relief, as a sudden unexpected weariness enveloped her. She had a desperate urge to lie down and fall fast asleep. Had she had this tiredness when she'd been pregnant with Lynn? It was such a long time ago she couldn't really remember.

It was a real effort to make conversation with the driver, who was full of chat. She'd be glad when she was home. The thoughts of the return flight and the drive home from the airport made her heart sink. Devlin longed for bed.

Later, as she sat waiting to board, relieved beyond measure that there was no sign of the Obnoxious One, she took her mobile phone out of her bag and dialled Luke's private line. Her number would come up, he'd know it was her.

'Hi Devlin. How did it go?' His voice had a smile in it and she smiled back.

'I miss you, Luke,' she said longingly, suddenly desperately lonely for him, as she walked over to a window out of earshot of the other passengers.

'I miss you too, but it won't be long until I'm with you,' he said comfortingly.

'Oh Luke, I don't know if it's my hormones, I'm blaming everything on them, but I'm as horny as hell and I wish I was in bed with you right now doing wild erotic things.'

'Don't say things like that,' he groaned. 'Now you're making *me* horny. I might go out and jump on Dianne.'

Devlin giggled. Dianne Westwood was Luke's highly efficient, glamorous PA. Unmarried, in her late thirties, she'd always had a major crush on him, despite his efforts to let her know in a kind way that she was barking completely up the wrong tree. Dianne thought that she concealed her feelings extremely well but her crush was very obvious. She detested Devlin and was always businesslike but exceedingly cool towards her.

'Well if you go out and jump on Dianne, I'm going to go back into Galway to jump on the landscape gardener I met today. He was *really* sexy,' Devlin teased.

'Who's he?' Luke asked.

'His name is Matthew Moran. He was a bit of all right.'

'You hussy. And a pregnant hussy at that. But a very sexy pregnant hussy,' he added huskily. 'I wish you were here. Let's stop talking about sex or I'll get nothing done for the rest of the evening and I've a meeting in ten minutes. I want to be able to concentrate. Tell me about what happened today instead.'

'OK, just this once I'll take pity on you but I'm going to talk dirty to you on the phone tonight—'

'Devlin stop it!' Luke laughed. 'Tell me about today.'

'I had a great day. I met Brendan Quinn and John Joe Connolly. Brendan had some excellent ideas. He's really in tune with the whole thing, which makes it so much easier. And you know John Joe. As quiet as ever. But he's sound.'

'He's a great bloke. I worked with him on the building sites here, he'd never let you down. I'm glad he's doing the job.'

'Me too,' Devlin agreed just as her flight was called over the Tannoy. 'Luke, I have to go, my flight's been called. Ring me tonight.'

'OK. Take care of yourself.'

'You too. I love you.'

'I love you too. Bye.'

She was so lucky, she thought, as she walked towards the queue at the boarding gate. She had everything. Luke was her soul mate as well as her lover and when they were apart she missed him like hell, she thought as she handed her boarding card to the air stewardess.

The flight home was smoother than the previous day's flight and the seat beside her was empty, which made it more relaxing. The tiredness swamped her again and she fell asleep soon after take-off in spite of her best efforts.

She woke to hear the captain announce that they were making their descent into Dublin airport and blinked rapidly, trying to focus. She hoped she hadn't been snoring.

The drive home was horrendous. The rush-hour gridlock was well under way. She got stuck in a traffic jam on the airport dual carriageway, and as the bumper-to-bumper traffic crawled along at a snail's pace she had to struggle to keep her wits about her, she felt so lethargic. She cursed herself for not leaving the car at home and taking a taxi. But then the queues at the taxi rank at the airport had been huge too, so it was six of one half a dozen of the other, she reckoned, as she inched past Whitehall church.

Peckish, but too tired to cook for herself, she stopped at the chippers and got a snack box.

'If Dianne could see me now,' she thought in amusement ten minutes later as she ate from the box with her fingers, not even bothering to put the chicken and chips on a plate. She dumped the empty box in the bin, had a quick shower, and was in bed by seven thirty.

Still, it had been a most productive day. One of the best she had ever put in, she thought with satisfaction. City Girl phase two was ready to roll.

Devlin picked up the phone and dialled Luke's number.

'Hello, love, I know it's early, but I just can't keep my eyes open. So do you mind if I don't talk dirty tonight, I just have to go asleep.'

'Spoilsport! What happened, horny?' he laughed.

'Pregnancy,' she murmured. 'It's amazing, Luke. One minute you're flying around the place. The next you're so zonked you'd sleep at the drop of a hat. I can't remember being like this when I was pregnant before.'

'Maybe you're doing too much,' he said, concerned.

'No, no,' she hastened to reassure him. 'I'm fine, honestly. This happens in the first months. It passes, so I'm told. I'll call you the minute I wake up in the morning and tell you *exactly* what I'd like you to do to me and *exactly* what I'd like to do to you. How about that?'

'Sounds good to me, Devlin.' Luke was smiling, she could tell.

'I love you, good night.'

'Good night, I love you too,' Luke echoed tenderly down the line.

Devlin fell asleep smiling, but it wasn't Luke she dreamed of, it was Matthew Moran who was looking into her eyes and telling her that he loved her.

Sixteen

Maggie applied her make-up carefully for her meeting with Marcy Elliot. She had taken great care when dressing and looked very chic in a slate-grey tailored trouser suit worn with a pale pink silk camisole. Her editor was a stylish, elegant woman. Maggie always made an extra effort when she was going to see her. She gelled her fringe and fingered her hair, trying to achieve a feathery effect. It had grown too long. It was practically a bird's nest. Time to get it cut. She noted with dismay the smattering of grey hairs among the rich gold and chestnut curls that tumbled to her shoulders. The time was coming when she'd have to consider her hairdresser's suggestion about tinting.

Maggie grinned. Her hairdresser, Nikki, was such a bossy-boots but she was the best in the world. Maybe it was time for a change of image, as Nikki was constantly suggesting. It might make her feel better psychologically. There was nothing like a new hairstyle to pick you up when you felt sludgy and unattractive and down in the dumps. Nikki wanted to cut her hair shorter but Maggie, for some strange reason, always felt naked if the back of her neck was bare. She'd get it cut before she went to Powerscourt

Springs, she decided. And, of course, she wanted to look her best when Alma arrived. Alma went to the hairdresser and beauty salon at least three times a week. She always looked terrific.

When Maggie had lived in Saudi, she'd done the same. It was a way of life. Now she was so busy she hardly had time to go to City Girl for a workout.

The phone rang. Maggie hurried to answer it, glancing at her watch as she did so. It was early, nine fifteen. She was meeting Marcy at ten thirty in the Shelbourne. She needed to get her skates on. If it was Nelsie on the phone ready for one of her long chats, Maggie would just have to cut her short and her mother wouldn't like that.

'Please don't let it be Ma,' she murmured as she picked up the receiver. 'Hello?'

'Maggie, I know this is bad form and short notice but could you possibly meet me for lunch rather than at ten thirty as arranged? Something's come up that I need to attend to,' Marcy said briskly.

'I'll have to be back here for twenty to three, Marcy. I have to pick Shona up from school.' Maggie tried to keep the irritation out of her voice. Did Marcy think that she was the only one with a hectic schedule?

'Don't worry, we'll have a quick bite to eat and I'll fill you in on developments.' Marcy was as businesslike as ever. 'How about if I meet you at one in the Shelbourne? We can eat there. I'll book a table.'

'OK, Marcy. See you then.' Maggie sighed.

'Fine so. Bye.' Marcy was gone, leaving Maggie staring at the phone in exasperation. How typical of Marcy. She had a knack of making Maggie feel completely and utterly insignificant and inconsequential.

It wasn't at all deliberate. It was simply that her editor had such a sense of herself and her own importance, it was inconceivable that someone else's time was just as important as Marcy's. It would never dawn on the other woman that Maggie might be insulted or inconvenienced by her 'something that had come up'. It would certainly never occur to Marcy that Maggie had to work around her children's school hours, and that her time was as worthy of consideration as Marcy's. But then Marcy didn't have children. She had no conception of what it was like to rear children and run a household. Marcy lived in a posh apartment in Sutton with her barrister husband. They had a part-time housekeeper who cleaned, shopped, and ironed, leaving both of them plenty of time to aggressively pursue their career ambitions.

What she should have done, Maggie thought glumly, was be assertive and say that the new arrangement didn't suit. But knowing Marcy she'd probably have said 'fine' and suggested a meeting later in the week. Maggie was so on edge about what was going on at Enterprise Publishing she couldn't wait that long.

'I bet Josephine Langley won't be palmed off with "a quick bite to eat,"' Maggie growled as she tidied away her make-up. Josephine Langley was Enterprise's most successful best-selling author. She'd made a fortune for the company and was the envy of every other author in the Enterprise stable. All of them, including Maggie, aspired to equalling her sales figures.

'Oh stop talking to yourself!' She glowered at her reflection in the mirror. She had a couple of hours to fill. There was no point in sitting down to write, she was too tense. She could change the sheets on the children's beds and put in a wash or she could make a big pot roast and freeze a couple of dinners or she could mend the rip in Michael's school pullover or . . . there were a dozen chores that needed her attention. None of them the slightest bit enticing. Besides, she didn't feel like taking off her grey trouser suit to do housework.

Impulsively she picked up her bag and car keys and hurried downstairs. Ten minutes later she was on the M50 heading for Glasnevin. If Nikki couldn't fit her in for a cut and blow-dry she'd drive into City Girl and see if Devlin could arrange a hair appointment for her. The bird's nest was getting to her.

Fifteen minutes later she parked down the small side road adjacent to the Botanic Garden Nurseries. She'd seen a warden give a ticket to a woman parked on the double yellows outside her hairdressers and she wasn't going to take the risk. She crossed the road and walked briskly past the off-licence and chemist. She needed Vick and junior aspirin, she remembered, she'd get them on the way back. She'd asked Terry three times to get them on his way home from work but he'd forgotten each time.

The salon was busy and her heart sank. It was a bit much to come without an appointment.

'Hi Maggie, you look the biz, are you off on a publicity thing?' Nikki greeted her.

'Well, I'm meeting my editor for lunch in the Shelbourne and the hair's gone bird's-nesty.'

'You can say that again,' the petite brunette said dryly. 'Take a seat, I can fit you in, but you're getting a radical change of image and you can start getting used to the idea right now.'

'Not short,' protested Maggie.

'Short! Sit!' Nikki ordered.

'Yes, Nikki,' Maggie said meekly. Despite her dread of short hair, the idea of a radical change of image was very seductive.

Two hours later she was staring shell-shocked at her reflection in the big gleaming mirror in front of her. The curls were gone and the grey hairs too, replaced by a sleek sophisticated cut, styled back behind the ears, to draw attention to her eyes and cheekbones. A feathery fringe softened the image but she was shaken none the less.

'It's so short,' she wailed.

'It's gorgeous. Very sexy.'

'Takes years off you.'

'It will be so easy to manage.'

'It's cool.'

Jean, Pauline, Louise and Laura, the other stylists, crowded around to have a look as Nikki stood, arms folded, smiling smugly, having got her own way at long last.

'It's you, Maggie. It's youthful and fresh and the next time you're in I might cut it even shorter.'

'In your dreams, Nikki.' Maggie grinned as she paid her bill.

'We'll see!' Nikki said coolly but she gave Maggie a warm hug before she left.

Maggie hurried back to the car. Her neck felt cold. She'd buy a scarf in town. Her head felt so light and shorn. It would take a while to get used to. It was so nice to have stylists that cared about their customers. Maggie always left Nikki's feeling like a new woman. Today she looked like one, she reflected, as she stared at her reflection in the rear-view mirror. The tint was nice though, rich but very natural-looking. Her first tint, that was a sure sign of middle-age and she wasn't even forty, she thought mournfully as she slid into the traffic and headed for the city.

It was just midday. She'd park in the City Girl car park, pop up and see Devlin and then walk across Stephen's Green to the Shelbourne.

'It's fabulous, Maggie!' Devlin exclaimed as Maggie walked into her office half an hour later. 'Turn around. Let me see.' Maggie laughed and put her hand to the back of her neck.

'It's too short.'

'No it's not. It's so sophisticated,' Devlin raved. 'It's so with it. It's perfect for you.'

'I got a tint,' Maggie confessed. 'I'm on the slippery slope.'

'Oh dear,' Devlin murmured. 'It's a beautiful shade. It's very natural.'

'I know, but still now that I've started I'll have to keep doing it. I don't believe in growing old gracefully. I'll fight it tooth and nail.'

'Me too,' Devlin said firmly. 'I don't care what the feminists say. The first sign of wrinkles and grey hair and I'm nipping it in the bud for my own sake. Are we very vain and shallow?' she asked, laughing.

'No. We're normal. We're human,' Maggie declared as she viewed herself in the mirror on Devlin's wall. 'Are you sure it's not too short?'

'No it's perfect. Now how did you get on with Marcy Elliot? What's happening at your publishers?' Devlin sat on the edge of her desk, bright-eyed and full of vitality, oozing chic in a taupe tailored suit. Maggie reflected that her marriage to Luke had been the best thing that had ever happened to her. No

153

longer restless and unhappy, Devlin had it all.

'Marcy changed the meeting to a lunch-time one. I'm meeting her at one in the Shelbourne which is a bit of a pain in the butt because I'll have to rush home to collect Shona from school, so I probably won't have time to come back over and tell you about it. I'll give you a ring tonight.' Maggie sighed.

'Oh! I was dying to hear what's going on,' Devlin said regretfully.

'Me too. It's very unsettling, Dev. I can't write. I'm worried about my new editor. What's he or she going to be like? I'm taking a break after this one. I'm whacked.'

'You can't do that,' protested her friend. 'Your fans will go mad. The pages you brought over on Sunday were brilliant. *Betrayal* is definitely your best yet.'

'Oh, do you think so, Dev? And you really liked the pages?' Maggie said eagerly, always glad to get a positive response to a novel in progress. Her greatest fear was that it would never be as good as her previous novels and that she was losing her touch. Praise and encouragement always gave her confidence a boost.

'I really liked them,' Devlin assured her. 'It's going to be a great book, so stop panicking and keep writing. It doesn't matter who your editor is, it's you that's writing it.'

'A good editor is like a good husband, Devlin. Supportive, encouraging, keeping you on the straight and narrow when you can't see the wood for the trees. I don't have that in Terry any more, that's why I valued Marcy so much.' To her dismay, tears welled in her eyes.

154

'Oh Maggie, Maggie!' Devlin shot up, horrified, and hurried over to her friend.

'I'm sorry, Dev,' Maggie sobbed. 'I don't know where all this came from. It must be PMT. It's just that I feel so stressed and then Terry goes and pulls the Al Shariff stunt and I know my feelings didn't even enter his head when he invited them. All he was thinking about was the good time he'd have with Sulaiman and showing off in front of Alma. And I just wonder how much longer I can stick living with him without going crazy. I don't want to be with him. I don't want to be married to him any more. I feel so angry and resentful. If it was just me, I'd be gone. But I have to think of the kids. They were so traumatized the first time we separated, I couldn't bear to put them through it again. But Devlin, if only you knew how much I long for a bit of support and thoughtfulness and kisses and cuddles. You know the kind of thing that makes all your hassles and troubles fade into the background, and you don't care what's happening on the outside because inside you feel cherished. I miss it, Devlin. I look at you and Luke and envy you so much, not in a bad way but in a way that makes me feel how empty my own life is. I'm sorry. I'm sorry. It has to be PMT or something. I don't usually do this.' Maggie's body shook with sobs.

'It's OK, Maggie. It's OK.' Devlin put her arms around her friend and stroked her back.

'Do I have to live the rest of my life with Terry because of vows I made years ago? I believed them when I made them. I didn't know all this was going to happen. I didn't know I'd stop loving him. How can God be so cruel as to want two people who have no feelings for each other to stay together? There's no love in that,' Maggie raged. 'I don't understand any of it. I tried my best to be a good wife and mother but am I supposed to be miserable for the rest of my life because the Church doesn't allow divorce? I feel completely trapped, Devlin. I feel all this pressure inside me. Sometimes I think I'm going to crack up.'

'I don't know what to say to help,' Devlin admitted. 'It must be horrible to feel so trapped. I'm sorry things are so bad between you and Terry. And I think it would truly be very wrong for you to feel that you have to stay with him for the rest of your life just so you can say "I kept the rules." I think Caroline is right sometimes that we all come into each others' lives for a reason and then we move on after we've learned whatever they have to teach us. Maybe Terry is teaching you that it's not wrong to put yourself first sometimes. You should talk to Caroline, she's good at this kind of stuff,' Devlin urged, desperate to help.

'Oh I don't know. I couldn't cope with being told that Terry is a great spirit and that we all knew what we were letting ourselves in for before we came to earth. Who in their right mind would have agreed to my life? If what she says is true, I'm sure I'd have wanted to be a perfect size twelve with straight hair, able to eat as much as I liked. And with someone sensitive, and supportive and dead sexy for a husband.' Maggie sniffed, wiping her eyes. 'Sorry, Devlin, this certainly wasn't on the agenda,' she said ruefully as she inspected the damage in the mirror. 'Look at the state of me. I can't waltz into the Shelbourne looking like this.' Mascara ran in streaks down under her eyes.

Her cheeks were blotchy, her eye-shadow smudged and her cheeks red and swollen.

'Stay calm, I'll get one of the girls to touch you up. Here, wipe off that mascara.' Devlin rummaged in her bag and produced make-up remover and a cotton pad.

'Thanks. You're a pal.'

Devlin gave her a hug. 'All I can say is that Luke and I will always be here for you and we'll do anything to help out when the Al Shariffs come.'

'Thanks, Devlin.' Maggie gulped. Where had that unleashing of sorrow and grief come from? What was wrong with her, losing control like that? 'Sorry for bawling all over you. I don't know why it happened.' Her hands shook as she poured some cream onto the pad.

'Maggie, you're under stress. You're unhappy. You're tired and unsupported. Why would you *not* burst into tears now and again? I don't know how you cope with the kids and your career and the state of your marriage. You carry it off really well. You're *entitled* to a Good-Cry-And-Get-It-Off-Your-Chest-Day every so often,' Devlin declared as she pressed a button on her intercom and asked for a beautician to come up to her office as soon as possible with her make-up kit.

'I'm awful. I never even asked you how you got on in Galway,' Maggie said apologetically. 'Did you have a good trip? Is it all working out?'

'It's going to be great, Maggie. When it's all set up we'll go down for a pampery weekend,' Devlin enthused. 'I was talking to the architect. It's going to be all wood and windows to make the most of that fantastic light. And the landscape gardener came up with some beautiful ideas. As well as making the most of the panorama he's going to develop some secluded little nooks and crannies where clients can go and sit and be alone to read or just to sit and think. It's going to cost a fortune and Andrew is whinging away but it will be worth it. But do you know something, Maggie? For the last couple of days this tiredness has come over me and I've just wanted to put my head down and sleep. I don't remember having that with Lynn,' Devlin remarked.

'Oh I had that with the twins. I'll never forget it. I used to be exhausted. I fell asleep at a dinner party in Saudi once. Terry was mortified. It passes after the first three months, though. And Devlin, my advice is, don't run yourself into the ground and take naps when you need them,' Maggie said firmly.

'Yes, nurse,' Devlin said meekly.

Maggie grinned. 'I mean it, Miss. I know you. Gadding about here and there, organizing this, developing that. This is the perfect time for you to learn to delegate—' A knock on the door interrupted her lecture.

'Perfect timing, saved from a sermon.' Devlin wrinkled her nose at Maggie as she opened the door to admit a white-coated beautician. 'Hi, Carla, can you do a quick repair job on Maggie? She has to be out of here in five minutes.'

'No problem,' the young woman said cheerfully. 'If you just sit here in Devlin's chair – the light is better – I'll fix you up now.'

Five minutes later Maggie, restored to her former glory, hugged Devlin. 'Thanks for everything. I'll be in touch.'

'Let me know what's going on. I'll be dying to

hear. And good luck. I'm sure it will all turn out for the best. Maybe your new editor will be dynamite! Maybe she'll take you to creative heights you've never been to before. Sometimes change is good,' Devlin encouraged. 'And don't forget, Luke and I will help out any way we can when the Al Shariffs are over. OK?'

'OK.' Maggie smiled as she waved goodbye and closed the door behind her. The relief of unburdening herself to Devlin left her feeling much less oppressed. Her friend was right. Keeping things in didn't help. A good cry helped the body and soul. The release of all that emotion had helped her clarify things in her own mind. She had finally admitted that she didn't want to be married to Terry any more. And while it didn't change her situation, the verbal acknowledgement of it meant that she could stop running away from it. That at least was something positive. And maybe Devlin was right about the new editor. She always had a very optimistic way of looking at things. Maggie hadn't thought of it in those terms at all. Maybe her creativity would be enhanced and she'd learn a lot more about writing. Perhaps things wouldn't turn out too bad after all.

Maggie hurried down the steps of City Girl – she didn't want to keep Marcy waiting. Then a thought struck her. Marcy had often kept her waiting. She slowed her pace. Typical of her, Maggie thought ruefully. Putting everyone else first. Well, not today. She wasn't going to arrive at the Shelbourne out of breath and all flustered. Marcy could cool her heels for a few minutes for once.

Seventeen

The Shelbourne was buzzing. Movers, shakers. Businessmen and women. Ladies who lunch. Legal eagles. Men about town. Politicians. Journalists. They all ebbed and flowed through the busy hotel and there, in the lounge, engrossed in a conversation on her mobile, a sheaf of papers on her knee, briefcase at her feet, sat Marcy Elliot, the epitome of the Nineties career woman.

Maggie had always admired her. Highly intelligent, sharp, tolerating no nonsense. Marcy was assertive and assured and always put herself first. Although she admired her, Maggie didn't like her the way she liked Sandra Nolan, the sales and marketing director. Sandra was warm and bubbly as well as being superb at her job. Marcy lacked warmth and empathy and Maggie found that hard to take sometimes. Nevertheless she was an exceptional editor and Maggie knew how lucky she was to have been given such an excellent grounding for her first three novels. Marcy had taught her a lot.

Today her editor was as elegant and stylish as ever, in a severe black suit with a cream camisole. Her cropped chestnut hair gleamed. Her make-up was impeccable. Her bright blue eyes shone with health.

Marcy was one of the most health-conscious people Maggie had ever met. She neither smoked nor drank. Didn't eat red meat, exercised daily and looked so fit and healthy that Maggie always felt stones over-weight and sludgy and flabby beside her.

Marcy saw her and beckoned imperiously for her to join her. Maggie hid a smile. Although she and Marcy were almost the same age, Marcy had an air of authority and self-assurance that made her seem years older.

'I suggest that we try and find a window that suits both of us sooner rather than later, Monica. Get your secretary to call me when you've had a chance to check your diary. Talk soon. Bye,' Maggie heard her editor say crisply before she ended the call. Marcy then turned her attention to her author and in her brisk, authoritative way said, 'Maggie, good to see you. *Love* the hair. It takes years off you. Let's head directly into the restaurant. I've booked a table in Number 27. I haven't eaten there before. I'm looking forward to it.' She swept her file of papers into her briefcase in one fluid motion.

She stood up gracefully and Maggie tried not to be envious of her supple, well-toned figure. 'I hope you're hungry. This is going on Enterprise's expense account and I, for one, intend making the most of it.' She swept ahead of Maggie and led the way out of the lounge and into the restaurant.

As they were shown to their table, Maggie, who hadn't dined in the restaurant previously either, was conscious that the majority of diners were men. She looked around to see if Terry was at any of the tables. He often had business lunches here. She couldn't see him, or, more likely in Terry's case, hear him, but she

161

silently applauded his choice of restaurant.

Number 27 was spacious, airy and ornately elegant, the high ceiling with its beautiful intricate plaster work a tribute to the timeless refinement of bygone days. Chandeliers sparkled. Mirrors gleamed on the walls, reflecting windows adorned with heavy swagged blue curtains. Warm yellow walls lent a cosy air. The pile of the carpet was so thick she could feel her heels sinking into it. She must jot down a few notes to remind herself of the décor, she thought. She could use it in a novel.

Pictures flashed into her mind's eye. Tara, her heroine in *Betrayal*, could be having an unexpected business lunch, just like Maggie, and she could discover her skunk of a husband, Jonathan, engaging in yet another tryst. It would be a good set piece and another chapter, Maggie thought happily, as she visualized the hugely satisfying emotional scene that she would later write. There was eating and drinking in it. Maggie smiled. She loved it when inspirations like this struck.

'What are you smiling at?' Marcy asked as Maggie sat down opposite her and took the menu from the attentive waiter.

'I was just thinking of a particularly meaty scene that I could write with Tara and Jonathan, set here,' she enthused. 'Tara could have a mid-morning meeting with a client changed to a lunch appointment. When she walks into the dining-room she finds Jonathan sitting with a stunning redhead gazing into his eyes, and this after he's promised her he's finished with the blonde bimbo mistress, Jill. And then—' A thought struck her. 'Oh but you won't be editing me any more. There's not much point in telling you about it,' she added regretfully.

'Let's order first, Maggie, and then we'll discuss what's happening. Have whatever you like. As I said, Enterprise is paying for this and I don't mind if they have to pay through the nose,' Marcy instructed tartly. Maggie's heart sank. She didn't like the sound of this. Marcy had always been Enterprise's champion. She had cared deeply about the company and had always been completely involved in matters pertaining to it. She and Jeremy Wilson, Maggie's publisher and Marcy's employer, were particularly close. There had been rumours of an affair. Watching them together over the years, Maggie couldn't quite decide if this was the case. She was more inclined to think that their closeness was because of a shared love of books and commitment to publishing.

Jeremy Wilson was not exactly God's gift to women, and Marcy's husband, Daniel, was rather dishy. If the relationship between Marcy and Jeremy was physical, Maggie would have been very surprised. Besides, Jeremy's second wife, Claudette, a feisty Frenchwoman, kept a fairly tight rein on him.

'I think I'll have the mushroom risotto and the vegetable lasagne,' Marcy decided.

'Maggie?' She arched an eyebrow at her author.

'Oh . . . aah!' Maggie had been so busy worrying about what was going on at Enterprise Publishing that she hadn't really studied the menu. 'Mmm . . . I'll go for the Caesar salad and the fillet of beef, please,' she ordered hastily, before handing back her menu.

'Would you care for some wine, Maggie?' Marcy asked.

'I'm driving today. I won't bother. Ballygowan Sparkling will be fine, thanks.'

'Two Ballygowans with lemon and ice please,' Marcy ordered.

The waiter smiled politely, took the menus and glided away.

'Why are you leaving?' Maggie was direct.

Marcy sighed. 'It's not my choice, to be honest. It's not what I want or what I ever envisaged. I helped Jeremy build up Enterprise Publishing. I signed up great, talented authors, yourself included. But quality was always of the utmost importance to me. You know that, Maggie.' Her tone was stern. 'I want to be proud of our product. I demand high standards.'

'I know that, Marcy. It's always been a challenge and a comfort to know that you demand and expect the best,' Maggie said warmly, and meant it. 'So what's changed?'

'An awful lot has changed, unfortunately, and certainly not for the better. Some of the manuscripts that are being accepted now are, quite frankly, *rubbish*!' Marcy tapped the fingers of one hand agitatedly against the table in a sharp staccato. Maggie couldn't help but notice. It was so out of character. Marcy was *always* extremely controlled. Maggie had seen her snowed under with work, a dozen books on the go, phones ringing non-stop. Constant interruptions. But she was never fazed. This was a totally new side to Marcy. She'd never seen her editor so fidgety or jumpy. It was unnerving.

'Go on,' she prompted.

Marcy inhaled deeply. 'You remember, a year ago, there were management changes. Jeremy remained as publisher but handed over the reins of MD to Claudette. Well she –' the *she* was uttered in a tone of utter contempt, emphasized with flared nostrils, tightening of the lips and narrowing of the eyes that left Maggie in no doubt as to how her editor felt about the current managing director – 'is making changes left, right, and centre. And, at the risk of repeating myself, none for the better. I can't work with the woman. She has no feeling for books. *Bucks* is her goal. Excuse the pun. Quantity not quality is her aim and frankly, Maggie, with her at the helm, Enterprise is going to go down the tubes. Believe me!' She waved a hand dramatically.

Maggie could see how Marcy and Claudette would clash. Both were domineering and bossy but, previously, Claudette had always remained somewhat in the background. 'But why did Jeremy make Claudette, MD?' Maggie was curious. Jeremy had always been very hands-on.

'He had chest pains eighteen months ago and was hospitalized for tests, as you know. He was diagnosed with angina. Claudette badgered him to make her MD. Not, I hasten to add, out of concern for Jeremy, she doesn't give two hoots about him. But she wanted to get her claws into the company good and deep. Jeremy has a daughter from his first marriage and Claudette is determined that she'll get nothing when Jeremy dies. She's going to swindle her out of that company good and proper. Claudette is a gold-digger and always has been and she's extremely manipulative.' Marcy was so angry her cheeks were puce.

Maggie was very startled at Marcy's vehemence. She really had it in for Claudette. The fireworks in the past eighteen months must have been mighty.

'How do you know that it isn't concern for Jeremy? How do you know all this?' Maggie broke a bread roll in half and began to butter it.

'Maggie, I've known them both a long time. I've known Jeremy longer than Claudette has. Marrying her was a big mistake, I could see it. She went after him for his money. He, of course, is so vain, he thought it was because she found him irresistible. The fool! Vanity was always Jeremy's weak spot. He should have bedded her but never wed her if it was sex that he wanted. But no, he had to make an idiot of himself and go galloping down the aisle at his age because his ego and his hormones were rampant.' Marcy was so indignant she had to take a sip of water.

Maggie was fascinated. Jeremy Wilson with rampant hormones. It was a faintly revolting thought. Jeremy, skinny, bony, with mottled hands and bad breath, Claudette deserved every penny she got if she had sex with him, Maggie couldn't help thinking. There was definitely a novel in this, she thought wryly, as Marcy resumed her tirade.

'Claudette never gave a toss about the company when Jeremy was in the full of his health, all she wanted to do was *spend* his money. His angina has concentrated her mind wonderfully. He is, after all, twenty years older than she is. Don't forget that. Enterprise Publishing is relatively successful. She sees the dollar signs. Don't for a minute think that when Jeremy pops his clogs Claudette is going to keep on the company. She's going to sell it for a mega profit to some big publishing conglomerate and then you can forget it, Maggie. Quality, good writing, style . . . out the window.'

'And can Jeremy not see what's happening to his company? Can he not put his foot down?'

Marcy shook her head. 'He doesn't *want* to see.

He's sold out. She's got to him. It's all about money now. You were lucky you signed your contract when you did. Don't sign another one with them. Angela Allen and Josephine Langley are leaving at the end of their contracts. They can see the writing on the wall.'

'Wow!' Maggie's eyes widened. This was shocking news. Angela Allen and Josephine Langley were Enterprise's top authors.

'I'm telling you, Maggie, that company is going to go down the tubes,' Marcy reiterated. 'To be honest, I know I said that Claudette will sell for a big profit but if Jeremy doesn't pop his clogs sooner rather than later, she might be on a hiding to nothing. If all the big authors leave there'll be no company to sell. Big conglomerates won't be interested in the smaller-fry authors. Ha!' Marcy gave a dry laugh. 'She'll be well and truly hoist by her own petard. And that is something I would dearly like to see.'

'And were you pushed or did you resign?' Maggie asked, agog.

'Nobody pushes me, Maggie,' Marcy said snootily, sitting back to allow the waiter to place her starter in front of her.

When Maggie was served and they were alone again, Marcy resumed their conversation.

'I resigned after the most horrible year I have ever put in. I can't continue to work there. I simply couldn't cope with the demands and changes when standards were slipping in every department. They've turned it into a Yellow Pack Publishers. The two proofreaders and the copy editor were let go. They're hiring freelance ones who are absolutely hopeless but needless to say much cheaper. And it's not that there aren't good proofreaders out there. There are, but the good ones are expensive and Claudette won't pay them. The woman is *such* a penny-pincher except when she's out buying her designer labels, of course.'

Marcy was going to town on Claudette. The knife was in deep, Maggie thought in amusement. She was sure her editor was exaggerating the situation, as was her wont. The trouble with Marcy was that she liked being in control. Unfortunately, now it was Claudette who was pulling the strings.

'I ended up proofing and copy-editing half the time. I don't have time for that, Maggie!' Marcy ranted. 'But I couldn't let manuscripts go to print in the state they were in. I couldn't stand over them. And I wouldn't do that to my authors. No author of mine is going to be taken to task and get bad reviews because of shoddy editing. I needed decent backup and I wasn't getting it!' Marcy shook her head as if she still couldn't believe what was going on. 'Sandra's going berserk too,' she added as she speared a mushroom. 'She's not going to stay much longer either.'

'What are you going to do?' Maggie asked glumly as she forked a piece of anchovy and nibbled at it. The Caesar salad was delicious but her appetite had waned after hearing such disturbing news. With Marcy gone, and Sandra going, Maggie knew she definitely didn't want to stay.

'I'm taking a couple of months off to review my options. Once the news is out that I've left Enterprise the offers will come flooding in, I'm not exaggerating. I'm a valuable commodity. I can spot best-selling novels and go with them. Some editors are good at spotting talent but not good at working on text. Some are great at text but don't have a commercial eye. I'm good at both. I'll have no problems getting work. I just want to be sure that I'm working for a publishing company that aspires to the same things that I aspire to.'

'What did Jeremy say when you offered your resignation?'

'Maggie, that was the day when I realized that Jeremy has no loyalty to anyone. I was with him for years. *Years.* And it meant *nothing.*' Marcy's eyes glittered suspiciously and Maggie saw the hurt reflected in them. What would she do if Marcy burst into tears? It was unthinkable.

The moment passed and Marcy regained her composure. She pointed her fork at Maggie. 'Never mix business and friendship. Friendship always loses out. Loyalty is to the dollar, not the person. Jeremy took my letter of resignation, wished me well in a cold sort of way. And that was that. Nothing more. Not even an expression of regret that our collaboration was at an end. But he couldn't look me in the eye. He knows full well that he's sold out and I'm glad I don't have to work with him any more. He's pitiful.' Marcy's tone oozed contempt.

'That's dreadful,' murmured Maggie. 'You both always seemed so enthusiastic about publishing and so in tune.'

'When Jeremy was in his prime, there wasn't a publisher who could touch him. He was a ground-breaker. But publishing's changed. It's all take-overs and international buy-ups. It's big business,' Marcy moaned.

Maggie could see that, to a certain degree, her editor was enjoying the drama of it all.

'Claudette, needless to say, is delighted by my resignation. I've been such a thorn in her side,' Marcy continued. 'She's been trying to get rid of me ever since she took over. She's assured me of an excellent reference. As if I'd take a reference from *her*. The woman can't even spell or punctuate. You should see the memos that she sends around the office. I always make it a point to edit mine and hand them back to her with the corrections in red biro. It drives her bananas. Childish I know, but it makes me feel good. I don't need references from the likes of her. My authors and their novels are testament enough to my track record.' Marcy's fingers tightened on her knife and fork and Maggie could see how deeply hurt she was, for all her bravado.

'I can't imagine working with another editor,' Maggie confessed. 'I always enjoyed our editing sessions so much.'

'As did I.' Marcy managed a wan smile. 'You're a good writer, Maggie. You write from the heart. Just watch your tendency to overuse adjectives and adverbs. Although you have much improved in that too.'

Maggie laughed. 'I'll never forget you and your red pen on my first day of editing. I was shell-shocked.'

'You survived and did very well. I'm proud of you, Maggie. And proud that I discovered such a talented writer. Perhaps we'll work together again. How many more have you to do for them?'

'One after this one.'

'That's not too bad. Never *ever* sign more than a two-book contract. You never know how circumstances are going to change. It's a nightmare to be tied up to a company that you don't want to be with. Have you heard about how there's ructions in

Bennett's Books? The auditors have been called in, there's wholesale fraud going on. Writs are flying, authors are suing, it's the talk of the trade.' Marcy was in full flow.

Maggie took a sip of her sparkling water and sat back as the waiter removed her plate. She might as well *try* and enjoy the rest of her lunch, and the gossip, it was the last one she'd have with Marcy as author and editor. Who knew what was in store for her now with Enterprise Publishing?

Terry panted hard and tried to suppress a groan. He was puffed. He glanced at the console in front of him. Four hundred metres. Only a quarter of a mile on level one of the incline and he was bushwhacked. Maybe he'd jack it in early and go and have lunch. There was a time when he could have run three miles on the treadmill and it wouldn't have knocked a feather out of him. Just worked up a light sweat, that was all. Once you hit forty it was downhill all the way, he thought grumpily.

He jabbed a stubby finger on the speed button and reduced it to a more tolerable level. He shouldn't be expecting miracles on his first day back at the gym. It was just that he needed to get fit fast. In a matter of weeks Alma Al Shariff would be a guest in his house, and he wanted to be looking his best. He'd always had a thing for Alma. She was a sexy bird. And she had a way of looking at you from beneath her lashes that was very come-hither. Terry *knew* she fancied him. Always had, he thought confidently, as he increased his incline to the second level and saw two red dots light up the console. In a week he'd be up to five and more, he vowed. Alma Al Shariff was going to see a lean, mean, fighting machine. Not a paunchy slob with love handles.

Terry sighed. The weight had crept on him so gradually. All the business lunches and expensive dinners. If Maggie was any good she'd take him in tow and make sure she cooked low-calorie dishes at home and encourage him to diet. But she didn't care any more. She had no time for him. It was the kids and her writing. He was just an afterthought. He wasn't used to being an afterthought, he thought resentfully.

Hell! He'd worked hard to give Maggie and the kids a decent lifestyle and a big house. OK, so he'd had a fling with Ria Kirby. Men did things like that and they meant nothing. Women took all this fidelity lark so seriously. There was not one man in his set who hadn't played around, although most of the lucky bastards hadn't been caught, he thought ruefully. If he had another affair it was Maggie's own fault. He wasn't getting tender loving care and consideration at home so he'd just have to look for it elsewhere. Sure they had sex, occasionally, when she wasn't moaning about being so tired. But her heart wasn't in it. It was purely mechanical. And very unsatisfying. She just lay there like a sack of spuds.

Sometimes she didn't even bother to fake it. That seemed worse than her not having an orgasm. The fact that she wouldn't fake it just showed that she didn't care about the way he felt any more. When their marriage had been good he'd prided himself on his abilities as a lover. Maggie knew that. Knew that it was important to him, but now she couldn't care less. What he needed, and needed badly, was a woman who was hot for him. A woman who would make him feel like a man again. But first he had to get fit and look fit.

He checked the mileage display. Eight hundred metres. Half a mile in seven minutes. Not bad for his first attempt. It had been years since he'd worked out. He slowed the treadmill to a crawl, wiped his forehead and took a drink. Next on his agenda was the abs toner. A couple of weeks doing that and his belly would be as flat as a pancake, he thought optimistically as he stopped the treadmill. He took a couple more slugs of water then walked into the exercise section, placed a mat on the floor, laid his head on the pad of the lightweight machine and began to exercise. Twenty reps later he was puffed and his stomach muscles ached. Just as well he was lying down, he thought dispiritedly, as he began another set. Only the thought of the flirty Alma kept him going.

Eighteen

Caroline sat fidgeting at her desk. She was supposed to be working out staff requirements for the new Galway project but her attention kept wandering and she simply couldn't concentrate.

It was almost a week since Mrs Yates had had her heart attack and she was making satisfactory progress, according to Richard's brief daily report.

Tension was high between them, almost as bad as when he had been hitting her and she'd been drinking. She hadn't suggested again going to the hospital with him and he hadn't invited her to and so a wall of resentment was being built between them, brick by brick. Caroline knew that unless she made a move he never would. What a fool she'd been to move back in with him after working in Abu Dhabi. To think she had actually made the break once, survived it and made a life for herself, and then she'd let it all slip away.

It was said that life presented the same lesson to you until you learned it. Now she was going to have to go through it all again. Devlin had suggested that she take a holiday as she hadn't had one this year. The thought was appealing. But where to go on her own and what to do?

A friend of hers, Monica Denton, whom she'd worked with in Abu Dhabi, was constantly trying to persuade her to come back out to the Gulf on another holiday, but the idea didn't really appeal to her. Her first visit to the Gulf had been wonderfully exciting and adventurous. The cultural differences had astonished and delighted her. The scents of jasmine and frangipani and other glorious exotic flowers had been intoxicating and she had enjoyed the whole experience, although in the end she'd been glad to escape the heat and humidity for the fresh tangy air of home. A year and a half later when she'd gone back for a ten-day visit it hadn't been the same. She'd been tired and stressed after a year without a holiday. In that twelve months she'd done a damn good job for Devlin, taking charge of the personnel administration in the three City Girl centres. After such hard work, she'd badly needed a break.

She shouldn't have gone to the Gulf for that particular holiday, she'd admitted to herself on the second day of her stay. The heat and humidity that left her feeling like a wet rag, the noise, the never-ending traffic that filled the city with stinking fumes, had got to her. It was far from restful. She would have been much better off on a beach in Majorca.

Monica and her American husband Wayne had felt obliged to fill Caroline's day with activities, when all she had really wanted to do was to laze in the sun and read and relax and avoid people. She met enough people at home, between work and Richard's ladder-climbing social life.

Unfortunately Wayne was a go-getter. He worked for a large multinational oil company. A high-flyer in his own eyes, he liked to see and be seen. He had the

175

biggest ego Caroline had ever encountered. He couldn't sit quietly for ten minutes but always had to be bustling about in his fussy irritating way, organizing this, that and the other. He was sure that Caroline was deeply impressed by their affluent lifestyle and nearly drove her insane with his boasting and bragging.

After ten days of parties, cultural events, coffee mornings, shopping, eating out and general socializing, Caroline was exhausted. Monica and Wayne seemed to have been going through a bad patch and had bickered constantly. The atmosphere in their big high-rise apartment that overlooked the Corniche had been tense. Caroline had found it stressful, to say the least, and had been glad to step onto the KLM airbus for the long tiring flight home.

'You'll have to come and stay longer the next time and we'll have to do much more sightseeing. We never got to Dubai, or Al Ain, this time,' Monica urged on the phone, two days later, as Caroline, still not unpacked, was thinking that she'd need a holiday to get over her holiday.

They phoned regularly to invite her back to stay with them and Caroline knew they couldn't understand how she wasn't jumping for joy at the idea of a holiday in such an exotic location. They were completely immersed in the frenzy of the expat lifestyle. They couldn't see beyond it. Monica and Wayne had forgotten how to relax. The older woman could not understand Caroline's need for solitude.

'You've changed so much, Caroline. You have to put yourself about. There are great job opportunities out here for someone with your experience. I could introduce you to so many influential people. What do you want to bury yourself in Dublin for the rest of your life for? Divorce the jerk. Come out here and find a rich husband and you'll be set up for life. You'll never get a man with your head stuck in those books. Come on, we should be out socializing, you can read any old time.'

Monica, in fairness, had a point. Caroline *had* changed.

Having reached the lowest point in her life with her suicide attempt and drinking, Caroline had come to an awareness of another aspect of her life which had opened a whole new world to her. In the depths of her misery and pain, when she had felt utterly abandoned and completely alone, one night when she'd been in the rehab clinic she'd fallen to her knees and asked the Almighty for help.

She'd cried her eyes out and whispered, 'God? Help me! Help me! Help me.' She'd cried all that night, great wrenching sobs that had shaken her thin, pain-racked body from head to toe, but in the morning, having slept for a couple of hours after dawn, she'd awoken feeling lighter, better, and almost serene. The great knot of pain, grief, and loneliness that had lodged in her breastbone seemed to have unravelled. And she had the strangest sense that she was not alone.

Later, after breakfast and a counselling session, she had wandered into the small library and had stood idly at the bookcase, perusing the titles. Almost as if she'd been drawn to it, she'd reached out and pulled out a book comfortingly title *Embraced by the Light*. It was the story of a woman, Betty J. Eadie, who had undergone a near-death experience that had changed her life.

Caroline had been unable to put the book down. Something in her changed that day: she became aware that life was much more than a physical journey. In time, having read many such books and having spent many hours alone, thinking, asking for help and guidance, she came to realize that her alcoholism had been a gift bringing a spiritual dimension and awareness to her life that she might never have experienced otherwise. In that light, she was able to see herself not as a victim but as a seeker on an incredible journey that unfolded and led her where she knew not, every hour of every day.

Along the dark parts of that long avenue she'd been brought to her knees, but she'd picked herself up, forged ahead and she knew now with certainty that whatever happened in her life, guidance was with her. All she had to do was ask.

It wasn't an easy journey. Trying to bear in mind *'This moment is as it should be'* when her world seemed to have started to fall apart again, and trying to *'Judge not, that you be not judged,'* when Richard was being a shit and Mrs Yates was controlling and manipulating all over the place, was extremely difficult.

Caroline sighed deeply as she reflected on her current situation. Intuitively, she knew that once she made the first positive step towards leaving, doors would open for her. It had happened for her when she'd left Richard before. She'd got the job in Abu Dhabi, and on her return Devlin had offered her the challenging position in City Girl. All she had to do was to make the leap of faith and leave Richard, and something would turn up. It was just a question of having the courage to do it.

She wasn't great on courage, she thought despondently, as she twisted and untwisted the telephone cord. Devlin had much more courage than she had. She'd gone and lived in a high-rise flat in Ballymun when she'd been a single mother with Lynn. And then when her baby and her aunt had been killed in that awful car crash, and she'd suffered dreadful injuries, she'd forced herself to go on living even though she wanted to die too. And now look at her, happily married, pregnant and successful beyond her wildest dreams. Only an incredibly brave person could have overcome what Devlin had endured.

When things had got rough for Caroline, she'd taken to the bottle, she thought in disgust.

'Now stop that!' she said aloud. It was very wrong for her to compare herself to someone else. Everyone had to tread their own path. She'd once again given into negative thinking. Enough was enough.

She said a little prayer, asking for courage, picked up the phone and took a deep breath. She flicked through her rolodex and found the number she wanted and dialled it.

'Murray & Murray, Estate Agents and Auctioneers,' a pleasant voice came down the line.

'Hello, could I speak to Olivia O'Neill please? It's a personal call,' she said crisply.

'Certainly. One moment and I'll connect you,' the receptionist said politely. 'Just hold the line.'

'Greensleeves' came tinnily over the airwaves as Caroline waited impatiently.

Olivia was a friend from way back when Caroline had worked in an estate agents. Although Olivia had moved from their old firm, she and Caroline had kept in touch.

'Hello?' Her friend's delightful Kerry lilt had never disappeared, even after twenty years in Dublin.

'Olivia, it's Caroline, I've a favour to ask.'

'Hiya, Caroline. Ask away,' Olivia said cheerfully.

'Well it's like this, Olivia. I'm leaving Richard and I want to buy a place of my own. I was wondering if you would keep an eye out for me,' Caroline explained.

'Well it's about bloody time,' the other woman said bluntly. 'I'm glad to hear it. Now if you can wait a couple of months there's a very nice new block of apartments and town houses coming onstream, not too far from your neck of the woods, down towards St Anne's Park in Raheny. You might consider them. I'd really advise you to go for somewhere new, you won't have to pay stamp duty as a first-time buyer and you won't have to upgrade or redecorate as you might with a second-hand property. But of course you know all that yourself, you being an old hand.'

'Yeah, an old, old hand. Practically geriatric.' Caroline grinned.

'So you're taking the plunge at last. Good on you, Caroline. It will be the start of a whole new life for you and I want to come to the house-warming party. You must know a few well-heeled eligible hunks you could introduce me to.' Olivia was a separated mother of two.

'Like yourself, Olivia, I know a few heels, eligible or not. The man will come when he's meant to.'

'I'm fed up waiting,' the other woman moaned. 'I went to a singles dance the other night, Caroline. Boy was that an experience! I met this guy – gorgeous-looking, late thirties – who spent the whole night talking about himself and his problems. He was married, separated for years, had one child, a boy. He'd been in a few relationships since but was currently single. By the time he'd told me that he'd never really loved anyone in his whole life, ever, I was nearly crying. I wanted to say, "You can learn to love me. I'll love you. I'll take care of you." Caroline, I'm telling you he pressed every single button and I was ready to jump in. You know me and my maternal instincts!'

'What happened?' Caroline asked. She'd never met anyone like Olivia for letting her heart rule her head.

'We made a date to go to dinner in Mario's. I did all the booking. I had several phone calls from him in the meantime and we talked and talked . . . all about him naturally . . . and then I sat waiting for him to collect me at seven, from my house. And waited . . . and waited. The fucker stood me up. And he looked so bloody respectable. Suit, tie, his own business. Imagine! Imagine being thirty-nine years of age and being stood up. It's outrageous. It's ridiculous. That happens to fifteen-year-olds, for God's sake!'

'Girl, you had a lucky escape,' Caroline retorted. 'He lied when he told you that he'd never loved anyone in his whole life. He's so in love with himself there's no room for anyone else. If he phones you again, do yourself a favour and hang up. You're not that desperate.'

'Oh yes I am,' wailed Olivia. 'I'm lonely, Caroline. I miss having a man around the house. I miss coming home and telling someone the news of the day. My kids are adorable but all they want to do is watch MTV and play on the computer. I hate sleeping on my own. It's cold. I want loving arms, a nice furry hairy chest, and long hard legs wrapped around me keeping me warm.'

'Did you ever think of trying the zoo?' Caroline teased, amused at Olivia's description.

'Bitch.' Olivia chuckled. 'What finally made you decide to call it a day with Richard?'

'Well, it was a joint decision originally, and we were going for a divorce as well. Richard was going to sell the firm and move to Boston, but then Mrs Yates had a heart attack after hearing the news, so he's not selling and he's not going and now he's iffy about the divorce too. If I don't do it now, I'll never do it. It would have been easier if things had gone to plan. He's kind of blaming me for Mrs Yates's heart attack.'

'Typical,' Olivia said dryly. 'But don't you dare take that guilt trip on board,' her friend warned. 'Great move on her part, though. She has him for life now.'

'Yeah,' Caroline sighed. 'It's a very destructive relationship and I'm not getting drawn in deeper than I am already. It's time to walk away.'

'Walking away is the hardest thing in the world,' Olivia said sadly and Caroline's heart went out to her. Olivia had been married to a gambler. She loved him deeply but he'd lost every penny they had. Because of his addiction they'd been in debt up to their ears. Caroline knew she still wept for him, even after three years of separation.

'Listen, why don't we have a night out? I promise I won't stand you up. I'll be at your front door at seven on the dot. I don't have a hairy chest but I could give you a hug if that would help?' Caroline suggested.

'I'd love it. When? Where?'

'Hell! Why not Mario's?'

'Why not?' Olivia laughed.

'Right! I'll check to see what the bookings are like and get back to you. Talk to you soon, Olivia,' Caroline said light-heartedly. Now that she'd taken the first step towards making the break, she felt as if a load had lifted from her shoulders.

Nineteen

'You haven't sold the firm, have you?' Sarah Yates
asked in a quavery voice.

'No, Mother, I haven't,' Richard assured her.

'And you're not leaving me alone to go to
America?'

'No.'

'And you're not going to get a divorce?' She fixed
him with a beady stare.

'No, Mother. I told you so last night and the night
before.'

He looked pasty-faced and unhappy, but it was
good enough for him, for giving her a fright like that,
Sarah thought unforgivingly as she lay back against
the crisp white pillows and closed her eyes.

'Are you all right, Mother? Should I get a nurse?'
he asked anxiously.

'No. I'm just tired. You can go now if you want to.
When you come in tomorrow bring me the blue
bedjacket that's in the middle drawer of my dressing-
table. And bring me my missal.'

She kept her eyes closed as she heard him put on
his black overcoat and only opened them when he
took her hand in his and bid her good night.

'Good night, Richard. Make sure Mrs Gleeson is

keeping the house clean and check the sideboard for dust. I don't trust her to dust properly when I'm not there to inspect.'

'Very well, Mother.' Richard gave her hand a limp squeeze.

She didn't return the pressure. Withholding approval and affection was the best way of dealing with Richard when he was recalcitrant. It was a method that had always worked, from the time he'd been a little boy.

She closed her eyes again when he slipped quietly out of the room. She was tired. But triumphant, she thought with satisfaction. Richard wasn't going anywhere. He wasn't selling his legal practice and he wasn't putting his immortal soul in danger and disgracing the family name by divorcing. The battle had been won. But at what cost?

A tear trickled down Sarah's cheek. She'd never been ill in her life. She'd been up and about two days after having Richard, at a time when women stayed in bed ten days and more after a confinement. She had always been strong and fit. Now she hadn't an ounce of energy and she felt as if she'd been run over by a bus. She'd never taken tablets in her life, now the nurses were giving them to her morning, noon and night and they were making her feel most peculiar. They were causing her to have strange, frightening dreams that disturbed her. But the worst thing of all was that the specialist had told her that she was going to have heart surgery when she was stronger. The idea of being cut open terrified her. She'd be lucky if she didn't die of fright first, she thought tearfully.

Stop that now, stop it, she ordered herself. She willed herself to a calmer state. There was to be no more talk of dying. She had no intention of dying. She had no illusions about what would happen if she died. That Caroline, the unscrupulous hussy, would convince Richard that a divorce was the best thing for him. She'd make him sell his practice and probably demand half of the proceeds, money to which she certainly was not entitled, and then she'd go off and leave him for some fancy man. She'd have won! That was unthinkable.

Another thought struck her. She should add a codicil to her will stating that Richard could only inherit her estate if he never divorced. That would sort that little matter, she thought grimly, as she drifted off into an unsatisfactory drug-induced sleep.

Richard pulled the collar of his overcoat up to his ears and hunched his shoulders miserably as he walked from the hospital to the car park. It was dark, cold, wet and windy. Litter swirled at his feet. He felt like crying. If only Charles were here to comfort and console him. But Charles, his dearest friend, his only friend, was dead and he was alone.

A strangled sob erupted from his throat, and he kept his head bent, his chin practically touching his chest, as he hurried towards the car, afraid he would be seen. It was so unmanly to cry. But he didn't feel manly at all. He never really had. He felt like a lonely, terrified little boy who was completely trapped.

Charles was the only one who had understood him. Charles was the only one who'd known every intimate thing about him. Only Charles knew how much he really hated his mother. But Charles was gone, dead and buried, taking that sinful secret to the grave.

Caroline probably knew, of course, she was very perceptive about things like that. She'd always stood up for him against his mother and he'd always resented it, because it made him feel weak and insecure. But at least he didn't have to put on an act with her. She knew him. And now she was leaving him.

Why was it that everyone he had ever loved or cared for had left him? he pondered, swallowing hard to try and ease the lump in his throat. His father, whom he'd loved. A gentle, caring man. Charles, who had been a father to him as well as a lover. Both dead. And Caroline, whose gentleness had drawn him to her the first time he'd met her. Even though he'd treated her appallingly, she'd forgiven him and become his friend. And now she was leaving him too. Betraying him, in a way, with all this talk of separation and divorce and moving on. She'd move on and feel contempt for him because he hadn't had the courage to do what he wanted to. And all because of that *witch* up in the heart unit.

Richard sat in his car and put his head in his hands and cried his heart out.

Caroline dived into the sparkling heated waters of the swimming-pool and swam its length energetically. She'd put in a hard day at work and she needed to unwind, so she'd left her office and taken the lift up to City Girl's roof-top pool, intent on having a good invigorating swim.

Staff could use the pool if there were less than ten clients in it at any given time, but senior management like Caroline could use it at will. It was a perk of the job. Tonight it was busy but not overly crowded.

She swam in rhythmic, even strokes, enjoying the feel of the water on her tense neck muscles. She and Devlin had had a very satisfactory meeting about Galway, and then Andrew had joined them and the fur had started to fly.

All accountants were the same, she reflected, as she cut through the water on her second lap. No imagination! Quantity at the cost of quality! Andrew couldn't understand the type of refuge she and Devlin envisaged for the new residential centre. Reiki healing, soma therapy, kinesiology, were all foreign concepts to him. Why couldn't they stick with the tried and tested acupuncture and reflexology therapies that they'd used so successfully to date, he'd wanted to know. If things went wrong with these strange therapies, would they be sued?

She knew he had his job to do, but nevertheless she was surprised at how suspicious he'd been.

'Are you sure it's not quackery?' he demanded. 'How can you prove these things work?'

'How can you prove they don't?' she'd shot back.

'Oh come on now, Caroline, I know you're into all this New Age stuff, but really we're talking about a business here,' Andrew retorted superciliously.

'Listen, Andrew, why don't you take a trip out to the RDS the next time the Mind, Body, Spirit exhibition is on and see how jam-packed it is. *And* see potential clients for City Girl Residential,' Caroline retorted.

'But they're all weirdos,' the accountant declared.

'Andrew, Caroline is right. We've got to move with the times. We don't want to miss the boat on this. We're being innovative here, so less of the weirdo stuff please,' Devlin said coolly.

'I see she's got you brainwashed too.' He scowled.

'That's enough, Andrew. These are the going rates for the type of therapies discussed. I'd like you to work out a salary and employment package and see how that fits in with our budget.'

'What does Luke feel about this?' Andrew persisted.

Caroline held her breath. Although he didn't realize it, Andrew had just crossed a boundary line and pushed too far.

'This is *my* project, Andrew. Luke respects my judgement and backs me all the way. I suggest you do the same. I'd like those estimates *today* please,' Devlin ordered, letting him know, in no uncertain terms, who was boss.

'Fine!' he said tightly, glowered at Caroline and marched from the office.

He had it in for her now, Caroline knew. She'd had a feeling before this that he resented her considerable input into management decisions, and her friendship with Devlin. It was all ego stuff, his ego stuff, and she wasn't getting into it, she thought determinedly as she finished another lap. She decided to do a visualization – that always helped considerably when she felt drained of energy because of a confrontation or power struggle. She imagined herself attached to the accountant by seven thin electrical cords, one for each chakra. Slowly, in her mind's eye, one by one, she unplugged each cord from him and watched him drift away from her. She sent him a blessing, asked for one for herself and immediately felt a sense of detachment from the situation.

It worked well with Andrew because she wasn't too pushed about him one way or the other, she

189

reflected wryly, but it didn't always work when she used it to try and detach from Richard and his mother. Still, she kept trying, and that was the main thing, she assured herself as she eased up and turned on her back and began a leisurely backstroke.

Richard had thawed a bit in the last few days. But he was miserable and Caroline knew that deep down he was still very angry.

Each evening after work he went to the hospital and it was often after ten when he got home. He would slump in front of the TV for an hour or two, sometimes making desultory conversation, sometimes not, depending on his humour.

She refrained from asking him about his mother. It was only a flashpoint between them. Nor had she told him about her decision to look at a property in the coming months. He had enough on his plate, she figured. There was a time and a place for everything.

He hadn't been too impressed when she'd told him this morning that she was going out with Olivia for dinner. She could read it in his eyes, as plain as could be.

How can you possibly go out and enjoy yourself and leave me in the lurch when I'm suffering? You should be suffering too!

Caroline sighed. She was determined to enjoy her night out and not to feel guilty about it. But in spite of her best efforts, every so often guilt niggled, even though she knew it was completely irrational and misplaced.

She climbed out of the pool, stepped into the poolside shower and let the jets cascade over her. Ten minutes in the sauna, ten minutes in the steam room and she felt like a new woman. She washed her hair, dried herself off, slipped into a towelling robe and strolled out of the pool area and up to the salon. One of the girls had promised to do her make-up for her.

Olivia had phoned earlier in the day to tell her not to bother driving out of town to collect her at seven. Her child-minder had offered to come early, so Olivia would meet her from work in City Girl.

Caroline had used the time for her swim and sauna and was feeling very relaxed by the time Olivia hurried in at six thirty.

'God! The traffic is atrocious! Caroline, you look stunning! I'm not going out with you,' she exclaimed in admiration at Caroline's simple, superbly cut, black long-sleeved dress.

'Don't be daft! You look fantastic yourself. I love that trouser suit on you.'

Olivia wore a tailored burgundy pure wool trouser suit. A rich black devoré scarf thrown casually around her neck gave the outfit an elegant finishing touch.

'I don't know what I'd do without swop shops,' Olivia admitted. 'I'd never own a "label" otherwise. My horoscope said my fortunes were changing. Do you think that means I'm going to meet a man tonight?'

'Who knows?' Caroline said lightly. 'Maybe we both might. I wonder what mine said?'

'I'd say it said something about buying property. Did you get the brochure I sent you? It's for new apartments in Malahide. I know you're not going to buy there, but it will give you an idea of what's on the market and the prices that they're going for. Your horoscope probably said something like "Saturn leaves Capricorn, Mercury is no longer retrograde and you are on the move." Imagine still reading horoscopes at our age. There's no hope for us.' Olivia giggled.

She had the most infectious giggle that Caroline had ever heard and she started to laugh herself. Her spirits lifted. It was going to be a good night and they were going to enjoy themselves.

'Let's hit the road,' she suggested, very relieved not to be going home to Richard and his moods.

They spent hours over their meal, gossiping, reviewing their current situations and flirting with the Adonis who was waiting on them.

'He's gorgeous!' drooled Olivia. 'Drop-dead *gorgeous*. I wonder is he married?'

'I don't know. I'd be surprised if he wasn't,' Caroline replied, admiring his neat ass and slim waist.

'I don't know about you, Caroline, but I really could do with a man sooner rather than later. I'm fierce lonely,' Olivia confided.

'At least you've got the children. I don't have that comfort,' Caroline sighed.

'I know,' Olivia said tipsily – she was on her fourth glass of red wine – 'why don't I just say the next time he comes to the table, "excuse me, Marco, but Caroline is in dire need of the juice of your loins. She needs bambinos."'

Caroline spluttered into her Aqua Libra. 'Livy don't you dare! You're outrageous!' she managed between snorts of laughter.

'I'd love to see his face though. He's a bit *too* aware of himself. Still, if I had buns like that I'd be aware of myself too.' Olivia took another slug. 'Look at us. Two beauties and not a man between us – well, you can't really call Richard a man if you know what I mean. He's a man, but not a man.' She giggled again. 'Sorry, Caroline, this wine's gone to my head. I think I'm a bit pissed. It's just that I haven't been out in ages.'

'Enjoy it,' Caroline urged. 'I wish I could have a glass with you. But going back on the sauce is the last thing I need.'

'You need a man and so do I. A real man with all his faculties in order and no baggage and no addictions. Now that you're finally coming out of purdah and getting the divorce there's no excuse. We really should go out more often. So let's try and start going out on the hunt at least once a week.'

'Where will we meet them? I'm not into the pub scene,' Caroline was dubious. 'And let's face it, Olivia, both of us come with baggage. In fact, I have excess baggage!'

'Don't worry about that,' Olivia dismissed that notion out of hand. 'They'll be so glad to have us, they'll *carry* our baggage!' she chortled.

Caroline burst out laughing.

'Now we want some nice rugged, lean, fit types,' the irrepressible Olivia continued. 'No more wimps in our beds! Down with wimps, I say. Wimp off, you wimp! We're all wimped out. Now where do we find real men, you ask? We could join a hill-walking club or go orienteering, or canoeing or even parachuting,' Olivia announced enthusiastically. 'Just think of the mega hunks we'd meet. Broad shoulders, hairy chests, hard muscular thighs. Wouldn't it be wonderful?'

'You *are* pissed, Olivia. This is the same Olivia who's afraid of flying! And the Olivia who took up badminton, played one game and never went back because it was "too energetic",' derided Caroline.

'I've changed. I'm into sports now. I do ten min-utes on the treadmill and ten minutes on the rowing-machine. I could hill-walk or canoe no prob-lem,' Olivia said expansively. 'Maybe we'll forget parachuting. A tad OTT,' she punned.

'We'll have this conversation when you're not under the influence.' Caroline grinned.

'Spoilsport,' Olivia chided, waving at the divine Marco.

He waved back and winked.

'Did you see that?' Olivia beamed. 'He fancies me. We could have a threesome. You can have the juice of his loins. I'll have his buns.'

'We're going home. It's half eleven. You told me the child-minder has to be home by twelve mid-week,' Caroline reminded her.

'All right, Cinderella, if you insist,' Olivia drained the last of her wine. 'I really enjoyed myself,' she declared.

'Me too. It was fun. We'll do it again soon,' Caroline said warmly. Olivia was right. They should go out more often. She so enjoyed this sort of socializing. It was much more relaxing than Richard's society bashes.

They strolled back towards Stephen's Green, laughing and chatting animatedly. Caroline had given Harry, City Girl's car-park attendant, her spare keys and he'd parked the car for her opposite the Shelbourne when City Girl had closed. He'd left a message for her on her mobile to tell her its location.

They had just passed the Shelbourne when a stocky, sallow-faced man greeted Caroline.

'How are you, Caroline? What are you doing out on the town without Richard?'

'Oh . . . Oh hi, Tony,' she said politely. She didn't really like Tony Macken, a legal crony of Richard's. 'Olivia, this is Tony Macken, Tony, Olivia O'Neill.'

'Nice to meet you.' He held out his hand to Olivia and held hers longer than was necessary, staring into her eyes.

'Why don't I bring you two girls into the Horseshoe Bar for a drink? It's early yet. It's the least I could do for Richard,' he invited suavely.

'Thanks, but Olivia has a babysitter and she has to be back. And I had a long day. I'm tired,' Caroline explained.

'Phone and say you'll be late, you silly girl,' he suggested chummily to Olivia. 'And what's this tired bit, Caroline? Don't you work in that beauty place that costs an arm and a leg? Sure that's a doddle. If you were battling judges all day you'd be tired. So stop making excuses. You beautiful girls can't go home at this hour of the night. It's preposterous. I insist you have at least one drink. And I won't take no for an answer.' He took Olivia by the arm.

Olivia froze. 'Excuse me,' she said politely. 'Let go of my arm. And could I just say to you, you patronizing git, Caroline and I are not girls! We're women. And were I to stay manless for the rest of my life, you'd still be the last type of condescending ignoramus I'd want to go for a drink with.' She turned on her heel and marched across the road to Caroline's car.

'A bit pissed is she?' Tony asked, gobsmacked.

'You're lucky she is,' Caroline retorted furiously.

'Because you got away lightly. But I'm not pissed, Tony. And you know something? She's absolutely right! You're rude, patronizing, and an ignoramus to boot. Goodnight, Tony.'

'What's up with you? PMT?' Tony called nastily after her as she walked across the road to join Olivia.

'Ignorant bastard!' growled Olivia as she sat in the car beside Caroline. 'Did you hear him? Did you hear him, Caroline? *Girls!* How dare he say your work is a doddle. Is he for real?'

'Yes, unfortunately. We'll probably get writs in the morning threatening to sue us for slander, libel and defamation of character or whatever it is they sue for.' Caroline grimaced.

'Don't be ridiculous, Caroline, the judge would take one look at him and one look at us and lock him up. In a mental asylum probably,' she added for good measure.

They guffawed, imagining the scenario.

'I was proud of you, O'Neill. I bet Tony Macken has never been called a condescending git before,' Caroline said in approval as she circled the Green.

'Imagine being married to that! And we thought we had problems. Poor, poor Mrs Macken,' Olivia said dryly. 'The old saying is true, there *is* always someone worse off than you.'

It was one of the most enjoyable nights out she'd had in a long time, Caroline reflected as she parked her car in the garage beside Richard's, having dropped Olivia home. She yawned. She was looking forward to getting into bed.

The light was on in the lounge, she saw with surprise, as she let herself into the penthouse. Her heart did a somersault. Maybe Mrs Yates had taken a turn for the worse and Richard was waiting up to tell her. Perhaps, when she'd been out enjoying herself, her mother-in-law had died.

Caroline took a deep breath and prepared herself for the worst.

Twenty

'Richard, is everything all right? You're up late,' Caroline said hesitantly as she walked into the room.

'What's this?' he demanded truculently, waving a large brown envelope at her.

'What do you mean, what's this?' Caroline answered irritably. 'How do I know? I haven't opened it yet.' Obviously Mrs Yates hadn't died. But Richard was in a foul mood about something. She started getting annoyed. She'd just had a lovely evening. How mean of Richard to go and spoil it.

'How can you be so selfish, Caroline?' Richard jumped to his feet, startling her, as he thrust the brown envelope at her. 'How can you be so self-centred as to consider moving out at a time like this? How typical of you. It's all me, me, me. You alcoholics are all the same. Everything centres around you. It doesn't matter what anyone else is going through. Your lives and your feelings are more important than anyone else's. That's what they teach you in AA, isn't it? Put yourself first and to hell with everyone else,' he ranted.

'What *is* wrong with you? What's this all about? Why are you saying these horrible things?' Caroline was completely bewildered by his onslaught.

'Don't put on your little-Miss-Innocent act with me, Caroline. You're just as sly and devious as anyone else out there. But I never thought you'd be so insensitive and so ungrateful, after all I've done for you. To go behind my back like this.' He waved the brown envelope aggressively close to her face.

'What are you talking about, Richard? I don't know what you're going on about.' Caroline snatched the envelope from him. It was already opened. She pulled out a brochure and saw an apartment complex advertised for sale. She turned the envelope over and saw that it was from Murray & Murray Estate Agents and Auctioneers. It was addressed to her.

Caroline was horrified. 'You opened my post!' she raged. 'That envelope was addressed to me. How *dare* you, Richard! That's outrageous. You've no business to do such a thing. What possessed you? How could you treat me with such a lack of respect? I can't believe this.' Caroline was so angry her voice was shaking.

'Cut the crap, Caroline. The truth is you're off sneaking around looking at places. What were you going to do, skulk off some day after I'd gone to work and when I came home you'd be gone? That's what you were going to do, wasn't it?' Richard said furiously.

'No it isn't. You know very well that I wouldn't do that, Richard. I told you I was going to leave. I'm not going to do anything behind your back. But I'm going. And I'm going to get a divorce. This marriage is over, Richard. If you could call it a marriage,' she added bitterly.

'You were damn glad to marry me when I asked you. You couldn't get the ring on your finger fast enough,' Richard retorted nastily.

'You should never have asked me.' Caroline rounded on him, equally angry. 'You used me so that you could carry on your relationship with Charles. It was despicable, Richard. You ruined my life.'

'What are you talking about?' he sneered. 'You couldn't wait to escape from the drudgery of looking after your father and your brothers in that crummy little house in Marino. I gave you a life of luxury—'

'A life of *luxury*,' Caroline scoffed. 'But what else did I have? Nothing. No cherishing, no loving. And no sex. Imagine what that's been like for me, Richard. You were all right. You had Charles. I had no-one.'

'What about that sleazy foreigner you picked up in London?' Richard said snidely. 'And I'm sure you weren't *lonely* in the Emirates. You married me because it suited you. So accept some responsibility for your actions and don't lay all the blame on me.'

Caroline felt a surge of pure hatred. It was so typical of Richard to play dirty if he felt he was losing an argument.

'You beat the living daylights out of me, Richard. Don't forget that,' she yelled, wanting to hurt him just as he had hurt her. 'You're a wife-batterer. Should I accept responsibility for that? That was all my fault too, was it?''

'Shut up! Shut up about that. You love to rub my nose in it, don't you. God Almighty I'll be well rid of you,' Richard snarled as he marched out of the room and gave the door a resounding slam.

Caroline's heart pounded so loudly she thought it was going to burst out of her chest. She felt faint after the unexpected vicious row. It had been brewing ever since Mrs Yates had suffered her heart attack, nevertheless Caroline was stunned by the ferocity of his anger and resentment. All the old wounds had been ripped open. The bad old days were back with a vengeance.

Caroline knew what was wrong with him. He was feeling out of control. Richard was such a controller. Now his mother had put paid to his future and he was going to be tied to her and to his firm, and it looked to him as though she, his only support, was walking away from him. She who had always deferred to him, was no longer deferential. He had lost his power over her too.

She had to move on, Caroline told herself yet again. She wasn't the timid, fearful, pathetic young girl he had married, any more. He couldn't handle that. Timid and deferential had suited him down to the ground because he'd never had that before and it made him feel powerful and strong. Sarah Yates had a lot to answer for, Caroline thought viciously. Tears welled up in her eyes. Why was this happening? Hadn't she learned enough through misery? When did the lessons come through joy? Serenity? She'd paid her dues and struggled to get her life back on an even keel. Why, when things had seemed to be going right, should it all go so wrong?

Richard was so angry he wanted to lash out and smash something. With great difficulty he resisted the urge to pick up the Belleek china bowl of pot-pourri on the hall table and fling it against the long narrow mirror on the opposite wall. He slammed his bedroom door and threw himself on the bed.

'Fucking bitch!' he muttered viciously. 'Poxy, fucking, ungrateful cow.'

Why did she have to throw it in his face that he'd hit her? Why couldn't she forget that it was all in the past? He'd felt like hitting her tonight, he raged. If he had stayed in the room any longer he would have. It would have been so satisfying to shut her mouth with a punch and watch the fear ignite in her eyes. Then she might have a bit more respect for him. Nobody gave a shit about him or his feelings. Not his mother, not Caroline, no-one. He felt like a nothing.

If Mangan and the rest of the law library lot saw him now, how they would revel in his misery. He wasn't particularly liked among his peers. He knew that. He was too ambitious. Too successful. Too envied. He could see behind their façade of hearty handshakes and hail-fellow-well-met crap. Little did they know, he thought sorrowfully. His life was a shambles. A disaster. And what had he got to look forward to?

Nothing.

Twenty-one

'Devlin, I've just had a call from a very irate woman in Galway, complaining that she's tried three times to book in for a full-body aromatherapy massage and she hasn't been able to get an appointment for a month. She claimed it's because all the manageress's friends are getting cheapies and there isn't room for anyone else. According to her, it's well known in Galway that if you know Ciara Hanlon, she'll look after you. She was hopping mad. I've told her I'll get back to her,' Liz informed her boss just as Andrew Dawson walked into Devlin's office.

'What was that?' the accountant asked sharply.

Liz looked at Devlin. She nodded and once again Liz relayed the message.

'I'll look into it today, Liz,' Devlin responded calmly but her eyes were on Andrew. He looked troubled.

'Fine.' Liz closed the door quietly and went back to her desk.

'What's wrong, Andrew?' Devlin asked.

'We have a problem, Devlin. It's very interesting that that call should come today. I've just been going through Galway's figures and comparing them with Dublin and Belfast for the last quarter. And something's not right. They're ordering double the amount of creams, waxes, oils and so on, but their figures don't tally. And the overheads are marginally higher than before. Electricity, heating and so on. I think there's a scam going on.'

'I don't believe it! There must be a mistake, Andrew.' Devlin was shocked. 'None of the girls would do anything like that.'

'Something's going on,' he reiterated.

'But who do you think is doing it? Or is there more than one? How? Why? This is *terrible*.'

'Well, you heard what Liz said. It sounds like Ciara is implicated,' Andrew said slowly.

'But she wouldn't do anything like that. She couldn't. She's an excellent manageress. She's done a great job in Galway,' Devlin exclaimed, unable to believe that the friendly, competent, stylish young woman who'd run Galway City Girl since its inception would be involved in dishonest business practice. It was unthinkable. Devlin had spent a lot of time in meetings and on the phone with Ciara in the past few months, and she'd been full of enthusiasm and plans for the new extension. Very much a company woman.

'Maybe someone with a grudge made that phone call,' Devlin suggested agitatedly.

'Something's not right with the figures, Devlin, I've had a feeling over the last quarter that something was going on but I wanted to make sure. We have to investigate it. Better to nip it in the bud now,' Andrew said crisply. 'Why don't you ring that woman and see what she has to say?'

'OK,' Devlin said slowly. 'I just can't believe that any of the staff would rip us off.'

'Devlin, we're not living in nirvana, unfortunately. Given the opportunity there's plenty of people out there ready to rip you off. Honesty in business is rare and you're lucky that you haven't come up against a crooked cookie before now. I'm going to see about putting someone in place to keep an eye on things. You call that woman.' Andrew hurried out of her office, anxious to get moving on the problem.

Devlin buzzed Liz on the intercom and asked her for the caller's number. She dialled with a hint of apprehension. She had a feeling that all was not going to be well.

A clear, well-modulated tone answered. 'Willowfield House. Hello?'

'Could I speak to Mrs Charlotte Adams please?' Devlin asked politely.

'Speaking,' came the crisp reply.

'Hello, Mrs Adams, my name is Devlin Delaney, I own City Girl. I believe you've had a problem booking a treatment. Perhaps I could help.'

'Oh . . . Oh yes, hello. Thank you for calling back,' the woman responded coolly. 'Well, I think you should know that there are some difficulties trying to book treatments.'

'It's a very busy centre,' Devlin pointed out.

'I realize that. But I've heard this discussed at lunches and dinners and indeed at my bridge club and tennis club, and it seems from what I can gather that if one is a friend of the manageress, there's no problem booking in. And seemingly some of the ladies have even had treatments on Sundays when the place is closed. How does one get into this clique? There's nothing I'd like better than a facial on a Sunday afternoon. I must say I'm not at all impressed, Miss Delaney.'

Devlin's eyes were out on stalks at her caller's information. Treatments being carried out on a Sunday! What on earth was going on? She gave no hint of her disquiet, however.

'I'll phone them myself and make sure you get an appointment, Mrs Adams. And I'd like you to have another treatment of your choice with our compliments. I'll inform reception in Galway,' Devlin responded courteously.

'Oh . . . well . . . That's most kind of you.' The tone became less snooty. 'I'm sorry to complain of course, it's rather irritating to have to do so. I know that Hanlon girl gives treatments in people's homes and I'm sure I could have booked her for one of them, but it's not quite the same as going in and having one in the luxury of City Girl's surroundings, if you know what I mean.'

'I do indeed,' Devlin said evenly. 'I'm sorry that you've experienced delays. I'll sort it this morning. If you care to ring reception after lunch they'll be able to book you in. Thank you for calling.'

'Not at all. Thank you for dealing with my complaint.' Charlotte Adams sounded much happier as she hung up but Devlin was extremely troubled as she put the receiver back. Her finger pressed another button on the console and Andrew's voice came down the line.

'Yes Devlin?'

'You'd better come in here, Andrew. Things seem to be going from bad to worse,' she said heavily.

The accountant's face grew grim a few minutes later as she relayed details of her phone call.

'Using the premises on Sunday, that would

account for the rise in light and heating bills. It would also account for the extra oils, waxes, and so on. I wonder does Madam Hanlon use her own supply of products when she's making her private calls, or does she use City Girl stock?'

'I can't believe it, Andrew. We gave her a great bonus this year and a brand-new car. Could there be a mistake?'

'Well, I've double- and treble-checked the figures and something's definitely wrong. It justifies an internal audit. But I want to catch Ms Hanlon red-handed. I know a firm who specializes in this kind of thing. I think we'll give them a shout.' He paced up and down, frowning.

'Will I say anything to Ciara about that Adams woman's complaint?' Devlin asked.

'Pass it off lightly. We don't want to get her suspicions up,' Andrew instructed.

'Maybe I should get Liz to phone reception and not speak to Ciara at all.'

'Good thinking, Devlin. If you were involved it would look as serious as it is and, as I say, we don't want Ciara Hanlon getting wind that anything is up. I'm setting up the investigation immediately. The sooner it's sorted the better, especially with the new development starting soon.'

'We'll have to give her the sack if we prove that she's ripping us off.'

'Yeah. And you're going to need someone good to take over down there. Someone you can really depend on. You'd better start thinking of a few names to put in the hat.'

'Right. Keep me up to date on any developments. I'll talk to Luke tonight or maybe I'll wait until tomorrow. I don't want him coming home to bad news, he's busy enough as it is.' Devlin was despondent.

'Don't take it personally, Devlin. These things happen in business,' Andrew advised.

'But I *do* take it personally, Andrew. Just because it's business is no excuse to steal from people and treat them like dirt. I gave that girl a position of trust. I paid her well. And gave her excellent perks. And she can smile at me and be nice to my face and pretend that she has my company's business at heart and all the time she is *stealing* from me. Stabbing me in the back. Being as two-faced as they come. I take that *very* personally, Andrew. There isn't one set of morals for business and another for relationships. It's all the one to me. I don't differentiate between business and personal relationships in the way I treat people. It's no different stealing from the business me and the private me. It's all the one and it's dishonest. There's no grey area in between,' Devlin raged. 'And don't tell me ever to get used to it because I won't.'

'I agree with you, Devlin,' Andrew said calmly, 'but you have to face facts, unfortunately. As I say, you're lucky that this is your first taste of . . . for want of a better word . . . fraud.'

'Well, I hope it's my last,' Devlin snapped. She glowered at the accountant.

'Talk to you later.' He ignored her anger.

'Sorry, Andrew,' Devlin apologized for outburst. It wasn't her accountant's fault that Ciara Hanlon might be a thief. It wasn't fair to take it out on him. But it left a sour taste in her mouth.

'We'll sort it out, Devlin. Don't let it get to you too

208

much is the best advice I can offer you. When you leave the office today put it out of your head.'

Devlin knew he was right. Taking work problems home was the worst thing to do. When she'd opened City Girl she'd lived and breathed it morning, noon, and night. It had almost cost her her relationship with Luke. You had to have boundaries.

She took a few deep breaths to try and get her anger under control. She was so mad with Ciara Hanlon she felt like getting on the next flight to Galway and confronting her with her treachery.

When she'd calmed down somewhat, she told Liz to ring Galway and organize the treatments for Charlotte Adams, and tried to put the problem aside for the rest of the day.

The traffic was so bad that evening that Luke was home before her, had the table set and the side salad prepared ready to accompany the steak she intended to serve.

'Hi, you look fraught,' he remarked as she dumped her briefcase in the hall and hurried into the kitchen to greet him.

'The traffic was woeful. I thought I'd have been home before you, sorry about that, Luke.'

'Don't be daft. The flight landed ten minutes early due to tail winds and the traffic from the airport was light enough at my end. I didn't have to cross town like you. Come here, wife, and kiss and hug me.' He caught her to him and enveloped her in a bear-hug. Devlin sank into his embrace gratefully. Luke was so solid and strong. When he had his arms around her nothing ever seemed as bad as she thought it was.

'I hope you're not overdoing it. You look tired—'

'Now, Luke . . .' Devlin admonished.

'Sorry.' He held up a hand.

'I'm pregnant. It's not an illness. It's a perfectly natural process.'

'I know. Don't give out to me. I just worry about you.' Luke rested his chin on her head.

'Well thank you, I know you do and that's nice to know. But I'm fine, really. The traffic was heavy and I was busy at work today but now I'm ready to flop with my gorgeous, kind, sexy husband.'

Luke laughed. 'OK! OK. I'll get the dinner.'

Devlin grinned. 'Well, you are gorgeous and kind and sexy but I suppose seeing as I *am* pregnant I could put my feet up . . .'

'Go on in and flop. Dinner won't be long,' Luke instructed.

'Ah, let's get it together. It's more fun.' Devlin leaned up and kissed him, just wanting to be with him.

'You sit on the stool and butter the French stick then,' Luke suggested as he prepared the baked potatoes.

They chatted companionably, filling each other in on the events of the previous days. Luke had been in London since Sunday and Devlin reflected how much she missed him on the days he was away and how empty the apartment was without him. It was the pattern of their life but it would have to change now that she was pregnant.

She didn't say anything about Ciara Hanlon and the trouble at Galway, there was time enough for that. All she wanted to do right now was relax with her husband and switch off. Andrew was absolutely right about not bringing work home. She pushed all thoughts of City Girl from her mind. Caroline was always saying how important it was to live for the moment.

This was her moment with Luke. Nothing was more important than that.

Twenty-two

The following morning the alarm clock woke her and she stretched out her hand to switch it off. Luke did likewise, reaching across her. Their hands reached the clock together. Devlin laughed. 'Morning,' she murmured drowsily as she turned and burrowed her face against him, the dark tangle of hair that covered his chest soft against her cheek.

'Morning,' he murmured back, holding her close. They lay, arms around each other, snoozing contentedly.

'I really don't feel like getting up,' Devlin mumbled after a while.

'Let's go on the mitch,' Luke suggested lazily.

'What!' Devlin exclaimed, intrigued.

'Let's bunk off and have a day to ourselves. We deserve it.'

'But I've meetings.' Devlin sighed.

'There she goes. My little workaholic. Meetings can be cancelled. The world won't stop revolving because Devlin Delaney missed a meeting, you know. Hard and all as it is to believe,' Luke teased.

'But Luke, that's no way to run a business. You wouldn't do it if we were in London,' she protested.

'I might, if I thought I was going on a dirty date with a sexy woman.'

'A dirty date . . . What dirty date?' she exclaimed.

'Are you going to lighten up and be a bit spontaneous instead of being little-Miss-Goody-Two-Shoes-Career-Woman?' Luke leaned on his elbow and looked down at her sternly.

Devlin laughed. She loved Luke's boyish streak. He always nipped it in the bud when she took herself too seriously.

'So we're going on a dirty date? Where?' Her eyes danced.

'Wait and see.'

'Don't be such a rotter. Tell me,' she demanded, pummelling him. Luke retaliated by tickling her unmercifully.

'Stop it, stop it,' she shrieked between guffaws.

'Am I a rotter?'

'No . . . No . . . you're a mad bastard,' she giggled.

'That's my wife . . . the lady.' Luke kissed her on the nose.

'Where are we going?'

'I told you, on a dirty date. Now let's go and have some breakfast and get going.' He got out of bed and pulled back the curtains. Devlin could see a deep pink streak in the eastern sky and the sun, a pale wintry yellow sphere as it rose on the horizon. It was a crisp clear morning that promised a fine day. She suddenly felt light-hearted. Imagine spending a whole day with Luke when they should be at work. What a treat.

She slid out of bed and put her arms around him.

'You know, you're very good at marriage,' she remarked.

'Am I?' He looked at her quizzically.

'You're much better than me at making time for us. I'd never have thought of taking a day off mid-week in a million years.'

'Life's too short, Devlin. It's allowed to have fun, you know.'

'I'm so lucky, Luke. Poor Caroline has never had what we've got and Maggie and Terry are poles apart now.'

'Yeah. It's sad. Terry's crazy to treat Maggie the way he does. He'll never find another woman like her. And those poor kids. He doesn't deserve them. I can't understand men who won't spend time with their children. I can't wait for our child to be born. And you're right, Devlin, we're lucky and we're always going to have fun days, you and me. Let's always make time for us, no matter how many children or how many businesses we have. And let's spend lots of time with our child.' Luke was serious as he took her face between his hands.

'I love you.' Devlin wrapped her arms around him. She felt completely happy. 'Take me back to bed and let's start the day *properly* . . .'

Two hours later they were driving under the M50 towards the North Road. 'Where are we going, Luke?' Devlin was consumed with curiosity.

'Patience, woman. We'll be there shortly.'

'Well it can't be Belfast, you'd never take this route. You'd go by the airport. This is the road to Ashbourne. Are we going to Ashbourne? Why would you want to go to Ashbourne?' Devlin's brow furrowed as she tried to work out where they were going.

'Come on, tell me,' she wheedled.

'Nope.'

'Why did you want me to wear my jeans?'

'I told you, we're going on a dirty date,' he said infuriatingly as they sped along the busy road.

'Why are we going down this side road?' Devlin was utterly flummoxed as Luke turned left and they drove down a narrow tree-lined country road.

Luke pulled onto the verge. 'Stay there for a minute,' he instructed. She watched as he opened the boot but she couldn't see what he was doing.

Moments later he was standing at her door, grinning at her expression, a pair of green wellington boots in his hand. He was already wearing his. 'Here, put these on.'

'Luke, would you tell me *what's* going on?' Devlin unzipped her ankle boots and pulled on the wellies.

'We're going to walk the land, wife.'

Devlin laughed. 'Is that right, husband?' She got out of the car and he tucked her arm in his.

'What do you think of this field?' he asked as he led her through a green iron gate.

'It's mucky,' Devlin said doubtfully as she sank to her ankles in thick creamy mud. 'What's so important about this field anyway?'

'This, my dear girl, is going to be my next project. It's for sale, it's been rezoned for building so I'm going to buy it and build houses on it. And you know the land my father left me in Meath? I'm going to do the same there. It's just an excuse to spend more time at home with you.'

'Oh Luke, that's brilliant! I hate sleeping on my own at night. You're such a good snuggler, you know.' Devlin's face creased into a broad smile.

215

'You're very good for my ego, Dev.' Luke smiled back at her.

'But sure I love you. It's as simple as that.' Devlin squeezed his hand as they began walking along the boundary.

'Do you know what I've always loved about you, Devlin? You're dead straight. You don't play games. I always know where I stand with you.'

'But Luke, you're easy to be straight with. You're the most honest and the most decent man I ever met. And you know I never thought I'd say this, but I'm glad now that I went through all that heartbreak and grief with Colin, because every day I'm with you I thank God for the gift of your love. If I hadn't gone through what I did, I don't think I'd really appreciate what I have now the way I do. And I'll never take it for granted. I'm really, really happy, Luke.'

'Me too,' Luke said as his arm tightened around her. They walked along the edge of the field listening to the birds chirruping in the crisp late autumn morning. They breathed the rich fresh country air with relish.

It was like being in another world. Devlin relaxed, letting the residue of guilt about taking the day off work flow away. Luke was right. Life was too short. Time together was precious. A cottage nestled into a small grove of trees in the adjoining field. A thin plume of smoke curled from the chimney. Devlin marvelled at how rural the scene was, so close to the capital.

'This would be a nice place to bring up children.' She spoke her thoughts aloud.

'Hmm, we're going to have to sort out our living arrangements.' Luke cocked an eye at her.

Devlin's heart gave a little flutter. Suppose Luke felt that they should live in London? Deep down she dreaded the idea of moving back to England but if it was what he wanted, it wouldn't be for selfish reasons. Devlin knew that. There and then she decided if he opted for London he'd get no arguments from her. She wasn't wimping out. She'd known Luke's business was in London when she'd married him. She'd known a time would come when they'd have to make a permanent home in Dublin or London. It would be much easier for her to operate from London and commute once or twice a week than it would be for him.

And don't ever act the martyr about it either, she warned herself silently.

'We should decide one way or another what we're going to do. I suppose London is the most practical option.'

There! She'd said it. She could almost feel herself holding her breath as she waited for him to agree with her.

'Do you think so?' He looked at her in surprise.

'Well, isn't it? Your business is there?' She was taken aback at his reaction.

'City Girl is here. That's as important.'

'I know that, I'm not saying that my business isn't as important to me as yours is to you. I just think it would be easier for me to commute on a permanent basis than it would be for you.'

'I wouldn't want you commuting, Devlin,' Luke said slowly.

'Why? Do you want me to give up City Girl and be a stay-at-home mother?' Devlin couldn't conceal her shock. This was one scenario she hadn't considered.

'Good God, Devlin, I'd never expect you to give up City Girl,' Luke exclaimed. 'I just don't want you commuting because it's exhausting as well as being a mega pain in the ass.'

'Oh!' she murmured. 'Well, I don't want you to be commuting either.'

'Tell you what, let's go on part two of our date and decide one way or another at the end of it,' Luke suggested.

'Where are we going now?' Devlin was mystified.

'You'll see. Come on let's go back to the car for the next leg of Reilly's Mystery Tour.'

'I give up. You're mad.' Devlin followed her husband as he strode across the field at speed.

Twenty-five minutes later he drove into Clontarf DART station and parked the car.

'Where are we going now?' she demanded.

'On the DART,' he said innocently.

'Where on the DART?'

'Here . . . there. Wherever we want.'

'But why?'

'There doesn't have to be a why. Be spontaneous, Devlin.' Luke grinned. 'Come on, if a DART goes by while we're down here I'm not waiting on another one. Day out's cancelled.'

'Is that right?' Devlin said tartly. 'Luke has spoken.'

'Correct. Get your ass out of the car, woman, and stop delaying.'

Devlin laughed as she got out of the car. 'One thing about being married to you, Reilly. I'm never bored.'

'One thing about being married to you, Delaney, neither am I.'

218

He paid for two return tickets to Dalkey and they hurried up the iron staircase onto the platform. The monitor indicated that a train would be along in three minutes and Devlin felt a thrill of excitement. She'd always loved trains ever since her childhood holidays in Rosslare Harbour, when she'd stood at her aunt's great picture windows and watched the boat-trains clickity clack along the viaduct. She never used the DART because it didn't run near Stephen's Green, but often, stuck in traffic on the quays, she'd watched the green trains glide over Butt Bridge with effortless ease and envied the passengers who'd be home long before she would.

From where they stood high up on the platform, Clontarf and Dublin Bay spread out in a grand panorama to the east. The sun sparkled on the glittering water and the twin red and white ESB chimneys stood stark against the deep blue sky, the spirals of smoke drifting in great white plumes into the blueness. There was a tremendous sense of colour and space. So different from London. After their conversation earlier, Devlin felt that they were going to live in Dublin. The thought made her happy.

'Here's the train,' Luke said, looking northwards. Seconds later the lime-green train pulled into the station and the doors hissed open.

'Let's sit on the left-hand side. It's got the sea view,' Devlin suggested. She led the way to an empty seat in the middle of the carriage and they sat smiling at each other like two little kids on a day out.

'The reason we're on the DART is that I want you to look at the areas we pass through and think about where you might like to buy a house.'

'*Are* we going to live in Dublin?' Her heart lifted.

'I think so, Dev. I'd much prefer to rear children here.' Luke looked at her questioningly.

'Me too,' she agreed. 'Are you sure about this, Luke, because you know you wouldn't get any argument from me if you wanted to stay in London.'

'I know that, love. But I'd like our children to grow up close to the sea and the countryside, and that wouldn't be the case in London.' Luke put his arm around her shoulder as the train moved off slowly and before long they were heading towards the Docklands.

'Where do you think you'd like to live? Do you want to join U2, Enya, and the rest of the celebs out in Dalkey and Killiney?' Luke enquired as they clattered along the tracks through the North Strand towards Amiens Street.

Devlin wrinkled her nose. 'Even though I grew up on the Southside, I like living on the Northside. I like Clontarf. I like Howth. And it's very handy for the airport. That's got to be an important consideration. You don't want to be sitting in gridlock every time you're coming or going to and from there.'

'You might change your mind when we get out to Dalkey and you see the views.' Luke smiled.

'Views aren't everything.' Devlin snuggled close. 'But I do love this one.' They peered out the window as the train left Amiens Street behind and slowly crossed Butt Bridge. The Liffey glittered in the morning sun, snaking its way up under O'Connell Bridge and east past the Customs House to the sea. 'This is the life isn't it? A whole day to ourselves, seeing the sights of Dublin on the DART. Are we wild or what?' She laughed heartily. 'I'd love Jean Mallen to see us. She'd be horrified. Imagine being caught on the DART. Just think what she'd write in that tacky 'social column', as she calls it.'

'That one! She's just a jumped-up little consequence with a chip on her shoulder. I saw her on a late-night chat programme the other night. All simpering and giggling. Someone should tell her TV's not her forte,' Luke scoffed.

'Neither's writing a social column,' Devlin said dryly and Luke laughed.

'Bitchy! Bitchy!'

'I know, but she is a bitch. She said awful things about Caroline in her column when she and Richard separated. She'll probably go to town on her this time as well. It's really unfair the way the press intrude on people's private traumas,' Devlin argued.

'I'm glad Caroline's going for the divorce. It's time she started afresh. She deserves so much better,' Luke remarked.

'I wish she could find someone special and settle down and have a family. That's all she's ever wanted.'

'Maybe it will happen. She's a lovely woman.' Luke smiled down at her. 'She's doing a great job in City Girl.'

'Yeah, she is,' Devlin agreed, suddenly remembering with a sinking heart the problems with Ciara Hanlon. She'd planned to tell Luke about it today, before he'd come up with his day-off brainwave.

She couldn't tell him about it now and ruin his fun. Today was their special day. Resolutely she pushed the problem to the back of her mind once more, as the train thundered past the Merrion Gates and the sea came into view. Luke pointed out a massive car boat heading for port and a cargo ship steaming towards the horizon.

They had a beautiful day, climbing to the top of Killiney Hill where the full panorama of Dublin spread out before them, and Wicklow to the south seemed just a length away. They had lunch in a little Italian bistro in Dalkey and afterwards strolled around the bookshops and a small art gallery, where Luke bought her a miniature painting of a delicate pink rose.

They got the DART back to Clontarf around four, before the rush hour. As the familiar weariness swept over her, Devlin tried to hide her yawns.

'You go to bed for a snooze when we get home, and we could go to Wong's for dinner if you like. Save us having to cook,' Luke suggested.

'That would be nice,' Devlin approved. She hadn't had Chinese in ages. Wong's roast-duck starter was especially tasty.

That night, as she sat in the dimly lit restaurant enjoying her meal, she reached out and took Luke's hand.

'It was the most perfect day,' she said simply. And meant it. Tomorrow and its troubles could wait.

Twenty-three

'We are so looking forward to seeing you, Maggie.'
Alma Al Shariff's husky tones, still with a trace of a
Cork lilt, floated across the air waves from Saudi as
clear as a bell.

Maggie was swamped with guilt. Alma sounded so
genuinely pleased to be visiting them. Maybe things
wouldn't be too bad after all. If only she could get a
few more chapters written she wouldn't feel so
harassed.

'We'll take you to dinner and the theatre and we'll
go shopping in Brown Thomas. We're going to have
a wonderful time, Maggie. Thanks so much for
putting us up. Suly is like a little boy at the thought
of it. Honestly, Maggie, he's driving me crazy these
days. There's a new guy in Oncology who's got it all.
Talent, looks, money, women throwing themselves at
him, and it's driving Sulaiman bananas. And you
know why? Because this new guy's young. Sulaiman
will be forty-five this year and he can't cope with it. I
caught him using my moisturizer the other day. Can
you believe it? Crazy! Crazy! Is Terry like that?'

Maggie laughed. 'Yep! He's taken to going to the
gym now. And he's off the drink until you come. And
he's taking some sort of ginseng supplement that

someone at work told him about. Don't ask me what it's supposed to do.'

'Maggie, guess what? Suly can't get it up any more. It's driving me nuts. I've gone past the sympathy stage. I mean is it me or what? Do you think he's lost interest? Or do you think he's having an affair and using it all up on someone else? I don't know what to think. What do you think?' Alma asked glumly.

Maggie threw her eyes up to heaven. Alma was always in the throes of a drama. No matter how personal her problem she'd share it with all and sundry. Maggie wouldn't dream of discussing her sex life . . . or lack of sex life with Alma. With Devlin and Caroline, yes. They were her dearest friends, but Alma came under the heading of friendly acquaintance. And *indiscreet* friendly acquaintance at that. If Maggie said that she and Terry were having problems, it would be all over the compound in Saudi. Still, it wouldn't be Alma if there wasn't a crisis in her life. How typical of her to think that Sulaiman was having an affair just because he was temporarily impotent.

'Look, Alma, maybe he's just tired and stressed out at the moment. I'm sure it's just temporary,' she soothed.

'Was Terry ever impotent?' Alma asked artlessly.

I couldn't care less any more, Maggie thought sourly. 'Not really, but then his job wouldn't be half as stressful as Sulaiman's. After all, he does have to make life and death decisions,' she said diplomatically.

'Yes well that's *his* problem and it's causing *me* problems,' Alma said tartly, as self-centred as ever, Maggie noted with amusement.

'Maybe the holiday will do you all the good in the world.' She twirled the phone cord impatiently. The day was running away with her and she was getting nothing done. She hadn't even started to write yet, but Alma was flowing. Their phone bill must cost a fortune. No wonder Sulaiman was stressed.

'Yes, Maggie, honestly, the thought of this holiday's keeping me going. Believe me. I can't tell you how much I'm looking forward to Ireland and the States. It will be such a delightful change from here. Listen, I've loads of scandal for you. Mina Farooq is pregnant, but Rameez isn't the father.'

'Really?' Maggie was taken aback at this news. Mina Farooq was a mutual acquaintance who'd been a theatre sister when Maggie worked in the hospital. She'd been a quiet, reserved Filipino girl, married to a Pakistani who worked in computers. 'Who's the father?'

'She fell head over heels in love with a Scottish engineer who was working in the desert and they had an affair. He was a hunk, Maggie. He fancied me too,' she added hastily. 'Imagine little Mrs Demure dropping her drawers for an engineer? Remember how straight-laced she was?'

'And what about Rameez? Does he know?' Maggie was astonished. Mina Farooq was the last person she'd have figured to have an affair.

'He's too busy having an affair with himself to notice what poor Mina's up to,' Alma retorted caustically. 'Of course he doesn't know. He doesn't think anyone else would even notice Mina, let alone find her attractive. You know the way he puts her down all the time. He's in for a hell of a shock when the baby's born. It's good enough for him. He's the pits. If I was married to him, I'd drown myself. She should leave him.'

'Why doesn't she?'

'The kids. Rameez would get custody. Even if he didn't he'd take off with them to Pakistan and she'd never see them again.'

'Poor Mina,' Maggie said sympathetically.

'That's not all,' Alma said dramatically. 'Remember Kenneth Fenlon, that sanctimonious little weasel from Accounts who never touched a drink and always looked down his nose at the rest of us who did?'

'I remember him,' Maggie made a face. 'Horrible little man. What's he done?'

'Someone planted a bottle of Scotch in his sports bag while he was playing tennis and tipped off the Muttawaah. He nearly had hysterics and you know what?' Alma let out a hearty chuckle.

'What?' Maggie laughed herself. This conversation was bringing back so many memories.

'He was deported!' giggled Alma.

'Never,' Maggie shrieked. 'I don't believe it. Oh I'd love to have been there for that.' Kenneth Fenlon had been universally disliked and with good reason. He was a sly, devious little man who distrusted everyone he worked with.

'And guess what else?' Alma was enjoying herself hugely, Maggie could tell.

'What?'

'He was on the fiddle. Mr Holier-Than-Thou had a neat little scam going in hospital supplies.'

'I knew it!' Maggie exclaimed. 'Didn't I always say that? That little wart was as shifty as they come. What's he doing now?'

'Well, here's the icing on the cake, Maggie,' Alma declared dramatically. 'I hear he's taken to the bottle. He lives near Beaumont hospital and Andy McLoughlin, an electrician over here, comes from around there too. The last time he was home he saw Kenneth in the local, pissed as a newt.'

Maggie guffawed. 'Well, well, well. How the mighty have fallen.'

'I thought you'd enjoy that, Maggie. You had a few run-ins with him, didn't you?'

'Didn't everyone in the hospital?' Maggie grinned.

Alma stayed on the phone for another half an hour, filling her in on all the news and gossip. The compound was a hotbed of intrigue and infidelities and always had been. Maggie was reminded of how claustrophobic she'd found it all. It had been horrible when Terry had started his affair with Ria Kirby, when she'd been pregnant with the twins. Everyone on the compound had known about it except her. She'd found out afterwards when she'd come back home to live and caught Terry and Ria making love in the shower one awful day soon after Ria had come back to Ireland.

Alma loved that kind of gossip and carry-on. She could never get enough of it. It was because her life was empty, Maggie had sometimes thought, when the other woman was delighting in some new scandal that rocked the unreal little expat world in the dry, dusty, arid country that would never be called home.

Alma seemed to be the woman who had everything. A tall, dark, handsome husband, who was wealthy and successful. Two children. Staff to take care of her every need. A very cosmopolitan lifestyle. Yet she wasn't happy. There was a restlessness about her that never left her. She was a real flirt too and had indulged in a few flings herself, Maggie remembered wryly.

It was all Sulaiman's fault for not paying her enough attention, she'd told Maggie crossly. She was a woman who *needed* tender loving care.

She was a very selfish and demanding woman would have been another way of putting it. Maggie refrained from saying so. She often wondered how Sulaiman put up with her attention-seeking ways. When Maggie looked at Alma she saw a woman who had never grown up emotionally.

Her own life might not be a bed of roses right now, but at least she accepted responsibility for it with some degree of maturity. Alma never faced her problems. She ran away from them and filled her life with superficialities in an attempt to deny their existence.

Maggie sighed as she glanced at the clock. It was too late to attempt any writing for now. It was almost time to do the school run and give the children their dinner.

The phone rang again. Maggie scowled. Sometimes that damn instrument was the bane of her life.

'Hello?' She tried to keep the impatience out of her voice.

'Maggie, howya, it's Orla. Thank God I got you, I've been trying for ages. Would you mind picking the kids up from school, I've got delayed in town but I'll be home as quick as I can.'

Maggie's heart sank. Orla Noonan, one of her neighbours, was a flaming great nuisance. She was always planting her kids on Maggie while she went off gadding about, enjoying herself. 'As quick as I can' could mean four hours later.

No! Maggie decided. Enough was enough. Orla had pulled this stunt once too often. She was fed up being used.

'Sorry, Orla,' she said crisply. 'I'm afraid I can't do it today, I'm going out.'

'Oh God, the kids will be in a panic, what will I do?' Orla fussed. 'You couldn't just wait for twenty minutes, Maggie? I'd really appreciate it, pet. I meant to be home, but there was a huge queue in the bank and then I had to change Sean's trousers in Marks & Spencers and you know the palaver that is. I went to the wrong place and queued for ages and then I had to go upstairs to Customer Services and I had to queue for another twenty minutes. You know the way they go mad at the school if you don't collect the kids on time.' Orla was not giving up that easily.

Maggie wavered. She knew what it was like queuing in banks and shops. Poor Sean and Katie would be waiting with anxious little faces for their mother to come and collect them. She was never on time and they frequently had to wait in the school office under the disapproving stare of the secretary. When Orla eventually came rushing in, it would be with some convoluted rigmarole that was blatantly untrue.

'Orla, twenty minutes max, and I mean it,' she said firmly, mad with herself for caving in.

'Oh you're a dote, Maggie. Thanks a million. I'll see you soon,' Orla trilled down the phone.

Maggie hung up, riddled with frustration. Why hadn't she stuck to her guns? Typical of her. But then she thought of Orla's two kids who were always being lumped from this one to that, and knew why. She was soft, some would say too soft. But where children were concerned who could be soft enough?

At least her three always had the reassurance that she'd be there for them after school, not like that flibbertigibbet Noonan who should never have had children in the first place because she hadn't the slightest interest in looking after them.

Orla Noonan emerged from the phone box beside the lifts in the ILAC and smiled at her sister. 'Everything's grand. Maggie's picking the kids up. Let's go and have a cup of tea, I'm parched. And I want to run into Hickeys to have a look at some material to make a flower girl's dress for Katie. Tara's asked her to be flower girl at the wedding.' She knew she'd promised Maggie she'd be home in twenty minutes, but a cup of tea would only take five and a quick browse through Hickeys another five. She'd scorch home then. The traffic wouldn't be too bad at this hour of the afternoon. Anyway Sean and Katie would be company for Michael and Shona if Maggie wanted to get a few pages written while she was waiting. Orla justified the delay to herself with ease as she and her sister headed for the Kylemore Café.

Twenty-four

An hour and a half later Maggie was sizzling with suppressed anger. Orla Noonan was a cow and a half. How dare she? How *dare* she treat Maggie with such contempt? Sean and Katie were having high jinks out in the back garden with Michael and Shona. She'd taken pity on them after the first half an hour and made up a plateful of chicken and salad sandwiches and, at Michael's behest, a flask of Bovril.

'We're at base camp, Mam. We're climbing Everest,' he explained. 'And it's thirty degrees below freezing.'

It *was* a cold day, Maggie acknowledged, although not quite thirty below.

'Would a few chocolate biscuits give you more heat and energy?' She arched an eyebrow at him.

'Sure would, Mam.' He grinned. Maggie grinned back at him. He had such a fertile imagination. He was his mother's son in that respect. She watched the children playing away at the side of the wooden shed in an old tent that had seen better days. In their minds they *were* at the foot of the Himalayas, not stuck in the back of a large garden in the Dublin suburbs. The sandwiches were given short shrift. She should have made a big hotpot, she thought, as she looked at Shona's red nose and cheeks under her woollen cap. The day had turned bitterly cold, wintry even, and the pale yellow November sun struggled to cast a faded light on the southern wall of the garden.

As the time ticked by, Maggie grew more angry by the second. Orla Noonan was a pig-ignorant selfish bitch and always had been, and this time Maggie was going to let her know in no uncertain terms that she had been taken for a ride once too often. No wonder none of the neighbours in their cul-de-sac had a good word to say about her. She'd tried it on all of them.

If it wasn't for the neighbours those poor children would never be fed and watered half the time. They were like little orphans sometimes as Orla skittered around the city entertaining herself. Billy, the father, a hulking great lump of a bloke, was never at home either. He worked seven days a week. At least, he told Orla he did, Maggie thought wryly. Their marriage was about as good as hers and Terry's and that wasn't saying much, she thought dispiritedly.

She glanced at the clock. Half three. Twenty minutes, my ass! Maggie scowled. Orla would arrive in her own good time with some outlandish excuse, as usual.

It was after four before Orla zoomed up the drive in her red Honda Civic and bounced breezily up to the front door.

'Terribly sorry, Maggie, pet,' she apologized profusely. 'But you'll never believe what happened. I was—'

'You're right, Orla. I *don't* believe you,' Maggie cut her off sharply. 'You've taken advantage of me once too often, but you won't do it again, believe me. Go back out to your car and I'll send the children out to you. And never, *ever* ask me to mind them again because the answer will be no.'

'Oh now, hold on a minute, Maggie,' Orla blustered, red-faced. 'You're being very unfair here. I do *indeed* have a genuine and legitimate reason for being late. You see the car in front of me in the ILAC broke down and blocked—'

'Out, Orla! You used that excuse three months ago to Judy next door. Just go. You're nothing but a user. You should be ashamed of yourself.' Maggie practically bundled the other woman out the door, she was so annoyed.

'There's really no need for this—'

'There *is* need. I've had it up to here with you,' Maggie snapped viciously. 'Into the car, Orla. I'll send the kids out.' She closed the door firmly in her neighbour's face. Orla was gobsmacked. Maggie didn't care. Years and years of being used had just come to a head. Too many people were taking advantage of her good nature. Now they could all go to hell. She'd had enough. She wouldn't take it out on the kids, of course. If they'd been in the house she certainly wouldn't have let them see the altercation. She'd have taken Orla aside into another room. She was glad they were outside. It had been childishly satisfying to shut the door in Orla Noonan's face.

'Katie, Sean, get your school bags, your mammy is waiting for you in the car,' she called out the back door.

'Aw Mam, can they not stay for another while? We're having a great game,' Michael protested.

Four eager faces turned towards her hopefully.

'No, Michael. I'm sorry, we're going out.' Maggie's tone was firm and he knew better than to argue.

233

'Where are we going, Mam?' Shona asked excitedly. 'I didn't know that we are going out. Can Katie and Sean come with us?'

For God's sake. I'll murder them! Maggie glared at her two.

'No, I'm afraid not today. Now you and Michael go inside and wash your hands and brush your hair, quickly. Sean, Katie, hurry up and don't keep Mammy waiting.'

Sean and Katie trooped disappointedly into the kitchen, followed by an equally disappointed Shona and Michael. Maggie sighed in irritation. Kids were never satisfied.

She opened the front door for them, relieved to see that Orla was sitting in the car. The other woman studiously ignored her as Katie and Sean opened the front passenger door and climbed into the back seat. Maggie waved at the children as Orla revved the engine and drove out of the drive with considerable haste. Her house was at the entrance to their small cul-de-sac and no-one could go in or out without Orla seeing them. Maggie would have to go out now. She'd said she was going out, not only to Orla but to the kids as well. There was no point in making a liar out of herself. She'd be as bad as Orla. She had no dinner preparations done either. She was damned if after being out for the next hour she was going to come home to get dinner.

She picked up the phone and dialled Terry's office.

'Hi, it's me. Will you get a chippie or a Chinese for yourself on the way home, I'm taking the kids over to Blanchardstown to get shoes and I'm going to take them to MacDonald's. I won't be cooking dinner.'

'A fat lot of good chips or Chinese are to me when

234

I'm trying to lose a bit of weight, Maggie,' Terry grumbled.

'Well get a Weight Watchers ready-made in the supermarket then,' Maggie snapped and slammed the phone down. The last thing she needed this day was Terry whinging. It was such a big deal because he was on a diet. The whole world had to muck in and help!

She felt the tension in the back of her neck, and in her jaw. There was a dull throb at the side of her temple. The starting of that horrible hormoney headache that no painkiller would shift. Her waistband felt too tight for her. She glanced at the calendar. Four days before her period. A good old dose of PMT to top off a disaster of a day. What more could she want?

The phone rang. She assumed it was Terry ready to give her a piece of his mind.

'Hello,' she barked.

'Oh . . . Um . . . hello. Could I speak to Maggie Ryan please?' a young female voice asked politely.

'Speaking,' she said in a more civil tone.

'Um . . . hello, Maggie. My name is Miranda Quigley. I'm your new editor. I'm just phoning all my authors to introduce myself. Perhaps you could come over to the office some day next week and we could have a chat.'

'Oh . . . hello, er . . . Miranda. I'd like to meet you very much. I'd value your input, to be honest. I'm a bit blocked at the moment,' Maggie confessed.

'I haven't had a chance yet to read the chunk of *Betrayal* you sent in. I've quite a few to catch up on,' Miranda said brightly.

Maggie's heart sank. This was the last thing she

needed to hear. 'Have you read any of my books?' she asked hesitantly.

'Um . . . actually no. But I will. Soon. Just keep writing, Maggie. We can cut anything that isn't working,' Miranda said airily.

'What type of books have you edited before this?' Maggie asked curiously. Miranda sounded so young to be an editor.

'Er . . . well actually I was in sales and marketing before this, with Lakelands Press. Unfortunately they've gone to the wall. However I've read and commented on plenty of manuscripts during my time there. This is my first time in editorial. I'm looking forward to it immensely.'

'I see,' Maggie said despondently. This was an absolute nightmare. She was being given a novice editor, untried, who'd never read any of her novels and who'd worked for a publisher who'd folded. Maggie vaguely knew of Lakelands Press, a small outfit who hadn't made any significant impact on the book trade although they plugged away and promised their authors the moon.

'Don't worry about a thing, Maggie. We'll get along fine.' Miranda spoke with all the confidence of youth.

'I'm sure we will,' Maggie responded with as much enthusiasm as she could muster.

'Great. Why don't you call my secretary early next week to schedule a meeting. It was nice talking to you. I'm looking forward to seeing you. I must rush. I have an acquisitions meeting to attend. It's my first,' Miranda bubbled.

'Enjoy it,' Maggie murmured. 'Bye.'

She stared at the phone as Miranda clicked off. There was only one thing for it. A Big Mac Meal . . .

Large. *And* ice-cream in caramel sauce. Either that or get thoroughly pissed. And how could she do that with three children?

'Come on,' she yelled up the stairs. 'We're going to buy shoes for Shona and have a MacDonald's in Blanchardstown.'

'I don't want to go, Mam,' Mimi yelled back. 'Rachel and I are doing a project. She's coming over in a few minutes.'

'You can do it when we get back. We'll only be gone an hour or so. We'll call in and tell her on the way.'

'We'll be gone more than an hour, Mam. We'll be gone ages. It's not fair, I don't want to go,' Mimi whined.

'Mimi, get your ass down here now and let's get out of here, pronto,' Maggie roared. 'Rachel can come another day.'

'There's no need to use swear-words. You're always giving out to us for using swear-words. You should practise what you preach,' Mimi said snootily from the landing.

'Just don't push me today, Mimi Ryan. I'm warning you,' Maggie snapped, at the end of her tether.

'There's no need to go ballistic! Chill out, Mam,' her daughter said pertly as she sauntered down the stairs.

'I'll slap your face good and hard if you speak to me like that again, you cheeky little brat. Do you hear me? You impudent little wagon,' Maggie exploded, her hands itching to thump her elder daughter.

Mimi burst into tears at the unexpected vehemence of the retort and the fury in her mother's eyes.

Maggie burst into tears as she realized how out of control she was and just how close she'd been to venting her frustration on Mimi and slapping her hard.

Shona burst into tears because her mother and sister were crying and she hated raised voices and rows.

Michael stood by looking helplessly at the trio, his eyes wide with panic.

'I'm sorry, Mimi, I shouldn't have said that.' Maggie tried to compose herself.

'I'm sorry too, Mammy, I didn't mean it. Really I didn't. I love you, Mammy.' Mimi flung herself into Maggie's arms and hugged her tightly, her thin childish arms like two vices around her waist.

This made Maggie cry even harder and she held her daughter close, trying to swallow her sobs. She knew she was frightening her children. It was the worst thing in the world to see your parents crying.

'Mammy, are you all right?' Shona asked anxiously between sobs.

'Now look what you did, Miss Mimi,' Michael accused gruffly. 'It's all your fault for being cheeky. You made Mammy cry.'

'You leave me alone, Michael Ryan.' Mimi howled even louder.

'Shush, shush, stop now. Come here, Shone, stop crying, pet.' She drew Shona into her embrace. *Get a grip, Maggie*, she pleaded silently and, with an immense effort of will, she composed herself. 'Come on now. I'm sorry I lost my temper. We'll go over to Blanchdardstown and have a nice time out for ourselves. We'll buy new shoes for Shona, new jeans for Michael, and a sweatshirt in Paco for Mimi. And then we'll have a MacDonald's. OK?' She gave a weak smile.

'Are you sure you're all right, Mammy?' Shona asked anxiously, raising a tear-stained face to hers.

'Yes, pet. I'm OK. Don't be worrying. Quick now, run up and get ready so that we're not heading into the rush-hour traffic,' she urged.

Subdued, they hurried upstairs. Maggie followed tiredly. She went into the *en suite* in her bedroom and closed the door. Leaning against the plane of the door, she felt it cool against her forehead. Tears brimmed up again and she thrust her face in her hands and cried as quietly as she could.

How could her life be in such a mess? How could she come so close to losing control that she had almost walloped her daughter? She knew kids could push you to the limit. But this had been too close for comfort.

To hell with the novel, if she didn't get it done in time, she didn't get it done. She'd have to ease off. It wasn't worth it when the children started to suffer.

But it wasn't just that. It was Orla's casual abuse of her, and Terry's me, me, me attitude. It wasn't as if he had to eat a takeaway that often, she thought resentfully.

'I'm sick, sick, sick of him,' she muttered, wiping the tears from her cheeks. He took her so much for granted. It was as if the separation had never happened. He knew she wouldn't put the children through that trauma a second time. As far as he was concerned, he was as safe as houses. Maggie could look after him. Cook for him, feed him, wash and iron, and look after his house and his children and he could just sit back and take it all for granted. She could have a humdinger of a row about it with him and point out all her grievances. But what was the use? They'd been through it before, many times. It was water off a duck's back, at this stage and not worth her energy.

She started to cry again. God, she was really losing it, she thought in desperation. She needed this like a hole in the head. She ran cold water into the basin, soaked her face-cloth in it and patted it along her face and neck. Her heart was racing. If she wasn't careful she'd be having palpitations. Stress and panic attacks. Perfect! What more could she wish for? The woman who had everything.

One thing was for damn sure, she was going to enjoy every minute of Powerscourt Springs with the girls. She was going to have every treatment she could possibly have. To hell with the cost. She'd worked hard to make her money from her novels – she was going to spend some of it on herself for once. The royalty cheque had arrived just in time.

At least that weekend was coming up soon. She needed it badly, because once that was over, she was going to have to make her Christmas cake and puddings, not to mention starting her Christmas shopping, so as to have time to entertain the Al Shariffs. She must tell Josie, her cleaner, to give the guest room and *en suite* a thorough going-over. She could start the Christmas cleaning a few weeks early too, Maggie decided, as she made up her face to cover the ravages of her weeping fit.

But now she was going to spend time with her children. Maybe Orla had done her a favour after all. Orla could go to hell. The novel could go on the back burner for a while. It was time to get her priorities straight.

Twenty-five

Maggie was tired when they got home from Blanchardstown, but she was happier. She'd taken the children to the pictures, much to their delight. As they sank back into the plush chairs of the big cinema with their popcorn, M&Ms and Coke, the anticipation on their faces and their pleasure at the unexpected treat went a long way towards restoring her equilibrium. Afterwards they'd gone to Clark's to buy shoes, and to Paco for Mimi's much desired sweatshirt, then finally to Dunnes for Michael's jeans. After that, as another little treat, she'd taken them to HMV to buy a CD each. They'd spent ages flicking through the racks, although Shona knew straight away that she wanted the Spice Girls. Mimi dithered between Robbie Williams and Celine Dion.

Michael couldn't make up his mind until he saw the Venga Boys and then he was happy. They sat in MacDonald's munching their burgers, all thoughts of the earlier upset forgotten as they discussed the film, their new CDs and what they were going to get for Christmas.

'You're very late. Where were you? I thought you were going shopping for shoes,' Terry growled when they walked into the sitting-room at nine thirty.

'We went late-night shopping, Daddy, an' Mammy took us to the pictures. An' then we went to HMV an' got CDs an' *then* we went to MacDonald's an' had a Big Mac an' now here we are,' Shona kindly explained.

'What's all this in aid of?' He glanced at Maggie.

She shrugged. 'Shona needed new shoes. Michael needed new jeans and Mimi needed a new sweatshirt so we went shopping and decided to treat ourselves as well.'

'I hope all the homework is done,' Terry said sternly.

Maggie felt fury rise. The nerve of him to say that. Who was it that did homework with the kids day in day out? Her. He was never there for homework. He was just saying that for spite, to get back at her for slamming the phone down earlier. With difficulty she kept her temper.

'The homework was done as soon as everyone came in from school, as usual,' she said pointedly.

'Yeah an' Michael could do sums that Sean Noonan couldn't an' they're in the same class, Daddy,' Shona piped up proudly.

'Were the Noonans here this afternoon? Billy Noonan called over. He wanted a word with you. I said you were out,' Terry remarked casually as he flicked channels from the settee where he was sprawled.

'Oh!' Maggie was surprised. What on earth did Billy Noonan want with her? she thought, puzzled. Then she remembered. Her heart sank. Surely Orla hadn't sent him up because of the row. Wasn't she well able to fight her own battles? The pair of them could get lost. She had enough on her plate, Maggie thought irritably.

242

'Come on, gang. It's late and there's school tomorrow. Go up and get ready for bed. Michael, you go into our *en suite* and let Mimi and Shona have the bathroom,' she instructed. 'Say good night to Daddy.'

They launched themselves on Terry with hugs and kisses.

'Tell you what? When lucky old Mam goes away on her girls' weekend we'll go to Fort Lucan for the day. How about it?' he suggested.

Howls of delight greeted this pronouncement and Maggie felt a stab of resentment. Typical Terry. His rare treats were always so spectacular they eclipsed her more mundane efforts, and were always much more appreciated by the children.

Don't be such a childish bitch, she chided herself silently, annoyed at her response.

'Dad, Fort Lucan's MEGA.' Michael was chuffed. 'When are you going away, Mam?' He turned to her eagerly.

'Soon.' Maggie smiled in spite of herself.

'Great,' he enthused. 'Night, Dad. I can't wait.'

'Or me,' echoed his siblings as they smothered their father with more kisses.

'Come on. Up to bed.' Maggie interrupted the love-in. She'd planned on cooking and freezing dinners for her weekend away but he was such a wonderful father he could do a bit of real parenting and cook himself, she decided there and then. And to really prove himself, he could do the supermarket shopping that weekend as well.

About twenty minutes later, as she was kneeling at the sock drawer getting clean socks and tights for everyone, the doorbell rang. Who's that at this hour of the night? she wondered absently as she took out two pairs of navy woollen tights for the girls and a pair of grey socks for Michael. If someone was selling charity scratch cards at this late hour they should be shot. If there was an old person living alone they might get a fright being disturbed at this time of night.

She heard Terry answer the door. Heard a man's deep voice. Her heart lurched as she recognized it. Billy Noonan.

She slipped quietly out of the girls' room and closed the door. Michael's light was already off. He was exhausted. Good! She didn't want her children to know anything of the row with Orla. That was between adults. As far as she was concerned her children could play with the Noonans for ever and a day.

Terry was just about to call her as she appeared at the top of the stairs.

'Billy wants a word with you. Come in, Billy. Stop standing there, man. Would you like a drink?'

'No thanks, Terry. This isn't a social visit,' Billy said frostily. He stared coldly at Maggie from behind heavy black glasses.

'Oh! Sounds serious. What's up?' Terry said jocularly.

'Billy come in out of the hall, please,' Maggie said coolly and marched into the sitting-room. Her neighbour had no option but to follow. Terry brought up the rear.

'Close the door please, Terry,' Maggie said politely.

'Oh! Right.' Terry was mystified. 'Do you want me to go?'

'Not at all.' Maggie felt icy calm. How *dare* Billy Noonan come calling at this hour, obviously intending to have a go at her. He'd picked the wrong woman to tangle with. She'd seen off a drug-crazed mugger in New York, in her youth. Billy Noonan stood no chance, she thought dismissively, as a spark of the old Maggie returned.

'What's your problem, Billy?'

'You called my wife a liar today,' Billy said truculently, his hands on his hips.

'Oh now, Billy, I'm sure there's some explanation,' Terry interjected hastily. 'It must be a misunderstanding, Maggie would never call Orla a liar.'

'Yes I would. And yes I did,' Maggie said coldly, ignoring her husband as she eyeballed Billy.

'So you did? You don't deny it,' Billy growled.

'What the bloody hell did you do that for?' Terry exclaimed in dismay.

'Because it's true.' Maggie rounded on him, furious at his lack of support.

'That wasn't a very nice thing to do,' Terry accused. Maggie gave him a withering look.

She turned back to her neighbour, who stood red-faced and hostile, staring at her.

'You'd better apologize for that, Maggie. I won't stand here and let you call Orla a liar.'

'Why? What are you going to do, Billy?' she demanded aggressively. 'Now you listen to me, and listen well. I called Orla Noonan a liar because she is one. And you know that as well as I do. I did her a favour today as I've done many times over the years. I picked your kids up from school and she told me she'd be here to collect them in twenty minutes. Over an hour and a half later, Billy . . . do you hear me? *An hour and a half later*, she arrived with some cock-and-bull story about getting stuck behind a broken-down car in the ILAC. It was one of her better lies, I'll grant you that. But she'd already told it to Judy next door, a couple of months back. And if you care to, we can ring the ILAC first thing in the morning and check the veracity of Orla's story. I'm sure they keep logs of any such occurrences.' Her eyes sparked with anger as she glared at Billy.

'Orla's very upset and I won't have you upsetting my wife,' Billy mumbled, taken aback at Maggie's fury.

'Well fuck Orla! And fuck you! What about *me*? What about *my* feelings?' she demanded. 'What am I? Good old Maggie-Doormat Ryan, here for everyone to walk all over? Is that what you and Orla think, Billy? Let me tell you one thing. I've given your children more dinners and done more homework with them than *you* ever have. You're so busy out working all day. So how dare you come into my house with a fucking *attitude!*'

Billy swallowed hard, his eyes blinking rapidly behind his glasses, his Adam's apple bobbing up and down. 'There's no need for such crude language,' he ventured weakly.

'Is that right?' snapped Maggie sarcastically. 'Says who? Let me tell you, Billy Noonan. There is need. *My* need. So fuck you and your sensitive ears. I've heard you curse a lot worse when your team is losing a match on TV. Don't give me that crap. And furthermore how dare you have the effrontery to knock on my door at this hour of the night and come into my house and have a go at me? You tell Orla Noonan to fight her own battles from now on, if she has the guts to. Now get out of my house. I'm a busy woman. I don't have time for this nonsense.'

Maggie marched over to the door and held it open.

She had an immense urge to kick Billy in his plump well-padded ass, as he slunk out the door followed by Terry.

She stood, pumped full of adrenaline, as Terry opened the front door for the other man. PMT was a great thing to have when you were letting fly and giving someone a piece of your mind, she thought with satisfaction as she heard Terry mutter something about it all blowing over.

In your dreams, you faithless bastard, she thought viciously. It was his turn next.

Twenty-six

'God almighty, Maggie, that was no way to speak to a neighbour! Your language is atrocious,' Terry fumed as he came back into the room.

'Well thank *you*! You gutless bastard. Thanks a million for standing up for me and taking my side. It does my heart good to know what a wonderful supportive husband I have.' Maggie turned on him savagely. 'How dare you tell me in front of Billy Noonan that I shouldn't have called that sly cow a liar? How dare you, Terry! You had no business undermining me in front of him—'

'For God's sake, Maggie, what the bloody hell has got into you these days? You're like a bloody demon,' Terry accused heatedly. Maggie marched up to him and eyeballed him.

'I'm sick of you. That's what's wrong with me. I don't want to be married to you. I wish I could leave you. But I can't because of the kids. You leave all the rearing of the children to me. You don't pull your weight in the house. You do fuck-all housework. You don't give me a chance to work at *my* career. You don't even take it seriously. You invited the Al Shariffs to stay for a week without even asking me. You—'

'Oh shut the fuck up, Maggie,' Terry snarled. 'I've had enough of this shit. If you're so fed up of it all why don't *you* walk? Why don't you go and get a place of your own on your fabulous royalties and see what it's like then, having to pay a mortgage. I'll get someone in to look after the kids. Do you think it's a joyride for me, living with you? Well believe me, it's as much an ordeal for me as it is for you.' He jabbed a finger in her face. 'Look what you've turned into. Your mother. A whinging, whining, moaning nag! You don't even turn me on any more. Having sex with you is like trying to ride a sack of potatoes. That's about as exciting as it gets nowadays.'

'Ha! Do you hear who's talking,' Maggie raged, incensed. 'Having sex with you is like having a withered old walrus on top of me. You're not man enough to satisfy me any more. You haven't in years. Go and treat yourself to some Viagra before you talk to me about sex.'

Terry flushed a dull deep red. Maggie knew she'd hit him where it hurt. But she didn't care. It had been deliberate. And a low shot. He'd always prided himself on his sexual prowess and his abilities as a lover. She wanted to hurt him as much as he had hurt her. And that was *exactly* the way to do it.

'And you know something else . . . dear . . .' she added sarcastically. 'I'm not going anywhere. Those children upstairs are going to live an untroubled life in this house until they've left school and have got jobs for themselves. But in the meantime, don't you ever come near me again. You can go and sleep with the potatoes out in the shed for all I care.'

She stalked out of the room, head high.

Terry glared after her. Right now he felt as though

he hated her. What a bitch! There was nothing wrong with him or his performance. Give him the right woman and he'd show her. Someone like . . . he cast around wildly for someone who'd turn him on. Alma . . . yes . . . Alma Al Shariff was a *real* woman. Not like Maggie.

What did she expect him to do? Stay at home and be a Mrs Mops? Someone had to earn a crust to pay the bills. Why could she never understand that? Why did she expect him to turn around and do housework and the like when he came home from work? He'd spent all day slogging his guts out to provide her and the children with a standard of living that was the envy of many of her friends and neighbours.

Housework and kids were primarily a woman's responsibility but Maggie had never understood that, Terry thought furiously. Well, she'd better understand it. It was her problem. Because from now on he was going to spend a lot less time at home. Who'd want to spend time with a menopausal old shrew? He was going to put himself out and about once more. A nice little mistress would do him all the good in the world. She'd appreciate him. De-stress him. Give him a few hours of R&R. He'd make it very clear from the start that she couldn't expect marriage. He'd tell her that he couldn't break up the home. There was no way he was going through the Ria Kirby experience again. Terry scowled as he thought of his ex-lover. She'd practically demanded that he marry her. Once her bloom had worn off she'd been as much a shrew as Maggie was.

One marriage in a lifetime was enough. In fact once was too bloody much, Terry thought glumly as he poured himself a stiff whiskey. Keep his exits free and clear but take what was offered. That was his motto. Maggie'd had her chance. Now she'd blown it. That was her tough luck.

Maggie felt exhilarated as she stood under the shower a little while later. The pretence was over. She didn't have to put on a front any more. She'd told Terry what she thought of him and he'd returned the compliment. It was over.

The relief of it was indescribable. She could move forward now with some degree of certainty. She no longer had to be a 'wife' to Terry. She didn't have to make the effort any more. She didn't have to have sex with him ever again out of a sense of duty or routine. She knew to expect nothing of him from now on. That was a liberation in its own way.

She wrapped a towel around herself and wiped the steam from the mirror. She looked tired. The lines around her eyes and mouth seemed much more pronounced. And she was carrying a half-stone too much weight. She did look about as sexy as a sack of potatoes, she conceded wryly, and she felt about as sexy as them as well.

She'd start cutting down, she promised herself. It was just that when she was under stress, she ate. Comfort eating. She could write a book about it and it would be a damn sight easier than writing her novel. She really should spend a bit more time at City Girl, she thought regretfully, as she felt the thickening of her waist and dried the soft swelling of her untoned tummy. She'd been so fit and healthy once upon a time. She'd like to get back to that. The gym regime was certainly starting to work on Terry. And he was watching what he ate. How long would this fad last. He'd never stick it over Christmas.

Maggie got into bed and switched out the light. She lay in the dark, her mind racing. The sooner she finished her book the sooner she'd get a portion of her advance on delivery. She could use that to get the attic converted. That's what she'd do, she decided. She'd get the attic converted into a lovely little studio for herself. She'd have her space to write in. And she'd put a bed up there. As far as the children were concerned she and Terry would still share a bedroom but once the three of them were in bed, she'd go up to her little haven and they'd be none the wiser. She'd even get a portable TV up there. Terry could have their big double bed all to himself, she thought nastily. The sooner the better.

She was going to finish that damn book come hell or high water. Forget about putting it on the back burner. Once it was done, she could collapse in a heap and take a break. And for the next one she'd have her attic room and space from Terry. It was definitely time to take some control back in her life. Maggie was asleep in minutes. She had the best sleep she'd had in months.

The following week she drove out to Enterprise Publishing for her first meeting with her new editor. She had another fifty pages written. She was delighted with herself. She'd got up at six every morning and had an hour and a half of uninterrupted writing. It was exhausting, but she kept pushing herself. The more she got done before the Al Shariffs came, the better. The sooner she got her advance payment, the sooner she could get the builders in.

It was strange not to be meeting Marcy. Maggie felt a pang as she entered the small car park. Marcy had been such a support. Somehow she couldn't imagine herself having the same rapport with the youthful Miranda.

She noticed Jeremy's Merc and Claudette's sporty coupé parked near the entrance. The odd couple were in residence, she thought with a grin, as she hurried across the tarmacadam in the teeth of a howling gale and lashing rain.

Joan the receptionist had the door open for her.

'Don't want one of our precious authors getting wet,' she laughed.

'Thanks, Joan. I've a meeting with Miranda Quigley.' Maggie ran her fingers through her wind-swept hair. 'There's been a few changes, I hear.'

'You can say that again,' the middle-aged woman said dryly. 'And not for the better either. I've never known such penny-pinching. Madame has taken over the reins with gusto. Here she comes,' Joan mur-mured.

'Aah, Maggie. How lovely to see you,' Claudette gushed as she sashayed down the stairs, followed by Jeremy. She was wearing a cream pure wool suit with black accessories and a black pashmina scarf thrown casually over her shoulders. She looked stunning, the epitome of French chic. 'How is the book coming along?'

'Fine,' Maggie said politely, surprised at the other woman's apparent warmth. On the few occasions that Maggie had encountered Claudette previously, Claudette had greeted her in a bored and offhand way. This seemed completely out of character.

'We must take you to lunch someday, mustn't we Jeremy?' she said in her attractive accented English.

'Ah . . . yes . . . yes of course, darling,' Jeremy

agreed. 'We'll be giving *Exposé* a big push. Dumpbins. Posters. The lot,' he added loftily.

'Lucky old *Exposé*,' Maggie said lightly.

'What . . . what?' blustered Jeremy, unused to authors being so dismissive about projected sales plans.

'My novel is called *Betrayal*, Jeremy,' Maggie said evenly.

'Oh yes. Yes. Yes. Of course, Maggie.' Jeremy peered over the tops of his bifocals. 'We have so many books coming out. It's hard to keep track. Just keep on writing. Have you met Miranda yet? A wonderful girl. Perfect editor for you. Young and with it. Keep you fresh for our younger market. Very important. Very important.'

'Personally I'd have preferred an editor with some experience,' Maggie said tartly.

'What . . . what! What do you mean by that?' Jeremy bristled.

'Miranda tells me that this is her first stint in editorial. I would have preferred a more experienced editor,' Maggie retorted.

'Miranda Quigley has the best credentials. We wouldn't have taken her on otherwise,' Claudette interjected coolly before moving towards the door.

'We'll see,' Maggie replied noncommittally.

Jeremy's eyes narrowed. 'Now, now, Maggie. We've never let you down. We've done very well by you. Everything will be fine. Now we must have a nice long gossipy lunch some day soon. Have you ever dined in Guilbaud's? Or perhaps *Les Frères Jacques*? I'll treat you to something really special,' he announced expansively.

'I've been to both of them. Yes.' Maggie was

damned if she was going to let Jeremy Wilson patronize her. *Something really special* indeed! As though she were some impressionable greenhorn.

'Good, good. We must arrange it.' Jeremy wasn't really listening as he progressed across the foyer in Claudette's perfumed wake. He never listened to people. Especially people he considered his inferiors. And they were many.

He threw his conversation at them like pearls before swine, Maggie reflected in amusement. She'd had the 'Jeremy treatment' before.

'Miranda is ready to see you now,' Joan murmured diplomatically.

'Aren't I the lucky one?' Maggie arched an eyebrow.

Joan's laugh echoed behind her as Maggie pushed through the swing doors to the editorial department. Three doors down to the left she stopped and took a deep breath. Miranda's name-plate, gleaming, had replaced Marcy's. Upon seeing it, Maggie felt highly indignant on her former editor's behalf. Marcy really had been treated badly by the company. Still, that wasn't the youthful Miranda's fault, Maggie chided herself. Maybe Miranda would surprise her and turn out to be a superb editor.

She knocked politely on the door.

'Come in,' chirruped Miranda gaily.

Maggie walked in and in spite of herself her jaw sagged slightly at the sight of her new editor.

Kooky! was the first word that sprang to mind. Miranda looked about sixteen years old. She wore a pink mini. Pink and green striped socks over tights. A green belly top and a long chunky black cardigan. She had a small blue stud in her nose. A mass of black curly hair framed a small heart-shaped face. Wide grey eyes blinked earnestly from behind round silver-framed glasses. She wore blue glitter nail varnish.

'Hiya, Maggie. It's great to meet you. Sit down.' Miranda waved airily at the chair in front of her desk.

'Thanks,' Maggie managed weakly.

'Straight away. *Lo-ve* what I've read so far. Are they new pages I see?' She pointed to the folder Maggie had laid on the desk.

'It's fifty new pages,' Maggie said, pleased at least that her new editor had liked the book so far.

'*Wond-er-ful*!' Miranda enthused. 'Would you like a coffee?'

'That would be nice,' Maggie agreed.

Miranda picked up the phone and pressed a button. 'Joan, could you be an *ab-so-lute* darling and bring us in two coffees, black for me, no sugar. Maggie?' She beamed across the desk at her.

'Just milk, please,' Maggie murmured, trying to imagine what Marcy would say if she could see her replacement. The office had been cleared of all her former editor's personal effects. Miranda had made the place very much her own. Little green china frogs dotted shelves and window-ledges. A huge, spotty, lurid green one held Miranda's pens on the desk. A variety of trailing ivys overflowed from various brightly coloured pots surrounded by more little frogs.

'I *lo-ve* frogs,' Miranda said cheerfully.

'They're very . . . colourful.' Maggie gave an inward sigh.

'Now then, Maggie.' Miranda sat up straight, all business. 'Have you any idea when you can deliver?

I'm getting pressure from above to have manuscripts in on time.'

'Well obviously, I want to finish this as soon as possible. But I do have family commitments. I have three children and it's difficult to write sometimes.' Maggie was defensive. She hadn't expected this. She'd been hoping for some constructive comments on the manuscript. She was well over halfway through it.

'I'm sure it is difficult. *Ex-treme-ly* so.' Miranda was full of sympathy. 'But big boss is putting the pressure on. You know what publishers are like.'

Big boss can get lost! Maggie thought crossly.

'Have you any suggestions about the manuscript itself?' She tried to keep her tone light but she was getting more irritated by the minute.

Joan arrived with coffee.

'Ah . . . you *dar-ling!*' Miranda oozed insincere charm.

'Sorry there's no biscuits,' Joan apologized to Maggie as she laid the tray on Miranda's desk. 'Cutbacks,' she added caustically, throwing her eyes up to heaven as she left the room.

'Now where were we?' Miranda ignored the receptionist's sarcasm.

'The manuscript,' prompted Maggie as she took a sip of her coffee. It was bitter-tasting. Even the coffee had deteriorated, she thought sourly.

'Oh, yes. Just keep writing, Maggie. It's fine.' Miranda gazed at her, wide-eyed.

'No suggestions?'

'Er . . . well maybe you might consider adding a few more sex scenes and er . . . hotting them up a bit. Sex always sells. Don't forget I was in sales and marketing.' She gave a tinkly little laugh.

'You're joking!' Maggie was affronted.

'Oh . . . er . . . no, actually.' Miranda was taken aback at Maggie's tone.

'Miranda. Let's get one thing straight, here and now. I don't write sex for the sake of "hotting up" a novel. I write it when it's part of a character's story-line and I write it in a manner that is germane to the character and the plot.' Maggie didn't try to hide her annoyance.

'Oh . . . of course . . . yes indeed.' Miranda retreated.

'I was wondering if you think I should develop Clara's relationship with Matthew. Or should I have it end badly and have her on her own again?' Maggie persevered.

'Oh *ex-cell-ent* suggestion.' Miranda grasped the straw gratefully. '*Won-der-ful*! That's the way to go. And perhaps Clara could have a few one-night stands,' she added hopefully.

Maggie had had enough. It was perfectly clear to her that she was getting nowhere fast.

'Fine, Miranda. I'll get on it. Thank you for your time.'

'Not at all, Maggie. That's what I'm here for. Any problems, just buzz me,' Miranda said earnestly, her little pixie face eager and serious.

'I will,' Maggie fibbed.

It wasn't the poor *child's* fault. She thought she could do the job. It obviously suited Jeremy and Claudette's pocket to employ someone like Miranda. They were probably paying her a pittance, Maggie fumed.

If she hadn't seen the chairman and his wife going out, earlier, she would have marched straight

258

upstairs and had it out with the pair of them.

Marcy was right. Get her contract finished fast and get out. It was obvious the way things were going at Enterprise. Downhill all the way.

'Thanks for the coffee, Joan,' she said on her way out.

'I bet you need more than a coffee after that editorial session,' Joan drawled.

Maggie laughed. What else could she do?

'I'll see you, Joan.'

'You might. And then again you might not. I'm job-hunting,' Joan whispered.

'The best of luck, then. Let me know if you're successful,' Maggie said encouragingly as she opened the door and made a dash through the rain for the car.

'You're on your own, Ryan,' she muttered as she reversed out of the parking space and headed for home. She had the afternoon to herself. The children were invited to a birthday party at MacDonald's in Phibsboro and were being picked up from school. Maggie was going to make the most of it. She didn't have to cook a dinner. She was going to order a Chinese for herself. Terry could join her if he wanted to. Tough luck if he was on a diet. Otherwise he could cook for himself. She was going to spend the afternoon writing. And she'd have to trust her own instincts for this book.

The answering machine's little red light winked rhythmically at her from the hall table. Maybe it was Devlin or Caroline or someone to lift her spirits, she thought optimistically as she hung up her wet coat. She'd turned her mobile off before she'd gone into Miranda's office and had forgotten to switch it back on again. She hoped it wasn't Terry. He always went ballistic when she didn't have her phone switched on.

She pressed the play button.

'Hello, Maggie. It's your mother.' Nelsie's disembodied voice filled the hall. 'I've been trying to get you all morning but you're out gallivantin'.' Maggie felt her blood pressure rise.

'Gallivanting my hat,' she snorted. Her mother continued. Nelsie never left a simple message, there was always a saga that would take up at least half the tape and sometimes more.

Maggie waited for the saga.

'Your father and I are coming to Dublin for the day. We're going to visit Kitty Bradshaw out in Beaumont. The poor craythur is having a CAT scan and all kinds of tests to see what's giving her the terrible headaches she's been having. I hope to God it's not a tumour or anything like that . . .'

Maggie threw her eyes up to heaven. Nelsie always went for the worst possible scenario. 'When they send you to Beaumont it's serious enough, I was told,' Nelsie continued cheerfully. 'Anyway I was wondering if you could put us up for the night because your father wants to go into that medical place on Talbot Street to get one of those backrests for his car and we could do that in the morning before going home. Oh and Maggie, we'll just have had a light lunch, you know the way your father doesn't like driving on a full stomach. It makes him drowsy. So would you mind putting our name in the pot when you're making the dinner. See you later, love. I'm hanging up now.'

Maggie stared at the answering machine and shook her head in disbelief. Was she the butt of some great cosmic joke? she wondered. Were the gods all up there laughing at her, wondering what little spanners they could throw in the works that constituted her miserable existence?

'I hope you're all having a bloody good guffaw, because I'm not amused,' she gritted as she went out to the freezer and took out a freezer bag of lamb pieces. A hotpot would be the handiest thing to prepare and she could have apple crumble for dessert, it was her mother's favourite.

Clara and her doomed relationship would have to wait until tomorrow, Maggie thought regretfully as she emptied a dozen potatoes into the sink and started to peel them. If her father was coming to dinner, there could be no skimping on the spuds.

It was bloody annoying. She'd have to be relatively civil to Terry in front of her parents. They'd been extremely cool with each other since the row. It was easier than having to put on a façade, that was for sure, she reflected, as her knife swiftly deskinned the potatoes.

Her eyes took on a faraway look. If Clara's relationship was going to end badly maybe she might just chuck up her job and have a whole new career change. And just when she wasn't expecting it, Mr Right could come into her life. The least she could do was to give the poor girl a happy ending. And she most emphatically would not be having a few one-night stands, she thought derisively, remembering Miranda's tacky suggestion.

As the potatoes were peeled and the carrots and turnips sliced, Maggie plotted her next chapter.

Twenty-seven

Devlin gingerly slid her toothbrush into her mouth and gave a quick brush up and down. Sometimes washing her teeth in the morning made her gag.

She tried not to think about it as she brushed briskly. But it was too late. She retched miserably. Maybe after the third month it would end, Devlin thought hopefully, ever the optimist. Everything was going to end after the third month. And that was coming up soon. The tiredness, the nausea, the craving for coffee. And then she'd sail through her pregnancy, she assured herself. Today the thought of going into the office made her feel tired. And that was most unlike her.

It was probably psychological, she reflected, as she carefully applied her make-up. She was dreading the result of the surveillance on Ciara Hanlon.

Devlin had more or less resigned herself to the fact that Ciara was ripping her off in a blatant and shameless manner. Andrew's surveillance operative had already ascertained that Ciara was working in City Girl on a Sunday.

The busy manageress had seen five separate clients between ten a.m. and four p.m. Andrew reckoned that because it was Sunday she was charging a minimum of thirty pounds per treatment. That was a cool one hundred and fifty pounds for her pocket. She could be charging forty to fifty pounds for the Repécharge facial, or the full-body aromatherapy massage. It was hard work. Devlin didn't deny that. Nevertheless, Ciara was using City Girl's facilities and products. Apart from the financial implications, the loss of trust was what Devlin found most difficult to cope with.

Having to speak to Ciara on the phone every day as she gave a progress report on the new building was extremely depressing and uncomfortable. Devlin longed to confront the younger woman straight out, but Andrew had cautioned her against it until they had the file ready to present to Ciara.

Caroline had been as shocked as Devlin, when she'd told her the sorry saga.

'That's a bummer, Devlin. It's hard to believe. I always thought Ciara was dead straight. And I liked her.' Caroline shook her head in disbelief. 'Unless you take Linda Woods from Belfast and promote Celine Massey to manageress you're going to have to advertise. You'll need someone fairly experienced to run the residential complex as well.'

'I don't want to take Linda from Belfast. She's doing an excellent job up there and besides, her mother's recovering from a cancer op. I don't think she'd be anxious to move yet.' Devlin sighed.

'What a horrible thing to do. How did she possibly think she could get away with it?' Caroline wondered aloud. 'She's on a very good salary. Her job is top-notch. Maybe she has some financial problems that we don't know about.'

'You could be right,' Devlin said with a glimmer of

hope. There had to be some reason behind the manageress's unacceptable behaviour. Maybe Ciara had a good reason for her extracurricular activities.

She'd mooted the notion to Andrew. The accountant wasn't inclined to such charitable sentiment.

'We'll see. She'll have the chance to explain herself,' was all he'd say. In the meantime, Devlin had had to deal with Ciara as though everything were normal and the worst thing was that in a couple of days' time she was going to have to take a trip to Galway to check out the progress on the new residential complex. That was going to be an absolute nightmare. Andrew was adamant that they had a watertight case against Ciara before they called her to account. He was right, Devlin admitted. They couldn't go flinging accusations around until they were absolutely sure.

It was distressing, nevertheless.

Devlin sighed as she squirted some White Linen on her neck and wrists. The joys of owning your own business! She was lucky to have got this far without too many misfortunes. She traced some lipstick across her lips, blotted it and glanced at her reflection in the mirror. She looked healthy and glowing, not at all like some unfortunate who had just deposited her breakfast down the loo and was suffering from severe nausea.

Luke was in the bedroom, flicking through papers in his briefcase, when she emerged from the *en suite*.

'Are you OK? Pity you haven't got dentures.' He grinned.

'Smart-ass. If you're not careful I'll puke all over you,' Devlin retorted. 'Go over to the other side of the bed and help me make it.'

'Yes boss!' Luke clicked his heels and saluted.

'Sorry. I didn't mean to be tetchy,' Devlin apologized.

'I'd probably be tetchy too if I was gagging every time I brushed my teeth. You're forgiven.' He eyed her quizzically. 'When are you going to tell me what's on your mind?'

'There's nothing on my mind,' Devlin said lightly as she plumped the pillows and tweaked the sheet. For some reason she'd put off telling Luke about Ciara. She knew it was ridiculous but somehow she felt that she'd made a major error of judgement in promoting and believing in Ciara. He might question her business sense. Basically, her pride was holding her back. She didn't want to look foolish in her husband's eyes. His good opinion, particularly of her business acumen, was important to her.

'Devlin, if you've nothing on your mind then I'm the Aga Khan. I wish you'd tell me what it is. I'm your husband, don't forget. Husbands *are* allowed to share.'

'I know that, Luke.' Devlin smiled. He knew her so well. She should have realized that she couldn't keep her worry to herself without him noticing.

'Well then?'

He came around to her side of the bed and sat down, drawing her down beside him.

Devlin took a deep breath.

'Ciara Hanlon's on the make. She's opening City Girl on Sundays to give treatments and Andrew thinks that she's using our stock on home visits. We've got someone down there compiling a report. We're going to confront her with it. That's it in a nutshell.' She looked at him and shrugged.

'How did you find out?' Luke frowned.

'Andrew noticed that the quarterly figures for Galway were higher than normal and the orders for oils, creams, waxes and so on were doubled. And then this woman phoned in saying that she couldn't get an appointment . . .' Devlin outlined the saga underlying Charlotte Adams's complaint.

'Get rid of her. Pronto.' Luke had a look on his face that Devlin rarely saw. Hard. Cold. Unyielding. Luke could be very tough in his business dealings. He had to be. The building trade was not for the faint-hearted. But this was different. Devlin still clung to the hope that Ciara had some reasonable explanation.

'Maybe she has some financial problems that we don't know about that necessitate her having to do extra work,' Devlin said earnestly.

'Devlin, Ciara Hanlon has her eye on the main chance. And she's taking the main chance at your expense—'

'Luke, we don't know that. The girl's entitled to the benefit of the doubt,' Devlin interrupted.

'Don't be a fool, Devlin. Whether she has problems or not, she's on the make. That's unacceptable. She's got to go,' Luke declared.

'I'm not making any decisions until I find out what's behind it,' Devlin retorted stubbornly.

'Devlin, I've been in business a lot longer than you—'

'Oh don't start that routine,' Devlin bristled, irritated at his response. Luke could be so damn inflexible sometimes. She was sorry she'd told him about Ciara Hanlon. She should have known what his response would be. Luke was uncompromising in his business ethics.

'Don't get all defensive, Devlin,' Luke said irritably.

'I'm not getting defensive, Luke. Just don't start being superior.'

'I'm not being superior. You always take that attitude when we're having a discussion like this,' Luke accused.

'Discussion! That's rich! You mean when you're *telling* me what to do,' Devlin said hotly.

'I'm not telling you what to do. I'm merely pointing out that whether you like it or not, you have to face facts. And the facts are that you have a dishonest employee. You can't let her off the hook. She has to accept responsibility for her actions. You're not doing her any favours protecting her from that. If people never have to accept that they've done wrong they just keep on committing the crime, hurting other people and ultimately themselves,' Luke said sternly.

'Oh for God's sake, don't lecture me about it. You're as bad as Caroline. That's just the sort of thing she'd say.' Devlin jumped up and stalked out of the room.

'Caroline has a bit of cop-on at least,' Luke thundered as he slammed his briefcase shut and grabbed his jacket.

'Look, I'll deal with this the way I see fit. Without any interference from you, Luke Reilly!' Devlin yelled.

'That's what I'm afraid of,' Luke retaliated nastily as he strode down the hall.

'How dare you, Luke. That's a cheap shot! I'm sorry I opened my mouth. I should have known. You're always the same. Patronizing and laying down the law.' Devlin was spitting feathers at this slur on her management abilities.

'For heaven's sake don't be so childish, Devlin. Business isn't for wimps. Sometimes you have to make tough decisions. If you can't see that, you're in trouble. I'll see you tonight.'

'Yeah, well at least I have a heart,' Devlin shouted at his retreating back. But the door was closed behind him and he was gone, leaving Devlin red-faced with fury.

'Arrogant bastard!' she swore as she snatched up her car keys from the table. Lecturing her like she was a . . . a . . . mere *novice*. She couldn't have run a thriving business for years if she'd been a softie. She'd made tough decisions in her time. She'd sack Ciara Hanlon if the circumstances warranted it.

The sooner this was sorted the better. She was heartily sick of it. It was making her uncomfortable at work, and now it had caused a row in her marriage. She and Luke rarely rowed but when they did it could be sharp and nasty. He liked getting his own way, that was the problem, she thought resentfully as she slipped into her trench coat and picked up her brief-case.

Luke had really gone beyond the boundary with his insulting remarks. He could damn well apologize. Just because once upon a time he'd known more about business than she had. Well, not any more. And he'd bloody well better recognize that, she raged as she locked the door behind her and waited for the lift.

And what was more, ranting and raving and barging out in a huff was no way to be treating her when she was pregnant. He might have some consideration, she thought with a sudden surge of self-pity. He could be such a mule sometimes. Well, this time he could piss off. She wasn't kissing and making up first.

Luke gunned the engine and drove out of the apartment complex at speed. Devlin could be damn well infuriating at times. And today was one of them. The trouble with her was she was so bull-headed she couldn't take constructive advice or criticism. Sometimes she couldn't see beyond her nose. Ciara Hanlon was taking her for a ride and if there were mitigating circumstances he'd eat his bloody hat. He'd been too long in the business not to know a rip-off merchant when he saw one. Give someone like Ciara Hanlon a chance and she'd do the exact same thing to some other poor sucker until someone got sense and put a halt to her gallop.

The trouble with Devlin was that she let her heart rule her head too much, and that was fatal in business.

He was tempted to give Andrew Dawson a call but if Devlin found out she'd hit the roof. City Girl was very much her baby. Luke was a sleeping partner, only involved when major decisions concerning expansion and the like were under discussion. Besides, a call from him would undermine her in the accountant's eyes. Devlin had told him of the comment Andrew had made when they'd been discussing the Mind, Body, Spirit aspect of the treatments. Devlin had been fit to be tied that evening. And rightly so. Andrew had no business putting Devlin down. Her instincts for City Girl were always spot on.

He couldn't possibly make the call, he thought regretfully. Because if he did he'd tell Andrew Dawson to call in the police and charge that two-faced Hanlon bitch with everything they could throw at her.

Twenty-eight

Caroline was just coming out the front door of her apartment complex as Devlin walked over to her car. It was nice they lived so close to each other. She paused and waited for her friend. Sometimes, if neither had meetings or appointments, they drove in to City Girl in the one car. Devlin needed her car today. She was going to be the guest speaker at a businesswomen's lunch in the Burlington. She wasn't sure what Caroline's agenda was.

'Do you want a lift?' she invited as Caroline joined her. 'I need my car for that lunch do in the Burlington, but I'll be going back to the office and I can give you a lift home.'

'Oh . . . OK, Dev, suits me. I'm not going anywhere today.' Caroline accepted the offer and got into the car beside her. 'Luke went scorching out in a hurry. I saw him from the kitchen window,' she remarked innocently.

'Huh!' Devlin gave an eloquent snort. Caroline looked at her in surprise. This was an unusual response where Luke was concerned.

'We had a row,' Devlin said glumly. 'And when I tell you what it was about you'll probably take his side.'

'Don't tell me then,' Caroline said matter-of-factly

as she rooted in her handbag for a tissue.

'Oh!' Devlin was taken aback by her friend's answer. This was annoying. She wanted to tell Caroline. She just didn't want her to agree with what Luke had said.

'OK,' she sighed, putting the car into reverse and manoeuvring out of her space.

'I like this car, it's very sporty,' Caroline said chattily as she fastened her belt and settled in for the journey across town. Devlin drove past the manicured gardens and slid her pass into the security gates. They glided open to allow her to emerge into the heavy morning traffic on the Clontarf Road.

'I'll change it after I've had the baby. It would be a nightmare trying to get a baby seat into this. It's so low down,' Devlin remarked as she scooted into the far lane and waved at the man who had courteously signalled her in.

'How're you feeling today?' Caroline asked sympathetically.

'Lousy. All I'm afraid of is that I'll throw up at that bloody lunch. I said I'd do it months ago, before I was pregnant. I couldn't very well ring up and cancel. That would let the whole side down,' Devlin said wryly. 'After all, us businesswomen can handle everything. We can make it in a man's world and have children and run a home. Just think what it would look like if the guest speaker wimped out because she was tired, queasy, and right at this moment couldn't give a toss about making it in business.'

Caroline laughed. 'I bet most of them would understand *exactly* how you feel. Don't be so hard on yourself, Devlin. Why don't you go home straight after the lunch and have a rest for yourself?'

'Oh, I can't do that. I'm off to Galway later this week and I need to prepare for that. And I've got some new suppliers to talk to and I've an interview with the *Business Review* magazine at four.' Devlin rattled off her afternoon's agenda.

Caroline shook her head. 'Devlin, we all make our own treadmills. You need to get off yours now and again. You don't have to say yes to everything. You need to take a little time out for yourself to prepare for your great event.'

'Yes, Mammy,' Devlin said irritably.

'Sorry! I didn't mean to lecture.' Caroline grinned.

'I'm sorry too. I didn't mean to snap,' Devlin apologized. 'It's just that Luke thinks I should throw the book at Ciara. Make no allowances. Get rid of her. In my shoes I guess he'd prosecute her. He says that if I don't make her accept responsibility for what she's done she'll never see the wrong in it, and she'll just go on doing it. Why should it be up to me?' she blurted out, unable to contain it any longer.

Caroline sighed. 'You know, they say that even the abuser becomes abused if the abuse is allowed to continue. By taking the less difficult path of letting her go and doing nothing about it you're enabling her to do it again. So you become the enabler. It's like in relationships where the husband is continually unfaithful to his wife and she knows about it. By not drawing a boundary and saying enough, it stops now or I leave, she continues to enable him to abuse her,' Caroline explained.

'Where do you learn all these things?' Devlin demanded. She knew in her heart and soul that what her friend was saying was true. What Luke had been saying was true. She just didn't want to have to be the one to do the nasty on Ciara.

Caroline looked at Devlin with great affection. 'Devlin, after what I went through I needed to find out why. I asked for spiritual help. I got it. I was given teachers, books to read. Many books to read. I have shelves of spiritual and metaphysical literature. Come over and have a look at them some day. There might be one that you're drawn to. That's the one you've got to read. When the pupil is ready the teacher will come. Ciara's a teacher for you. And you're a teacher for her.'

'And are you saying to me for example that poor Lillian O'Carroll should up sticks and walk away from Alastair?' Devlin asked, puzzled. 'I know he treats her dreadfully and rubs her nose in it in the most callous way, but she'd lose everything.'

Lillian O'Carroll was a mutual acquaintance of theirs, a well-known socialite and charity fund-raiser. Her husband, a lawyer, was consistently unfaithful and made no effort to conceal his affairs. She frequently met his lady friends at parties.

'Devlin, Lillian is not a victim,' Caroline said firmly. 'That's where you're making the mistake. She knows about Alastair's carry-on, she turns a blind eye to it. Her silence and acceptance of the situation enables it to continue. Alastair has never been called to account. In return she gets the big house, the swanky car, the credit cards, her horse, the kudos of being Mrs Alastair O'Carroll. And yes, knowing Alastair, if she gave him an ultimatum she'd probably end up with feck-all. But there is a relationship that is going nowhere. There's no growth. There's no love. No respect. No harmony. If she said enough was enough and she left him it would be such a huge step,

274

to leave all that horrible energy behind her. Her life would change immeasurably. Doors would open for her. New people would come into her life. It would be the hardest thing in the world to do, but once she took that leap of faith it would be the best thing that ever happened to her. That's why I'm divorcing Richard. I'm closing the door on that sorry twisted mess, otherwise I'll stay stagnant and frustrated and unhappy,' Caroline finished ruefully.

'You're very brave, Caroline,' Devlin said.

'I'm not brave at all. I'm petrified,' Caroline confessed. 'It's easy to talk about all these things. It's easy to know what's the right thing to do. It's the doing of it that's so hard.'

'You and I are so different,' Devlin smiled. 'When I was going through my traumas I dealt with it all externally. I worked my butt off so I wouldn't have to think. You dealt with all your stuff internally, if you know what I mean. You went right in there and coped head-on with all the emotional stuff. I just ran away from it.'

'Everyone's different, Devlin. We all have our own paths to follow.'

'Yeah, well I'm good at running away from mine and I wish I could run away from the Ciara Hanlon débâcle.' Devlin sighed despondently as she turned off the roundabout at The Point and drove along the North Wall.

'Look, I'm in charge of personnel, if you want me to sit in on the interview with Ciara, I will. And at the end of the day you make the decision that you're most happy with and that you can live with,' Caroline said supportively. 'Things will work out. Don't worry.'

'I hope so.' Devlin was unconvinced. One way or the other it was all going to be a load of hassle.

Luke didn't phone as he usually did, at least once, and she was too stubborn to pick up the phone and ring him herself. He was in the wrong upsetting her, she thought self-righteously. Besides, she still wasn't sure about the correctness of his and Caroline's reasoning. Surely it would be much more compassionate to just sack Ciara without a reference and give her a chance to start afresh. The Lord always showed mercy and compassion to sinners.

She dialled Caroline's extension and put that argument to her. Triumphantly, it had to be said.

'You're right, Devlin,' Caroline agreed cheerfully. 'But He loved the sinner, not the sin. And don't forget, He showed righteous anger in the Temple when he horsewhipped the sellers. Mercy and compassion is one thing. Letting people get way with wrongdoing is another.'

'I can't *believe* I'm having this conversation!' Devlin declared in exasperation. 'I must be crazy. I don't even go to Mass.'

'What's that got to do with anything? You could go to Mass three times a day and still be a horrible, judgemental person,' Caroline pointed out reasonably. 'Look at Mrs Yates. She practically lives in the church but she hasn't an ounce of Christianity in her. It's what's in your heart that counts. And Delaney, you've got a big heart. Now I'm going. I've got to work out Christmas holidays and bonuses. Bye bye. Maybe I should give up City Girl and go into spiritual healing. What do you think?' Caroline teased.

'I think you'd be very good at it, actually,' Devlin said seriously. 'Will you put the Light around me or whatever it is that you do? I'm off to give my talk.'

'Will do. You'll be fine. I'll see you this evening.'

'Thanks, Caro. Bye.' Devlin put the phone down and sat staring out the window. She could listen to Caroline for hours, talking about the spiritual stuff. It was very interesting to hear of her friend's experiences, but somehow she just couldn't seem to adapt it to her own life. Still, she felt vaguely comforted that Caroline had put the Light around her, it sounded so protective and Caroline had great faith in it. If it was good enough for Caroline it was good enough for her, Devlin thought with a smile as she got her coat and briefcase and headed out to the lift.

The traffic was dire. She should have taken a taxi, she reflected, as she crawled past the Shelbourne. Caroline was right, she should start making life simpler for herself. She might start going home early from the office on Fridays, she decided. She could spend time reading the stack of books and magazines that she'd never managed to get to. The thought cheered her up immensely. How nice it would be to miss the rush-hour traffic on Friday evenings and instead be curled up on her big comfy sofa in front of the fire, reading and snoozing and tuning out completely.

What was the point in being successful if you didn't reap the rewards of it?

It was a question she asked her audience of smart, highly intelligent and successful women, after they'd enjoyed a tasty lunch. Her speech had turned into an entertaining and lively question-and-answer session and as the women shared their experiences with each other, Devlin forgot her worries over Ciara Hanlon

277

and thoroughly enjoyed herself. It was with regret that she had to leave the vibrant group to be back at the office for the interview with the magazine *Business Review*. The reporter was lazy and ill-prepared and Devlin had to struggle to contain her impatience as she answered questions she'd been asked dozens of times before. It was a rare interview where she was asked an original and intelligent question, she thought wryly as she went onto autopilot, only for the witless fool of a reporter to discover twenty minutes later that his tape recorder's batteries were flat. Devlin felt like ramming it down his neck.

'It was a great lunch,' she told Caroline as they drove home, 'but the interview was crap. The jerk kept calling me Delvin. I bet he'll have it spelt wrong the whole way through the interview. I corrected him a dozen times if I corrected him once but in the end I gave up. And when he found out that his batteries were flat I nearly went bananas.'

By the time she got home she was whacked. Luke wasn't back yet so she headed for the shower. She wasn't hungry. The lunch had been filling. He could look after himself for once, she thought tiredly as the hot jets of water flowed over her body. She dried herself and wrapped herself in her towelling robe, trying not to get lockjaw from her prodigious yawns.

She'd have a ten-minute rest, she decided, too weary even to draw the curtains. She could see the lights of Dublin twinkling in the distance. She'd just lie quietly in bed and look at them. Devlin crawled under the covers and stretched her weary limbs. It had been a very long and eventful day. She was asleep in seconds.

* * *

He should have phoned, Luke chastised himself as he sat in bumper-to-bumper traffic on the N11 coming up to Cornelscourt. He'd been so annoyed with her this morning he hadn't bothered. Then around lunch-time he'd decided to give Devlin a call but she wasn't at her desk and her mobile had been switched off and that had really made him mad. If she wanted to be *that* petty . . . forget it! Then he'd remembered that she was speaking at a lunch engagement and later she had an interview with a Sunday paper, and he'd felt bad about the way he'd thought about her.

He'd bought her two dozen pink roses as a peace-offering. He hoped they weren't withered in the boot.

He was nearly withered in this traffic, he thought irritably as he tapped his fingers impatiently against the steering-wheel. He had the usual East Link traffic snarl-up to deal with yet. It would be a good hour before he was home. Luke sighed. He was tired and hungry. Maybe he should give Devlin a call, find out where she was and tell her he was on his way. If she was too tired to cook they could eat out.

He called up her mobile number and frowned as it went into divert straight away. She must be still tied up.

He was surprised to see her bag and briefcase in the hall when he got home. He'd tried her mobile every so often and still got divert. He'd assumed then that he'd be home before her. The only light on was the small lamp in the hall. Darkness in the lounge and kitchen. No sounds or aromas of cooking. No light from the bedroom and the curtains weren't pulled. She hadn't been in there.

She must have gone out, he thought crossly as he

plonked the roses into the sink and filled it with water. That wasn't very nice. The least she could have done was to phone him and let him know that she wouldn't be in for dinner. He could have got himself a takeaway or stopped off at Wong's or the little Italian place they liked. Just because they were having a row didn't mean that all communications had to break down.

Strange for her to come home and leave her bag and briefcase in the hall though, he puzzled as he rooted through the fridge.

Caroline's! he thought triumphantly. That's where she was. She was probably eating there too. Leaving him to starve! His stomach rumbled. He was ravenous. Maybe there was some of that tasty lamb casserole that she often made and froze. He searched the freezer and found the container he was looking for. Perfect! Luke shoved it in the microwave and while it was heating he buttered a big chunk of Vienna roll, lashed on some blackcurrant jam and munched away hungrily. He set a tray, poured himself a beer and when the casserole was heated he served it out, carried the tray into the lounge, switched on the gas fire and the TV and plonked into the armchair. There was a match on. What more could a man want? Luke thought happily as he settled down to an evening of peace and quiet.

By eleven, he was knackered. Devlin and Caroline must have settled in for a session. He wasn't waiting up. He had to be up at the crack of dawn to go to London. He tidied away after him and put his dishes in the dishwasher.

He was just about to put on the main light in the bedroom when he heard a sound. A little cough.

Startled, he looked at the bed. In the light from the hallway he could see Devlin curled up under the covers. She'd been here all along and he hadn't realized it.

She must have gone straight to bed when she came in from work. She'd been telling him how tired the pregnancy made her feel. His heart softened. He'd been a bit rough on her this morning. He was tempted to wake her up and apologize. But that wouldn't be very fair, he thought regretfully, as he listened to her even deep breathing. She was obviously whacked. If he woke her up she might not go to sleep again.

He left the light off and went into the *en suite* and had a quick shower before sliding into bed beside her. He put his arms around her and she snuggled in against him, still asleep. Luke yawned. They'd make up in the morning and it would be all the nicer. He was asleep in minutes.

Twenty-nine

Devlin yawned and stretched. And blinked. Daylight showed through a chink in the curtains. How could it be bright? She'd only got into bed for a nap. And she hadn't pulled the curtains. Luke must have done that. She turned her head to look at the small travel clock beside the bed. Five to eight. She sat up, puzzled. It couldn't be five to eight in the morning, could it? She surely hadn't slept round the clock?

She scrambled out of bed and pulled back the curtains. It was daytime. Raining and blowing a howling gale. A miserable sort of day. People were leaving for work. She should be showered and dressed at this stage.

'Oh Lord,' she muttered as she ran her fingers through her hair. She hadn't heard Luke come in. Hadn't heard him come to bed. And she hadn't heard him get up this morning.

A thought struck her. Luke was going to London today. She wouldn't see him again until the end of the week. Devlin burst into tears.

He'd gone to London without saying goodbye. Without making up their row. He'd never done that before.

She sat on the bed and put her face in her hands

and cried. He must be as mad as hell with her. Well, he could go to hell himself. The next time he phoned she'd hang up. And he could stay in London for all she cared.

Devlin wiped her eyes. What on earth was wrong with her? Where had all this weeping come from? Her hormones were running rampant.

A wave of nausea swamped her and eventually receded. Devlin crept back in under the bed covers. She remembered Caroline's words about treadmills being of your own making. Maybe today she'd step off hers. She'd phone Liz and tell her that she wasn't coming in. She just felt too lethargic to make the effort. You had to listen to your body sometimes.

She lay quietly with her hands on her tummy, stroking her palms across it. She had to think about the baby too. Maybe a day of peace and calm would restore her equilibrium. She was going to Galway in two days' time, that would be difficult and tiring. At least Caroline was coming with her this trip. They were taking the morning train and flying home the same evening.

The rain battered off the window-pane and the skies darkened. A rumble of thunder in the distance signalled worsening weather. Devlin felt snug and cosy. She'd be mad to get dressed and go haring into City Girl when she could stay at home and read *Memoirs of a Geisha*, curled up in bed while the rest of the world galloped along on their treadmills. It was like staying at home sick from school. If her audience of successful businesswomen could see her now, they might not be too impressed. Devlin gave a wry smile. Anyway, who was to know? She rarely took a day off. She was entitled.

Her stomach gurgled. She was hungry. It had been a long time since she'd eaten. She'd feel better after she'd had some toast. She always did. And today, seeing as she wasn't going into work, she'd just lick some toothpaste around her teeth instead of brushing them. That way she'd get to keep her breakfast down.

She headed into the kitchen and came to a full stop in front of the sink. Two dozen tightly budded pale pink roses filled the basin. A note was propped up against the kettle.

A lump in her throat nearly choked her. Luke had bought her pink roses and she'd been thinking he was the worst in the world. How disloyal of her. She should have known better. Tears spurted from her eyes again.

'This is ridiculous,' she sobbed. She opened Luke's note.

Dear Sleepy Head,

I wanted to wake you up this morning to say goodbye but you were fast asleep and I just couldn't bring myself to. I hope you like the roses. I didn't mean to upset you. I love you. And don't worry about the other thing. You do what you think fit. I'll call later.

Love Luke.
XXXX

'Oh Luke, I love you too,' she hiccuped as she raced over to the phone and dialled his mobile number.

'You're in the land of the living,' he greeted her, and she could hear the smile in his voice.

'Oh Luke, why didn't you wake me up? I wanted to say goodbye to you.'

'Are you crying?' Luke said.

'Not, not really. I got the roses,' Devlin sniffled.

'Aha! So there *are* waterworks. I know you. You cry at the National Anthem.' Luke laughed.

'They're beautiful. Thanks.' She was feeling a hundred times better just hearing his voice.

'Sorry I didn't call yesterday. The phone was off all afternoon. I should have phoned earlier in the morning but you know yourself . . . I needed time to cool down.'

'*You* needed time to cool down. *I* was fit to burst,' Devlin snorted.

'I know . . . that's why I got out while the going was good,' Luke teased.

'Listen, buster. You had me up to ninety.'

'Ah, you should have gone up to a hundred while you were at it,' Luke retorted good-humouredly.

She burst out laughing. You couldn't win with Luke.

'Did your lunch and interview go well? What did they ask you?'

He was always so interested in what was going on in her life, even after all the years they'd been together. She told him all that had happened the previous day. 'And I'm taking today off,' she added. 'I'm just going to laze at home all day.'

'You're having me on.' She could hear the disbelief in Luke's voice.

'I'm not. It's a horrible day. It's raining and blowing a gale and there's thunder in the hills and I just

285

decided to step off the treadmill for once and take it easy.'

'You're dead right, Devlin. I never thought I'd see the day. My little workaholic is getting sense at last. That's great news. You have a lovely long lazy day and think of me over here working my fingers to the bone, with my nose to the grindstone and my shoulder to the wheel.'

'Yes, dear,' Devlin said smugly.

When she eventually hung up, she was beaming. She hated rowing with Luke. It always threw her off kilter. It wasn't that they didn't argue. They had mighty arguments on a variety of topics, but that was fun and she loved pitting her wits against him, especially when he conceded the point. But a row was a different kettle of fish. It wasn't in her nature to fight. She'd seen too many rows when she was a child, when her mother was drunk and out of control. Rows brought up old buried fears. They made her feel insecure. Even with Luke. And that was crazy because she felt safer with Luke than she did with any other human being. Luke gave her the freedom to be totally herself. That was the greatest gift of all.

She spent a thoroughly relaxing day, reading and dozing as her body caught up on some much needed rest. It was nice to be alone for a while. It was such a contrast to the buzz and bustle of the office.

Later in the afternoon, she slipped into a track suit and lit the fire and lay on the sofa, looking out through the big floor-to-ceiling French windows at the white-capped waves that frothed and bubbled along the deserted shore. She was glad the weather was so bad. It made her day off all the more enjoyable.

The following day when she went into work she felt the better for her little break. She was going to take the odd day off here and there for the next few months, she decided, as she ran up the stairs to Caroline's office.

'Ciara's just been on the phone,' Caroline said dryly.

'What does she want?'

'Just checking that I had got the copy of the report she had written about our new staffing requirements.' Caroline waved the neatly typed and bound report at Devlin.

'Pity she won't see it all come to fruition,' Devlin said coldly. 'I don't know how I'm going to be able to be nice to her. I wish she was gone.'

'Look, why don't I take her off your hands tomorrow for as much time as I can. We can spend a couple of hours discussing staff requirements. You talk to the builders and the suppliers. We're stuck for time anyway, so it suits our purposes to hold separate meetings.'

'I don't want you to be stuck with Ciara. I'd like you to see what's going on.' Devlin frowned.

'This report is very thorough, I'll give Ciara that. It will be very helpful to us. We might as well make the most of it. So this time wearing my "personnel co-ordinator" hat I'll get the staff side sorted, leaving you free to concentrate on everything else.' She grinned. 'So I'll be ahead of myself, so to speak. And when I go down the next time, because my job will be done I'll be free to sit in on your meetings. OK?'

'Have I any choice in the matter?' Devlin retorted.

'Not really, no,' Caroline said firmly.

'You're very bossy.'

'Comes with the job.'

'OK, Caroline. As long as you don't mind,' Devlin agreed.

'As I say, Dev, it suits our purposes to have it this way. I'll tell you though,' she said, changing the subject, 'I think it's a great idea to go to Powerscourt Springs. It will be very interesting to see residential in action.'

'Yeah, and I'm really looking forward to flopping. It's going to be so nice for the three of us to be on our own for a while. It's ages since we've spent time together. It's just what we need.' Devlin took Ciara's report from Caroline and longed to throw it in the bin. Nevertheless, Caroline was right. Ciara was good at her job and if her points were pertinent it would be foolish to ignore them.

The manageress was all smiles when she greeted them in the foyer the following morning.

'Devlin, Caroline, great to see you. Progress is excellent as you can hear.' She made a face at the sound of drilling and banging that throbbed dully through the double-glazed doors. 'We're well on target.'

'Morning, Ciara.' Devlin had to struggle to keep her voice civil. Seeing Ciara in the flesh, knowing what she knew about her, was more difficult than she'd expected.

Why? she wanted to ask. *I was good to you. I gave you an opportunity. Why are you ripping me off?*

'Ciara, we're actually going to split up. You and I are going to discuss your report. Devlin can hold her meetings without us. We'll get more done seeing as our time is limited,' Caroline interjected smoothly.

'Oh!' Ciara was taken aback. 'I think I should be at

Devlin's meetings. I am the manageress and I need to keep abreast of things. The interior designer is coming today to show samples of curtain and furnishing materials. He wants us to make our selection as soon as possible so that she can get the furniture organized and ordered. And then later I've made arrangements for the three of us to have lunch in Kirwan's Lane. I've booked a table.'

Devlin's eyebrows rose. Lunch in Kirwan's Lane would go on expenses, of course.

'Ciara, we're here to work, unfortunately. Caroline and I have a lot to get through today. I can deal with the interior designer. And I'm sure you can organize something tasty from the kitchen,' Devlin said coolly.

'Of course. But I would like to be involved with the interior design and I thought it would be nice for the three of us to have a *working* lunch somewhere special. It's one of the in places in Galway. It's good to be seen there. A lot of our clientele dine there,' Ciara pointed out a tad sulkily.

'Well, today time's of the essence. Another time,' Caroline said lightly. 'And of course you'll be involved with all aspects of the new development, that's why I want to spend time with you on the report. Now, I think we should give Devlin your office for her meetings and you and I can go over to that nice little corner and perhaps Mona would bring us some coffee.' Caroline smiled at the receptionist. 'And tea for Devlin,' she added blandly, remembering that Devlin had given up coffee for her pregnancy.

Ciara was furious at the way Caroline was taking over, Devlin could see it in her eyes.

'Good thinking, Caroline,' she approved briskly. 'Presumably John Joe is on site?' She turned to Ciara.

'Yes, Devlin, he knows you're coming. Will I bring you out?' she said sweetly, eager to please.

'Not at all, Ciara. I'll find him. You go off and work on the report with Caroline. I'll mosey around and see what's going on.' Devlin smiled brightly as if she hadn't a care in the world.

'Oh!' The younger woman was disappointed. Things weren't going to plan at all.

'See you later,' Devlin said cheerfully as Caroline and Ciara moved over to one of the sofas in a corner of the foyer.

You better have good reason, Hanlon! Devlin thought resentfully as she crossed the reception area. Ciara didn't look like someone with the weight of the world on her shoulders or some big burden that was causing her dishonesty. The sooner it was all out in the open, the better.

Thirty

Devlin cheered up considerably as the builder led her around the site, explaining everything in his rich Connemara accent as he went along. Even though it was all scaffolding and bricks and mortar at this stage she could visualize the finished product, and she knew without doubt that it was going to be a beautiful building.

The day flew. And it turned out much better than she'd expected. She hardly saw Ciara at all. The interior designer, a young Galway man named Finn Kennedy, was full of enthusiasm and ideas. He and Devlin spent an immensely satisfying two hours discussing every aspect of the interior design of the new building. They eventually decided on a selection of fabrics that were suitable for their requirements and within the budget allotted for furnishing.

Following her meeting with Finn she had a meeting with a tile supplier for the treatment rooms, then meetings with gym-equipment suppliers, sauna and Jacuzzi installers and kitchen-equipment suppliers. The new wing was to house a state-of-the-art kitchen to service the residential dining-room plus the existing dining-room. In between she grabbed a quick meal of poached salmon served with a mixed salad.

By the time the car came to collect them to bring them to the airport, Devlin was exhausted but exhilarated. Ciara hovered around, clearly annoyed at her exclusion from the key meetings.

'We'll talk soon, Ciara,' Devlin said noncommittally to her discomfited manageress, knowing that the next time she spoke to her would be to terminate her employment.

'OK, Devlin. I'm sorry I didn't get time to discuss matters. I hope you enjoyed the meeting with Finn,' she said tartly.

'I did. Immensely,' Devlin retorted.

'Thanks for all the hard work, Ciara. It was a very profitable meeting,' Caroline said smoothly.

'Not at all.' Ciara was polite. 'We must have covered everything,' she added with a hint of sarcasm.

'We certainly have.' Caroline ignored her tone.

Devlin turned to Caroline. 'We should go. Didn't you want to stop at that little shop at the Spanish Arch to get a present for Shauna Cleary's baby's christening?'

'Yes I do. Thanks for reminding me.'

'We'll get the driver to stop. Have to go. Thanks for looking after us, girls. We'll be in touch.' Devlin included the reception staff in her goodbyes and hurried out to the car, assailed by a myriad of emotions. It could have been the biggest success of her business career but Ciara's behaviour had taken the gloss off it, and she was still at a loss to know why.

Caroline asked the driver to stop at the curio shop and got into the car beside Devlin.

'Are you OK?' she asked as they pulled away from the complex.

'I'm tired,' Devlin admitted. 'But my meetings went well. I'm happy with the work I got done. How did you get on?'

'Fine.' Caroline nodded imperceptibly in the driver's direction. She didn't want anything getting back to Ciara or any of the staff. It was better not to discuss the situation in front of a third party.

Devlin copped on immediately.

'Good. A satisfactory day then.' Devlin leaned back in her seat and yawned. Tiredness seeped through her. She longed for her bed.

When the driver pulled up to let Caroline out Devlin decided to get out and breathe in some fresh sea air. It was a chilly evening and the breeze from the sea was stiff and invigorating. She was leaning against the car, inhaling the salty seaweed-scented air, when a tall, loping figure caught her eye. Her eyes narrowed as she followed his progress towards her. He was walking a golden retriever and as he came nearer to her she recognized Matthew Moran, the landscape gardener.

He walked like a panther, gracefully but full of restrained vigour, and again she was reminded of how attractive he was. Dead sexy actually, she thought to herself, wondering why she found him so attractive. She'd never felt attracted to any other man since she'd been with Luke, but Matthew Moran certainly pressed a button somewhere. She knew nothing about him or his personal life other than that he had come highly recommended and had a thriving practice.

'How are you, Devlin?' he said in his delicious West of Ireland accent.

'Hello Matthew. How's it going?' Devlin smiled.

He smiled back at her, his eyes crinkling in his tanned weather-beaten face. He had a lovely smile. Sort of shy, she decided. She had to find out more about him. Her chance would come when he was working on the grounds. It gave her a secret little buzz to find another man attractive. Just because she was married didn't mean she couldn't stand on the sidelines and look, she thought, as she met his gaze. He had such blue eyes. Very penetrating eyes. But there was a sort of a sadness about him that was intriguing.

'Have you been inspecting the new building?' He nodded in the direction of City Girl.

'I just came from there. It's coming on great,' Devlin said.

'He's doing a good job. At least with John Joe you know it will be well built,' Matthew remarked.

'What's your dog's name?' Devlin asked.

'This is Goldie,' Matthew said, patting the dog's head. Goldie turned and licked him affectionately.

'She's a lovely dog.' Devlin patted the soft furry pelt.

'She is that.' Matthew smiled down at the dog and again Devlin was struck at how his smile changed his austere features.

Just then Caroline hurried down the steps of the shop and over to the car.

'Sorry for keeping you, Devlin. Hello?' She smiled at Matthew.

'Caroline, this is Matthew Moran. He's landscaping City Girl for us. Matthew, this is my friend and colleague, Caroline Yates.'

'How do you do, Caroline?' Matthew politely held out his hand and dwarfed Caroline's in his.

'Nice to meet you. I saw your plans for the garden.

294

It's going to be beautiful,' Caroline said warmly.

'Thank you. I hope so. Well, ladies, nice to see you. Safe journey.' Matthew raised a hand in salute, obviously tired of small talk, and then he was gone, striding into the distance with the dog trotting at his heels.

'He's nice, isn't he?' Devlin said dreamily as she watched him go.

'Hmm. What do you think? I got a little china piggy bank and a little bracelet. Do you think that's OK?' Clearly Matthew hadn't made the impression on Caroline that he'd made on Devlin. Caroline held out her packages for inspection, but Devlin was gazing after Matthew's retreating figure.

'Devlin?' Caroline queried again.

'Oh! They're lovely.' Devlin came back to earth.

'We should go. We'll be heading into the rush hour. Andrew would go bananas if we missed our flight and had to book into a hotel for an overnighter.' Caroline grinned.

'Andrew's a buzz-killer,' Devlin retorted.

'What?'

'A buzz-killer. I heard Andrea Kearney saying it about Gary Nolan. Good, isn't it?' Devlin giggled.

'It certainly describes Gary Nolan to a T.' Caroline laughed. 'He could do with a personality transplant, he's such a stuffed shirt. It *does* describe Andrew a bit. He takes himself *very* seriously. Do you know what I should do?' Her brown eyes danced with mischief.

'What?' Devlin grinned.

'You know the way he's slightly suspicious – to put it mildly – of some of our new therapies? Well, I could have him come to my office and walk in to find me sitting under a pyramid twirling a smudge stick. I'd love to see his face. Maybe I'll give him a dream-catcher for Christmas.'

'If he ever makes a crack again like he did the day he asked me what did Luke think of my plans, he'll be getting a gift voucher for a colonic irrigation from me,' Devlin declared. She wouldn't forget that slight in a hurry.

Relieved that the stress of pretending that every-thing was normal with Ciara was over, Devlin relaxed and unwound on the drive to the airport. Caroline was a great pal, she thought gratefully, as her friend went to get them a cup of tea while they waited for their flight to be called. Having her take Ciara off her hands had been a big bonus that had made the day a lot easier on her. And she'd done it in such a pro-fessional way, Devlin was full of admiration for her. Caroline was a great asset to the company as well as being her best friend.

She fell asleep on the flight home, resting on Caroline's shoulder. And even in the car home from the airport, she felt drowsy and glad that she wasn't driving.

'Are you hungry? Would you like to stop some-where and have a bite to eat?' Caroline asked kindly.

'I just want to go to bed, Caroline.' Devlin yawned. 'I'm so tired in this pregnancy. It's unbeliev-able. It just washes over you in waves. You literally want to put your head down anywhere and sleep.'

'Don't come in tomorrow.'

'I can't take another day off. And besides I'm tak-ing Friday week off when we go to Powerscourt Springs. I'll be in tomorrow. I'll be fine after a night's sleep,' Devlin assured her.

'Well, just take it easy,' Caroline warned. 'We can manage to survive the odd day that you aren't around.'

Devlin laughed. Of that she had no doubt.

An hour later she was tucked up in bed, sipping the hot chocolate that Caroline had made for her. Her eyelids drooped and she turned off the TV, unable to concentrate on the documentary she was watching. She switched off the light and lay in the dark, reviewing the events of the day. Ciara had been so brazen. Didn't she have any qualms at all about what she was doing? She had looked Devlin straight in the eye with not a flicker of discomfort. She was a strange girl, that was for sure. How would she react when she was confronted with her wrongdoing?

Deny it all, probably, Devlin thought wearily as she closed her eyes and slipped into sleep.

Those fucking rich bitches! Just who did they think they were? Swanning down from Dublin. Taking over and telling her what to do on *her* patch. Ciara counted the takings from the day's business and with huge resentment put the cash into the safe ready to be lodged in the bank the following morning.

The day had been a disaster. She'd been stuck with Caroline Yates for practically the whole time. Caroline had wanted estimates of how many treatments the new wing could expect to cater for. She'd wanted to work out how many new housekeeping staff would need to be employed. What ground staff would they need? Ciara had gone into all that in her report but Caroline had nit-picked her way through it until Ciara was fit to be tied.

Devlin had gone ahead and had the meeting with

Finn Kennedy and had made selections without even asking her opinion. That just wasn't on. She was the manageress, for God's sake. This was her City Girl. She'd earned the right to be involved in all decision-making. Today she'd been treated like some little skivvy. And then to top it all she'd had to cancel lunch. She'd been so looking forward to making an entrance into the restaurant with Devlin and Caroline. She'd told lots of those snooty dames who came to her for private treatments that she was bringing Devlin to lunch. They all knew of Devlin Delaney, the celebrity from Dublin who was a *close* friend of Ciara's. She'd actually told a few white lies to several of them and said that Devlin was going to make her a director of the company.

And so she should be a director! Ciara scowled as she slammed shut her creditors' ledger. She worked her butt off so that pair could live in the lap of luxury, wear posh clothes and drive swanky cars. It was on the backs of Ciara and the rest of City Girl's employees that those two were living a fabulous lifestyle, Ciara thought with mounting fury as she glanced through the rota that the salon manageress had made out for the following day.

But her time was coming, Ciara vowed. One day she would have her own emporium and it would be far superior to anything Devlin Delaney could ever aspire to. She was biding her time. She wanted to see how the new wing panned out. She wanted to see residential in action and she wanted to get names and addresses of customers that she would take the greatest pleasure in poaching when the time came.

Ciara knew that her dream was not going to happen overnight. She would wait until everything was right. In the meantime she would line her pockets, absorb everything, and then the rewards that she so richly deserved would be hers.

She hurried down the maple-floored hallway to the supply room beside the treatment rooms. She selected three soft fluffy towels in different colours. Devlin always insisted that they buy best-quality goods. She needed a few new towels for her home treatments. A supply of new robes had arrived, she noted. Once Roisin, the salon manageress, had marked them off, Ciara would nick one. She already had quite a supply for when she opened her own palace of luxury.

She switched off the lights and walked out to the foyer. The emergency lights cast a muted glow. Ciara stood a moment in the deep silence. By seven in the morning the building would be vibrant and alive with career women doing their workouts and lapping the pool before heading off to their desks. Later the society dames would arrive for their facials and de-stressing treatments

And Devlin Delaney would be swanning around doing damn all really, except making even more money. Whoever said that life wasn't fair knew exactly what they were talking about, Ciara reflected as she turned the lock in the door and walked out to her company car with her nicked goodies under her arm.

She didn't see the watcher in the distance or, later, note that she'd been followed home.

Thirty-one

Caroline slid her key reluctantly into the front door of her apartment block. Home was the last place she wanted to be. She'd enjoyed her trip to Galway. It was exciting watching the expansion of the company and being part of it. It was a terrible pity that Ciara Hanlon was defrauding Devlin. She was exceptionally bright and focused. Had the circumstances been different, Caroline would have really got a buzz out of their morning's work. She'd enjoyed Devlin's company too. They didn't often get a chance to spend a whole working day together. They were a good team, she thought with satisfaction.

Now she was coming home to an empty flat. And when Richard did come in after visiting his mother he would be surly and uncommunicative and not at all pleasant to be around.

She took the lift up to the penthouse. She was feeling peckish. Devlin had been too tired to go somewhere for a meal and Caroline wasn't in the humour for cooking. Besides, she needed to do a shop, there was very little in the fridge and not a lot in the freezer either. She prowled restlessly around the rooms, before deciding to phone Olivia. Maybe her friend was free and they could go and have a meal somewhere.

'Hi, it's me. I'm just in from Galway and I was wondering if you'd eaten. And if not would you like to come out for a bite to eat?' she asked hopefully.

'I've a chicken korma simmering on the pan. Why don't you get your ass over and join us?' Olivia invited hospitably.

'No, no, I wouldn't gatecrash your evening meal,' Caroline demurred.

'Don't be silly. There's loads. Come on. It's been a while since we had a natter,' Olivia urged.

'Are you sure?' Caroline wavered.

'Of course I'm sure. See you in a while.' Olivia rang off.

Caroline cheered up instantly. It was nice not to have to eat alone. She'd have a good laugh with Olivia. She unzipped the skirt of her grey business suit, unbuttoned her jacket and grabbed a pair of jeans and a sweatshirt out of the wardrobe. Ten minutes later after a quick shower she was dressed and ready to go.

She wrote a note for Richard and left it on the hall stand. It was out of habit, really, when she thought about it. It made no difference to him where she was these days. He was giving her the cold treatment.

As soon as their weekend in Powerscourt Springs was over she was definitely doing something about moving out. She'd had enough. Living with Richard and his resentments was extremely draining. But it was her own fault for putting up with it, she told herself firmly as she locked the door behind her and set out to dine with her friend.

* * *

'Richard, pass me that notepad. I'm going to write a list of instructions for Mrs Gleeson and you can give them to her tomorrow. And please check that she has carried them out before I get home,' Sarah ordered as she held out her hand for the notepad that was only inches away from her on her bedside locker.

Richard uncoiled himself from the armchair he'd been lounging in beside his mother's bed and did as he was bid.

'And turn down that television. I'm fed up with the North and Kosovo. And refugees. Is there no Christianity left in the world?' she grumbled.

Richard turned down the news. He was looking very down in the mouth, she noted, as she began to write her instructions for the housekeeper.

'You don't have to sit here night after night.' Sarah gave a martyred sniff. 'If it's an ordeal for you, I'd rather you didn't come. I don't want to put you out, Richard,' she added petulantly.

It was all right for him, he wasn't stuck in a nursing home feeling weak and tearful, wondering what was in store for the future. That was, if she *had* a future. She was beginning to have serious doubts. They'd brought her back to the hospital for a morning and given her a thing called a stress test and nearly killed her. It was outrageous. She'd written to the consultant and the matron and given them a piece of her mind.

Mr Collins, her consultant, had been most apologetic after he'd received her missive. But he'd told her it was necessary and that the results had been better than he'd hoped. He had told her that she could go home next week, but Sarah wasn't sure that she was up to it. She liked knowing that there was a bell beside her bed which would summon help if she felt she needed it. She wasn't looking forward to spending the nights on her own. She was trying to pluck up the courage to suggest to Richard that he come and stay with her for a while, but she had to pick the right moment. There was no point in asking him when he had a puss on him. He'd only say no and then she'd be stuck.

'Would you like me to ask one of the night nurses to get you a cup of tea?' She changed her tack.

'No thanks, Mother. I had something to eat in town. I don't want a cup of tea.'

'Would that . . . that lazy lump not have a bit of dinner ready for you when you come in from work?' Sarah injected a note of sympathy into her voice. 'It's a disgrace.'

'She works too, don't forget,' Richard said flatly.

'Huh! A woman's place is in the home. And a wife's place is taking care of her husband.' Sarah sniffed. Working women did not impress her one little bit. It was just an excuse to escape their responsibilities and gad about.

'You could always come and have dinner with me in the evenings, when I get home. I could employ Mrs Gleeson full-time and she could cook dinner for us.' Sarah sat up straight in bed, her eyes bright. If she got him to come for dinner she could always say that she felt a little weak and he'd feel obliged to stay.

'Do you think Mrs Gleeson would take on the job full-time? Doesn't she have family commitments? A deserted daughter or something?' Richard countered.

'She'd be delighted to take the job if the money was good enough. Those sort of people can never get

303

enough money,' Sarah declared confidently.

'It would be good if she could work longer hours for you.' Richard stood up and began to pace up and down.

Sarah suddenly realized that she had made a big mistake. If Hannah Gleeson came to work longer hours, Richard would feel he was off the hook and probably visit less and less.

'Maybe not, though,' she said hastily. 'I find her tedious sometimes. We'll see.'

'But Mother—'

Sarah raised a hand. 'Not now, Richard. I'm tired. You may go.' She used her weaker-than-weak voice.

'I'll see you tomorrow then.' Richard didn't argue. He gave her a lacklustre kiss and hurried out as if he couldn't wait to be rid of her.

Sarah lay in bed frowning. What was she to do? How could he even consider allowing her to go home alone? If he was married to any kind of a proper wife she'd ask Sarah to come and stay with them for a while. But that was out of the question, with Madam Caroline. She had burnt her bridges and Sarah would never give her the time of day again.

She turned to the picture of the Sacred Heart, with a sword piercing Jesus, that hung on the wall opposite the bed. Why had He seen fit to send her this great cross? Had it not been enough to take her dear husband from her and leave her with a young son to rear? A son who had turned into an ungrateful pup who considered her no more than a nuisance.

'It's too much to expect of a poor soul. Too much, dear Lord. Have mercy,' she prayed fervently as she reached for her rosary and settled down for the comforting ritual of her nightly prayers.

Richard's footsteps echoed down the parquet floor and he wrinkled his nose at the smell of age and infirmity which seeped through the closed bedroom doors and which no amount of disinfectant and polish could disguise. It was an expensive nursing home, no common-or-garden kip for Sarah, but nevertheless it was a depressing place and he hated his visits. He'd end up like his mother, he often thought. Lonely, unwanted, alone. He was riven with conflicting emotions. He wished he could leave her there to rot, yet he felt driven to sit with her, hour after hour, night after night.

He was certainly going to ask Mrs Gleeson to work longer hours, no matter what his mother said. She was an honest dependable woman and God knows she'd put up with his mother when many more would have simply thrown in the towel.

Eventually he'd have to get a live-in housekeeper, but that was a bit down the road. One step at a time, he told himself wearily as he got into his car and started the ignition.

Caroline wasn't home, he noted twenty minutes later, as he drove into the complex. She'd gone jaunting off to Galway with Devlin Delaney. He had papers to work on. A particularly tough family-law case had been taxing him for the past week and he sorely missed Charles's expertise and advice.

He took out the worn faded photo of Charles from his wallet and stared at the much loved face. When did grief go? How long did you have to carry it inside you, twisting your gut, stabbing your heart, aching, needing? The loneliness so fierce it was a physical pain. How was it possible to miss another human so much? How much longer could he carry on this façade of a life, without going mad?

He put the photo back in his wallet. Charles was gone and nothing was ever going to bring him back. He was on his own.

'Face it,' he growled as he took his briefcase and locked the car.

He read Caroline's note on the hall table.

She was having dinner with that estate-agent friend of hers, no doubt plotting what property to buy.

Hadn't she the carefree life? he thought resentfully as he flung his briefcase onto the sofa and poured himself a double brandy. It was the least he deserved. First thing tomorrow he was going to contact Hannah Gleeson. She could name her price. Anything would be worth it to get Sarah off his back.

Thirty-two

'I'll see you on Sunday evening.' Caroline stood at the door of the kitchen with her coat on, ready to depart for her weekend away with the girls. Richard sat at the table drinking black coffee. He barely acknowledged her goodbye.

'Richard, *please* stop being like this. It makes life very uncomfortable. It's so unnecessary. It's not my fault that your plans didn't work out. Please stop taking it out on me.' Caroline was at her wit's end. How much longer could this awful coolness between them last? Why couldn't he make the effort? Didn't it bother him?

'Well, you'll be moving out soon. So what do you care?' Richard said sulkily.

'Richard, don't be so childish,' Caroline said in exasperation. 'You were OK with it when you were supposed to be moving to Boston. We discussed it over and over. Just because your plans changed why should mine?'

'That's right. Think of yourself. Me. Me. Me,' Richard sneered.

'Oh forget it.' Caroline turned on her heel and walked out. If she stayed to argue the toss any more there'd be a full-scale row. He'd done enough already to ensure she couldn't go off to Powerscourt Springs with an easy mind.

Disheartened, she picked up her case in the hall and closed the door behind her. If Richard wanted to hold a grudge and keep her frozen out there was nothing she could do about it. She visualized him surrounded by light, and did the same for herself, as she descended to the foyer in the lift. The more attention you gave to negative energy like that, the bigger it grew. She had the choice to carry it with her for the weekend or let it go and not link into it.

Caroline took a deep breath. This was *her* weekend. She'd been looking forward to it for ages. Richard had to deal with his stuff, she couldn't do it for him. She'd tried to make up and he wouldn't make the effort.

'Forget it, now,' she told herself very firmly. She was going to enjoy every second of her time with the girls and try and put all thoughts of her unhappy situation out of her head.

Richard stood at the kitchen window and watched Caroline reverse her car over to Devlin's apartment block. He was filled with resentment and rage. His mother was in a nursing home putting him under fierce pressure. He'd had to cancel his plans to go to Boston and live a life unencumbered with all the trials that weighed him down here. And did Caroline give a damn? She did not.

It obviously didn't bother her that he was miserable and unhappy. She was far too busy enjoying life. Socializing with Olivia O'Neill night after night. Waltzing off to a health farm with that other pair. Viewing properties. Making plans to ditch him and leave him alone to get through his ordeals by himself.

Mrs Bloody Gleeson had been on holidays when he'd phoned last week. She was due back this weekend. *Holidays!* Benidorm! A funny time to be going on holidays. She'd probably got a cheapie off season. Maybe it was a good thing though, he mused as he rinsed his cup under the tap. She might be skint and in dire need of money. She *had* to agree to his offer. It was imperative that Sarah have full-time daily care. Hannah Gleeson was the best woman for the job.

'Have a ball, Devlin. Tell Caroline and Maggie to do the same. And take it easy. Rest up. Don't be doing aerobics and toning and that kind of stuff.' Luke enveloped her in a bear-hug.

Devlin laughed. 'I've no intentions of doing aerobics. A swim in the pool is the most energetic thing I plan to do. Besides, I got enough exercise this morning, Mr Sex On Legs.'

Luke's eyes twinkled. 'I don't have time to go to a gym. You have to keep me fit. It's your wifely duty.' His arms tightened around her. 'It was good, though. Wasn't it?'

'Yeah it was.' Devlin snuggled in close. Luke bent his head and kissed her, his tongue probing and teasing as his hands slid up under her jumper and cupped her breasts.

Devlin responded instantly, her nipples hardening under his erotic feather-like touch as his fingers slipped inside the flimsy material of her bra. Quivers of desire shot through her and she pulled away, breathless.

'Will you stop it, Reilly,' she protested, grinning. 'You're making me horny.'

'What do you think you're doing to me,' Luke said huskily as he held her tighter against him. She could feel his hardness and it turned her on.

'Oh Luke, that's not fair!' Devlin muttered as she drew his head down and kissed him passionately and then pulled him down onto the carpet.

'Wanton woman.' Luke grinned as he unbuttoned her jeans and slid them off, and groaned as she wrapped her legs around him.

It was quick and passionate and thoroughly satisfying. Devlin lay panting in his arms afterwards, grinning from ear to ear.

'Not bad for an old married couple,' she murmured breathlessly.

'Just ring the undertakers for me, now. You have me worn out, woman.' Luke kissed the top of her nose.

'You started it,' Devlin said indignantly.

'I only kissed you.' Luke feigned innocence.

'And you did other things. And you know how my wits desert me when you do those things to me.' Devlin buried her face in his neck. She loved his neck. It was such a strong, solid neck. A manly neck.

The doorbell shrilled.

'Oh crumbs! Quick, let me up! It's Caroline.' Devlin started to laugh as she pushed Luke off her and pulled on her briefs and jeans.

'Look at the head on you. Brush your hair for God's sake! And don't forget the back of it. It's always a dead give-away.' Luke couldn't hide his amusement.

310

Devlin hurried over to the intercom. 'I'll be down in two seconds, Caroline.'

'No hurry, the car's out the front,' her friend's voice echoed tinnily through the intercom.

Five minutes later, hair brushed, eyes and cheeks glowing, Devlin emerged on to the steps of the apartment block. Luke followed with her case, which he stowed in the boot that Caroline had already opened.

He kissed Caroline affectionately and she returned his hug.

'Girls, there's no need to tell you to have fun. That's a given. Caroline, don't be surprised if she's talking to you one minute and she's asleep the next. It can be very disconcerting. And for God's sake don't talk business. That Galway person is not to be mentioned. Work is out of bounds.'

Caroline laughed. 'Whatever you say, Luke. You know Devlin *always* does what I tell her to.'

'Lucky you, she never does what I tell her to. But I love her all the same.' Luke held the car door open for Devlin. 'See you Sunday,' he said. His eyes were warm and loving and Devlin felt completely happy.

'He's lovely, Dev. You're very lucky,' Caroline said as she drove to the security gates.

'I know,' Devlin acknowledged. 'It just gets better and better. I'm crazy about him.' She turned to Caroline. 'How was Richard? Any improvement?'

Caroline shook her head. 'No. He has to blame someone because everything's gone wrong. And at the moment that someone is me. The sooner I move out the better. After this weekend I'm going to go serious house-hunting.'

'Us too,' Devlin said. 'The only thing is that we've decided to hang onto the apartment until the house is completely ready to move into. So if we buy a second-hand house and have to redecorate I won't be stuck with builders and painters and plasterers and whatever.'

'You're right. That would be an awful pain in the butt, especially with a new baby to look after. It's a nice option to have.'

'Are you going to go for something new or second-hand?' Devlin asked as Caroline drove out onto the main road.

'I don't know yet. I'm just hoping that I'll see something and know that it's perfect for me.'

'It's a lousy time to be buying property. The prices are astronomical,' Devlin reflected.

'I know. Just my luck. We missed the boat there, didn't we?' Caroline smiled wryly at her.

'Successful businesswomen, my hat! And we're going to end up paying a fortune for property. We'll need to work twice as hard to pay the mortgages.' Devlin grinned. 'I hope the successful author is all ready for the weekend.'

'Well, if anyone needs a pampery weekend, she does.' Caroline turned left at Copeland Avenue and headed for the M50 to collect Maggie.

'I've taken a chicken casserole out of the freezer to defrost for your dinner tonight,' Maggie informed her husband as she sat at the kitchen table sewing a button that had just fallen off, onto the sleeve of Michael's school shirt.

'And what's for tomorrow and Sunday?' Terry scraped the merest hint of low-fat spread onto his one slice of toast. Secretly Maggie was impressed. He'd really stuck to his diet and it showed. He'd lost over a stone and had toned up considerably. She begrudged him every ounce of his weight loss.

'You're going to Fort Lucan tomorrow, I presumed that you'd be treating the kids to a meal out. And Sunday you can cook what you like. There's lamb and beef in the freezer,' Maggie said coolly.

'*Cook*!' Terry looked at her askance. 'Did you not cook up a meal and freeze it?'

'I cook practically three hundred and sixty-five days a year, Terry, it won't kill you to have to get a meal ready for one day.' Maggie bit the end of the thread and wound it around the button.

'There you go, Michael.' She handed the shirt to her son, who was standing in his pants and vest.

'Thanks, Mam. You are coming back on Sunday, aren't you?' His big blue eyes looked at her solemnly.

'Of course I am, pet. I'm just going away with Devlin and Caroline for the weekend. Of course I'm coming home. Where else would I be going, you silly billy?'

'Just checking that it wasn't for a longer time,' he explained earnestly. But Maggie understood the reasoning behind his questioning. There was still an underlying insecurity in Michael that went back to their separation. No doubt he'd picked up on the cool atmosphere between herself and Terry of late. Michael was an awful worrier. God knows what notions were running around that head of his.

'I'll ring you every night from the health farm and I'll bring you back a present,' she promised.

'Thanks, Mam.' Michael flung his arms around her and she held him tight, his cow-lick brushing her cheek, his face sticky from his porridge and honey.

'Go and wash your face before you put your shirt on.' She smiled at him and loved him with all her heart.

'Mam, Lisa Dunne is having a slumber party tomorrow night. Can I go to it?' Mimi twirled into the kitchen in her ballet shoes.

'Ask Daddy, he's minding you tomorrow.' Maggie glanced at Terry. Let him do a bit of parenting for a change.

'Can I, Dad?'

'Are there any boys at it?' Terry asked, sternly.

'Don't be silly, Dad. What would we want *boys* at a slumber party for? It's for girls. It's for *fun*!' Mimi said indignantly, wrinkling her nose in distaste at the idea.

Maggie hid a grin. Thank God her elder daughter wasn't into boys yet.

Terry arched an eyebrow at Maggie.

'It's fine with me. The Dunnes are a nice family.'

'OK,' Terry agreed and was rewarded with a kiss from Mimi.

'Tomorrow is going to be a perfect day,' she declared. 'Fort Lucan *and* a slumber party.'

'Can Kerry come and stay the night if Mimi's going to a slumber party?' Shona lifted her head from a puzzle on the back of the cornflakes box that she was trying to work out.

Terry shook his head at Maggie. 'Not a good idea if you're not here,' he murmured.

'No love, Daddy will have enough on his hands, but I bet he'd let you get some videos,' Maggie said brightly.

'But I want Kerry to stay, 'cos she's my best friend.' Shona pouted.

314

'I know, pet. When I come back, we'll have her over to stay,' Maggie soothed.

'Mimi gets everything she wants and I get nothing!' Shona stomped out in high dudgeon.

'I just think it's better, considering the day and age that we live in, for you to be here when the girls' friends are staying over,' Terry pointed out.

'You're right. It's terrible. But what can you do?' Maggie shook her head. For once they were in accord over something.

'Don't worry. I'll make a fuss of her, she'll be fine.' Terry shrugged into his suit jacket, picked up his briefcase and headed for the door.

'Will you be leaving your mobile switched on?' he asked.

'No. How could I if I'm having treatments done? Or if I'm in the pool or Jacuzzi.'

'It's well for some,' he remarked dryly.

'I'll phone the kids at night. You can leave a message for me if you have to. I'll check them every so often.' Maggie ignored his tone.

'Fine. See you Sunday. What time will you be home?'

'Whenever,' Maggie said evenly. She was damned if she was tying herself down to a time.

Terry scowled, and walked out of the kitchen. She heard the front door close.

'I'll have a wonderful time. Thank you so much for your good wishes,' she muttered under her breath as she cleared dirty porridge dishes off the table and began to stack the dishwasher. Josie her cleaning lady would be here any minute but Maggie hated her coming into a mess and always tried to have the breakfast dishes cleared away before she arrived.

Three-quarters of an hour later her three children were safely deposited at the school gates, and then and only then did Maggie finally feel a sense of anticipation creep up on her.

She drove quickly home and just as she was entering the cul-de-sac Orla Noonan was driving out. Orla nearly got a crick in her neck turning away.

'Up yours,' said Maggie, unimpressed. Orla was for the birds and she could fly away with them for all Maggie cared. She was going away with friends. *Real* friends. She pulled up in the drive and hurried into the house, anxious to be ready when the girls arrived.

She checked her case to make sure she had everything and glanced at her laptop, neatly put away in its travel bag.

Should she or shouldn't she?

She was going on a break, she reasoned. That meant a break from writing as well as family. Only it would be the ideal opportunity to fit in a few hours' writing in peace and quiet with no interruptions. She was desperately anxious to get the book finished. She was on the last lap. Another thirty thousand words and she'd be done.

Then she could get the builders in to do her attic conversion. She hadn't told Terry of her plans yet. Time for that when the book was ready to go to print.

'You're not bringing your computer,' protested Devlin when she saw Maggie's luggage.

'Come on, Maggie. This is a pampery weekend,' remonstrated Caroline.

'I know, girls. I might get a few hours done early in the morning and then I wouldn't feel so guilty about not working,' she explained weakly.

'And Luke Reilly calls *me* a workaholic,' Devlin

teased. 'Get in the car and relax, for God's sake.'

'I'm perfectly relaxed,' Maggie retorted.

'Well, would you ever take off your rubber gloves, then. Or are you bringing them with you?' Devlin asked quizzically.

'Oh! Oh sorry,' Maggie said flustered. 'I was just cleaning the downstairs loo, before Josie cleans it, if you know what I mean.'

'Maggie, you're the only woman I know who cleans the house *before* the cleaner comes. You're a hoot!' Devlin said fondly. 'Come on. Get your ass in gear. We're out of here now.'

'Some things never change, Caroline. Remember how bossy she was when we were in the flat in Sandymount?' Maggie drawled. 'How high will I jump, Delaney?'

Devlin laughed. 'As high as I tell you if it means you're going to relax and enjoy yourself.'

Maggie removed her gloves, washed her hands, brushed her hair and called goodbye up the stairs to Josie.

'Let's go.' She beamed. 'I'm ready for this.'

'Me too,' Devlin echoed. 'I know I have treatments in City Girl but I always feel a bit guilty. Silly, I know. But there it is. So I'm really going to give myself up to a thorough pampering.'

'This brings back memories.' Maggie sat back in her seat and stretched. 'Remember the trip we did for our girls' weekend away to Rosslare and Caroline drove us in her brand-new Fiesta all those years ago?'

'Yeah and remember the shrieks of us when she passed the little old Methuselah on the tractor,' Devlin guffawed.

317

'This is going to be fun!' Caroline grinned. 'Did anyone bring a sin bag?'

'Oh Lordy! Remember the sin bag on the Shannon? We simply have to stop and fill up with goodies. It wouldn't be a girls' weekend away without a sin bag,' Maggie declared. 'After all, we are going to a *health* farm.' They shrieked with laughter as the years rolled away and they felt as young and carefree as they had been when they'd first become friends.

They stopped in Avoca Handweavers to shop and have a giggly, giddy lunch. Maggie treated herself to a set of beautifully cut champagne flutes with an eye to the Al Shariffs' arrival. Devlin bought Luke a chunky-knit jumper and Caroline bought a wooden salad bowl and matching salt and pepper set for her new home. It was delightful to meander around the displays knowing that there were no demands to be made on their time.

It was with mounting anticipation that they drove along the winding country roads of Wicklow until they turned into the long curving drive, set in acres of lush meadows, that led to the attractive cluster of whitewashed buildings that was Powerscourt Springs Health Farm.

Thirty-three

'This is very nice,' Caroline said admiringly as they followed the small white signpost and turned left for Reception.

'I love the horses.' Devlin observed the quietly grazing animals with delight. 'We won't be able to have horses, our grounds are so small. And they've got ducks too. Did you see them in the little stream? This is going to be a hard act to follow.' She glanced at Caroline with a wry smile, all her competitive juices flowing.

'Never mind, Devlin. We'll stick some goldfish in the pond and maybe a frog or two,' Caroline countered.

'Maybe we could get a pair of swans!' Devlin suggested seriously.

'Matthew Moran – he's a very sexy landscape gardener,' she turned back to explain to Maggie, 'if I wasn't mad about Luke I'd set my cap at him, anyway he's putting in an ornamental pond. Maybe he could get me two swans. What do you think, Caroline?'

Caroline wasn't listening. She was performing a complicated backing manoeuvre into a parking space between a Saab and a BMW. The small circular car park was almost full.

'Sorry, Devlin. What did you say?' She straightened up the wheels and switched off the engine.

'I was thinking that perhaps Matthew Moran might get us a pair of swans for the pool.'

Caroline laughed. 'Now Devlin,' she warned,' stay calm. There's no need to go overboard.'

'Look at the gym,' Devlin said enviously. 'Look at those fabulous floor-to-ceiling windows. Look at the view.' The three of them gazed in delight at the stunning uninterrupted views of the gently undulating Wicklow hills stretching as far as the eye could see, no matter what direction you looked in. The grounds surrounding the complex were well tended, filled with rockeries and shrubs, and seasonal flowers.

'It's like a little paradise set in the middle of the country where no-one can get at you,' Maggie exclaimed in delight as she resolutely switched off her phone. 'Come on, girls, phones off,' she ordered.

Devlin and Caroline complied without dissent.

'Let's check in,' Devlin suggested happily.

'This is what I was born for.' Maggie grinned as she got out of the car and took long deep breaths of fresh air.

The reception area was very welcoming and enticing. Wood and glass filled it with natural light. The highly polished floors gleamed, mirrors sparkled, plush sofas invited guests to sink into them. An enormous cut-glass chandelier dominated the ceiling, radiating golden sparkles in the glass of the floor-to-ceiling double doors.

I'm having one of them, Devlin thought privately. And then was amused at her childishness.

The staff at reception were very friendly and

welcoming. Devlin, Caroline and Maggie were shown to their room and invited to come to the lounge, when they had settled in, for coffee and an introductory tour and consultation.

'I love the décor. This is a very cosy room,' Maggie approved when they were on their own. Decorated in warm tones of yellow and gold, it was a light, airy room that was fresh, restful and soothing. The three beds with their striped yellow and gold covers looked so inviting that Maggie lay down on the nearest one, said, 'This is mine, wake me up when it's time to go home,' stretched luxuriously and closed her eyes.

'The bathroom is dotey,' Caroline announced as she unpacked her toilet bag.

'Look at the view. This place is magnificent,' Devlin remarked, drawn to the window like a magnet. 'I'm really glad we came.'

'Me too,' echoed the others.

'Come on, let's go for coffee and the consultations. Have you decided what treatments you're going to have?' Caroline picked up one of the brochures. 'I'm having the manicure and pedicure, for starters.' She perused the glossy leaflet intently. 'The Honey and Almond Body Polish sounds gorgeous.'

'I like the sound of the Peppermint Twist, and the Thermal Mud Treatment. Oh and look at the Repécharge Four-layer Facial, and you get a scalp and hand massage as well,' Maggie enthused as she read out the details.

'Oh I'm going to have that,' Caroline agreed eagerly. 'I've had it in City Girl a couple of times and it's divine.'

'I suggest we all have the Body Exfoliant first. It

'leaves your skin so fresh and clean,' Devlin added her contribution.

'Good thinking! And we should have a swim, sauna and a Jacuzzi before we have any treatments,' Caroline declared.

'Is anyone going to do the walk, or the body-toning and aqua aerobics?' Maggie asked.

They looked at each other and laughed.

'Well, it *is* a pampery weekend,' Caroline pointed out.

'The emphasis seems to be much more on relaxation than killing yourself on the treadmill and stepper,' Devlin noted. 'I like that. We'll bear that in mind, Caroline. Sometimes a health farm can sound so regimented and killjoyish.'

'Come on, let's go down to the lounge and get organized,' Maggie urged. 'I'd love a Jacuzzi.'

An hour later they swam leisurely up and down the pool, their soft luxurious towelling robes draped over three chairs. In each robe's pocket reposed a three-day timetable of head-to-toe treatments that had been worked out for each of them by one of the therapists.

They were in the seventh heaven as they swam in the heated pool and listened to the soft pitter-patter of rain against the enormous French windows that overlooked the grounds.

A while later, Devlin sat dangling her legs over the edge of the Jacuzzi, while Maggie and Caroline luxuriated in the bubbling hot cauldron as powerful jets of hot water soothed their tired, stressed bodies.

'Am I dreaming this?' Maggie murmured contentedly.

'Even though I've done all this kind of thing a

thousand times in City Girl, I really feel I'm switched off completely here,' Devlin admitted.

'Yeah, but you or I can't totally relax in City Girl. You're the owner and employer. I'm one of the bosses. It's different,' Caroline observed. 'Here we're just clients to be looked after.'

'They do a very good job of looking after you. The atmosphere is excellent. Clients' requirements are a priority. I'm impressed. And you know what?' Devlin grinned.

'What?' Maggie grinned back.

'Within ten minutes of putting on the robe, I forgot that I was here to suss out the place and get ideas for Galway. I intend to forget about work completely.'

'Atta girl,' Maggie encouraged. 'Let's have another swim.'

By six thirty that evening they'd been exfoliated from head to toe and had soothing moisturizing creams massaged into their skin to leave it soft and silky. They'd each had a back massage.

'I feel so clean. My skin feels so soft,' Maggie rubbed her arm against her cheek. 'This has been a fabulous day.'

'I'm glad we got a three-bed room.' Devlin smiled at her friends. 'It wouldn't be the same otherwise.'

'Me too,' agreed Maggie.

'It's nice and informal here, isn't it? Not at all posh or intimidating,' Caroline remarked as she slipped into fresh underwear and sat at the dressing-table to dry her hair.

'I like the fact that you can be weighed and measured and have all your meals calorie-counted and go on a diet if you want to, but it's not a regimented system. The emphasis is much more on de-stressing and unwinding. Definitely I think that's the way we should go, Caroline. The more I see the more certain I am that it's right for us,' Devlin commented as she rummaged in the wardrobe.

'What are you wearing for dinner?' Maggie asked.

Devlin took out a pair of cream linen trousers and a chocolate-brown silk shirt.

'That's what I'm wearing.'

'I'm wearing trousers too, and my little lilac cardigan,' Caroline said.

'Those little cardigans are lovely on you. I'd look like Dolly Parton in one,' Maggie said enviously, eyeing her voluptuous curves in the mirror.

'Oh Maggie, I'd love to have a figure like yours. It's dead sexy,' Caroline declared.

'You mean I'm a stone overweight,' Maggie said dryly.

'No, no!' protested Caroline. 'Remember when I was really fat, Dev, it was soft blubbery fat. Wasn't it?' She looked at Devlin for confirmation. Devlin nodded.

'But even if you are a few pounds overweight it suits you. You're statuesque. You can carry it. If I put on weight, it's blubber straight away.' Caroline sighed.

'Terry really stuck to his diet and it shows. It really gets up my nose. I'm so jealous. Isn't that the pits?' Maggie said as she slithered into a silky black shift dress and put on a short-sleeved white jacket, trimmed in black.

'I think unconditional love is when you can be *truly* delighted for someone when they lose weight, especially if they're not your favourite person in the world,' Caroline commented wickedly as she applied lipstick.

'Then I'll never achieve unconditional love,' Maggie laughed. 'Because I begrudge every ounce Terry's lost, and you know who makes me sick now to look at her?'

'Let me guess,' Devlin grinned as she slipped a gold bangle over her wrist. 'Marie Grimes.'

Marie Grimes was a lady who lunched a lot in City Girl and considered herself to be an A-list socialite.

'Oh yes, she *is* sickening since she went on the NuTron diet. God, if I hear what she's allowed on her green list and not allowed on her red list once more, I'll throw up,' Caroline exclaimed vehemently. 'If she wasn't such a boasty bitch it wouldn't be so bad.'

Maggie winked at Devlin. 'But she's a great spirit though, Caroline, isn't she?'

Caroline flung a pillow at her. 'Smart wagon,' she laughed.

'I don't know about you two but I'm starving. I wonder what's for dinner?' Devlin held the door open and they trooped out into the quiet carpeted corridor.

The menu was mouth-watering.

'I'll have the Warm Salad of Summer Asparagus,' Devlin ordered. 'And the Filet of Beef glazed with honey and mustard.'

'I'll have the Baked Scallops with a sesame crust and lime sauce. And I'll have the Char-grilled Tuna Steak,' Caroline decided.

'And I'll have the Scallops and Beef,' Maggie smiled.

'And we'll all have the Plum Tomato Soup spiked with basil,' Devlin added.

'And to drink?' the restaurant hostess asked pleasantly.

'Sparkling water will be fine.' Maggie glanced at the others, who nodded their assent.

'Look at the desserts, Dark and White Chocolate Mousse and it's only 145 calories,' Maggie exclaimed while they waited for their first course.

'Warm Pears served with Passion Fruit Sorbet, sounds yummy,' Devlin murmured.

'Try the home-made brown bread with walnuts,' Caroline urged, tucking in. 'It's scrumptious!'

The meal was delicious and they lingered in the small, intimate, candle-lit dining-room enjoying the relaxed hum of conversation, enjoying the soothing ambience and most of all enjoying each other's company.

By eleven they were tucked up in bed, hardly able to keep their eyes open. Devlin was asleep in minutes. Caroline and Maggie chatted quietly for a while longer until great yawns got the better of them and they switched off the lamp.

'God be with the days when we'd party until four and five in the morning and fall asleep when the milkman was starting his rounds,' Maggie murmured.

'They were good times,' Caroline smiled in the dark.

'They were, and we didn't really appreciate them,' Maggie said regretfully.

'That's the way with life, unfortunately. Good times will come your way again, Maggie,' Caroline said encouragingly.

'I hope so. It's hard, Caro,' she confided. 'I'm lonely. I long to be loved.'

'Me too,' came the whisper from the other bed. 'Devlin is so lucky to have Luke. Our day will come. Night, Maggie.'

'Night, Caroline. See you in the morning.' Maggie turned over and pulled the covers over her ears, luxuriating in the comfort of a bed to herself. Moments later she was asleep, and before long Caroline's breathing turned deep and even as she joined her friends in slumber.

The following morning, Maggie, awake since six – force of habit – had written two thousand words, Devlin had had a swim and walked a mile on the treadmill, and Caroline had had a lie-in, before they sat down to breakfast at nine. All the guests were in their robes and the day guests were arriving and being shown around.

Great banks of inky clouds gathered behind the hills but occasionally the sun would burst through, shining on the purple-green slopes, as the three women sat at the table in the window alcove and drank in the beauty of the panorama in front of them.

Later, Caroline and Maggie helped themselves to coffee from the table outside the dining-room and the three of them made their way to the plush peach and gold lounge, where towelling-robed guests relaxed and chatted and read or snoozed as they waited to be called for treatments.

Five minutes after they'd sat down and flicked through the day's complimentary newspapers, they were all collected by their individual therapists.

Devlin was having the Four-Layer facial, Maggie the Peppermint Twist, and Caroline the Honey and Almond treatment.

They joined up again for lunch, and feasted on a

delicious buffet of salmon and quiche and a variety of salads made with the freshest ingredients, that brought them back for more.

Afterwards they curled up on the sofas with their books, and snug, warm and cosy, they chatted lazily and watched the dark purple clouds unleash the torrents of rain they had been holding all day. Before long they were all snoozing, completely and utterly relaxed after their exquisite treatments of the morning.

Sometime later, as Maggie drifted off to sleep under the comforting hands of the therapist who was giving her the full-body aromatherapy massage, she vowed that she was going to treat herself to another long weekend in this nirvana, when she had the book finished, the Al Shariffs were gone and Christmas was over. As months of tiredness eased out of her bones she was so glad she had discovered the place that she could come to when she felt worn out, drained, and longing for a break from her non-marriage. This place would get her through things, she vowed to herself. It would be her haven. Her reward for hard work. Here she would enjoy the fruits of her labours and not feel one bit guilty at spending some of her royalties on herself.

It didn't matter whether Devlin or Caroline came, although it was lovely being with them, she acknowledged. This was a place you could come to with friends or alone. And, come hell or high water, she'd be back.

Devlin lay with her eyes closed, listening to the soothing music as the therapist lightly cleansed the area around her eyes. She was having the Eye

Treatment and it felt so refreshing and relaxing she wanted to sleep.

This had been a brainwave, she thought with satisfaction. The three of them hadn't been as relaxed in years. She could see the difference in Maggie already. What was the point of being successful if you didn't splash out on yourself now and again?

They really should do this more often. Although once she had the baby she'd be tied. The thought gave her a little pang. Even though she longed to have this much wanted child she knew her life would change completely. It would no longer be hers. She and Luke would not have the luxury of spontaneous living, she thought, smiling, remembering their day 'on the mitch'. They should make the most of the next few months together and she should make the most of every second of this weekend, she thought drowsily, as the therapist smoothed cool cream onto her skin with a feather-light touch. Her rhythmic circular movements were almost hypnotic.

Caroline felt the heat of the green thermal mud seep deep into the lower curve of her spine. Warm towels kept the rest of her body snug. The nagging ache that sometimes plagued her receded gently, soothed by the deep-heat treatment.

Once, when she had gone for acupuncture for her back, the acupuncturist, a wise and spiritual woman, had asked her gently, 'What burdens are you carrying that are too heavy for your back?' The question had made her cry as she finally acknowledged that yes, she had burdens, and it wasn't giving into weakness to admit it, instead of putting on a façade and pretending that everything was all right.

Richard was a heavy burden, she thought sadly.

One she shouldn't be carrying. Her back had only started to trouble her again recently, since the row over Mrs Yates.

I have to let him go, she told herself for the thousandth time.

Oh Lord, let me do it gently and with kindness. Guide my path. Show me Your Divine Plan. She prayed with heartfelt emotion in that peaceful little room, knowing that every prayer was always heard and an answer always given.

Thirty-four

Hannah Gleeson put on her best pure wool coat – a present from her daughter, before the bowsie husband had deserted her – her red felt hat and her black gloves. She dabbed powder on her cheeks, reddened her lips with Max Factor lipstick, squirted Lily of the Valley perfume on her neck and wrists and stood back to admire herself in the mirror.

She was pleased with what she saw. She looked every inch a lady, she thought approvingly as she stepped into her good Sunday shoes. The black patent ones, all shiny and bright.

Today was an important day. She wanted to look her best. And she did look her best. She'd come back from a winter week in Spain where the sun had shone on her, even though it had rained cats and dogs here at home, she'd been told. Winning five thousand pounds on a Prize Bond she'd held for over twenty years had been the greatest occasion of her life. She still had four thousand left, even after giving her daughter and herself the week away.

But something almost as good had happened to her two days before she won the money. Something as unexpected as it was welcome. The answer to prayer. A cross taken from her.

Hannah smiled at herself, pleased that her perm had taken so well. She was going visiting and she looked every *inch* a lady, she told herself, reassuringly, once again.

'Yeu won't look down yer high and mighty nose on me, madam,' she declared aloud. 'The time has come for me to give yeu a piece of my mind, yeu little ould nettle. Yeu bould ould rip! And if it gives yeu another heart attack it will be good enough for yeu. And I won't be savin' yer life either.'

Raising her chin, Hannah picked up her new shiny patent bag that she'd bought in Spain to match her shoes and marched out of her bedroom, the light of battle in her bright blue eyes.

Sarah sipped her cup of tea and nibbled daintily at a biscuit. She was feeling stronger today. The hairdresser had come yesterday and set her hair and Richard had bought her a new bedjacket that looked most fetching. It was soft pink angora wool and she was very pleased with it. He'd told her that he'd picked it himself. She knew that wife of his hadn't. She was off down at a health farm, spending all his hard-earned money. Richard had told her that she had gone with friends.

Boozing friends, no doubt. Sarah sniffed. They were most likely up to their tonsils in drink. Once an alcoholic always an alcoholic, in Sarah's eyes. She'd never believed that Caroline was on the dry. She was glad to know that her despised daughter-in-law was away. She was going to ask Richard to take her out for the day tomorrow. She'd go to Mass in the nuns' chapel downstairs and then have her lunch. Sunday lunch was the best lunch of the week here. Then Richard could collect her.

He could bring her home so that she could check that Mrs Gleeson was cleaning the house properly. And then he could give her tea in his apartment, seeing as that hussy wouldn't be there. Sarah liked the view from Richard's penthouse. She liked looking down on the world.

The maid came to take the tray away. 'A very nice elevenses, dear,' Sarah said graciously. 'But the spoon was stained. Please make sure that I get *clean* cutlery, in future. I've had a very serious heart attack, you know. An infection could kill me.'

Pity it doesn't, the young girl thought glumly as she removed the tray. Matron would be told about the spoon and she'd get a telling-off . . . yet again. And it was all that crabby old bat's fault. She had a good mind to mix Epsom salts in with the sugar and give the old witch a right dose of the scutters.

Sarah, ignorant of planned revenge attacks, flicked on the TV and settled back to enjoy a gardening programme. If only her garden looked as well. Nolan would want to have pruned the roses and put down the polyanthus by now, but he was probably taking it easy while she was away.

She'd be able to check up on that tomorrow. And she'd have stern words with him if everything wasn't up to standard. Gardeners weren't indispensable, she'd warn him. It was good to keep staff on their toes.

The nurse came in and plumped up her pillows and straightened up the bedspread.

'Everything all right, Mrs Yates?' she queried.

'Everything's very nice. Perhaps you might get me the *Irish Times*. I do enjoy the Weekend section.' Sarah smiled sweetly.

'Did you not order one last night?' the nurse asked.

'I wasn't in the humour last night. I didn't think I'd be able for it. But I do feel a little stronger today. I'm not putting you out, dear, am I? Matron has told me to ask for whatever I need.'

'I'll get someone to get one for you.' The nurse's lips tightened. That Yates bitch was the bane of her life.

'Thank you, dear.' Sarah settled back comfortably on her freshly plumped pillows. Being in a nursing home was rather like being in a hotel, she mused. It wasn't at all frightening, like the hospital had been. She was going to make the most of her last few days.

A smart rap on the door startled her.

'Come in,' she quavered. It could be her consultant. It didn't do to sound too hale and hearty.

Hannah Gleeson marched through the door, all dressed up.

Sarah felt a little self-conscious. This was rather unexpected. She would have preferred to have known about her housekeeper's visit in advance.

'Mrs Gleeson, how kind of you to come and visit. I'm afraid I can't talk very long. I'm still quite ill you see. Sit down for a few moments though, seeing as you've taken the trouble to come.' Sarah waved royally at the chair beside the bed.

'I won't sit if yeu don't mind. This isn't a social visit.'

Sarah's head snapped around at her housekeeper's tone. 'I beg your pardon, Mrs Gleeson,' she said sharply.

'Well I don't grant yeu me pardon, yer ladyship.

Yer high and mightiness.' Hannah's broad Dublin tones held nothing but contempt.

Sarah couldn't believe her ears at her house-keeper's impertinence. Before she could say anything, Hannah advanced towards her, a finger wagging.

'I'm here ta tender me resignation. I'm finished working for yeu, thank God and His Holy Mother, because yeu've been a crown of thorns around me head. I've hated every minute I've been stuck in that mausoleum of yours. And yeu,' she advanced at Sarah, who shrank back against the pillows, 'yeu are nuttin' but an ignorant mean ould bitch who wouldn't give yeu the steam of yer piss. Bad scran to yer mother for bringing yeu into the world ta tor-ment the likes a me an' mine. Yeu think yer a lady! Yeu don't know the meaning of the word. Yeu weren't brought up, yeu were dragged up.

'But I'm going ta work for a lady. A real lady and she only lives four doors down the road from yeu. The one yer always giving out about. Mrs O'Donnell.

'I met her on the street one day and we got chat-tin' and in the heel of the hunt she offered me a job and the wages are much better than what I ever got from yeu. So yeu can stick yer job up yer snooty tight little arse, Sarah Yates, and yer airs and graces with it. Airs and *disgraces* would be more like it. Because that's what yeu are. A disgrace. And God help the poor craythur who comes ta take me place.'

With that she threw her set of keys to Sarah's house on the bed, turned on her heel and marched out the door, leaving Sarah grasping her throat in shock. Perhaps she was imagining all of this. Maybe the drugs were causing her to hallucinate. The slam of the door told her she was not imagining anything. Hannah Gleeson had abused and insulted her up to her eyebrows and she on her sickbed. Sarah felt a dizziness overcome her. She picked up her bell and kept her finger pressed firmly on the buzzer.

Hannah Gleeson felt as though a weight had been lifted off her shoulders. And what was even more . . . she had reclaimed her pride. Her dignity.

For years she had suffered Sarah Yates's insults. But she'd finally had the last word. It was the best day of her life. Even better than winning the Prize Bond, Hannah thought in elation, as she walked down the drive of the nursing home without a backward glance.

Thirty-five

'But I thought she was much better. She was in very good form yesterday evening.' Richard was irritated and perplexed as he spoke down the phone to the staff nurse from the nursing home.

'It's just a slight temperature and we've given her a mild sedative. It's nothing to worry about. She'd just be better off not having any visitors this afternoon. I'm not talking about you, of course,' she added comfortingly.

'I'll be in after lunch,' Richard said flatly and hung up.

This was a bloody nuisance. He was fed up to the back teeth visiting Sarah in the nursing home. It took up the whole afternoon or evening, week in, week out.

He'd seen her improving. He'd half expected her to be discharged at the weekend. Once Mrs Gleeson took up full-time work he could scale down his visits to his mother. Where was that woman? he wondered in irritation. He'd spent the whole morning phoning her but there was no answer. He wanted to sort out her new working arrangements. The sooner the better.

He tried again. No luck.

It was raining, a steady downpour that did nothing to improve his humour. The dull greyness of the day oozed into the penthouse like a miasma. He snapped on a lamp in an effort to dispel the gloom. There was nothing that whetted his appetite in the fridge or freezer. He supposed he should go shopping. Lunchtime on Saturday was not the ideal time to go shopping in Superquinn in Sutton. Richard sighed. He couldn't be bothered.

No doubt Caroline was tucking into gourmet light-cal food in Powerscourt Springs, with not a care in the world, he thought resentfully. He paced up and down restlessly. He could work on his briefs, he supposed. The courts had ruled against him in his last three cases. He was losing his touch. He glanced at his briefcase. Sod that, he thought. He couldn't care less if he lost every case from here to kingdom come.

He'd buy the paper, have a sandwich and cup of coffee in the Yacht, go and visit his mother and if the weather improved he might go into town for an hour or so and have dinner somewhere later on.

'Mega exciting life, Yates,' he muttered. When Charles had been alive they'd gone to the theatre, films, art exhibitions, all the city's cultural activities. Caroline had been with them, of course. 'The decoy', she always called herself. He'd had a busy life. He'd been involved in politics. He'd networked actively. These days he couldn't be bothered. The spark and the hunger had gone out of him once Charles had died. Now it didn't matter any more.

Two hours later he stood at his mother's bedside. She was wearing the new pink bedjacket his secretary had chosen for her. He'd lied and told her that he'd picked it himself. She'd been pleased at that.

Her eyes were closed. She looked a little pale. Maybe she was going to snuff it. A treacherous hope flared for a second. It would solve everything for him. He'd leave the damn country and never set foot in it again. And Caroline could go fuck herself, he'd never speak to her again. Deserting him when he needed her most.

Sarah suddenly opened her eyes and impaled him with a laser-like stare. 'Richard you're going to have to find me a new housekeeper. Hannah Gleeson will not be setting foot in my house again.'

'What?' he exclaimed, astonished.

Sarah sat straight up in bed, her eyes bright beads of temper. She didn't look at all like someone who was going to snuff it.

'That woman had the cheek to come in here to me in my sickbed, and give me the greatest mouthful of impudence. I have been treated with *such* disrespect.' Sarah was still livid, despite her sedative.

'But what did she say?' Richard was mystified.

'She told me she was leaving. That O'Donnell woman four doors down from me has offered her a job. And *then* . . .' Sarah inhaled deeply. 'Then she called me such dreadful names. She said I was a crown of thorns around her head. Can you credit that? *I* was a crown of thorns? After all I've done for that woman. I gave her ten pounds extra every Christmas as a bonus.' Sarah was pink with indignation. 'I wouldn't repeat her other vulgarities. I'm well rid of her, Richard. Kindly place an ad in the *Irish Times* and specify highest references only.'

'And what will you do until you get someone new?' Richard couldn't hide his dismay. What on earth had possessed Mrs Gleeson?

'You'll just have to come and stay with me for a week or two. I can get the mini-maids to come twice a week and you can collect something for us from the delicatessen some evenings. You can get some of those nice chicken dishes out of Marks & Spencers and some of those baby potatoes.' Sarah had it all planned.

Richard said nothing. This was a nightmare. His mother was never going to get someone to keep house for her. Who in their right mind would want to work for such a virago? He was up the creek without a paddle.

'Maybe you should sell the house and think of finding a good-quality nursing home to stay in,' he ventured. 'You like this place? And the care is very good.'

'Indeed and it's not,' Sarah snapped. 'I got dirty cutlery today and I was waiting an hour and a half for an *Irish Times*. And I'll thank you not to suggest selling your father's house again. Of course you'd like to wash your hands of me and incarcerate me in a home, wouldn't you? I'm just a nuisance to you now,' Sarah said self-pityingly. 'You never like to be put out.'

'I'm just thinking of you, Mother,' Richard gritted.

'You mean you're just thinking of yourself. Go on. Get out of here. I'd be better off dead.'

'Mother I—'

'Get out,' she screeched.

Her face was contorted with anger, her finger shaking as she pointed to the door. It was very rarely that Sarah lost control. But when she did it was not a pretty sight.

Silently Richard picked up his overcoat. He left the room and didn't look back.

There was nothing he could do or say to salvage the situation. He didn't care any more. Hannah Gleeson had been his one faint hope that there was a glimmer of light at the end of the tunnel. Now that light had been well and truly extinguished.

Sarah wouldn't go into a nursing home. No-one would ever stick working for her. There were no options. No alternatives. Nothing. It was all going to be left to him.

He walked out of the nursing home like a man in a daze. There was *one* thing he could do, he thought despondently, as he switched on the ignition and reversed out of the parking space.

It would be a solution of sorts, he acknowledged grimly. He straightened up the wheels and drove off, noticing as he did so that a glorious vivid rainbow arched across the sky. Richard smiled at the irony of it as he eased into the flow of traffic.

Thirty-six

The cottage had a rustic charm that appealed to Luke. The wood and stonework lent a warm homely air. They'd have to extend up and out but that wouldn't be a problem. He hoped Devlin liked it. He felt that she would. He stepped out into the garden, neglected, overgrown, but nearly a half an acre with massive potential. And the view, even when wreathed in mist and rain, was stunning. On a clear day they'd be able to see as far as Wicklow. It hadn't been raining when he'd driven up here. There'd been a huge rainbow over to the east when he'd set out to view the house but within five minutes of reaching The Summit the mist had closed in again and the rain began to pelt down.

Misty views or not, it was a hot property. Sites like this on Howth Head were few and far between. If Devlin liked it, he'd match any bid.

'I'd like to bring my wife to see it, she's away at the moment,' he told the estate agent who'd shown him the property.

'That's no problem. Just phone me when it suits you and we'll fix a time,' the young man said affably as he locked the door after them.

'I'll do that, so,' Luke agreed.

It was getting dark as he drove down the narrow winding road. Lights twinkled in windows, casting warm shadows. Below him, Dublin glittered through the mist.

He was tempted to leave a message on her mobile. Now that he'd discovered this little gem he wanted her to see it so they could put in an offer as quickly as possible.

She'd be home tomorrow. Time enough until then. He'd warned the estate agent not to let it go until he'd offered for it. His stomach rumbled. He was peckish. He turned right and headed for the harbour. There was a nice seafood restaurant there that he liked. He could have dinner and save himself cooking.

Devlin rang him just as he had ordered his coffee. He moved out to the reception area to talk to her.

'Luke we're having an absolute ball,' she enthused. 'We all had full-body aromatherapy massages today and we're so laid back the thought of putting clothes on over all those lovely oils is just not on, so we're staying in our robes and having dinner sent to the room.' He smiled at the evident pleasure in her voice.

'I've just had a feast of monkfish, but I'm fully dressed.' He laughed.

'Where did you go? Howth?'

'Yeah. I was out and about so I decided to eat out. What's the weather like down in Wicklow?'

'Oh, it's lousy,' Devlin assured him. 'But it's perfect for us, all wrapped up in our robes looking out at it. Winter is a much better time to come to a health farm than summer. We'll have to come down for a weekend before the baby's born. It would be the most divine place for you to relax.'

'Yes, dear.' Luke humoured her. Health farms weren't exactly his cup of tea.

'Oh, here's our dinner. The girls all said hello. I love you. Talk to you tomorrow,' Devlin said hastily.

'Enjoy it. I love you too. Bye.'

Luke put his phone back on his belt. He was delighted Devlin was enjoying herself so much. She sounded rested and relaxed. She was a gas woman, telling him he needed to relax. She was far more driven than he was.

He finished his coffee and ordered another one before paying his bill and setting off for home. The traffic was quite heavy on the Dublin Road, with people going into the city for Saturday-night entertainment.

Ten minutes later he swung right into the apartment complex and saw in surprise that the security gates were open. An ambulance, fire engine, and squad car, all with lights flashing, were clustered in front of one of the garages. What was going on? Luke wondered. Had there been a fire? As he drove nearer he saw with some concern that it was the Yates's garage. He slowed to a halt and got out of the car. A man's body was being placed on a gurney. It was Richard. He was unconscious.

'Move on please, sir. There's nothing you can do here,' a policeman ordered politely.

'This man's a friend of the family. I should contact his wife,' Luke said. 'Is he all right? What is it? A heart attack?' He sniffed the air. There was an awful smell of carbon monoxide. It suddenly hit Luke like a sledgehammer. Richard had tried to top himself.

The gurney was lifted into the ambulance, the doors closed as Luke looked on in shock. Then it was gone, speeding away into the night.

'It would be helpful, sir, if you could contact the lady straight away. And perhaps you would confirm the name and address for me,' the guard said, opening his notebook.

'Yes of course,' Luke responded, dazed, giving the details required. 'What hospital has the ambulance taken him to?'

'The Mater's on call today, sir.'

'OK. I better go and contact Caroline.' Luke felt sick for her. Yet another ordeal for her to endure. Richard could be brain-damaged. How could she leave him after this? She'd always live in fear that he'd try it again.

'Why, God?' He raised his eyes to heaven as he got into the car and drove over to his own block. 'She's such a good, decent person. Why don't you pick on someone your own size for a change?' he demanded angrily.

What was the best way to deal with this? he wondered. It would take too long for him to go down and collect her. Time was of the essence. But he didn't want her driving up to Dublin in turmoil. Devlin had her phone off. She'd only switched it on to call him. There was nothing for it but to ring reception and get Devlin to phone him back.

The receptionist was most helpful when he told her that he needed Devlin to phone him urgently, without Caroline knowing. 'Her husband's had a bit of a turn,' he explained. 'But I don't want her to be upset.'

'Don't worry, I'll get your wife to come to

345

reception on some pretext and she can phone you from the office,' the woman assured him.

It seemed to take for ever, but it was only five minutes before the phone rang and it was Devlin, frantic.

'What's wrong, Luke?'

'Devlin, you've got to get Caroline to the Mater as soon as you can. Richard's been taken there by ambulance. I'll meet you there. Ring me when you get to Cornelscourt and I'll leave home then.'

'What's wrong with him?'

'I don't know.' Luke was evasive.

'I'd better get Caroline to phone the hospital immediately,' Devlin said.

'No, no, don't do that. They won't tell her much over the phone anyway,' Luke said hastily.

'Is he dead, Luke?' Devlin asked, horrified. 'Luke, please tell me what happened.'

There was silence for a minute as Luke struggled to formulate a reply that wasn't a lie.

'I don't know if he's dead. I saw him being taken off in the ambulance. He didn't look good.'

'But did he collapse or what?' Devlin persisted. 'What will I tell Caroline?'

'Tell her that he's taken a turn and been brought to hospital. And if she asks if it's serious, say serious enough. It would be cruel to lead her up the garden path and give her false hope.'

'Oh Luke, he is dead, isn't he? Poor Caroline.' Devlin started to cry. 'You're hiding something from me.'

'Devlin, please don't cry,' Luke said desperately. 'Honest to God, I don't know if he's dead or not.' He took a deep breath. There was no point in hiding the truth from Devlin. It might be better if she knew now, so that she wouldn't get such a shock at the hospital. 'Devlin, he tried to commit suicide. He was taken from the car in his garage suffering from carbon-monoxide poisoning.'

'Oh Jesus, Mary and Joseph,' Devlin whispered. Her knees shook and she had to sit down.

'Poor Richard! Poor Caroline. Oh Luke, this is terrible. This is unbelievable.' She was distraught.

'I know, love. Just get back to Dublin as soon as you can. I want to be with you and Caroline.'

'OK, Luke. We'll get there as quick as we can.'

'Drive carefully. Maybe you or Maggie should drive,' Luke suggested.

'OK. Bye.' Devlin hung up.

Luke pitied her having to tell Caroline such news. He wished from the bottom of his heart that he was with them.

Thirty-seven

Devlin sat, numb, as she tried to digest what Luke had just told her. Richard had attempted suicide! How could he do such a thing? Apart from what he was feeling himself, he must have known what it would do to Caroline.

You don't have time to sit here. Get up. You've to tell Caroline. Time for whys later, the reasoning part of her brain said. Devlin took several deep breaths and stood up. Her heart was galloping. Her mouth was dry. She swallowed.

The girl on reception looked up from her work. Her face fell when she saw Devlin's expression.

'Not good news?'

'No, I'm sorry. We have to get back to Dublin right now. Could you prepare our bill? Put it all on my credit card. We can work it out between us later,' Devlin said hurriedly.

The walk to the room seemed like forever and when she reached the door, she stood uncertainly for a moment. What words would she use? How did you tell your best friend that she was going to get yet another slap in the face from life? And a very vicious slap at that.

She took a deep breath and opened the door.

Maggie and Caroline were laughing together. Both of them looked at her in anticipation. They thought she had gone to reception to change her timetable of treatments for the following day. When she saw the look on Devlin's face Maggie jumped off the bed.

'What's wrong, Dev?' She was at her side in an instant.

'Caroline, we have to go back to Dublin. Luke phoned me—'

'Oh hell! Did Mrs Yates die?' Caroline groaned. 'Did Richard tell him?' She frowned. 'God, you'd think he would have phoned to let me know. Maybe there's a message on my phone. I'll check it.' She got up from the bed and rooted in her bag, looking for the mobile.

Devlin went over and put her arms around her. 'It's not Mrs Yates, Caroline. It's Richard,' she explained gently. 'He's had some sort of a turn. Luke saw him being taken into an ambulance on a stretcher. He's gone to the Mater. Luke's going to meet us there.'

'Is it a heart attack?' Caroline was white-faced and stunned. 'This is terrible. He wouldn't speak to me when I left. He wouldn't make up. I walked out and told him to forget it.' She burst into tears.

'Come on, Caro. Get dressed quick. We'll know more when we get to the hospital.' Maggie took over. She knew by the expression on Devlin's face that worse was to come.

'But did Luke say how he was? Was he conscious?' Caroline asked frantically as she pulled her robe off and began to dress.

'He was unconscious, Luke said.'

'Maybe I should ring the hospital?' Caroline looked questioningly at Maggie.

349

'No!' Devlin said more sharply than she had intended. 'I mean we can do it in the car. We should just get a move on now and get going. I'll help you pack.'

'Caroline, go into the bathroom and wash your face, you can't go into the hospital covered in oils and creams,' Maggie ordered kindly.

'Oh! Oh! Right.' Caroline rubbed her oily face.

'What the fuck is wrong?' Maggie whispered when the *en suite* door closed behind their friend.

'Richard tried to commit suicide in his car. In his garage,' Devlin whispered back.

'I don't believe it!' Maggie's jaw dropped. 'Oh the bastard! The selfish fucker! If he's not dead already he will be by the time I get my hands on him,' she raged.

'Maggie! That's horrible. Poor Richard. Imagine how desperate you'd be to want to do a thing like that!' Devlin protested heatedly.

'Poor Richard my arse! How could he do a thing like that to Caroline? Imagine the guilt trip she's going to go on. She'll never leave him now. He knew exactly what he was doing. The bollix,' Maggie hissed furiously as she threw her clothes into her bag. 'This is just another way of manipulating her, the way he's always done. This is just a play for sympathy. He wouldn't have the guts to do it properly.'

'Luke said that he looked very bad,' Devlin argued, still whispering as she pulled her jeans on.

'Look if he'd wanted to commit suicide he'd have gone somewhere isolated. Not a garage in the middle of an apartment complex where anyone could find him,' Maggie snorted.

This hadn't occurred to Devlin. Her heart lifted.

'Maybe they got him in time, then,' she said hopefully.

Caroline emerged, red-eyed, from the bathroom before Maggie could answer. Devlin's heart went out to her. She put her arms around her.

'Come on,' she said comfortingly. 'Everything will be all right. Do your thing with the Light. Put the Light around him.'

'I've tried,' Caroline gulped. 'Devlin, I'm scared. If anything happens to Richard I don't know how I'll live with myself. He told me that I was self-centred and a typical alcoholic. He said it was always about me, me, me. Maybe he was right. Maybe I didn't support him enough with what was going on with his mother.'

Maggie looked as if she was going to burst when she heard this. Devlin flashed her a warning glance to stay silent.

'We're practically ready to go. I'll drive,' she offered, taking Caroline's bag.

'No I'd prefer to drive myself. It will keep my mind off things,' Caroline said.

'OK. I'll pay the bill. We can sort it later.' Devlin held open the door.

'I'm really sorry to have ruined the weekend,' Caroline apologized tearfully.

'Don't be ridiculous, Caroline. It's not your fault. Come on, let's go,' Maggie said briskly, leading the way.

It took just a couple of minutes for Devlin to settle up and pay by her credit card. Maggie and Caroline had the bags loaded and the engine running when she emerged into the cold damp night.

They left their luxurious haven, lost in their own

thoughts as Caroline drove through the murky mists along the winding country roads. At last they joined the N11 near the Avoca Handweavers, where they had had such a jolly lunch the day before.

Once they got onto the dual carriageway, Caroline put the boot down and sped towards Dublin at ninety miles an hour, while Devlin and Maggie sat silently hoping that she wouldn't crash the car on the greasy roads.

Caroline had never felt so apprehensive in her life. Or so lonely. *Please let him be all right. I'll make it up to him. I won't leave him. I'll do what he wants*, she bargained silently as she sliced through massive puddles enveloping the car in spray. Her mind was a whirl. Was this happening because she had tried to walk away from her marriage? But all her spiritual books had led her to believe that it was wrong to stay where there was no love and growth and positivity. Had she just been applying these beliefs to suit herself?

No! These self-doubts were just fear and ego. It was wrong of her to start blaming herself, she assured herself. She knew in the core of her that she had been taking the right step. There was a reason for everything. There was a reason for all of this. She just couldn't see it yet.

Please give me courage, she prayed silently as the dual carriageway turned into a motorway and she increased the pressure on the accelerator.

Devlin rang Luke at Cornelscourt as arranged. She could see Caroline biting her lip, trying to keep her composure. The nearer they got to the hospital the paler she looked. Devlin felt her stomach tighten and lurch as she wondered what they would be told. She prayed that Luke would be there before them.

He was. Standing in his heavy dark overcoat, the rain plastering his hair to his head, he was waiting for them outside Accident and Emergency.

'Luke, Luke. How's Richard? Is he all right?' Caroline jammed to a halt and jumped out of the car.

'They wouldn't tell me anything, love. Because I'm not related. I'll come in with you now.' Luke put his arms around her.

Devlin and Maggie got out of the car. Luke kissed them both and led them into the antiseptic hall of the A and E. He spoke to a nurse, who looked at Caroline with sympathy and asked them to follow her. Maggie's face fell as they were led into a small side room. Her stomach tightened with dread. She knew what was coming. She'd led people into small side rooms when she was a nurse. And always to prepare them for or tell them the worst. If Richard had been in the ICU, or a ward, they would have been informed.

'He's dead, Maggie, isn't he? That's what they're going to tell us here.' Caroline turned to her friend, uncertainty written all over her face.

'I think so,' she answered quietly. There was no point in lying. Maggie put her arms around her as a chaplain and a staff nurse came into the room.

'I'm very sorry, Mrs Yates,' the chaplain said.

Caroline let out a loud wail. 'Oh no. Oh God, please. Not like this. Don't do this to me.'

'Shush, Caroline. Shush.' Maggie held her tightly. Devlin started to cry. Luke put his arms around his wife.

'What happened to him? He was young. Too young to have a heart attack.' Caroline shook her head in disbelief. 'Maggie, he can't be dead.' She couldn't take it in. Richard wasn't even forty. His mother should be dead. Not him.

The chaplain looked at Luke. 'Mrs Yates . . . Ah—'

Luke shook his head. He walked over to Caroline and took her hand. He eased her down on the small sofa and sat beside her. 'Caroline,' he said gently but firmly. 'Caroline, look at me. Richard didn't have a heart attack. He committed suicide.'

Caroline looked at him uncomprehendingly. 'Committed suicide,' she echoed.

'Yes, love, he inhaled the fumes from his car exhaust.'

'Richard committed *suicide*?' She stared into Luke's kind amber eyes. He nodded gently, stroking her hand.

Caroline felt smothered in darkness. Richard had committed suicide. He'd been driven to take his own life because she had been so selfish as to not help him carry his burdens. She had been so busy standing up for herself and her rights she hadn't seen the despair and emptiness that had lurked behind his coldness and anger. Charles, the one person in the world whom he had truly loved, had died and he'd had to endure the grief of that, silently and alone. She had been a selfish bloody bitch these past few weeks. Caroline flayed herself mercilessly. Now Richard was dead and it was all her fault.

Devlin covered her face and wept. She couldn't bear to watch the pain, and horror and hurt and bewilderment in Caroline's eyes.

Maggie bit her lip, regretting the words she had uttered in anger to Devlin less than two hours ago.

'Luke, Luke. What will I do? It's all my fault.'

Caroline's face crumpled and she collapsed in his arms, sobbing and muttering incoherently. It was all her fault for seeking to let him go. God had taken her at her word.

'It's not your fault. It's no-one's fault,' Luke comforted her, stroking her back as you would a child. He held her close and she clung to him desperately. This couldn't be happening. It was all some terrible nightmare. Richard couldn't be dead. He was in the middle of a family-law case. It was highly intricate.

He wouldn't commit suicide in the middle of a case. It wasn't his way. It was too untidy.

'There must be a mistake. Richard wouldn't leave a case unfinished.' She lifted her tear-stained face from Luke's shoulder.

'Love, there's no mistake and when you're ready you'll have to identify him. You're his next of kin. Then they have to do a post-mortem because of the circumstances of his death,' Luke said quietly.

'Oh! Oh!' Caroline hung her head as his words sank in. Richard really was dead. She was going to have to identify him. She had to face it. She couldn't run away from it. She took a deep breath.

'Will you come with me, Luke?'

'Of course I will. Will we go now?'

She nodded silently.

'This way, Mrs Yates.' The staff nurse led them out.

All Caroline was conscious of, on that long walk to the room where Richard lay cold and still on a gurney, was the pressure and strength of Luke's hand in hers. She gripped it tight and tighter still as she looked down on the face of her dead husband. His eyes were closed, his cheeks a strange waxy colour. His lips bluey-white. There was nothing left of the

355

Richard she knew. Nothing of the Richard with whom she had shared such a turbulent life.

Where was his spirit now, she wondered, hardly able to breathe with grief and regret. Had Charles met him on the threshold of his next great journey? Could he see the whole picture of his life now and know the reasons for everything that had ever happened to him? Was he finally at peace? Had he seen the face of God? Had he felt the most pure and unconditional love that was the birthright of every soul that was ever created?

'Goodbye, Richard. I'm sorry,' she whispered as she traced her finger gently along his cold cheek. 'Be at peace.'

A thought struck her. Deeper dread enveloped her.

'Does his mother know?' she asked Luke.

He shook his head. 'I don't imagine so. Who would know to tell her? No-one would be told until you were. You're the next of kin.'

'She wouldn't want to see me. She wouldn't want to find out that Richard is dead from me,' Caroline fretted as Luke led her from the room.

'Why don't you ring the nursing home and ask them to tell her doctor to break it to her when he considers the time is right. At least she's in the best possible place if she takes a turn or anything,' Luke suggested.

'What am I going to do about the funeral? She might want to arrange it.'

'He was your husband,' Luke pointed out.

'You know the sort of marriage we had, Luke,' Caroline said miserably. 'And anyway, the last thing I want to do is to fight with that woman over Richard's funeral. It would be so unseemly. It would be just like

356

her to die for spite and then I'd have her on my conscience as well.'

'Caroline, this was not your fault. You can't let yourself think like that,' Luke reiterated.

'Oh Luke, if you were in my shoes you wouldn't say that.' Caroline started to cry again.

Luke put his arms around her and held her close, not knowing what to do or say to console her.

'Come on,' he said after a while. 'Let's get you home to bed. You won't have to worry about the funeral for a day or two yet. They won't release the body to you until the post-mortem has been conducted.'

'If the shock of his death doesn't kill her, knowing that he committed suicide might. Sarah will never get over that. She always worried about what the family and neighbours would say. They'll have plenty to talk about now. And so will the crowd in the law library. The gossips will have a field day when the news gets out,' she said bitterly.

'What do you care about any of that, Caroline? Those people know nothing and it's none of their business. Don't give them a second thought,' Luke advised as they reached the room where Devlin and Maggie were waiting.

'You must stay with us for as long as you want, Caroline,' Devlin said. 'Come on home. It's late.'

'I suppose I should ring my dad and the boys, as well as the nursing home.' Caroline tried to sort out her priorities.

'Caroline, there's nothing anyone can do tonight. Why don't you try and get some sleep, and phone people tomorrow,' Maggie suggested.

'Yeah, you're right. It's not going to make any

difference now. But I'll phone the nursing home. I don't want Mrs Yates to say that I kept Richard's death from her,' Caroline said tiredly.

'OK, but we can do that at home,' Devlin said firmly.

'I'll drive your car home, Caroline.' Maggie held out her hand for the keys. Caroline gave them to her without argument. She felt she was in some sort of dank fog. She couldn't think straight, let alone drive a car.

'Maggie, you're welcome to stay the night too if you want. We've loads of room and Terry wasn't expecting you home until tomorrow evening.' Devlin looked hopefully at her friend. Maggie was great in a crisis. She always seemed to know what to do and what to say.

'Of course I'll stay. I'll give Terry a ring just to let him know. Come on, let's get you and Caroline home. It's been a long day.'

None of them could argue with that.

As Caroline walked out into the drizzly cold night she knew the nightmare was just beginning. And a major player in the nightmare would be the mother-in-law from hell.

Thirty-eight

Sarah patted her hair into place and lay back against her pillows ready to receive a visit from her consultant. An unexpected visit, to be sure. He didn't usually call on a Sunday. It must have been after her little turn following that upstart Gleeson's visit. And then of course there was Richard and the upset he'd caused her. Sarah's mouth tightened into a thin line. He was ready to put her into a home, the ungrateful pup. She'd had to ask the nurse for extra sleeping-tablets after that upset.

She could hear Mr Collins's firm brisk footsteps on the lino'd corridor. She recognized his walk. She'd been listening out for it here and in the hospital for weeks. The consultants always had a very decisive confident sort of walk, Mr Collins especially so.

He was rather early. It was only five to eight. Her breakfast tray was still in the room. They really ought to come at a more civilized hour, she thought crossly, as the footsteps drew nearer. Should she close her eyes and pretend to be asleep? She certainly didn't want to give him the false impression that she was as bright as a button. She fluttered her eyelids closed, heard the knock on the door and then the matron's voice calling her name.

Her eyes flew open. Matron, too, on a Sunday. She was getting the treatment. And rightly so, Sarah thought, extremely pleased at this extra bonus.

'Good morning, Matron. Good morning Mr Collins.' She made sure not to sound too bright.

'Good morning, dear. How are you today?' Matron asked.

'Not too bad, Matron. Yesterday wasn't the best of days.' Sarah smiled wanly.

'But a little stronger today?' Matron queried.

'A little,' Sarah agreed.

'Now dear, we want you to be very brave. Mr Collins and I are with you but we have some bad news for you, which I know you wouldn't want us to keep from you any longer.' The matron gripped her hand tightly.

Sarah suddenly felt very frightened.

'What is it?' she whispered and her heart began to pound. She was going to die. They were going to tell her that her illness was terminal.

'It's about Richard—' Matron began.

'Richard!' snapped Sarah, relieved beyond measure that Matron wasn't giving her a death sentence and annoyed that the nun had given her such a fright. Richard was probably in a huff because she'd told him to get out and he wasn't going to visit. She'd been half expecting that, she thought, as she lay back against the pillows.

'I'm afraid Richard died last night,' the matron said gently.

Sarah looked at her uncomprehendingly.

'Did you hear me, dear? Your son died last night. We got the phone call late and decided against waking you. I'm very, very sorry. If there is anything we can do, don't hesitate to ask.'

Sarah looked at the matron and then at her consultant. He had taken her other hand in his. Richard was dead. Her Richard. He couldn't be. It was all a big mistake. She tried to open her mouth to tell them so but she couldn't speak. She tried again. She saw Mr Collins looking at her with concern. She saw his lips moving but she couldn't hear what he was saying. A great roaring in her ears almost deafened her and then blackness engulfed her and she knew no more.

'She's still in a coma then?' Devlin said to Caroline as they drove to the funeral parlour to finalize the arrangements for Richard's funeral.

'Yeah! They don't know if she'll come out of it. It was a massive stroke. It's so ironic. She's alive still, and Richard's dead partly because of her. If she had died after her heart attack Richard would still be alive. He'd be in Boston and he'd be happy,' Caroline said flatly.

'Well, at least you got to make the funeral arrangements,' Devlin murmured.

'And I'm glad of that, Dev,' Caroline said vehemently. 'She would have wanted him buried out in Sutton in the family plot. He'd never have got away from her. This way he'll be as free as a bird with the one he always wanted to be with. And if she comes out of the coma and objects, it will be too late and there'll be nothing she can do about it.'

When Caroline had got the news that her mother-in-law had suffered a stroke on hearing the news of Richard's death, she had decided there and then to take charge of the funeral arrangements despite what any of the Yates relatives might say.

Once Richard's body was released for burial she had arranged for him to be cremated in Glasnevin. She knew if Sarah had been conscious she would have freaked.

Sarah didn't believe in cremations, even if the Church now allowed them. If a burial was good enough for the Lord it was good enough for everyone else, she was fond of saying. Sarah would never have allowed Richard to be cremated.

But Caroline knew exactly what she was going to do with his ashes. She was going to mix them with the tiny container of ashes that Richard had kept after he had scattered the rest of them on Killiney Hill as Charles had requested. It had been their favourite place. They had walked it's length and breadth many times together. Now they would be there together for eternity. Free and at peace.

She would do this one last thing for Richard, no matter what the objections.

They arrived at the funeral parlour to find a photographer lurking around the building.

Devlin cursed under her breath. But Caroline sat motionless and expressionless as the flash bulb went off in her face.

'Bastards!' Devlin swore as she swerved and drove past. The news of Richard's suicide had been leaked, and reporters and photographers had staked out Caroline's apartment and phoned constantly looking for information.

She had blanked them out completely. Detached herself from everything except the need to arrange a farewell to her husband that would have been everything he wished.

The undertaker was kindness and compassion

personified and Caroline was happy to take advice from him. Between him and Luke they had organized everything and taken much of the burden from her shoulders.

The removal of the remains from the funeral parlour was taking place the following evening, followed by Mass and the cremation service the next day. She would keep going until it was over and then she could collapse in a heap, she promised herself. But she had to keep going. Her greatest fear was that Sarah would revive and raise an objection to the cremation.

Sarah's brother, Richard's uncle Gordon, had told Caroline in no uncertain terms that cremation was against the wishes of the entire Yates family and that he was seriously thinking of taking legal advice on the matter.

'I'll get an injunction to stop the cremation,' he threatened.

'You do that, Gordon, and it will be all over the papers. The family name will be disgraced even more,' Caroline snapped, knowing exactly where the family Achilles' heel was. It was bad enough having news of Richard's suicide and the subsequent nasty conjectures plastered all over the newspapers. It would be an even worse nightmare to give the tabloids the juicy titbit that there was a family row going on about the burial.

Gordon Yates had stomped out of Devlin's apartment red-faced and puffing, but there'd been no more talk of injunctions. And Caroline had felt a fierce sense of triumph on Richard's behalf. She'd heard of injunctions to stop burials and cremations. If Gordon had gone to court she didn't know what would have happened. But her threat had seen him off. Bullies always backed down when confronted.

'The cheek of him, anyway,' she said to Devlin indignantly. 'He never even went in to see Sarah after her heart attack. He was no help to Richard at all. He didn't want to know. So stuff him.'

'He'll be first into the church, you wait and see,' Devlin prophesied. And she was right.

Gordon and his pasty-faced wife and their four pasty-faced sons were seated in the front row of the church when Caroline arrived with her father and brothers in the black limo, having followed Richard's hearse from the funeral parlour.

She was affronted. How dare they!

Without pause she genuflected and slipped into the front seat of the first row on the other side of the aisle. There was an audible gasp from the mourners behind Gordon's pew. Caroline had set the cat among the pigeons. Whom did they go to pay their respects to? The wife or the family?

Caroline couldn't care less. She knew that most of the people in the packed church were there out of a sense of duty or curiosity. Richard had had no close friends. He was respected but not particularly liked in his profession, and the rows full of the *crème de la crème* of Dublin's movers and shakers, with their faces suitably arranged in masks of solemnity, impressed her not one whit.

How sad it was, she thought, as the priest began the prayers, that there were so few in the church who would truly mourn Richard. To go through life and not be mourned at his passing, and to have touched so few lives, was a sad reflection on his own existence.

They thought he had it all. Success. Wealth. Looks.

The irony of it was that he had nothing in the end. Love was all that mattered in life.

None of them could figure out why he had committed suicide. Speculation was rife, money problems being the most eagerly discussed. How they would love revelations of a big cash scandal to top it off.

Let them speculate all they liked. Richard was free of all their pettiness now, Caroline thought, as she looked at the simple teak coffin that she had selected for him.

When the service was over, she sat beside her father and brothers and shook hands with everyone who came to offer their commiserations. It all became a huge blur. The myriad faces and 'I'm sorry for your troubles' ebbed and flowed with an air of unreality.

It was at the funeral Mass the following morning that her composure cracked, when the choir began to sing 'Be Not Afraid', the opening hymn that she had chosen.

Oh Richard! Richard! Not even a note to say goodbye. After all we'd been through together. I deserved that at least. She silently reproached him as she buried her face in her hands and wept. He had been found in his car clutching a photo of Charles. She had put the photo in the coffin with him, on his heart, with his hands crossed.

At least he'd had one great love, she reflected, as she stood silently alone with him for the last time. She had never known the great love of a man. Not the kind of love Luke had for Devlin. And she had never opened her heart and poured her love onto someone, and that was the great grief of her life. It was ironic that Richard had had that kind of love and she hadn't.

Her father patted her on the back awkwardly, and for his sake she tried to compose herself. Time enough for tears and self-pity when she was on her own again. She could weep and wail all she wanted with not a sinner to hear her.

Later, during Holy Communion, the choir sang 'Here I am Lord', and she took some measure of comfort from it. She had kept the readings simple. Luke had done the first reading and a cousin of Richard's the second. She had asked the priest to keep his sermon short and to dwell on the compassion and mercy of God. Devlin and Richard's secretary had brought up the gifts at the offertory. There was no-one else she felt she could ask. She only wanted people who felt some regret at Richard's passing. And Devlin had been truly upset.

The prayers at the end of the Mass gave her great solace, especially when the priest asked the angels to lead Richard to Paradise. She knew in the heart of her that Richard's soul was safe and happy and she tried to hold onto that thought later on in the crematorium, as the red curtains slowly closed behind the coffin as it slid out of sight. She felt some of the tension seep out of her. Richard's funeral had passed without incident.

Sarah was still in a coma.

Again people came to pay their condolences, and then it was time to go to the hotel where she had ordered a buffet lunch for the mourners who had filled the church.

'Look at them stuffing themselves, you'd think they never got a bite. Look at William Casey.' Devlin nudged Caroline and discreetly pointed to where the rotund barrister, who earned a fortune at tribunals, was tucking into a mound of food on his plate. 'I bet he goes up for seconds,' she whispered.

In spite of herself, Caroline chuckled and grinned at Devlin when William did indeed go up for seconds . . . and thirds.

'Look at Sophie Harris,' Maggie murmured, nodding in the direction of the tall, striking businesswoman who was a client of Richard's. 'She's had a face-lift.'

'Do you think so?' whispered Caroline, diverted.

'Look. There's not a crow's-foot in sight and her eyes have that slightly startled look because they're pulled so tight. And she's had a boob job. They're like Twin Peaks,' Maggie scoffed. 'And wearing a mini at her age! She's worse than Madeline Albright.'

'Jealousy'll get you nowhere,' Devlin teased.

'Bitch!' hissed Maggie and the three of them grinned, glad of the light relief to break the awfulness.

That night, when it was all over, Devlin and Caroline sat curled up in the big easy chairs in Devlin's lounge. Luke had gone to bed.

'I should go back to the apartment really. I just dread the thought of it.' Caroline sighed.

'You know, I don't think you should ever go back there. You never liked it from the minute you moved in there. It was always Richard's apartment. Maggie and I will sort out Richard's clothes and belongings. We can give his clothes to a charity shop. We'll file his papers in boxes until you decide what to do with them. If I were you I'd put the apartment on the market next week and close that chapter of your life.'

'It's like running away,' Caroline said.

'No it's not. It's moving on. And now you can do

it freely with nothing to hold you back,' Devlin argued.

'I don't know if I'm up to looking for a place yet. I don't know where to turn, really,' Caroline confessed.

'Well, I know exactly where you're going, Caroline,' Devlin said firmly. 'You, my dear, are getting out of town. You are going to nurse Galway through the Ciara Hanlon débâcle. You are going to move lock, stock, and barrel, office, paper-clips, everything, to Galway until it's ready to open and then you'll have had some breathing space to decide what to do with yourself.'

Caroline stared at her.

'Am I being bossy?' Devlin made a face.

Caroline smiled. 'No. You're being the best friend anyone could have.'

'What do you think? We need someone really good in Galway. Morale is going to be crap. But only if you want to go, Caroline. It just came to me last night in a flash. I thought a complete break from Dublin would be just what you need. And Maggie and I would visit often. And I know you love Galway.'

Caroline sat in the firelight and felt the hairs stand up on the back of her neck. In an instant her intuition urged her to say yes. She had read many times that when something felt very right you should always follow your gut instinct, no matter how off beam the idea seemed.

She heard herself say yes without hesitation.

'Do you mean it? Are you sure?' Devlin's eyes were bright with delight.

'I think it's a wonderful idea,' Caroline said simply. 'You get the most magnificent flashes.' She grinned.

'Now there's no rush. I want you to take time off and relax,' Devlin said hastily. 'Besides, I've to sack Madame Hanlon yet.' She made a wry face.

'Are you sure, Devlin?'

'Look, Caroline, with computers, e-mails, modems, it doesn't matter whether you're in Dublin, Belfast, Galway or the moon. You can do your job anywhere. So who better than you to get Galway up and running and back on track?' Devlin said matter-of-factly. 'Now off to bed with you. It's been a tough few days. You can stay in bed all day tomorrow if you want to. I'm having a lie-in, that's for sure. I'll meander into the office around noon.'

'You're very good to me, Devlin. And Luke. I'll never be able to thank him for all he's done for me.' Tears sprang to her eyes.

'We love you, Caroline. That's what friends are for. And you know something,' she rubbed Caroline's shoulders. 'One day your Luke is going to come. And I'll be there cheering.'

A while later, as she lay in bed, weary to her bones, Caroline pondered Devlin's words. Would she ever be lucky enough to meet a man like Luke?

Such a thing to be thinking and Richard hardly gone to his maker, she chastised herself.

Whatever about finding a man, she knew that going to Galway was the right move for her. As she closed her eyes to drift off to sleep, Caroline had the strongest image of a door closing gently, and another one opening to a place that was full of light.

Thirty-nine

It was a raw icy Sunday. The roads were slippery and Devlin was glad that she wasn't driving. Caroline was driving them to Galway, ten days after Richard's funeral. Her car was packed with clothes and boxes of books and personal possessions. Andrew's car, ahead of them, carried the overflow.

They were on their way to confront Ciara Hanlon, hoping to catch her giving private treatments. If it so happened that she didn't show up, Devlin intended helping Caroline to settle into her new home. They would confront Ciara the next morning.

Caroline would be overseeing the management of Galway City Girl, as well as her own job, from tomorrow onwards. She didn't seem at all worried about the extra workload. She was going to have her own PA, nevertheless she was going to be extremely busy.

Devlin thought ruefully how much she would miss her. It had always been so nice to share the journey into work, or to have coffee together or lunch. It was good looking out the window in the mornings and seeing the light on in Caroline's kitchen. That would have all changed anyway in the next couple of months. Caroline had always intended moving out and Devlin herself would be moving into a new house eventually. She gave a little smile as she thought of the beautiful cottage that Luke had discovered the day Richard committed suicide. It had real character and a magnificent garden and Devlin had fallen in love with it the minute she'd seen it. They were putting an offer in for it.

It was all change, Devlin reflected. For all of them. Galway would be good for Caroline. There were no memories of Richard in Galway. She could start afresh. The rich sea air might put some colour into her grey gaunt cheeks. Devlin had never seen her friend look so haggard.

Her thoughts turned to the ordeal facing her.

It turned out that Ciara had been stealing from City Girl on a regular basis. There was photographic proof of her leaving the building with large items. That had sickened Devlin. Apart from using City Girl's facilities on a Sunday, actually physically robbing her had hardened Devlin to take the course of action she was now following.

Ciara Hanlon was going to get the shock of her life this morning, Devlin thought grimly. The manageress had no idea that Devlin, Caroline and Andrew were paying City Girl a visit. Devlin hoped they caught her red-handed. She wouldn't be able to deny it. It would also be much easier to deal with the confrontation without the rest of the staff knowing that something was going on. If it turned awkward, Devlin did not want guests and staff to witness a spectacle.

'I wonder will she be there?' she mused.

'I'd imagine so,' Caroline replied as she skirted a pothole.

'You don't have to be there, Caroline,' Devlin said.

'Why not? Staff are my area of responsibility,' Caroline pointed out.

'I know but with everything that's happened—'

'Devlin, the only thing that's kept me sane these past few days is my job. The only way I've been able to cope with my guilt and my sadness is to put it aside for a couple of hours and immerse myself in the plans for operating the residential complex,' Caroline interrupted. 'It was great that we got to see Powerscourt Springs. They have the balance just right and there's a few things I might incorporate in our operation. If you agree, of course.'

'Well, I'm glad work's helping. And of course I'll be interested to see what ideas you come up with, but Caroline, you've got to stop feeling guilty,' Devlin urged. 'Didn't you once say to me when I was asking you why God allows awful things to happen to people, you said that He never interferes in our lives unless we ask and that we all have free choice?'

Caroline was silent for a while. 'That's right,' she agreed eventually. 'We have free choice to do the things we do for good or bad. That was a gift we were given.'

'And so Richard's choice was to commit suicide,' Devlin said quietly.

'Yes. But I could have helped him make a different choice maybe.'

'Caroline, that sounds like spiritual arrogance to me, if you don't mind my saying so,' Devlin retorted. 'You can't take the responsibility of his choice on your shoulders. You're always saying that each of us is on our own path and that's why it's wrong to judge, aren't you?'

'Umm?' Caroline wasn't sure where the point was leading.

'Well, stop judging Richard. And respect his choice,' Devlin said simply. 'His path was his path. Your path is yours. I don't know half as much about this kind of thing as you do, but I bet for you to be blaming yourself for another soul's behaviour is very wrong.'

'That's put me in my place,' Caroline snapped.

'I don't mean it like that, Caro, you know that,' Devlin protested. 'I'm only trying to help.'

'Try and imagine if Luke had committed suicide,' Caroline's tone was sharp. 'Try and imagine how you'd feel then, especially if you were estranged. It's easy for you to sit there and talk about *my* spiritual arrogance . . . if you don't mind my saying so.'

Devlin grimaced. 'I'm sorry, Caroline. I didn't mean to upset you. I was just trying to help. And you're right. I couldn't possibly imagine what you're going through. If anything happened to Luke I'd probably kill myself,' she added unthinkingly. And then realized what she'd said. Her hand flew up to her mouth in horror. *You jackass. What a totally insensitive thing to say*, she thought in dismay.

Caroline turned to look at her. Their eyes met and to Devlin's immense relief her friend burst out laughing.

'Oh, Caroline, I'm so sorry. What a thing to say,' she apologized, mortified.

'Delaney's famous size elevens right in it,' Caroline grinned. 'You should see your face. It's scarlet.'

'I'm mortified,' Devlin admitted, touching her flaming cheeks.

'Don't be silly, Dev. I feel so sorry for people trying to find the right thing to say to me. Poor Olivia couldn't handle it at all. If it wasn't for you and Maggie I would have gone mad. I know Maggie's furious with Richard and I'm glad that she is, in a strange sort of way, because she didn't shell out any empty platitudes, she just said nothing and looked after me. The three of us have never had to put on a façade with each other. So don't start now.'

She gave Devlin a wry smile. 'I never realized I was such a preacher about the spiritual stuff. I'm sorry if I've rammed it down your neck.'

'Oh, I love talking to you about it, Caroline. It makes you look at life with such a different perspective,' Devlin said slowly. 'And I just said those things back to you because I figured you were in such a fog with all that's happened, you forgot them or couldn't see them. It makes such sense to me hearing you say it. I hoped I could do the same for you.'

'It's much easier to read about it and hear people talk about it. But when it comes to the crunch and you have to try and apply it to your own life in a really difficult time like the one I'm going through, it's hard,' Caroline confessed. 'Everything you said is true. And I was judging Richard exactly as you said I was. And I've no business to.'

'Just don't be so hard on yourself,' Devlin said. 'Mind, I'm someone to talk about spiritual arrogance, when I get my hands on Ciara Hanlon God knows what I'll do or say? Why would she pick the path of deceit and thieving?' Devlin wondered. 'It's all terribly complicated, isn't it?'

'You can say that again,' Caroline agreed whole-heartedly, as she geared down to observe the speed limit coming into Galway.

Ciara buttered her toast and sipped her orange juice. She yawned. She was dead tired. She'd been at a very glamorous party the night before and had got off with a fine thing from Malahide. He was a banker, he'd told her. He was staying with friends in Galway for the weekend. He drove a fabulous Jag. His name was Robert McKenna. He was in his thirties and most important . . . single.

He owned his own apartment in the Marina in Malahide. And it was obvious he was very well off. He was impressed when she'd told him that she was the manageress of City Girl. He knew all about Devlin Delaney and her property-developer husband. He thought Devlin was pretty cool with a good business head on her shoulders.

He was also mega impressed when she'd given him an all-over body massage with lashings of oil, before she'd given him the ride of his life.

He was desperate to see her again. But Ciara knew the value of playing hard to get. She'd turned down his invitation to lunch and dinner today. He could drive over from Dublin the following weekend and she might fit him in for dinner on Saturday but he'd have to ring to confirm, she'd told him.

He wasn't used to being treated like that, obviously, and he'd been all over her trying to get her to change her mind and spend Sunday with him, but she'd been resolute. Besides which, she had three clients booked in for appointments.

Thank God they weren't massages, she thought

gratefully, nibbling on a slice of banana. She was whacked. Massages were tiring to give. She had one four-layer facial. One manicure and pedicure. And one eyebrow and eyelash tint and lip and chin wax. Her first appointment was at ten. She'd be home by one thirty. She was going to spend the afternoon in bed and catch up on some much needed rest.

Ciara had no doubts that Robert would phone her. She had long-term plans for him. It would be very handy being involved with a banker when it came time to open her own emporium.

Maybe that time was going to come sooner rather than later. Maybe Robert McKenna would be exactly the step up she needed on the business ladder.

Ciara smiled at her reflection a little later as she applied her make-up carefully. It was extremely important to look well groomed and immaculately made up when dealing with clients. It gave them confidence in you. They felt that they, too, could look that good after a treatment.

Brenda Regan was her first customer. She was a rich, raddled old peahen with suitcases under her eyes. A ten-layer facial wouldn't have any effect on her leather skin, Ciara reflected as she pencilled her eyebrows. Brenda was *so* superior. But she was a hell of a good tipper and she was right up there at the top of the social ladder. Her husband owned a chain of hotels. Brenda was a regular and very valued customer.

Ciara glanced at her watch. Almost nine fifteen. She'd want to get a move on to have the heating on and the towels warming on the radiators to cover Brenda's flabby shoulders. It was just as well she had her private clients to keep her hand in doing treatments. As manageress she never did anything like that. Her work was all administration. She yawned again and looked longingly at her rumpled bed. She'd got precious little sleep in it last night. She was going to work her butt off for the next few hours and make up for it this afternoon.

Andrew lugged Caroline's boxes into the lift of the apartment complex that was to be her new home. He was followed by Devlin and Caroline with their hands full.

'When the cars are unpacked I'll walk over to City Girl and see if Ciara's on the premises. As soon as I see a client go in I'll phone you on the mobile and you can come over and we'll get it over and done with,' Andrew suggested.

'Maybe she won't have booked in clients today,' Devlin ventured.

'Why should today be any different from any other Sunday, Devlin? She'll have a client at ten, as usual. Ten, eleven, twelve, every Sunday morning. That's the pattern that's shown up from surveillance.'

The lift doors slid open and Andrew groaned as he lifted the boxes. He was a slight, skinny man. Physical fitness was not his forte.

'That will give you muscles, Andrew.' Devlin grinned as she unlocked the door to the top-floor apartment.

Caroline looked around in pleasure. 'This is beautiful, Devlin. Look at the view.'

The complex was set on the banks of the Corrib. The wide floor-to-ceiling windows overlooked the weir at the mouth of the river. To the left was the Spanish Arch and the Long Walk that led to City Girl. Luke owned several apartments in the block, including the one that was to be Caroline's home for the next few months.

'It's handy being married to someone in the property business,' Devlin smiled. 'He has places everywhere. You should see the ones he owns in Cork.'

'Belfast is the place to buy now,' Andrew panted as he dropped his load to the floor.

'He has some there too,' Devlin said airily as she laid a bag containing Caroline's shoes on the sofa.

'Let's have a cup of tea before we do anything else,' Caroline suggested.

'OK, you stick the kettle on and I'll bring up the rest of the stuff,' Andrew ordered.

'I won't miss him,' Caroline said dryly as she opened the doors of the well-equipped kitchen cupboards and located cups and saucers.

It was after nine before they had their tea and a Danish. Devlin wasn't really that hungry. She was dreading the ordeal ahead of her. Caroline only ate because she knew that Devlin was watching her eagle-eyed.

'You will look after yourself? And eat in the dining-room, and eat properly,' Devlin warned.

'I will. I'm just not hungry these days. But when I get into a routine I'll be fine.' Caroline rinsed her cup under the tap.

'If you need more personnel, another secretary or whatever, let us know,' Andrew said kindly, making Caroline feel like a heel. He wasn't the worst really.

'I will. Don't worry,' she assured him.

He glanced at his watch. 'I'd better go. I'll call as soon as the client goes in.'

'This is horrible isn't it?' Devlin said twenty minutes later, as they waited for her mobile phone to ring.

Caroline looked up from where she was kneeling, on the bedroom floor, placing underwear into a pine chest of drawers.

'That girl is such an idiot,' she said angrily. 'She had it all and now she's blown it.'

The phone rang, its melodic tone making Devlin almost jump out of her skin, even though she'd been expecting it.

'She's there. And a woman driving a Merc has just gone in. Time to go,' Andrew said firmly.

'OK, we'll be there in a minute.' Devlin clicked off. She felt sick.

'Are you sure you want to come? I'm the employer. It's my business. I don't expect you to, Caroline.' She stood up to go.

'I told you before, staff are my responsibility. Let's get it over and done with.' Caroline picked up her bag.

'I've never sacked anyone before,' Devlin said ruefully as they descended in the lift.

'There's a first time for everything, unfortunately. You've been very lucky, I suppose.' Caroline held open the door of the foyer and a gust of salty sea air chilled them.

'How did she think she could get away with it?' Devlin fretted as she got into Caroline's car for the short drive.

'Let's see what she has to say for herself. It will be

379

interesting, to say the least,' Caroline said calmly as she started up the engine.

Devlin sat tensely, her hands clasped tightly for the couple of minutes they were in the car. Now that the time had finally come to deal with Ciara, she didn't feel at all tough and hard. She heartily wished that she was a million miles away.

Forty

Ciara smoothed cool cleanser over Brenda Regan's face. She lightly massaged the area around her eyes. In the background soothing piano music played on tape. Squalls of rain beat against the window. The room was snug and warm. Ciara stifled a yawn.

A smart rap on the door made her pause in mid-massage. She glanced up, startled.

Who the hell was this? She'd locked the main door.

'Excuse me a moment,' she said calmly to her client. Wiping her hands on one of the fluffy towels she walked over and opened the door.

Caroline Yates was standing outside. Ciara was gobsmacked. What on earth was Caroline Yates doing in Galway? She'd just been widowed. Her rich husband had topped himself. She stepped outside and closed the door of the treatment room behind her.

'How did you get in?' she asked inanely.

'I have keys, Ciara,' Caroline said coolly.

'I'm terribly sorry about your bereavement. It must be very tough.' Ciara spoke in a low respectful tone.

'Thank you. It is,' Caroline said quietly. She changed the subject. 'I'm sure you want to know why I'm here.'

Ciara's brain raced into action. Something was certainly up, judging by her boss's tone and cool demeanour. The best thing to do was to act as though everything was normal.

'I'm giving a treatment at the moment, Caroline,' she said calmly. 'There was some mix-up yesterday and this woman was overbooked so I offered to do her myself today. Overbooking's so sloppy and it gives a bad impression. I wanted to reverse it.'

'Is that right?' Caroline had to admire the younger woman's fast thinking. 'Well, I'm afraid you'll have to discontinue the treatment. You can give us the client's name and address and we'll see that she gets a free treatment next week,' Caroline responded evenly.

'It's a bit awkward, Caroline. Could you give me another twenty minutes?' Ciara said smoothly. But she was beginning to feel extremely uneasy.

'I'm afraid not, Ciara. Please convey our regrets and offer the client the free treatment and follow me down to the office when she's gone,' Caroline instructed crisply.

'Very well.' Ciara was most put out. What the hell was going on? She watched Caroline walk back towards reception. It was imperative that she contact her other two clients and cancel their treatments. Fortunately she had numbers for both of them. Just as well she'd brought her handbag with her mobile phone in it to the treatment room instead of leaving it in her office. That would have been tricky.

'Mrs Regan, so sorry for the interruption. Something's come up and I can't continue the treatment.' Ciara oozed regret as she wiped the cleanser off her client's face.

382

'Oh how annoying,' Brenda Regan pouted. 'And I was enjoying it so much.'

'I know, but I'll tell you what. I'll arrange for you to have a free facial whatever day suits you next week. How about that?'

'I'm very busy next week,' Brenda said petulantly. She sat up and shrugged off the towels.

Oh shut up and get out, Ciara thought agitatedly. 'Well, whenever it suits you,' she pacified.

Brenda got into her blouse and pulled on the lilac jacket of her Michael H. suit.

'I take it I don't have to pay for the *little* you did do?' she said frostily, patting her hair.

'Of course not, Mrs Regan, and I'm *terribly* sorry,' Ciara grovelled as the other woman swept out of the room and down the corridor. Ciara unlocked the main door and let her out. Caroline's car was parked beside Brenda's Merc.

Why she was in Galway, Ciara could not fathom. Unless she had come to get away from all the press hassle in Dublin. Maybe she was spending a few days in the Great Southern. But what did she want in City Girl that had made her come on a Sunday? Ciara was mystified. Perhaps there was a simple explanation. Maybe Caroline had merely gone for a walk and seen the two cars in the car park and the lights on in the building.

She was very pleased with her quick response about Brenda Regan having a treatment because of overbooking. That was inspired, Ciara congratulated herself, as she dialled the manicure and pedicure client to cancel. She was extremely fortunate to reach both women and rearrange their appointments. That was a relief, she thought as she slipped her phone into her bag. One overbooking was a reasonable explanation – if the other pair had arrived it would look a little suspicious.

Taking a deep breath to compose herself, Ciara hesitated outside her office. Should she knock, she wondered briefly.

Definitely not, she decided. After all, it was *her* office. She marched in only to come to a full stop when she saw Devlin, flanked by Caroline and Andrew Dawson, waiting behind her desk.

'Oh!' she exclaimed, flustered. 'What's going on?'

'Perhaps you might care to tell us, Ciara,' Devlin said and her eyes were hard, her tone ice-cold.

'What do you mean, Devlin?' Ciara widened her eyes and feigned innocence but her heart sank.

'Cut the crap, Ciara. We know all about your little Sunday sessions and your private treatments using City Girl stock, and we also know that you've been stealing from stores. Perhaps you'd care to explain.' Devlin stared hard at her.

'There's some mistake—'

'There's no mistake, Ciara.' Andrew tapped a beige file on the desk in front of him. 'We have dates, times, places. We have photographs and we have the figures to prove that you've been running a very profitable little scam for yourself. We've had you under surveillance for quite some time now.'

Ciara paled.

For a moment Devlin felt sorry for her, but then the young woman's face twisted in contempt and she turned to Devlin.

'You put me under surveillance after all I've done for you. After I've worked my butt off for you and this goddamn gold mine of yours. And you begrudged me my little nixers so much that you got someone to spy on me,' she spat.

'Ciara, you were getting very well paid. Over the odds in fact. And doing the odd nixer is a hell of a lot different from defrauding your employers,' Devlin retorted angrily.

'Defrauding your employers,' mimicked Ciara. 'Well fuck you, you rich bitch, sitting on your ass all day long. Swanning around the country in your swanky sports car. And *you*,' she pointed a finger at Caroline. 'Aren't you the lucky one. A rich widow who didn't have to lift a finger to make a fortune. Why should you and her,' she stabbed her finger in Devlin's direction, 'reap all the rewards of our hard work? You don't know what it's like trying to save for a mortgage, knowing that you're going to have to borrow at least a hundred thousand pounds because property has gone up so much. You don't have to shop for clothes in Dunnes Stores because it costs a fortune to keep a car on the road, seeing as I only get so much towards running it from you greedy crowd of fuckers,' Ciara shouted.

Devlin jumped to her feet, incensed. 'How dare you, Ciara Hanlon. How *dare* you speak to Caroline like that. You insensitive little bitch! And how dare you use my success as an excuse to cheat and steal from me?

'I can tell you one thing. You're far better off than I ever was at your age. I know what it was like to be practically penniless. I was a single parent in Ballymun flats. I couldn't even afford to buy clothes in Dunnes Stores, let alone run a car. But I didn't go out and steal from people or blame them for my circumstances. I took responsibility for my life and did something with it. You've been given every chance and opportunity. You've a job and a lifestyle that are the envy of many, but you've ruined it because of greed and jealousy. Whatever I got I worked for and I won't let an avaricious, lying little thief like you rob me blind and expect me to sit there and take it.' She was shaking with anger.

'Right! I'll go then. I resign. Stuff your job. Here's your keys.' Ciara jumped to her feet and flung her bunch of keys on the desk.

'I'm afraid it's not that simple, Ciara,' Andrew said coolly. 'The police would like a word with you. I called them earlier. And they have a warrant to search your house.'

'You've called the police!' Ciara couldn't believe her ears. 'I don't believe you. You're lying! You're just trying to frighten me.'

She turned to Devlin. 'You wouldn't go that far. You wouldn't be that much of a bitch!'

'It's not a question of being a bitch, Ciara,' Devlin snapped. 'We discussed long and hard as to whether we should call in the police. Personally I would have preferred not to. But I have an obligation to protect other employers and also an obligation to you to show you how serious your crimes are. You can't just expect to say "stuff your job" and walk away from what you've done. From what I've just heard it seems that anyone whom you perceive to be rich is a legitimate target, because you feel life owes you more than what you've got. I'm sorry, Ciara, that's not the way it works.'

'Don't you bloody well preach to me, Devlin Delaney. Who the fuck do you think you are? Miss High-and-Bloody-Mighty. You can go and get lost.

I'm getting out of here now and you can't stop me,' Ciara's voice was high and shrill. She ran from the office, down the hall and with trembling fingers unlatched the door. Andrew followed with the folder. He had seen the squad car out in the car park.

Ciara saw him coming and hurried out the door intent on getting to her car, only to come to a halt when she saw the two uniformed guards approaching.

'Oh fuck,' she muttered. There was nowhere to turn.

'Come along Ciara.' Andrew placed a firm hand on her wrist as the guards came abreast of them.

'Here's the file that I spoke to you about. This is the lady in question,' he told the older of the two guards.

'Very well, sir. Miss, come with us, please, we'd like you to answer a few questions down at the station,' the guard said politely.

Andrew took a white envelope out of his pocket and handed it to the former manageress. 'Devlin suggested I compile a list of solicitors in Galway, you might need to call one if you have none of your own.'

'That was very thoughtful,' sneered Ciara.

'It was, actually, Ciara. Personally I wouldn't have bothered. You don't deserve it and you're not worth the trouble,' Andrew said with contempt.

'Up yours,' Ciara snarled as she was led away.

Devlin and Caroline watched from the office as the squad car sped off.

Devlin was as white as a ghost. 'She was vicious, wasn't she? It was unbelievable. She feels that she's entitled to what she's robbed. Luke was right. She'd just go and do the same thing to someone else if we hadn't called the police. She doesn't think that she's done anything wrong at all.'

'That's the frightening thing,' Caroline remarked. 'She's bright, she's well educated. But she has no conscience about what she's done. Her resentment and greed are so great they've twisted her thinking completely. Life will have some hard lessons to teach her.'

'What a waste,' Devlin sighed as Andrew came back into the room.

'Let's go. Caroline and I will clear out Ciara's belongings tomorrow and go through the books here. I'll go down and check into my hotel and we could meet up around one thirty or so and have a bite to eat.'

'OK,' Caroline agreed. Devlin nodded. She was shattered.

'Come on, Dev, you should rest for a while,' Caroline urged. 'We had an early start.'

They left the building and locked the doors behind them, all of them relieved that the matter was finally at an end. Whatever happened to Ciara was out of their hands now.

It had been the longest, most frightening day of her life. Ciara sat shivering on her bed, numbed and shocked. She'd actually been locked up in a cell and charged by the police. They'd thrown questions at her hour after hour from that bloody file that Andrew Dawson had given them, and then they'd come and taken all the stuff she'd taken from stores and carted it off to the station. And *then* they'd locked her up in a smelly little cubbyhole that had nearly freaked her out.

Fortunately bail had been set, an amount that she could afford, thanks to the solicitor she'd hired. She'd been free to go. And not a minute too soon.

Ciara took a long slug of brandy as she looked at her bulging suitcase. She was finished here, her great plans up in smoke. She had a second cousin in London. She'd take a flight from Shannon tomorrow because come hell or high water, Devlin Delaney was not going to get the better of her. She could stay with her cousin for a day or two until she got a place of her own. She still had a couple of thousand pounds in her bank account. She'd withdraw it from the bank first thing and then drive to Shannon airport and a new life. With her experience in the beauty and leisure business she'd get a job no problem, Ciara thought confidently. She'd have to start from scratch again, that was the only thing. Still, there'd be more opportunities in London than in this kip of a country where the same clique, the exclusive circle, were the only ones who could make it.

She'd start all over again, but unfortunately she'd never be able to come home to rub that bitch Delaney's nose in it. Ciara Hanlon was a wanted woman. A woman on the run!

Later that night as Devlin and Caroline sat in front of the fire in Caroline's new apartment, sipping hot chocolate and eating chocolate biscuits, Caroline turned to her friend.

'I was a bit surprised that you didn't let Andrew challenge Ciara,' she said curiously.

'Oh I was tempted to, believe me,' Devlin admitted. 'But it would have been running away, I'm the boss when it suits me, kind of thing. I didn't want

Andrew to think I couldn't hack it. Or Luke, come to that. But especially Andrew. It does him good to know who's in charge every now and again. I know he thinks he knows better than we do. You've seen him at meetings.' Devlin made a face.

'I've seen him all right. Sure doesn't he think I'm away with the fairies with all my "New Age Claptrap",' Caroline said caustically.

'Do you think that Ciara will ever come to her senses? Or will she always have that huge chip on her shoulder?' Devlin wondered.

'Who knows? Choices and paths and all of that,' Caroline smiled.

'She was a brilliant manageress.'

'Yeah, she was. But if it was going to happen I'm glad it happened before we opened the new wing,' Caroline reflected.

'That will be our fresh start,' Devlin declared firmly.

'Yes, Dev, it will. City Girl's and mine,' Caroline agreed, and for the first time in a long while she felt optimistic.

Forty-one

Where had the time gone, Maggie thought in a panic as she flung a selection of Mr Kipling's tarts, teacakes and cherry buns into her shopping trolley. The Al Shariffs were coming tomorrow and she wasn't one bit organized.

'Have Yourself A Merry Little Christmas' wafted gaily through the store greatly adding to her irritation.

'Piss off,' she muttered, causing an elderly man pushing a trolley adjacent to her to give her a strange look and move off smartly.

So much had happened in the past few weeks. Their trip to Powerscourt Springs. Richard's death and funeral. Caroline moving to Galway. Now the arrival of the Al Shariffs was on top of her and she seemed to have nothing done. Maggie felt utterly overwhelmed. She ticked off biscuits and cakes from her list and headed for the meat counter. Her heart sank when she saw the queue. She'd be here all morning. She'd thought the queues wouldn't be too bad if she went shopping immediately after dropping the kids to school. It looked as though every other mother had had the same idea.

Two trolleyloads later she headed for the

off-licence. Another queue stretched in a long snaky line.

'To hell with this,' she muttered. Terry could call into an off-licence on the way home, she still had to buy a Christmas tree and decorate the house.

She drove home and unpacked the car. Dozens of white plastic bags of shopping filled the hall. Her heart sank. The thought of unpacking everything and finding room for groceries, and filling the fridge was so off-putting, she was tempted to go straight back out again and buy the Christmas tree.

She compromised and packed all the fridge and freezer food away, and then took off to try and find a particularly good and voluminous tree to impress the Al Shariff children.

'Get the biggest one you can find, Mam,' Michael had urged. 'So they can see what a real Irish Christmas tree looks like.' The children were very excited at the impending arrival of the Al Shariffs. Between that and Christmas they were up to ninety and driving Maggie bananas.

Terry was working flat out, or so he told her, so that he could take some holiday. You'd think he was doing her an enormous favour by taking the few days off, when it was all his fault in the first place that the Al Shariffs were spending so long with them. Maggie pondered this resentfully as she went through serried rows of sweet-smelling pine trees, looking for the one that would make Michael proud.

A tall, perfectly shaped specimen caught her eye, and she asked the young lad looking after them to hold it out for her. It was lovely, she had to admit. With a magnificent bushy bottom and a perfect symmetry.

392

'How much?' she asked.

'Thirty pounds, mam.'

'You're joking!' Maggie was horrified. Thirty pounds for a Christmas tree. It was daylight robbery.

'It's a particularly fine tree, mam.' The young fella went into his sales patter.

'Oh just give it to me.' Maggie didn't have time for this. 'Put it in the boot for me and I hope you enjoy your holiday in the Bahamas. I won't be able to afford a holiday after this.'

The young lad laughed. 'And a happy Christmas to you too, mam,' he said cheerily as he swung the tree with effortless ease into the boot of the car.

Unable to see out the rear-view mirror and with the boot of the car hopping up and down, Maggie crawled home at five miles an hour. She was panting and scratched to bits by the time she managed to extract the tree from the boot. The young lad who had sold it to her had made it look so easy, but it was a mighty tree and at one stage Maggie had her arms around it trying to keep it upright and it was like doing a crazy waltz in the driveway as the tree went one way and she hung on grimly trying to straighten it up. Orla Noonan *would* have to be sweeping her garden path, Maggie thought irritably, as she tried to look as though waltzing around her drive with a Christmas tree was the most natural thing in the world.

Orla and Billy had never spoken to them after the 'incident'. But Maggie didn't get hung up on it. It was their loss. To be a friend you had to behave like a friend, and Orla Noonan had never managed that. The children still played on the street together and Maggie was glad of that. At least her neighbours weren't so petty as to bar all contact.

She finally managed to haul the tree into the garage. She'd decorate the rest of the house but Terry could put up the tree, she decided, as she gazed at her scratched hands.

No doubt Alma would have the perfect manicure, she thought wryly. Alma was always creaming her hands and elbows. Maggie was hoping to get her hair cut first thing in the morning to look a bit presentable.

She worked like a Trojan for the rest of the day, putting away the shopping and decorating the house. Normally she enjoyed putting up the Christmas decorations but today she was too harassed. As the tin of snow got blocked for the umpteenth time, as she sprayed icicles on her red-taped decorated porch, she cursed like a trooper and longed to fling it out the window.

'Mam! The porch is MEGA!' Michael enthused when he arrived home from school. His eyes were alight with excitement and pleasure and, for a moment, all her hard work was worth it as he and the girls went from room to room exclaiming with delight over the decorations.

When she actually sat down for a quick cup of coffee after giving the children their dinner, she realized that she wasn't quite as disorganized as she'd thought that morning. The guest-rooms were all ready, beds changed, furniture polished until it gleamed. Her grocery shopping was all done. The house was decorated, apart from the tree. She'd made a dent in her Christmas shopping. All the Al Shariffs' presents had been bought. She'd been so impressed with the gifts in Avoca Handweavers she'd driven down one morning after Richard's funeral and bought all round her. Scented candles, room scenters and pot-pourri were big this year and Maggie had been ruthless, refusing to be sidetracked and ticking names off her list with a vengeance.

She still had her parents' presents to get. Her mother wouldn't thank her for scented candles. She liked Maggie to pick clothes for her, and her father was always happy to get a jumper and a good detective novel.

After she'd got her hair done in the morning she'd take a scorch out to Blanchardstown. Roches Stores would have plenty of clothes that would suit both her parents. She could buy the book in Easons and she could go into Paco and buy something for under the tree for the girls. That would be another few chores off her 'Still to Do' list.

Tonight she had to do her Christmas cards. If she didn't hurry on and write them, her friends and relations might get them in time for New Year. She eyed her laptop, packed neatly in its carrier.

So much for her novel. She was writing in fits and starts, which was very frustrating, and she knew the chance of her getting anything done in the next two weeks was highly unlikely. She was going to miss her deadline for sure, but there was nothing she could do about it, she thought glumly.

Her thoughts turned to the meal she would serve her guests on their arrival. They'd be flying all night with a flight change at Heathrow and their plane got into Dublin at four thirty. Maggie had decided to bring her three to the airport in her car and Terry could go in his. The airport at Christmas time was always spectacularly decorated and the kids were looking forward to the treat with great anticipation.

She'd decided, seeing as it was possibly the one day that she could get away with it, to serve Marks & Spencers chicken korma which was particularly tasty. She'd defrost a couple of cartons and some ready-cooked rice, add some fresh herbs herself and serve a side salad. Alma would never know the difference. It was cheating, she knew, and the old Maggie would never have done it, but times were different and this was the new Maggie. She'd warn Terry to say nothing.

After that it would be all home cooking or eating out. She had several chicken, lamb and steak dishes precooked and frozen so that would make life a little easier, nevertheless she would have to do the full Irish breakfast every morning. Sulaiman was particularly addicted to bacon, sausage and fried brown bread, and could never get enough of it when he was in Ireland. It was just her luck that he didn't practise his dietary laws, she sighed, as she cleared away the dinner dishes and switched on the dishwasher.

The kids were fighting over what to look at on the TV. Michael wanted to watch the five o'clock *Star Trek* on Sky, Mimi wanted to watch MTV. Normally she would have gone in and mediated and sent one of them upstairs to watch the portable in her bedroom but she was too tired to move, and she'd started writing her cards. She let them at it, with the consequence that there was a full-scale battle raging when Terry came home from work minutes later.

'For fuck's sake, Maggie, would you do something with that lot,' her husband snarled as he flung his briefcase down by the door and went to the fridge and poured himself a glass of orange juice.

'You do something with them, they're your

children too for crying out loud. I've done all the grocery shopping, half the Christmas shopping, your family's presents included, and I collected that god-damn tree and decorated the house today and if you're not bloody careful, I'll drive to Galway tomorrow and spend the next two weeks with Caroline and you can deal with the whole shaggin' lot yourself,' Maggie exploded.

Terry's cheeks turned a dull puce with temper. He marched out the door and seconds later she could hear him roaring at the kids. The TV was switched off and they were ordered to their rooms to do their homework. Silence reigned in the Ryan household.

She kept her head down, busy with the cards, while he put his dinner in the microwave and set a tray for himself.

'The tree's in the garage, I couldn't manage it myself. All the lights and decorations are on the land-ing,' she informed him coldly. He ignored her and took his dinner tray into the sitting-room.

'Suit yourself,' she muttered. If he didn't put the tree up it could rot in the garage for all she cared.

Three quarters of an hour later she heard much cursing and swearing as he hauled the tree in from the garage and tried to get it straight in the stand. Maggie grinned. If it fell down on top of him it would be good enough for him. Twenty minutes later he ram-paged into the kitchen. 'Half those bloody lights aren't working. Where's the spare bulbs?'

'You put the lights away last year,' she said calmly. It was the same *every* single year.

'I can't bloody remember.' Terry was working him-self up into a right rage.

'Try the toby jug on the glass cabinet,' Maggie said

sweetly. The spare bulbs had been kept there for donkey's years but he never remembered.

Silence reigned once more in the Ryan household until Terry tripped coming down the stairs and a box of baubles spilled all over the place, some getting trampled underfoot as he slithered to the bottom. A stream of obscenities rent the air.

Maggie threw her eyes up to heaven. Once Christmas was over she'd a good mind to take off to Galway as she'd threatened. Between Terry and the Al Shariffs she'd be lucky not to end up in an asylum.

Forty-two

'Maggie, your hair is gorgeous cut short.' Alma Al Shariff rushed out into Arrivals and swooped on Maggie, enveloping her in a warm embrace as waves of Chanel No 5 wafted into the air. Alma had obviously sprayed herself with perfume after disembarking.

'Terry, my good buddy!' Sulaiman left his luggage trolley and advanced, arms outstretched, to embrace Terry, kissing him on both cheeks.

Dublin airport was pandemonium. There was hardly room to move with the crush of people gathered around Arrivals.

'Terry, Terry!' Alma shrieked and launched herself on him, much to his delight, Maggie noted sourly. Alma was wearing skintight jeans, a black skintight polo that hugged every voluptuous curve, and a pink pashmina shawl. She looked slim, trendy, perfectly made up. A million dollars. Her blonde hair tumbled over her shoulders in the same style that Maggie remembered.

At least I've changed my hairstyle, tumbling curls are so bimboish, Maggie thought childishly, annoyed with herself for her envious reaction to the other woman's slenderness.

'Hi, Maggie!' Sulaiman beamed, greeting her in his attractively accented English. His curly beard tickled her cheek as he kissed her warmly.

Maggie hugged him back. She liked Sulaiman and now that they were here, she was glad to see him. He'd aged, she thought, noting the liberal streaks of grey in his black hair, and the heavy jowls his beard couldn't conceal.

'My God, Maggie,' shrieked Alma. 'Look at the size of those children!' She enveloped each of them in a monster hug, kissing them exaggeratedly, much to Michael's dismay.

'Darlings, come and say hello to the Ryans,' she urged a tall black-haired boy and a pretty blonde younger girl. 'Ali, Noori, say how do you do.'

Behind them a rotund middle-aged woman was struggling to stop parcels falling off one of the heavily laden trolleys. 'You remember Mrs Ling.' Alma smiled at Maggie.

'Hello Mrs Ling, let me help.' Maggie deftly repacked some of the packages and smiled at the Filipino maid.

'Let's get out of here,' Terry urged. 'It's bedlam.'

'You should have seen Heathrow.' Sulaiman threw his eyes up to heaven. 'It was a nightmare from start to finish.'

'I hate that airport. I dread changing terminals,' Alma declared as they pushed their way through the throngs. 'Isn't it lovely the way they have the airport decorated here. It's so nice to be welcomed home. The snowmen are fantastic. The kids were enchanted. I'd love it if it snowed for them. They've never seen snow,' Alma confided to Maggie as they followed their husbands and children.

'Are you not cold, Alma?' Maggie asked curiously. She'd expected the other woman to be wearing her fur.

'Not really, pashminas are really warm and besides I've got thermal long johns and a body suit under the clothes. Sulaiman is going to buy me a new fur coat in the States,' she confided.

Maggie was sorry she'd asked. Long johns and a body suit, and the woman still looked that slim. It was sickening.

'Sorry it's a bit of a trek,' Terry apologized. 'We took the two cars so that the kids could come and parking was a nightmare. We're in block C on different levels, unfortunately. We'll put some of the luggage into Maggie's car and perhaps Mrs Ling could go with her, and we'll follow.'

'Fine, fine.' Sulaiman beamed happily. 'Are we having rashers and sausages for breakfast tomorrow?'

'We are, good buddy, we are,' Terry said expansively, trying to keep his eyes off Alma's slim rounded ass.

'Excellent! I've been looking forward to this since we made our booking.'

'I figured that you'd be tired, so we'll have dinner as soon as we get home and you can go to bed whenever you like,' Maggie suggested.

'That sounds like heaven. And I'm starving. We had meals on all the flights but I just couldn't eat them,' Alma remarked.

Maggie felt like a heel. She should have provided something home-made, she berated herself. But it was too late now. The korma was defrosted and the salad prepared with just the dressing to be added. She'd shove a few garlic breads into the oven. That would add a bit of bulk to the meal.

'Mommy I'm tired,' Noori whinged. 'I don't want to have dinner. I just want to go to bed.'

'That's fine, pet. You can go straight to bed when we get home,' Maggie said sympathetically.

'You can play with my Sindy disco tomorrow if you want to,' Shona offered good-naturedly.

'Sindy's for kids,' Noori said with snooty superiority.

'Oh!' Shona was crestfallen.

Little Madam, Maggie thought crossly. Noori hadn't changed a bit from what Maggie remembered of her.

'I'll play with it with you, Shona,' Mimi said kindly. It was all right for her to call her sister a kid, but not for anyone else to.

Shona's face lit up. 'Thanks Mimi,' she said happily. Shona hero-worshipped her older sister and thought anything she did was cool.

'Here's the car,' Maggie said hastily as they reached the Golf.

'What a small car,' Ali remarked dismissively. 'We have a four-wheel drive for when we go to the desert and a Mercedes for town.'

'How nice for you, Ali, we don't have any deserts here.' Maggie's tone was bright, if a tad brittle. *More's the pity, or I could bury you in one*, she thought silently.

'But you might get to see snow?' Michael chipped in earnestly.

'I'd like that.' Ali's tone changed. 'My parents have promised me that we will see it in America.'

'Well if it comes when you're here we'll build a snowman. My dad builds *mega* snowmen,' Michael assured him.

'And can we throw snowballs?' Noori's superiority vanished.

'You might not like throwing snowballs, Noori,' Mimi said coolly. 'You get wet and there's lots of screaming. You might think it was just for kids.'

Maggie hid a smile. *Good girl, Mimi*, she thought.

Noori flashed Mimi a filthy look and ignored her. 'Mommy when can we get out of this place?' she whined.

'We're going now, darling.' Alma gave an expressive shrug. 'She's exhausted,' she said by way of mitigation.

'I know,' Maggie said. The child had had a very long overnight flight, a change of terminals and another flight. Her whinging was understandable. Maggie was always good at making allowances. They packed the Golf and Terry and the Al Shariffs went off to locate his car. No doubt Ali would be disappointed in that too, even though it was a Saab 95.

The traffic seemed even worse than usual. The congestion at the airport roundabout was chaotic. Poor Mrs Ling sat in the front seat beside Maggie, her eyelids drooping, her head nodding. There was nothing worse than the tiredness of travelling, Maggie thought sympathetically, as she crawled along at a snail's pace.

They didn't do too badly once they got onto the M50 and as soon as Maggie got home she unpacked the boot with Mrs Ling, and immediately turned her attention to dinner. The chicken korma in its attractive serving dish was ready to pop in the microwave, and by the time Terry arrived about ten minutes later an appetizing smell was wafting through the kitchen.

'Your tree is beautiful,' Sulaiman enthused.

'It's a real tree!' Noori's eyes nearly popped out of her head. 'We only have an artificial one.'

Michael looked chuffed. 'And look at our holly and our mistletoe, that's real too.'

'The mistletoe certainly is, Alma.' Terry winked.

Alma giggled and gave a provocative pout. 'It's a long time since I was kissed under the mistletoe.'

'Terry, could you put the dressing on the salad, and open a couple of bottles of wine,' Maggie cut in. If he thought he was going to act the idiot and stand around flirting with Alma while she did all the work he was sadly mistaken. He'd been ogling her from the minute she'd arrived.

'Sure,' he said lightly and winked at Alma again.

'Now we must give out the presents,' Noori proclaimed bossily. 'Mrs Ling, what bag are they in?'

Poor Mrs Ling went rooting and the next ten minutes was bedlam as the Al Shariffs exchanged Christmas gifts with the Ryans and paper and ribbons went everywhere.

Dinner was a lively affair. Sulaiman and Alma ate every scrap with evident enjoyment, and everyone seemed to have got their second wind. Maggie, after her second glass of wine, began to relax. She'd been worrying needlessly about the dinner, she chided herself silently.

The children went off to play with the computer and Mrs Ling, at Maggie's urgings, went to bed. 'We'll put the children to bed,' Maggie said kindly, 'won't we, Alma?'

'Of course we will. We'll all be in bed soon anyway,' Alma agreed.

'Thank you, ma'am,' Mrs Ling murmured and

slipped out of the room in her quiet unobtrusive way.

'We're going to the theatre tomorrow night—'

'And the pub?' Sulaiman enquired eagerly.

'And the pub,' laughed Maggie. 'And then Terry and Sulaiman can go and play golf one morning and you and I can go shopping. We'll bring the kids to Fort Lucan, an adventure centre, one day and the pictures another, and you and I can go into City Girl and have some treatments one morning before you go.' She turned to Alma.

'Lovely.' Alma gave a little wriggle. 'I'll have a full-body massage,' she said huskily, looking directly at Terry.

'Sounds very nice too.' Terry poured her another glass of wine. 'Have some more pavlova,' Maggie urged. *And put on an ounce!*

'No thank you, Maggie. I'm as full as an egg. I shouldn't have eaten any dessert at all.' Alma patted her non-existent tummy. 'I'll be getting fat.'

'Indeed and you won't, Alma,' Terry said gallantly. 'You look very well. Doesn't she, Maggie?'

'Oh, very well,' Maggie agreed politely.

'You look very well yourself, Terry,' Alma flirted.

Terry puffed out his chest. 'I work out as often as I can and play the odd round of golf,' he boasted.

'Suly's getting very flabby,' Alma said tartly, giving her husband an elbow in the stomach. 'You hear that, darling. Terry works out. You haven't worked out in years.'

'I don't have time to. I'm working myself to the bone to try and keep up with your spending,' Sulaiman retorted.

Terry guffawed. 'I know exactly what you mean,' he said chummily, much to Maggie's annoyance.

'Give over, I pay my own way. I'm a best-selling author, you know.'

'I'm never allowed to forget it.' Terry raised his eyebrows to heaven.

'Huh!' Alma glared at her husband. 'You'd think that we were paupers the way you go on,' she snapped.

'We will be, the way *you* go on,' Sulaiman snapped back. Alma bristled.

'Let's get the children to bed and go into the sitting-room and have a brandy,' Maggie suggested diplomatically. 'I forgot to tell you, Devlin's throwing a party in your honour on Saturday night.'

'Oh how wonderful! I adore parties,' Alma exclaimed. 'I'm so looking forward to seeing her. It's great news about her baby. And so sad about poor Caroline. How is she?'

'She's putting one foot in front of the other and getting on with it. It's very difficult for her but she's transferred to Galway City Girl. It's becoming residential, so she's overseeing that,' Maggie explained.

'Such a tragedy though. Did he leave a note? Do they know why?' Alma was dying to hear the gory details.

"No. Richard was depressed. It's one of those things. Let's get the children to bed.' She changed the subject. She had no intention of discussing Caroline or the tragedy with Alma.

'Will she be at the party? I'd like to see her,' Alma asked.

'No. It's a bit soon for her to be going to parties. She's just been bereaved in the most tragic circumstances, after all. Besides she'd have to travel up from Galway and it's a long drive,' Maggie pointed out.

Alma could be so obtuse at times. Imagine thinking that Caroline would even *want* to party at such a time.

'I'll have to get something to wear!' Alma declared.

Sulaiman looked sceptical but said nothing. Alma ignored him. 'Can we go to Brown Thomas? I adore BT's,' she begged.

'Sure. Maybe we could do that on Friday morning and bring the kids to the pictures Friday afternoon, and the guys can go and play golf.' Maggie drained her glass. 'Let's put the kids to bed. Terry, will you put the dishes in the dishwasher and we'll go and settle down for a natter,' she said easily. Terry needn't think that he was getting off scot-free. She was determined that he was going to pull his weight.

Fortunately, after the wine and the brandies, the other couple began to yawn prodigiously and by eleven, when Maggie suggested that they retire, they agreed tiredly. Maggie couldn't believe her luck to be in bed by eleven forty-five. The first day over, only six more to go, she thought drowsily as she drifted into sleep.

Forty-three

By the time Saturday arrived, Maggie was exhausted. She chickened out of Fort Lucan, much to Terry's annoyance.

'You have to come,' he hissed as he tied a knot in a refuse sack. They were on their own in the kitchen. Sulaiman and Alma were getting dressed and Noori and Ali rampaged up and down the stairs playing hide and go seek with Shona.

'Look, I've a load of washing to do. I've to collect your shirts and the rest of the ironing from the cleaners. I've to do a supermarket shop. I want to get tomorrow's lunch prepared, because I'll be drinking at Devlin's party tonight and I'll most likely have a hangover. It won't kill you to go without me. You've been getting off lightly as regards the kids. We took them to the pictures yesterday and to McDonald's. And if that young one asks me once more is it going to snow, I'll freak.' Maggie was at the end of her tether.

'Let Mrs Ling do it!' Terry growled.

'Terry Ryan, I will not! That poor woman has enough to do with those children.' Maggie was scandalized that he'd even consider asking the poor woman to do her housework.

'Oh! OK then!' Terry said with bad grace and stomped out to the shed with the refuse sack. Maggie heard a crash and rushed out into the hall. Pot-pourri lay scattered all over the carpet and the china bowl was smashed into smithereens.

'It was her fault,' Ali said shrilly, pointing to Shona.

'It was not, Ali Al Shariff,' Shona protested indignantly. 'You knocked against the table.'

'But you were chasing me, I was trying to get away from you.'

'Just go and get ready to go out, the pair of you.' Maggie gritted her teeth as she got down on her hands and knees and started picking up the fragments. Mrs Ling hurried to her assistance.

'Let me help, ma'am,' she offered.

'Thank you, Mrs Ling,' Maggie said gratefully, wondering how the woman remained so placid and even-tempered. If she had to take care of Alma and those two wild kids, day in day out, she'd crack up.

'Did you do this, Ali?' Sulaiman appeared at the top of the stairs. He at least chastised the children now and again.

'It was an accident,' sulked Ali. 'It was her fault,' he added spitefully, pointing to Shona, who promptly burst into tears and ran up to her room.

'It's OK, Sulaiman. It's just excitement. Fort Lucan will be the perfect place to get rid of excess energy,' Maggie said lightly.

'It's a pity you can't come. Alma and I would like to take you to lunch.'

'I really need to catch up,' she explained. 'I need to do a shop and collect stuff from the cleaners.'

'How about we take you out to dinner tomorrow

night?' Sulaiman got down on his hands and knees to help.

Maggie smiled at him. 'That would be lovely, Sulaiman. Thank you.' She was very fond of Sulaiman. He was a most generous man, and, to give her her due, Alma shared that trait. It was a shame their marriage seemed as rocky as hers and Terry's. They'd been sniping at each other since they'd arrived. It was uncomfortable.

She and Terry were making an effort and an unspoken truce was in effect.

It was with a huge sigh of relief that she waved them all off eventually. The silence was balm to her soul. She went into the kitchen, made herself a cup of coffee, took a chocolate-covered Kimberly out of the big Christmas biscuit tin, and sat down at the kitchen table and wilted.

Four days gone, only three to go, she comforted herself. And after that, never again. Not that Terry would be asking them to stay for a week again, she grinned. He was beginning to wilt too.

The phone rang. It was Devlin calling for her daily update, wondering how things were going.

'They're driving me nuts, Devlin,' she wailed. 'I hardly have time to pee. I went shopping with Alma yesterday and she must have tried on fifty dresses before finally deciding on the first one she saw. That was after we'd traipsed through every shop in Grafton Street. Then we took the kids to the pictures and Ali thought the film was too childish and moaned his way through it. Noori made herself sick eating M&Ms. They're fighting like cats and dogs with my lot. Alma is prancing around the house in her negligee and Terry is watering at the mouth. I'm telling you, I'd nearly get a novel out of it.' She laughed. If it wasn't for Devlin she'd be lost.

'Look, tonight you won't have to worry about a thing except enjoying yourself, and at least you're having a break from them today. I know you're up to your eyes. But you've passed the halfway mark. It's all downhill from now,' Devlin consoled.

'I know. And I enjoy Alma and Sulaiman's company. It's just a bad time to visit. Miranda Quigley phoned me looking for a delivery date for the manuscript, and it's just driving me crazy that I can't have a good run at it and finish the damned thing.' Maggie sighed.

'It will get done, stop panicking. You might even get a few pages written today.'

'Yeah, if I get myself in gear I just might.' Maggie felt a spurt of adrenaline. 'I'll go and get myself organized. See you around eight.'

'You're taking a taxi, aren't you?' Devlin said.

'I sure am, honey, I intend to get poleaxed,' Maggie informed her hostess.

'Lucky you, I'd love to get tiddly,' Devlin confessed.

'Just think, you're halfway there too,' Maggie soothed. That hadn't been the most tactful thing to say to a pregnant woman on the dry.

'At least the tiredness is gone. That was a killer. Anyway, I'll let you go, Maggs, I've to clear up the kitchen before the caterers come. See you tonight.'

Maggie finished her coffee, tidied up the house and put her washing in the machine. She was at the supermarket an hour later. She raced up and down the aisles and was lucky that the queues weren't as bad as she'd expected.

411

By one thirty Maggie was sitting at her computer, her fingers flying over the keyboard as she made the most of her precious little nugget of time. She was on the closing chapters of her novel, tying up loose ends. She knew where she was going and it was a joy to write, unlike at the beginning of the book when she was much slower, and unsure of what was happening.

She wrote fifteen pages with exhilaration, delighted with herself that she could go to Devlin's party with a clear conscience, knowing that she had worked well. The peace and quiet was a rare treat.

Her family and guests arrived home from Fort Lucan around four, the children bubbling to tell her of all they had done. After a quick cup of coffee she whisked Alma off to Nikki's, where they both had their hair done, and a sense of light-heartedness began to envelop her as she dressed for the party later that evening.

'I'm looking forward to this,' she confided to Terry as she applied her foundation.

'Me too. Devlin and Luke always throw a good bash. It will be nice to get out of the house. The kids are a bit wearing.' Terry poured aftershave onto his hands and smoothed it in to his cheeks. It was Fabergé. Alma had told him she liked the smell of it. *He* liked the smell of her Chanel No 5. She was a dead sexy woman. And the way she wriggled that ass of hers was an occasion of sin, he thought longingly.

'I just hope Alma doesn't get into a discussion about politics,' Maggie lowered her voice 'She's got very trenchant views, hasn't she? I got such an ear-bashing on the way home for some off-the-cuff remark I made. I was sorry I opened my mouth, I can tell you.'

'She argues her point in a very feisty manner.' Terry defended his new heroine.

'Come on, Terry, she rams her opinions down your neck,' Maggie retorted, unimpressed with 'feisty'.

I wished she'd ram her tongue down my neck, he thought, but he just muttered a non-committal 'umm', and carried on with his ablutions.

Maggie applied her eye-shadow with care. She wanted to look her best. Alma was wearing a stunning black off-the-shoulder cocktail dress, the one she'd bought in BT's, so Maggie had decided against wearing a dress, knowing that she couldn't compete in the figure stakes. She was wearing a pair of black trousers that were extremely flattering to her long legs and a royal blue silk top with a deep plunging V at the back. It was understated but very sexy. She intended to wear her highest heels.

'You look nice,' Terry said when she was ready, but she knew that he said it automatically. It meant nothing.

She didn't really care one way or the other whether he thought she looked nice or not. Nor did she care that he was constantly ogling Alma. She merely found his behaviour irritating.

'Thank you,' she said politely. At least the tenuous harmony between them at the moment was better than the bickering they'd been going on with.

Alma lay back into the frothy bubbles of her scented bath. She was looking forward to Devlin's party with great anticipation. Devlin had style and class – her party was sure to be a buzz. Alma enjoyed parties. She loved being the centre of attention and having men dancing attendance on her. It was nice to feel wanted and desired. It made her feel sexy and womanly. She gave a deep sigh and blew a dusting of foam off her nose.

She might as well be a nun for all the sex she'd had this past year, she reflected glumly. Sulaiman was a disaster in bed and he just wouldn't talk about it or go and see a doctor or even take Viagra. When she'd suggested that, he'd freaked.

'You expect me to take drugs. Men have died taking Viagra,' he'd raged. She should have known better. He wouldn't even take an aspirin for a headache. He was a doctor, for God's sake. He prescribed drugs day in, day out. What was his problem?

Alma soaped herself lazily. She was enjoying the break in Ireland. Terry and Maggie had gone to a lot of trouble to make sure their visit was a success. They couldn't do enough for them. Terry was being *so* attentive. He fancied her rotten. He couldn't take his eyes off her and he was always making sexy suggestive remarks, when Sulaiman and Maggie weren't around, of course. It was very gratifying. It was a pity he wasn't living in Saudi any more. She was enjoying their flirtation.

Later, downstairs, Terry poured some drinks while they waited for the taxi. Sulaiman was already sitting on the sofa, all dressed in a lovely grey suit.

He stood up when Maggie entered. 'You look stunning, Maggie,' he complimented her and gallantly kissed her hand.

'Thank you Suly, you look very dashing yourself,' she said gaily, and accepted a gin and tonic from Terry. Moments later, Alma made her entrance. Terry's eyes nearly popped out of his head as he took

414

in the apparition in front of him.

The black cocktail dress moulded every curve like a second skin. The off-the-shoulder neckline emphasized the creamy curve of breasts, the slit in the chiffony skirt showed tantalizing glimpses of black-stockinged thigh when she moved. Her blonde hair curled alluringly over her shoulders. A diamond necklace sparkled at her throat. Alma looked like a Hollywood star.

'Wow!' breathed Terry.

'You look fabulous,' Maggie said as Alma did a twirl.

'Nice dress,' Sulaiman approved.

'Have a drink.' Terry was practically slobbering.

'Thank you, Terry, you look *very* handsome,' Alma purred, accepting her drink. She sat on the arm of the sofa and crossed her legs provocatively. Maggie felt like slapping her. How could she behave so tartily in front of her husband? Poor Sulaiman, she'd done nothing but complain about him since she'd arrived.

That's their problem, not yours. Forget it, she told herself sternly.

'I just want to make sure Mrs Ling knows where to contact us if she needs us.' Maggie got up and headed towards the door.

'Don't fuss, Maggie, she won't need us,' Alma said airily.

'Just in case,' Maggie said firmly.

'Make yourself at home, Mrs Ling. When the children are in bed relax and have whatever you want, won't you,' Maggie told the maid after she'd written down Devlin's phone number and her own mobile number.

'Thank you, ma'am. I will. Have a nice time.'

'We will,' Maggie said cheerfully as the doorbell rang. 'Here's the taxi. Good night, everyone,' she called. The children were playing a new Playstation game that Terry had treated them to. They galloped downstairs to say good night.

'You look lovely, Mammy,' Shona said.

'Are they *real* diamonds?' Mimi asked Alma, round-eyed.

'Yes they are, darling. Do you like them?'

'They're gorgeous,' breathed Mimi. 'You must be very, *very* rich.'

Sulaiman laughed. 'I wish,' he said.

'Come on, rich man, let's go.' Terry patted his friend on the back and they trooped out laughing and looking forward to the revelries of the night ahead.

Forty-four

'Devlin, you look radiant. Congratulations on your wonderful news. Both of you.' Alma embraced Devlin warmly and then kissed Luke. 'Thank you so much for having this party for us. We are having the best time. I'm so glad we're home for Christmas. I'd forgotten how evocative it is. I love hearing all the Christmas carols and songs everywhere I go.'

'Let me take your shawl, Alma. Sulaiman, how are you?' Luke held out his hand and shook the other man's firmly.

The party was in full swing. A hum of gaiety and a buzz of conversation floated out from the lounge. A waitress in a black dress and a little white apron took Sulaiman's coat and Alma's pashmina from Luke, and held out her hand for Maggie's and Terry's coats. Another waitress carrying a tray of champagne glasses came over to them. The golden liquid sparkled and bubbled under the light of the chandelier.

'Oooh, champagne. I adore it.' Alma took a glass and sipped eagerly.

'Maggie?' Devlin urged.

'I will, thank you.' Maggie grinned and took one of the slender flutes.

'No need to ask us,' chuckled Terry as he handed a glass to Sulaiman and took one for himself.

'Come into the lounge,' Devlin invited. 'You know some of the people here. They've been at our summer barbecues.'

'Are the Madigans here?' Sulaiman asked. Andy Madigan was, like him, a kidney specialist. They had a lot in common. Sulaiman was always trying to persuade his Irish colleague to come out to Saudi.

'They are.' Devlin smiled, leading the way. 'And so is Walter Whelan. You beat him at Scrabble at that wild party in Maggie's house a couple of years back.'

'Remember that party! We were all smashed.' Alma giggled.

'Excellent!' Sulaiman's eyes brightened. This was going to be a good night.

They walked into Devlin's sitting-room and Alma gasped. 'Oh Devlin, what a magnificent tree. And what beautiful decorations.'

'The tree was Luke's doing! You should have seen him trying to get it up in the lift. My husband doesn't do things by halves,' she said fondly. 'He brings home half a forest.'

'It's only a twig, girl,' Luke declared with a boyish grin.

'It's a mighty twig!' Maggie murmured in awe.

'Well, you know me, Maggie. I have to outdo the neighbours,' Luke said straight-faced and Maggie burst out laughing. The six-foot tree, adorned with tiny gold lights and dozens of little red and gold bows, was reflected in the big patio doors and massive bevelled mirror over the mantelpiece. The effect was stunning.

'It's a beauty!' Maggie congratulated Luke.

'I know,' he said smugly.

'Andy Madigan!' Sulaiman made a beeline for his colleague and was embraced in a giant bear-hug by the red-bearded six-footer.

'Sulaiman Al Shariff, when are you going to leave that safe little job of yours and come over here and do some cutting-edge stuff?'

'Ha,' scoffed Sulaiman. 'When are you going to be a big boy and leave Mammy's apron strings and come to the desert and sit under starry skies drinking home-made liquor?'

'Sure I can do that on Dollymount strand.' Andy laughed.

'Alma, what a divine dress. Welcome home for Christmas.' Mary Madigan kissed the younger woman warmly. 'Did you know that Wendy Gaffney's gone out to Saudi as a theatre sister?'

'Yes would you believe, I bumped into her in the souk and . . .'

'That's Alma and Sulaiman taken care of,' Devlin murmured out of the side of her mouth, as she put a hand in the small of Maggie's back and propelled her towards the window.

The doorbell rang. 'I'll get it, I know you two are just bursting to have a little natter,' Luke offered.

'I'm going to get a beer, this fizzy stuff does nothing for me.' Terry drained his glass.

'Come with me old son, there's beer, shorts, anything you want.' Luke pointed him in the direction of the bar, set up in the dining-room and staffed by a pixie-faced little waitress.

'Nice waitress,' Terry approved.

'That's Terry taken care of,' Maggie said dryly.

'He'll be off to practice his charms on her. Poor thing.'

'You look fantastic, Maggie,' Devlin eyed her friend up and down. 'You've lost weight.'

'Do you think so?' Maggie was delighted. 'You know they're the three best words in the English language. Better even than "I love you."'

'Depends who's saying the "I love you."' Devlin's eyes strayed towards Luke, who was laughing heartily at something the new arrivals at his side had said.

'Still mad about him after all these years?' Maggie smiled down at her friend.

'I'm so lucky,' Devlin said simply. 'Can you see my bump?' she asked expectantly.

Maggie laughed at the tiny rounded curve of tummy that Devlin was so proud of.

'Dear, if I had a tummy that size I'd be ecstatic,' she said acerbically.

Devlin laughed. 'Ah stop it, you know what I mean.'

'I'm telling you it's a boy! You're carrying to the back.' Maggie had had this conversation a dozen times before.

'Do you really think so? I was huge with Lynn. I waddled!' Devlin gazed down at her little protrusion.

'Definitely!' Maggie said firmly.

'I feel great. That tiredness just vanished. It actually happened the weekend we were away in Powerscourt Springs.' Devlin took an onion tartlet from the canapés tray resting on a side-table and demolished it in two bites.

'It's an awful shame Caroline's not here. It's weird driving past the apartment.' Maggie selected a smoked-salmon-mousse delicacy and munched away.

'At least she's settled into Galway. And she's so busy she doesn't have time to dwell on things too much. She won't come home to Dublin for Christmas. Her father wants her to stay. We want her to stay. But she's adamant. She's staying on her own in Galway. I just don't understand it. If I were in her shoes I'd want to be with my loved ones.' Devlin sighed and bit into a stuffed mushroom.

'She can be as stubborn as a mule sometimes when she gets a notion. But you know Caroline. She's very self-sufficient. She likes solitude.' Maggie went for a tiny portion of crispy duck.

'It seems so lonely. I kind of feel guilty because I asked her to go to Galway.'

'Don't, Dev. It was the best thing you could have done for her,' Maggie said firmly as she licked her fingers. 'For God's sake get these things away from me before I eat the whole tray. It's a great party and thanks a million for having it. It will be the highlight of the visit. I was going to do a small dinner the night before they go but I told Terry we'll have to go to a restaurant. You couldn't have a little soirée in peace with those kids. They'd be up and down whinging and whining, looking for drinks. Looking for stories. It wouldn't be worth it. So we'll eat out. Will you and Luke come?'

'We'd love to. They seem to be in good form. That's a super dress that Alma's wearing,' Devlin remarked.

'Don't talk to me about that dress.' Maggie made a face. 'I've got the blisters on my feet still. Hasn't she a fabulous figure though. I'd give anything to have a figure like that.' Maggie sighed. Alma was perched on the arm of a sofa with her legs crossed to give the best view of her thigh. A cluster of men stood around her, entertaining her. She was like a queen bee.

'She wears her make-up very heavy though. That lip pencil went out with the button boots. Very dragqueeny around the mouth! And that Farah Fawcett blonde hair went out in the Eighties,' Devlin observed.

Maggie snorted. 'You bitch, Delaney. Terry thinks he's died and gone to heaven. She prances downstairs every morning in this black wispy thing that floats around her and shows off her boobs. He's shameless. He just sits there looking at them and of course she's sticking them out all over the place. I don't know how Sulaiman puts up with the way she behaves.'

'Maybe he doesn't care,' Devlin said.

'Oh he does, I think. She told me that he couldn't get it up any more and it's as if she flaunts herself to let him see what he's missing. It's a weird relationship. Almost as weird as me and Terry.' She made a face.

'Things no better?'

'No. The pretence is over. I told you, as soon as I get the book handed in, I'm getting my own room up in the attic,' Maggie said firmly.

'Oh look, here's Janice Sullivan. We're in for a laugh. I'm really glad she could come. She and Alma always get on great at the barbecues. I'd better go and start circulating for a while. I'm being so rude. As soon as your visitors are gone we'll try and have our Christmas lunch. Caroline has to come up to Dublin to sort out some business stuff and she wants to scatter Richard's ashes on Killiney Hill. We'll fix it for then,' Devlin suggested as Janice bore down on them.

'Girls! Wait until I tell you. I don't know if you've

422

heard,' Janice was bursting to tell them some snippet of gossip she'd picked up. 'Paula Walls has left Dan and has gone to live with Norma Kennedy . . . as a *couple*!'

'*What!*'

Devlin and Maggie exclaimed simultaneously. This *was* gossip of the highest order.

'Yes it's true.' Janice was highly satisfied with the impact her bombshell had made. 'Seemingly . . .' She went on to regale her two friends with the steamy details of Dublin's latest society scandal.

It was that sort of party.

By eleven everything was humming along, chat and laughter raising the rafters. A magnificent buffet of hot and cold food had been served and Maggie was delightfully tipsy.

She was having a ball chatting with friends of hers and Devlin's whom she hadn't seen for ages. She was talking to an interior-designer friend of theirs when Sulaiman came up to her, looking extremely agitated.

'Can I interrupt you for a moment, Maggie?' he asked.

'Of course,' she said, surprised. 'Excuse me, Rosie.' She moved away to a quiet corner.

'What's wrong – is everything OK?' Sulaiman's eyes were bright and his cheeks flushed. He'd been drinking quite heavily.

'No, Maggie, everything is not OK,' he said distractedly, his accent becoming more pronounced. 'My wife and your husband are in a room down the hall and they have been there for the past fifteen minutes. I'm going to go in.'

Maggie felt her stomach lurch. She'd hardly

noticed Terry all evening, she'd been too busy enjoying herself.

'You're making a mistake, Sulaiman. I'm sure you are,' she murmured, scanning the room to see if there was any sign of the two. 'Are they in the dining-room?'

'I'm telling you, Maggie, that slut has gone into a room with Terry, I saw them with my own eyes. And he is supposed to be my friend.'

His voice was getting louder.

'Shush, Suly. You must be mistaken,' Maggie said in desperation, sure that Terry wouldn't be so stupid as to go canoodling with Alma at Devlin's party.

'I'm *not* mistaken,' Sulaiman raged. 'And I will prove it to you.' He barrelled down the room towards the door, with Maggie in tow.

'Is everything OK, Maggie?' Luke was at her side. He'd seen Sulaiman's agitated conversation.

'No, Luke. He thinks Alma and Terry are in a room together. He's going to cause a scene,' Maggie whispered as she hurried after Sulaiman.

'This is the room,' Sulaiman announced at the top of his voice and shoved open the door.

Maggie nearly died. Terry was groaning on top of Alma, on the bed, and she had her long legs wrapped tightly around his back.

Sulaiman's face darkened terrifyingly and he made a lunge at Terry.

'You bastard!' he roared.

Alma screamed.

'Hold on now, Sulaiman.' Luke caught the other man.

'Let go of me. Let go of me.' He struggled. But Luke was a powerful man and held him back.

'You slut! You *whore*!' he ranted, beginning to curse in his native tongue.

Terry struggled to get up and rearrange his clothes, his face ashen.

'Don't you call me those names, Sulaiman Al Shariff,' Alma spat as she sat up, tousled and dishevelled.

'What good are you to me? I'm a woman, I have needs. A limp dick is no good to me,' she screeched drunkenly. 'That pathetic floppy little . . . little leek can't give me what I need. I need a real man,' she yelled.

Someone tittered nervously in the background as people gathered to see what was going on.

Sulaiman gave a great roar, shouted something in Urdu and lunged at Alma.

'No, Sulaiman. No! Come on. She's drunk. She doesn't mean it.' Luke manhandled Sulaiman out the door. Curious guests parted to let them through. Devlin stood wide-eyed, with her hands over her mouth in horror. Her eyes met Maggie's.

Maggie stood rooted to the spot. How could Terry humiliate her like this in front of Luke and Devlin and their guests? How could he shame them both and embarrass their best friends?

'You!' she pointed a finger at Alma. 'Don't come back to my house tonight. And *you*!' Her voice dripped with contempt, her eyes were like flints as she regarded her husband. 'Don't make the mistake of thinking that I give a damn who you fuck. She's welcome to you. You can fuck the man in the moon for all I care, but I think you're despicable to do what you've done to a friend. And to do it here in Devlin's and Luke's is as tacky as you are.'

With as much dignity as she could muster, she walked down the hall, followed by Devlin.

'I'm so sorry, Devlin. Just let me get a taxi and get out of here.' She was shaking.

'I'll drive you home. I haven't been drinking. You're not getting a taxi after that shock. God Almighty, I could strangle Terry. The fool!'

Andy and Mary Madigan came up to them. 'Maggie, we'll take Sulaiman home. He can spend the night with us. It might make things easier all round,' Mary said gently.

'That's very kind of you, Mary. Thanks.' Maggie was touched by the other woman's thoughtfulness. 'I'm terribly sorry about what happened.'

'Tsk, it's not your fault, pet. Things will sort themselves out,' Mary said diplomatically.

Luke and Sulaiman were out on the landing beside the lift. The older man was crying, sobbing like a child.

'You heard what she said. I'm not a man. I can't please her. I wish I were dead. I thought Terry Ryan was my friend.'

'These things happen, Sulaiman. There was drink taken. It was a party. It meant nothing, I'm sure.' Luke tried to console his distraught guest.

'Come on, Suly. Come home with us.' Andy took his colleague by the arm. 'Have a good night's sleep. Things will look different in the morning.' He led Sulaiman into the lift and Luke gave a sigh of relief as the doors closed and it began its descent.

'I'll take Alma to my house,' Janice offered.

'That's Paula and Norma knocked off the front page,' Maggie said sheepishly.

'Oh don't be silly, Maggie! This couldn't *possibly*

426

compete with Paula and Norma. You're not in the same league at all,' Janice retorted crisply. 'Chin up,' she said kindly. She went off in search of Alma, who was weeping drunkenly in the bathroom.

'Come on, Alma. You're coming to stay the night with me. You can sleep it off.' Janice rapped smartly on the door and marched in.

'Oh Janice, this is the worst night of my life,' Alma mumbled.

'Nonsense! Come on.'

'I'm going to be sick,' Alma wailed.

'Well throw up in the toilet, Alma,' Janice ordered, turning her around and sticking her head down the loo.

Alma retched miserably.

Good enough for you, thought Maggie unsympathetically as Janice closed the bathroom door. She never wanted to see Alma Al Shariff again.

Forty-five

By the time she got home, Maggie was drained and exhausted. She'd told Terry not to come with her. He was the last person she needed right now.

Devlin had wanted to drive her home but Maggie was adamant. It was too late. Devlin was pregnant. A taxi was fine.

The other guests had started to leave. Terry slipped away after mumbling an abashed apology to Devlin and Luke. Maggie's taxi arrived and she slid into the back seat gratefully. She was stone-cold sober again. Tired as she was, she was too wound up to go to bed, despite the fact that it was almost one a.m. With grim determination she set about packing her guests' bags. She didn't want to see them again. She just wanted them out. There was no question of them remaining in her house for the rest of their stay.

She threw Alma's toiletries into her toilet bag with a vengeance and then packed away her clothes into her suitcase. An hour later, the bed was stripped. The suitcases were in the hall and only the heavy scent of Alma's perfume lingered in the room as mute testament that she had ever been there.

She put the sheets in the washing-machine, switched off the lights and dragged herself up to bed.

Surprisingly, she fell asleep instantly, worn out.

Terry poured a shot from the bottle of whiskey he'd ordered from room service, undid his tie and kicked off his shoes. He lay back in the hotel armchair.

He'd really cocked things up tonight, he thought ruefully. Shagging Alma in Devlin's guest-room had not been a good move, although it had been incredibly exciting until they'd been interrupted.

The woman was hungry for it. There was nothing more satisfying than an eager woman. Now, though, he'd be in the doghouse. Maggie would never forgive him for embarrassing her in front of so many people. And he'd never be able to look Luke and Devlin in the eye.

He'd been lucky to get a room in a hotel at this time of year. Otherwise he'd have had to bunk down in the office. He'd have a nice lie-in in the morning, he decided. There was no point in going home early. The Al Shariffs would have to collect the kids and their luggage. He certainly didn't want to have to meet Sulaiman again. The man would kill him.

Terry felt a stab of shame. Suly was a nice man. It was a pity he'd discovered them. If he hadn't, there'd be no harm done.

Alma had been truly pissed to say the things she'd said. It was an awful thing to do. To take a man's pride away like that. 'Limp dick'. What a slur!

Poor Suly. It was a shame for him. He probably knew full well what he was missing. Alma was a real goer in the sack. Terry sighed. He wasn't at all sorry that he'd had the experience. He was just sorry he'd been caught.

* * *

Alma Al Shariff snored noisily on Janice Sullivan's guest bed. She was as drunk as a skunk. The minute the fresh air had hit her when she'd left Devlin's apartment all she wanted to do was sleep. She'd fallen asleep as soon as she lay down on the bed, wrapped in Janice's quilted dressing-gown. Her sleep was dreamless and untroubled.

Sulaiman Al Shariff cried his eyes out in the Madigans' guest-room. Curled up in a ball in the bed, he dug his fists in his eyes and wept brokenheartedly. He had failed his wife. She had shamed him. When they got back to Saudi from America he was going to divorce her and take the kids to Pakistan. His mother and sister could rear them. Alma was not a fit mother. She would pay the penalty for her betrayal.

Devlin and Luke lay cuddled in each other's arms in the silence of their apartment. The detritus of the party had been cleared away, the caterers and guests long gone.

'Poor Maggie,' sighed Devlin. 'It will be all over Dublin. Terry is such a selfish bastard.'

'And Alma's an almighty bitch. I know she was drunk, but to say those things to her husband in front of people was the lowest of the low.' Luke tightened his arms around her. 'That poor man was shattered. If I hadn't held him back he would have killed one or other of them.'

'Just as well you're good and fit,' Devlin murmured, resting her cheek against his chest.

'It took me all my strength. Sulaiman's no lightweight,' Luke said ruefully.

'It was very kind of Andy and Mary to take him home. And Janice certainly took no nonsense from Alma. Did you see the way she frogmarched her out to the lift?' Devlin giggled.

'Janice is a good egg,' Luke smiled. 'She said to me when she was going, "Luke darling, you throw a great party. I'll never be able to outdo it."'

'I wonder where will they go? They'll hardly get flights on standby at this time of the year.'

'Well, they can't stay at Maggie's, that's for sure.' Luke yawned. 'Go to sleep, wife. I don't know about you but I'm beat. It was a long day.'

Devlin lay in his arms and listened to his low rumbling snores. She could never conceive of Luke betraying her the way Terry had betrayed Maggie.

It was horrible watching her friend's marriage disintegrating. This had been a dreadful year for her two best friends. At least it was nearly over. Maybe things would change for both of them now that, through strange quirks of fate, they were free to move on.

'Maggie, where's Mommy and Dad? And why is all our luggage in the hall?' Noori came scooting downstairs looking extremely perplexed.

'Come and have your breakfast, Noori. You have to leave today. Your parents will collect you.' Maggie pulled out a chair at the kitchen table.

'But I don't want to leave. I want—'

'Eat,' Maggie ordered, putting a bowl of cornflakes in front of her young guest.

'But—'

'Not another word.' Maggie's tone was so grim Noori gulped and began to eat.

'Ah, Mrs Ling,' Maggie greeted the maid. 'There's

431

been a change of plans and you'll be leaving today, if you want to go upstairs and pack after you've had breakfast.'

'Very well, ma'am.' Mrs Ling sat down and calmly buttered some toast. Hers was never to reason why. If her employers wanted to go to Timbuktu she would simply pack her red tartan case and go. While Mrs Ling and the children were having breakfast, Maggie went into the sitting-room and dialled the Little Chef Motel in Swords. They had two rooms available so she booked them provisionally.

Then she rang the Madigans and asked to speak to Sulaiman. He was very subdued.

'Sulaiman, I've booked two rooms in the Little Chef Motel in Swords. They accommodate five people each. It's near the airport if you want to try for an earlier flight to the States. Or you can try yourself for hotel rooms. You might have trouble getting them so near to Christmas. I have all your luggage packed. And the children will be ready and waiting.'

'I'm very sorry about all this, Maggie,' he said miserably. 'You are in the same boat that I'm in.'

'I know, Suly. We just have to get on with it. I'm sorry that you can't finish your stay here.'

'That would be out of the question, of course. Do you know where my wife is?'

'You can call her at this number.' Maggie read out Janice's number and repeated it for him to write down.

'I'll call a taxi and I'll be there within the next hour,' Sulaiman said heavily. 'Thank you, Maggie. Again my apologies.'

'It's not your fault, Suly. Goodbye,' Maggie said sadly and hung up.

Alma groaned as Janice shook her awake. Her head felt as if it were going to explode. Her tongue felt two sizes too large for her mouth, which tasted like sawdust.

'Your husband phoned. He's collecting the children, Mrs Ling and your luggage from Maggie's. He wants you to take a taxi and meet him at the Little Chef Motel in Swords. It's close to the airport,' Janice added helpfully.

'I know where Swords is.' Alma ran her tongue around her teeth and nearly gagged. 'What does he want me to go there for? Why is he collecting the children and our luggage? What am I doing here?'

'Don't you remember last night? Er . . . you and Terry,' Janice said delicately.

'Oh my God.' Hazy memories floated back. Alma put her head in her hands. 'Oh God.' She looked at Janice. 'I guess Maggie won't ever speak to me again.'

'I guess not,' Janice agreed dryly.

'Could you remind me of the worst thing I did?' Alma asked heavily.

'Well, you and Terry were . . . um . . . doing it and Sulaiman and Maggie caught you. And then you cast some rather uncomplimentary aspersions on Sulaiman's . . . er . . . manhood.'

Alma drew a deep breath and winced. 'What was the worst thing I said?'

Janice cleared her throat. 'I . . . er . . . think you made some reference to his "limp dick".' Janice's tone was matter-of-fact.

Alma paled. 'Oh!' she whispered. 'In front of everyone?'

'In front of everyone,' Janice corroborated.

'He'll never forgive me for that,' Alma murmured.

'Possibly not,' Janice said cheerfully. 'Would you like a fry for breakfast?'

Forty-five minutes after his phone call, Sulaiman arrived to collect his family and their luggage. 'Mrs Ling, take the children to the car, please,' he ordered. Ali and Noori were subdued when they heard their father's tone. They followed the maid to the taxi, heads down. They knew something was up.

'We're going directly to the motel. Alma is taking a taxi from Janice's, she'll meet us there. That's all I know. I'm sorry, Maggie.' Tears darkened his eyes. Maggie threw her arms around him, distressed for him.

'She was drunk, Suly, she didn't mean it.'

'Oh yes she did, Maggie. Yes indeed she did. If it wasn't Terry it would have been someone else. I'm going to divorce her and let her go find what I can't give her. I can't forgive the hurt and shame she's brought me. Every time I look at her, I'll remember. I can't live like that.'

'I'm sorry, Sulaiman, I really am. Take care of yourself.' Maggie kissed him on the cheek and watched him leave. He walked like a man who had the weight of the world on his shoulders.

'Why did they have to go, Mam? What's wrong with Sulaiman?' Michael asked her when she walked back into the kitchen.

'They had to get to America sooner than they thought,' Maggie fibbed. 'Sulaiman was upset leaving.'

'And where's Alma?' Mimi wanted to know.

'She didn't feel too good at the party so she stayed

434

the night. She's going to take a taxi to meet the others.'

'She was nice,' said Shona. 'Where's Daddy?'

'He had to go into work.'

'On a Sunday?' Shona was aghast.

Drat! thought Maggie. She'd almost forgotten that it was Sunday. 'The alarm went off,' she lied. 'Quick, if we put our skates on we'll make twelve Mass and we won't have to go tonight. Hurry on and get ready.'

She ran upstairs and had a quick shower. When she was dressed she phoned Terry on his mobile.

'The coast is clear,' she said sarcastically, when he answered. 'Sulaiman and the kids are gone. You're safe to come home. I told the kids that you had to go into work to turn off the alarm. We're going to twelve Mass and then I'm taking them to Eddie Rocket's for lunch. You can get something yourself.'

'Look, Maggie, we have to talk,' Terry said earnestly. 'I was drunk, that's all. I—'

'Terry, I have absolutely nothing to say to you about the matter. I couldn't be bothered. You can do as you please. Go where you like as long as you carry out your responsibilities to the kids. And you'll be sleeping in the guest-room until I get my attic room built.'

'Your attic room?' Terry was mystified.

'As soon as I get my next advance cheque I'm getting a room built in the attic for myself. Our marriage is finished. When our children are reared and on their way I intend to divorce you. Unfortunately that will be a long way away. In the meantime, the less I have to be with you, Terry, the better. Goodbye.'

She clicked off and stared down at the phone.

'Put that in your pipe and smoke it. You did me a

favour, you bastard. You got rid of the Al Shariffs for me. I have three days extra to write,' Maggie muttered as she picked up her bag and her car keys and went down to tell her children that she was treating them to lunch.

Forty-six

It was a glorious winter's day. The sky was a vivid blue. The sun cast prisms of silver light onto the waves that sparkled as far as the eye could see. The Sugar Loaf and Wicklow hills were etched so clearly against the sky Caroline could see the shades of lavender, green and gold of the fields spread like a patchwork quilt across the countryside.

She was alone on Killiney Hill except for a woman walking her dog. It was the week before Christmas. It was hard to believe that Christmas was almost upon them and that her life had changed so radically. Richard was dead. She was a widow. And she was working and living in Galway. All in the space of less than two months.

Sometimes Caroline felt that she was living in a dream. She hugged close the silver urn containing Richard's ashes. Today she was going to let go of all the grief and bitterness and hurt that his death had caused her. Today she was going to set Richard free to be with Charles.

Today was the day that she was going to start afresh. Although at the time she'd been annoyed with her, Devlin had been absolutely right. She had to respect Richard's choice. If she kept immersing herself in guilt and bitterness she would never learn from the experience and never move on.

In her darkest nights after Richard's death she had felt deserted by God. But all the while Devlin's words kept coming back to her and, slowly, the fear and panic and guilt began to ease. It helped that she was up to her eyes at work.

There'd been huge shock when the staff had arrived the morning after Ciara's dismissal to find Devlin, Caroline and Andrew sitting in the office. Devlin had called a staff meeting and told them that Ciara had been dismissed for pilfering and that from now on management would report to Caroline. Ciara's job would be filled after interviews were held. In the meantime, it was business as usual.

The first week had been very unsettling for Caroline. The staff all knew of her tragedy and were awkward with her. But gradually routines were adhered to and the staff found out that Caroline was a very different kettle of fish from Ciara. The former manageress, it seemed, had been somewhat of an autocrat, whereas Caroline preferred teamwork. She initiated regular staff meetings and made sure that they knew her door was open to them with any problems they might have.

The new building was progressing on time. They were still on target for an April opening. After that, Caroline knew she'd have to decide whether to stay in Galway or move back to Dublin. She had put all her business in the hands of her solicitor. Richard had left her everything. The apartment, his law firm, his savings, investments and insurance policies. Overnight, Caroline had become a very wealthy woman. It was something she didn't give a lot of thought to.

Sometime in the future she'd deal with it. In the meantime she was immersed in her work.

Caroline had decided against selling the firm while Sarah was still in a coma. If her mother-in-law came out of it, she'd send her solicitor to meet with her and see what her thoughts were on the matter. Meanwhile, after the shock of Richard's death had sunk in, the partners had absorbed his work and for the foreseeable future the business would continue as normal.

Richard's uncle had pestered her after the funeral to know what her plans were, until Caroline, finally pushed to her limit, had told him to contact her solicitor and to leave her alone.

Galway was such a respite in that respect, Caroline mused, as she watched a green DART train snaking along the tracks towards Bray. No-one knew her. She was anonymous and for the time being that suited her very well.

She took the lid off the urn and looked at the fine grey ash inside. It was hard to believe that this was all that was left of Richard's earthly form.

'Be happy, Richard. Be with Charles for ever. Be with God,' she whispered. She leaned against the railings that protected onlookers from the drop, raised the urn high, and shook the contents in the air to be carried on the breeze. She stood for a long time gazing out to sea until, eventually, the cold made her shiver and she knew it was time to go.

She had done her best for her husband, now it was time to do the best for herself.

She had arranged to meet Devlin and Maggie for lunch. Devlin had filled her in on the 'incident'. She felt terribly sad for Maggie. People envied her.

Thought she had it all. They didn't know the reality of her life.

'Hello, Maggie, are you OK?' she exclaimed when she walked into the small Italian restaurant in Temple Bar.

'I'm fine,' Maggie said stoutly. 'Don't you worry about me. What about you?'

'I'm fine too.' Caroline smiled.

'How did the the . . . how do I put it?' Maggie paused.

'The scattering of the ashes?' Caroline said easily as she slipped into her seat.

'We'd have gone with you, you know,' Devlin interjected firmly.

'I know, Dev. And thank you. It was just something I had to do on my own. And it was all right. I'm really glad I did it. I sent a letter to Mrs Yates, should she ever come out of the coma, trying to explain why I did what I did. But frankly I don't care what she or any of them say. This isn't about any of them. It was about Richard. And who he was and what he was. He's with Charles now and I'm glad. They're free,' Caroline said defiantly.

'Are you sure you wouldn't come and stay with any of us for Christmas?' Devlin urged.

'Honestly, girls, I'd really prefer to stay in Galway and get it over with. It would be much easier for me,' Caroline declared briskly. 'Now let's order lunch.'

Caroline had driven back to Galway that evening feeling that a weight was lifted from her shoulders. She could move on. She was touched by the girls' invitation to spend Christmas with them. But she wanted to be alone. It was the easiest way to get through it.

At the time she'd felt it was the right thing for her to do, but on Christmas Eve she began to wonder if she'd made a big mistake. City Girl had closed at one, the staff excited and looking forward to the break. The building was silent and empty as she made the last checks before locking up.

Devlin would be the only one of the three of them having a good Christmas, she reflected sadly as she walked past the new building which was soon to be roofed. It would be difficult for Maggie but at least she had her children. And Christmas really was for children.

Would she ever have a child of her own? Right now it seemed very unlikely. Out of nowhere it came, that painful grievous thought that brought a lump to her throat and tears to her eyes.

'Oh stop feeling sorry for yourself,' she muttered as she walked along by the sea with her head down, blinking away the tears. She was so distracted she wasn't looking where she was going and she almost collided with a golden retriever on a leash. A tall, lean man in a green anorak was holding the leash.

'Sorry! Sorry, I wasn't looking where I was going,' Caroline apologized.

'That's OK,' the man said and Caroline recognized him.

'Oh! Mr Moran, isn't it? Our landscape gardener.'

'And you're Mrs Yates? We met before, briefly.'

'Yes I remember, I was down here with Devlin a while back.'

Caroline tried to regain her composure.

'And you've been bereaved since then.' His blue eyes were kind. 'I'm very sorry for your troubles, Mrs Yates.' There was such compassion in his voice she hung her head and started to cry again.

'There's a seat over there, perhaps you'd like to sit down,' he said calmly.

Caroline shook her head. 'I'm sorry,' she managed.

'There's nothing to be sorry for. Grief is grief, it comes to us all in one way or another,' he said quietly. He stood almost protectively at her side until she had stopped crying.

'Are you all right now?' He showed no embarrassment or discomfort at her display of emotion.

'It still catches me unawares. And I suppose with it being Christmas and everything.'

'The first one is always the worst.'

Caroline looked at him in surprise.

'My wife died four years ago. She was killed in a car crash the day after her fortieth birthday.'

'I'm sorry, Mr Moran.' Caroline looked into his blue eyes and had the strangest feeling that she knew him from somewhere.

'That's the way it goes.' The man shrugged. 'And the name's Matthew.'

'And mine's Caroline.'

They smiled at each other. His smile changed his features completely. He looked younger, less intense.

'So, are you going to Dublin this evening?' They turned and began to walk towards her apartment, the dog trotting along beside Matthew.

'No. I'm staying in Galway.'

'With friends?'

'No. I don't really know anybody here,' Caroline murmured. 'I just want to get the day over with. Have you family to go to? Children?'

'No, no children. My father's alive still, he lives

about five miles from here. I'll spend Christmas with him,' Matthew said.

'Have a happy one,' Caroline said as they reached his blue Peugeot station wagon.

'You live in the apartments over there, don't you? You don't have too far to go now,' he said diffidently.

She nodded. 'How do you know I live there?' She was curious.

Matthew laughed. 'You get to hear things when you're working around. Galway's not that big.'

Caroline smiled. 'I suppose you're right.'

'I have to get a move on. Take care.' Matthew opened the car door for the dog, raised his hand in casual salute and then he was gone, his car disappearing into the darkness.

Caroline felt better for being in his company. She couldn't explain why. She just did.

Forty-seven

New Year's Eve dawned bright and clear. Caroline lay in bed watching the sun streaming through the window. Her bedroom overlooked the river. The sun's sparkles danced up and down on the waves as it flowed along towards Galway Bay.

It was cold. Caroline snuggled in under the quilt of the double bed and yawned. She might go back to sleep for another snooze. She was dreading today. New Year's Eve had always been so lonely for her. This one would be a thousand times worse.

Christmas Day hadn't been too bad, she'd simply spent the day in bed watching TV. It had passed over her as though she were detached from the frenetic gaiety of it all. She had done a lot of sleeping the few days she'd been off work. She'd been content to do so. Her body obviously needed the rest after all the shocks and changes it had absorbed in the past few months. She yawned again and drifted off to sleep.

When she awoke the second time, the central heating had kicked in and her apartment felt nice and warm. She liked this apartment, she thought, looking around her bedroom with its pine dressing-table and chest of drawers. A large pine wardrobe was crammed with clothes.

She padded out to the sitting-room. A plump buttercup-yellow couch with a thin blue stripe, and two large armchairs in the same fabric, dominated the room. A pine dresser, a bookcase, a TV unit and a nest of tables completed the furnishings. Blue-and-yellow patterned curtains hung at the windows, the walls, a pale cream with the tiniest touch of yellow, lent the room a warm glow.

She had made the place her own with bowls of pot-pourri and scented candles dotted here and there. Her only ornaments, some cherished pieces of Lladro, were all that she had taken from the apartment in Dublin.

Nestled in a small alcove off the sitting-room, a round pine table and six chairs made up her dining area. The apartment was small and compact, but Caroline felt more at home here than she ever had in the big penthouse in Clontarf.

She made herself a cup of coffee and nibbled on a croissant. Later she sat in one of the big comfortable chairs and watched the stunning panorama from her window. She could look across the river to the Claddagh and Galway Bay. She might take up painting in the New Year, it would be a new interest, and she'd never be stuck for views. That was her first New Year's resolution, she decided.

She had just had lunch, around two, and was working on some revised costings for staff salaries when the doorbell rang. Caroline was startled. Who on earth would ring her doorbell on New Year's Eve in Galway?

She hurried to the intercom, picked it up and pressed the button. The screen blurred into view and to her astonishment she saw Matthew Moran standing outside.

'Matthew!' she exclaimed in surprise. 'Come in. I'm the top floor. First door to the right.'

She was standing with the door open when he loped out of the lift a few moments later. He carried two circular containers. 'These are for you for your balcony,' he said.

'Oh!' She was speechless. The gesture, so unexpected, so thoughtful, so caring, touched the core of her. Caroline was not used to the kindness of men.

'Let's put them on the balcony,' Matthew suggested easily.

'Of course.' Caroline hastened to the French doors to unlock them. Matthew laid the containers onto the tiled balcony.

'These are polyanthus.' He indicated a round tub edged with delicate yellow and purple plants. 'The little fellows in the centre are bachelor's buttons.' He nodded at the small red, white and blue flowers. 'And this is a cordyline.' He placed the larger tub with the spiky green plant in the centre of her balcony. 'That will make you think that you're abroad.' He smiled, and Caroline was struck by how genuine his smile was.

'Thank you very, very much, Matthew.' She was overwhelmed.

'Not at all. You're welcome. I planted up a garden for a woman whose husband died, the first year that I was in business. It was the middle of winter. She told me that caring for the shrubs and plants that I

446

put down for her kept her going. The thought of seeing them in flower in the spring was the one thing she focused on to get her through the hard times. I never forgot the excitement of her when she called me to tell me that the first snowdrops were out. So there you go. I'll pot up a few containers with spring flowers for you, to join these lads,' he said matter-of-factly.

'Thanks very much. You're very kind.' Caroline couldn't quite take it in.

'I see you're working,' he noted as he stepped back into the sitting-room.

'I was just doing a few figures. Putting in the time really,' Caroline confessed. 'I hate New Year's Eve.'

'Look on it as just another day,' Matthew advised. 'If you're not too busy I have Goldie down in the car with me. We're going for a walk. You're welcome to come.'

Caroline looked at him, his lean, handsome face and kind blue eyes, and knew that it was no coincidence that Matthew Moran had come into her life. She had just finished reading the book *Anam Cara*, or Soul Friend, by John O'Donohue, in which he described how two souls who have been looking for each other for eternity can meet in the most commonplace way. And when they meet, there is an instant act of recognition. An ancient knowing. On Christmas Eve when she'd bumped into Matthew she'd felt she knew him.

Now she was certain of it. She'd met an Anam Cara. A lightness settled on her soul. She felt a lovely tranquillity.

'I'd love to go for a walk,' Caroline said easily.

Sarah Yates blinked her eyes and blinked again as the brightness of the setting sun slanted in through the window and made her squint. She lay perfectly still, looking around her, trying to figure out where she was. She was in hospital, not the nursing home. She was in a small cubicle. She could see the nurses at their workstation.

Sarah felt terribly weak. She heard a nurse wish another nurse a happy New Year.

New Year! How long had she been here? She was shocked. She tried to remember what had happened to her to cause her to end up in hospital. A distant memory floated closer. Something about Richard. There was something wrong with her son. What was it? Sarah closed her eyes and concentrated hard. Her face contorted with the intensity of trying to remember.

She opened her eyes in horror. Matron had told her that Richard was dead. And worse than that, he'd committed suicide. Her heart began to pound, a tear trickled down her cheek. Her son, her reason for living, her dearest pride and joy, was dead. She was alone.

'Nurse,' she called. 'Nurse!' But all that came out were strange disconnected guttural sounds. Sarah had lost her speech.

'We're very antisocial. We could have gone out. We had enough party invitations, God knows.' Luke smiled down at Devlin, who was resting against him as they lay stretched out on the sofa in front of the fire. The lights from the tree cast a warm, intimate glow.

Devlin yawned. 'I'm whacked,' she murmured.

'It was an early flight home,' Luke conceded. They had flown to Brussels to Devlin's parents the day after Stephen's Day, and stayed a couple of days with them.

Lydia and Gerry had been delighted to see them. They were ecstatic at the news of Devlin's pregnancy and had made such a fuss of her, she was quite overwhelmed. It had been a lovely couple of days, but she was glad to be home and looking forward to sleeping in her own bed.

'It was nice that we had the photo to show your parents.' Luke massaged her shoulders.

'That photo is your pride and joy, isn't it?' Devlin turned her head and smiled at him. He was talking about the photo of the baby they'd got at her scan just before Christmas.

'It's magic.' Luke kissed the top of her head. 'It made the baby very real for me.'

Devlin felt a burst of happiness. It had been truly joyful to see Luke's reaction to the heartbeat and the sight of their little baby in her womb. Watching him experience the miracle of it all, Devlin had been overcome with emotion and burst into tears.

'What's wrong? Why are you crying?' His excitement had turned to concern.

'I'm just crying because I'm so happy. And I'm so glad that you're the father of my baby, because you are going to be a *spectacular* father.' She gulped.

Luke laughed and put his arms around her. 'You're just biased,' he teased, but he had looked at her with such love in his eyes she'd started bawling again, much to her mortification.

A fluttery little ripple tickled her stomach. 'Quick

Luke, feel it. The baby's kicking again,' she said excitedly, guiding his hand down to her tummy, loving the warmth and strength of his hand against her skin.

'I bet it's a boy,' she said. They hadn't asked to know the baby's sex. They wanted a surprise.

'I don't mind what it is. I'm just dying to see it.' Luke was as excited as a child as he felt his baby's energetic little kicks.

'We've had such a wonderful year. Haven't we? As a couple, I mean. I'm not talking about Richard and Ciara Han—'

'Forget her.' Luke put his hand over her mouth.

Devlin wriggled free. 'Imagine her doing a runner, though.'

Luke shrugged. 'Are you really surprised?' he asked.

'No, I suppose going on past behaviour, I'm not,' Devlin agreed.

'I have a surprise for you.' Luke looked down at her.

'What?' Her eyes lit up.

'I'll tell you at midnight.'

'Midnight!' Devlin exclaimed. 'I don't think I can last that long.'

She gave a yawn that nearly ended in lockjaw.

'Well, maybe you're right. I'm bushed myself. Will we go to bed?' Luke yawned too.

'We're a disgrace.' Devlin grinned.

'I know. Imagine going to bed at half ten on a New Year's Eve. We won't tell a sinner.' Luke pushed her up and stood up himself and stretched.

'Am I still going to find out the surprise?' Devlin demanded.

'Close your eyes. And open your hands and see what God will send you,' Luke repeated the old childhood rhyme. She stood expectantly like a child, while he reached down behind the cushions of the sofa and produced a small gift-wrapped box and placed it in her cupped hands.

'God, Luke. I didn't get you a New Year's Eve present,' Devlin said in dismay.

'This is just a once-off,' he said lightly. 'Go on, open it.'

Devlin tore the paper off the box. Luke always gave great presents. They were always so thoughtfully chosen.

She peeled back several layers of tissue paper and gazed in puzzlement at a bunch of keys on a rusty key ring.

'A bunch of keys. You messer, Reilly.' She laughed at the absurdity of it.

'They're not any old keys,' he said indignantly.

Comprehension dawned. 'The house? Did we get the house? I thought there were problems.' Devlin gazed down at the box, stunned.

'There were, but they've been sorted. It's ours. They closed before Christmas but I didn't tell you until everything was settled. I wanted it to be a surprise.'

'It's the best surprise I could have. It's wonderful. We're going to have the best year ever.' Devlin flung her arms around Luke's neck and kissed him joyfully.

Soft music played, candles flickered, the scent of aromatherapy oils wafted around the luxurious bedroom. It was almost midnight. Ciara knelt over the

451

florid heavyset young man in the bed and massaged his back. He was very rich, she comforted herself, as her hands slid over a fat roll of flesh. Very rich and very available. A very rich, available, fat man. A Greek businessman. And he wanted her.

Ciara sighed. This wasn't the way she'd expected to be spending New Year's Eve. Still, she could be in jail, she told herself briskly as she began to massage the back of Fat Boy's legs. She called him Fat Boy in her head. It gave her a sense of control.

She'd stayed with her cousin in Ealing for three nights on her arrival in London and got herself a job and a flat in west London. The beauty salon she worked in was extremely busy. It was like working on a conveyor belt. In – treatment – out, next customer, in – out, all day long. Far from what she was used to. She had no intentions of staying there long. It was much too exhausting. And besides, she was *Management*.

She'd met Fat Boy at a wine bar and they'd got talking. He wore gold everywhere. A gold Rolex. Gold medallions, gold signet rings, gold pinkie rings, gold bracelets. He drove a new Mercedes. She was playing hard to get. String him along and he was hooked. He was a damn sight richer than Luke Reilly and Devlin Delaney, Ciara thought disdainfully. He had oil tankers! He was a relative of a big Greek shipping family. He'd shown her a picture of his villa on Rhodes and his house in Athens. And this plush pad was his London home.

He groaned under her touch. Maybe tonight she should go further, she decided, as she slid her oily hands lightly along his inner thigh. Fat Boy gave a strangled gasp and then a horse-like snort. Ciara smiled. She intended to be Mrs Fat Boy before the New Year was very much older. She'd divorce him after a few years, when she was sure of a decent settlement.

Maggie sat red-eyed and weary at her computer. Her wrists ached, she had a thumping headache but she didn't care. Her fingers flew over the keyboard as she wrote the last chapter of *Betrayal*.

Terry and the children were watching a block-buster movie in the sitting-room. She was in the kitchen. It was the quietest New Year's Eve that she had ever spent. For the last ten years she and Terry had thrown a party for both their families. It had become the norm. 'Maggie's Party'.

On Christmas Eve, fed up to the back teeth with acting happy families, Maggie had informed Terry that she was not having a New Year's Eve party. They could tell the relations on Christmas Day when they went visiting.

He'd been horrified.

'But we always have a party. People refuse invitations to other people's parties to come to ours. We have to have it. It's expected.'

'Well, I'm fed up of people expecting things of me. You have one if you like. I'm having no hand, act or part in it. If you decide to have one, I'm going to Galway to Caroline.'

'I can't have a party on my own. It would look very odd. What would I tell people?'

'Tell them the truth. That you're a shit and our marriage is over. We're only staying together for the kids,' Maggie retorted.

'Smart bitch,' he snapped.

Maggie ignored him and walked out of the kitchen.

'But why aren't you having one, Maggie?' her brother and mother echoed when she told them the news as they gathered in Nelsie's front parlour for elevenses. A Christmas tradition.

'I have to get my book finished. I've missed my deadline. They're hollering for it,' Maggie said calmly.

'But what are we going to do for New Year's Eve?' her sister-in-law demanded.

'Have one of your own,' Maggie suggested sweetly. That soon shut her up.

It had been a difficult Christmas Day for her, but she'd made the effort for the children's sake and to them it had been Christmas as normal with all the attendant excitement.

The next few days, apart from family visits, had been quiet. The children were happy to watch TV and play with their Christmas presents. Maggie sat down to some serious work, pushing herself into the early hours to finish her novel. Her commitment to her readers and her pride in her work wouldn't allow her to give anything less than her best, but there were times when she longed to fling the computer out the window and pack the whole lot in.

The day after the Al Shariffs left, Marcy had phoned her to tell her that she was with a new publishing company and that when Maggie was free of her current contract, she would be a very welcome addition to their stable of authors.

Maggie was flattered. Marcy would only poach authors who she considered to be good. Flattered as she was, though, she'd turned down the offer.

'Once I'm finished with Enterprise, I don't know

if I'll continue writing, Marcy. It's too much pressure. My kids are losing out. I'm losing out. I might write a book at my own pace and *then* sign a contract. I don't know. This book hasn't been a happy experience at all. That's not the way it should be. I want to feel the joy of writing again.'

'You will, Maggie, under the hands of a good editor,' Marcy assured her. Maggie laughed.

'Presumably that's you?'

'Correct,' Marcy agreed. 'I'll get you back on track.'

'I don't think so, Marcy. I've thought about this long and hard. I need to give the time to my kids instead of brushing them off and telling them to be quiet. It's wrong. I'm a mother first and a writer second.'

'I'm disappointed to hear you say that,' Marcy said regretfully. 'You're making great strides in your writing career. Your sales are excellent. The only way you can go is up. When you leave Enterprise, of course,' she added acerbically.

'The only "up" place I'll be going is to the Golden Gates if I don't quit this stress and get a life, Marcy.' Maggie laughed. 'I'll keep in touch.'

'Do that,' said her ex-editor glumly.

Maggie smiled as she typed in the last quotation marks and full stop. She was finished. Finally finished. Enterprise could go whistle for their next one. Although, knowing them, they'd threaten to sue it out of her. Well, they could try, she thought grimly, as she saved her work and began to print out.

This year was for her children. If she could fit in a few pages every day, fine. If she couldn't, tough.

* * *

Alma Al Shariff slipped into the dress that she'd worn to that awful party at Devlin's. It was a pity about the bad memories. But the dress was stunning and she needed to strut her stuff tonight at the college dance. Sulaiman had told her on the plane to New York that he was going to divorce her. He had said it simply and plainly, 'I'm going to divorce you,' and then he had picked up his paper and ignored her for the rest of the long-haul flight. Fortunately Mrs Ling and the children had been in the opposite row. They hadn't heard the pronouncement.

It was essential that Alma meet a new man in the next couple of weeks. A new rich man with all his faculties in order. If he couldn't perform, bye bye. Celibacy was not her thing. Nor was being on her own with hardly any money, which was what would happen once Sulaiman divorced her. Alma sighed deeply. She was scared . . . very scared. But she could never let that show. Neediness and fear made men run very fast . . . in the opposite direction. So tonight she was operating on all thrusters. Alma raised her chin, stuck out her boobs, made sure the slit in her skirt was straight against her thigh and prepared to make her entrance.

Sulaiman Al Shariff downed another whiskey as he waited for his wife to finish preening so they could go to the goddamn faculty party. He was not enjoying America. The pace of life was too fast. The competition was fierce and much was expected of one. He longed to be under the stars in the desert, happy in his own little world. But he would never be happy again. Alma had seen to that. After the divorce came through he'd have to go home to Pakistan so that his mother and sister could look after his children. That would be a big upheaval, one thing in life that Sulaiman hated.

The year ahead couldn't possibly be worse than the one that was ending tonight, he mused.

That had been the mother of all years.

Forty-eight

Galway City Girl was buzzing. Devlin was hosting the party of parties, a huge luncheon to celebrate the grand opening of the first City Girl health farm. On time and just slightly over budget.

The rich, the famous, the movers and shakers had been invited by the PR firm Caroline had chosen to promote the new complex. A pianist played soft music. Waitresses moved between guests, offering selections of delicious canapés. Sun spilled through shining windows over the polished wooden floors. The bay windows overlooked a frothy blue sea. Guests stood mesmerized by the views.

Champagne flowed.

'Congratulations, Devlin. It's beautiful. The building is magnificent.' Maggie hugged her friend warmly. 'I wish you the very best of luck with it. You and Caroline have done a brilliant job.'

'Thanks, Maggie.' Devlin hugged her back. 'I'm chuffed with it. It's turned out better than I ever expected. Talking of Caroline, where is she?' Devlin scanned the huge throng but couldn't see her friend.

'She's out there.' Maggie grinned. 'With your land-scaper. Look.' She nodded towards the window.

Outside, Caroline was looking at something in a bed of daffodils that Matthew was pointing out to her. She was laughing.

'There's something going on there,' Maggie declared.

'What? Caroline and Matthew?' Devlin's jaw dropped.

'Have you not noticed them together? They're very comfortable with each other. They seem to have a great bond. She's very happy in his company,' Maggie observed.

'Good Lord!' Devlin had been so engrossed in sorting out the last-minute hiccups and overseeing everything, she hadn't really been taking much notice.

She felt a moment of pique. Matthew was *her* fantasy. *Her* little flirtation. And Caroline had swiped him. She saw Matthew smiling down at her friend and felt ashamed of her childishness. How could she be so mean? It probably went back to the days of their youth when Devlin could have had any man she wanted and Caroline had never had a boyfriend. Now Caroline had turned the tables on her in the strangest way. It was going to take a little getting used to.

'Just what she needs,' Maggie said firmly, mistaking the reason for Devlin's frown. 'I've never seen her looking so well and so healthy. They go for a lot of walks together, she told me.'

'She never said anything to me.' Devlin was a tad put out to have missed out on this. 'But then I suppose we've been so up to our eyes every time I come to Galway we haven't really had a chance to have a heart-to-heart. I haven't been down as much in the last few weeks, because of my sciatic nerve. It's killing me.'

'You poor old thing. There's nothing worse than that pain.' Maggie patted her friend's bump.

'It won't be long now, another couple of weeks. I won't be sorry when it's all over.' Devlin sighed. 'I feel as if I've been pregnant for ever. I suppose I'd better go and put myself about and charm the pants off potential guests. He made a great job of the grounds, didn't he?' Devlin said, looking out at the vista of daffodils, heathers and snowdrops and crocuses that graced the garden.

'It's paradise.' Maggie sighed wistfully. She'd love to spend a week here.

'Yes it is,' Devlin agreed. 'Oh Lord.' She groaned. 'Here's that awful woman from that ghastly newspaper. I'd better go and be nice to her. I'm really looking forward to our dinner tonight.'

'Me too,' Maggie said. 'Dinner at Caroline's will be the perfect end to a perfect day. Is Luke staying over?'

Devlin laughed. 'He is not, he said he wouldn't dare sit in on our dinner tonight. Especially when we haven't been together for ages. If you don't mind I'll go home with you tomorrow.'

'Lovely, so it's just going to be the three of us. A good old girlie night. My favourite! Go be nice,' Maggie joked and didn't envy Devlin in the slightest as she went to greet the journalist.

She'd be talking to journalists too soon for her liking. *Betrayal* was scheduled for an autumn publication. She'd have to grit her teeth and do her interviews and then see them describe her novel in print as 'trashy', 'pulp fiction', 'bonkbuster', without even having read it. The joys of it all, she thought wryly, as she sipped her champagne and gazed out to sea. Still, her attic was converted. She had a room of her own. It had its compensations.

Outside, Caroline drew a deep breath of satisfaction as she looked at the façade of the beautiful building that housed the new health farm.

'It looks good, doesn't it?' She turned to Matthew.

'It's a fine building. Devlin should be proud. And you too.' He looked very handsome in his suit, such a change from his familiar jeans.

'Aren't you going in to hobnob with the rich and famous?' he asked.

'I know I should. It's much more peaceful out here.' Caroline smiled.

'I suppose you'll go home to Dublin now that it's all set up,' he said casually.

Caroline was silent for a moment, then she said quietly, 'I was thinking that I'd like to live here permanently. I was thinking of buying a place of my own actually. I really like Galway. I'm happy here.'

'Are you, now? That's good, Caroline. We'll get plenty of walks done, so.' Matthew smiled down at her.

Caroline smiled back. 'Plenty,' she agreed.

The candles were lit, the scenters fragranced the air. The smell of roast lamb and rosemary permeated the kitchen.

Devlin, Maggie and Caroline were in their towelling robes. The three of them had had a massage to

461

ease away the stresses and strains of the lunch do. It had been after six thirty when they left City Girl. Caroline had insisted they get changed.

'It's a relaxing girls' night. What could be more relaxing than sitting in our robes?' she declared, kicking off her high heels the minute she got in the door. The other two followed her example, needing no second urging.

'I'm having a glass of wine tonight, to celebrate.' Devlin patted her tummy. 'The first of my pregnancy. I don't think that's too bad.' She and Maggie were lounging on the sofa as Caroline put the finishing touches to the meal.

'It's fine. One glass won't do any harm,' Maggie assured her. 'And if anyone deserves to celebrate you do.'

'I think we all have something to celebrate,' Caroline said as she carried a tureen of steaming home-made potato soup to the table. 'I made this because I know it's your favourite,' she said to Devlin.

'That's my pal.' Devlin grinned as she sat down at the table. 'Are you celebrating something other than the birth of our latest venture?' She arched an eyebrow in Caroline's direction.

'Yes,' Caroline said firmly. 'I've made a decision about my life which I think is cause for celebration for me.'

'What?' Maggie and Devlin asked simultaneously.

'I'm staying here, in Galway. If that's OK with you?' she said as she ladled the soup into bowls.

'It's fine. But do you mean for good?' Devlin was a bit taken aback.

'I'm going to buy a place here. I love it. I'm very

happy here and I never thought I'd be saying that, almost five months ago.'

'Would this happiness have anything to do with a certain Matthew Moran?' Maggie asked slyly as she buttered some brown bread.

Caroline blushed.

'Did you see that, Devlin Delaney?' Maggie teased. 'Did you see that blush? That reddener?'

'I certainly did. What's going on here?'

'There's nothing going on,' Caroline laughed. 'He's a lovely man who came into my life at a time when I was on my knees. He helped me to pick myself up and dust myself off and get going again.' She sat down and began to eat her soup.

'And that's it,' Maggie said, puzzled.

'No. It's very special. I *knew* the minute I spoke to him on Christmas Eve. I felt as though I'd known him all my life. I feel very safe with him. I can talk to him for hours and he can talk to me. I never had that with Richard. I never had that with a man before. It's lovely. I know you'll laugh at this, Maggie, but Matthew has a beautiful soul. You can see it in his eyes. He's a very "good" person.'

'I know what you mean, Caro. Luke has that quality too. It's a sort of a strength that's very reassuring,' Devlin interjected.

'Yeah.'

'I wish I could meet someone with a beautiful soul.' Maggie sighed, feeling quite left out.

'You have three beautiful little souls in your care,' Devlin pointed out gently. 'But I know it's lonely. Someone's there for you, Maggie.'

'Can you feel it in your waters?' Maggie grinned.

'I can feel it in me waters,' Devlin confirmed.

'Have you started the next book?' Caroline asked Maggie.

'I have not. I'm taking a break. The well's run dry. It will have to fill up again. I'm doing all the things I missed doing. I've got a life again. I'm going swimming with the kids. I'm working out in City Girl. I'm meeting friends. I'm reading other people's books. I've got some balance back and I feel much better.'

'You look great,' Caroline approved. She hadn't seen Maggie since before Christmas. 'And your room's finished?'

'It certainly is. It's lovely, isn't it, Devlin?'

Devlin nodded. 'It's a real little haven away from everyone. When you do get back to writing again it will be perfect for you.'

'I don't know if I want to write there, actually. I want a place that's just for me, if you know what I mean.'

'I can understand that feeling. Maybe you're right, Maggie. Keep it for yourself,' Caroline agreed as she cleared away the dishes. 'What does Terry think of it?'

'I've never asked him up to see it. It's off limits to him. I think he's seeing someone. He comes home very late several nights a week.' Maggie popped an olive into her mouth.

'Oh!' Caroline placed the roast lamb on the table. 'And you don't mind?'

'I couldn't give a hoot,' Maggie said airily and they all laughed. 'Well, it keeps him out of my hair and that suits me,' Maggie said firmly. 'The kids are happy enough and that's all that matters. I'll never put my writing before them again. Time enough for that when they've upped sticks and left. Talking of upping sticks,' she changed the subject, 'how's the house coming along, Devlin?'

'It's fabulous. The new extension's almost ready. The whole place has been gutted, rewired, new heating, the works. We hope to be in by July.'

'That's a good time to be moving in. The baby will be nearly two months old,' Maggie remarked. 'He'll be fine and hardy.'

'Is it a boy?' Caroline asked eagerly. 'Did you ask?'

'No. Maggie just insists I'm carrying to the back and she maintains it's a boy.'

'We'll see.' Maggie forked some garlic potatoes into her mouth. 'This is delicious, Caroline. I'm really enjoying myself. Thank you.'

'Me too,' echoed Devlin.

'Any word of Mrs Yates?' Maggie asked.

'I told you she's out of the coma. She's paralysed down one side. And she's lost her speech. She's in a nursing home. I won't sell the business as long as she's alive. I don't need the money and it would only agitate her. I wouldn't do that to her with the state she's in.'

'A sad end to a pretty empty life,' Maggie reflected.

'Did you ever hear from the Al Shariffs?' Caroline passed the gravy boat around.

'Not a peep. I don't know if they're dead or alive or on the planet. I don't know if they ever got divorced. I know nothing, nor do I care to,' Maggie said cheerfully.

'Ciara Hanlon hasn't been caught yet,' Devlin said out of the blue.

'You never escape the Law of the Universe, or

Divine Justice if you care to call it that. Even though you might think you've got away with things,' Caroline said.

Maggie threw her eyes up to heaven. 'She's off,' she declared and they all laughed heartily, happy to be together catching up on all that was going on in their lives.

Forty-nine

Devlin walked around her new house with an air of great anticipation. Everything was coming along nicely. All the walls were plastered, the new windows were in. Her state-of-the-art pine kitchen was being installed today.

They'd decided on pine because it suited the character of the cottage. The utility room off the kitchen was tiled all over, ready for the washing-machine, tumble-dryer and chest freezer. Upstairs in the new extension the huge master bedroom and *en suite* were ready for decoration. Three other new bedrooms had also been built on. She was trying to decide which one she'd put the baby in when it was old enough to go into a room of its own.

'Mind yourself there now, Mrs,' one of the builders said anxiously as she stepped over a loose timber. They didn't like to see her coming, Devlin knew. Not because they were afraid that she would find fault with their work but because they were afraid that she'd have the baby any second. In the last two weeks she'd bloomed dramatically. The baby's head was engaged. She could go any time.

Devlin heartily wished that the whole ordeal was over. She wasn't particularly looking forward to the birth. She'd had a hard time with Lynn and now that she was so much older she worried constantly.

What if she gave birth to a handicapped child? How would she cope? Would she have the strength to deal with it? She'd confided these fears to Maggie, who'd assured her that every mother had the exact same fears. Her friend urged her to try and put them out of her head.

The baby kicked lustily. It was a very active baby and she was glad of that. It reassured her that for the time being, as far as she knew, all was well.

Luke, although he did his best to hide it, was apprehensive. She knew he was worried that he wouldn't do enough to help her on the day.

At her prenatal classes there'd been a big laugh from the expectant couples when the midwife had told the husbands under no circumstances were they to tell their wives or partners to push.

Devlin had made him promise not to look at her lower regions.

'Just look at my face, won't you, Luke. I don't want you to be turned off sex for life.'

She'd read an article that said that men who were at their baby's birth were much slower in responding sexually to their wives afterwards than those who were absent.

'I promise I'll just look at your face. Whatever you want me to do, Devlin, I'll do,' he assured her earnestly. He'd arrived home from London two days ago with a Winnie the Pooh wall chart, a set of Winnie the Pooh Babygros, and a gorgeous Winnie the Pooh teddy bear.

He couldn't go into town without buying

something for the baby, and eventually she had to put her foot down. His excitement was infectious and she was dying for the moment that he would hold their child.

'I'm off, Mr Fleming,' she called out to the foreman, and hid a grin at the look of relief that crossed his face.

'Take care now, Mrs Reilly. Maybe you should stay put now until the baby's born and you'll have a nice surprise then when the place is all ready for you,' he suggested delicately.

'Perhaps you're right,' she agreed. There was no point in aggravating the poor unfortunate. In future she'd keep her visits until the evening when they were gone, when she could look around in peace.

It was a warm day, one of those lovely early summery days that come in May, so she drove down to the harbour and went for a walk along Howth pier. It was nice to feel the breeze on her face. At least her sciatic nerve had calmed down once the baby had shifted position. All in all, apart from the awful weariness in the first three months, and the drama of washing her teeth, she'd had a very good pregnancy. But the pressure was intense now and she'd be glad when she had her figure back, she reflected as she watched a woman wheeling a toddler in a buggy.

She walked back along the top wall to enjoy the view of the sea. Midway, she felt a little tired so she sat down on one of the wooden seats in the shelter of the wall and viewed the peaceful scene in front of her. Seagulls circled and dived into the glassy waters, a ship on the horizon glided past. It was strange to be a lady of leisure, keeping in touch with the office through fax and phone.

She'd stopped going into work two weeks ago. It was important, her gynaecologist said, to rest and prepare physically and mentally for the birth. Devlin knew she was right.

The seat was a bit damp, she felt, so she shifted position, only to suddenly freeze in shock as a puddle of water formed at her feet.

'Oh God, what a place for it to happen,' she muttered, and then realized that it would have been a thousand times more mortifying if it had happened in front of all the builders. Slowly, she made her way back along the pier, wondering if people could see the big wet stain on her maternity dress.

A calmness descended on her. This was it. There was nothing she could do. She was not in control any more. The baby and her body would have their way.

She was so calm, or rather so reluctant to go to the hospital, she made herself a cup of tea when she got home. The contractions had started, but it would be hours before anything happened, she assured herself. After all, she was no novice. She'd given birth before.

She phoned Luke, who was on site in Ashbourne.

'I'm coming, I'm coming, I'm coming,' he said frantically.

'Lucky you,' Devlin teased.

'*Devlin!* This is no time for messing. You're having a baby,' he gabbled.

'Yes, dear,' she said soothingly.

'Just sit down and don't move,' he ordered. 'I'll be home in a minute.'

'Yes, pet,' Devlin murmured, as she rinsed her cup and saucer and wiped down the counter tops. A contraction caught her by surprise and she gave a little gasp.

'Are you all right? Are you all right?' Luke was roaring down the phone.

'Luke. Calm down. I'm fine. Now drive carefully. I don't want to be widowed, thank you very much.'

'Right, right. I'm on my way.'

He was ashen-faced when he got home. 'Now stay calm,' he urged. 'I'll get your case. Now where is it?'

'Right here beside me on the sofa, dear,' Devlin said calmly.

'Oh! Oh! I didn't see it.' He grabbed the handle. 'Come on, let's go.'

'Luke,' Devlin reached up and took his face in her hands. 'Please calm down. I'm fine. This is the moment we've been waiting for, let's enjoy it.'

'I'm just worried, that's all. I'd like to get you to the hospital.' He took a deep breath. 'I'm calm.'

'Good,' she said.

Five hours later the contractions were coming hot and heavy. Devlin groaned as the pain engulfed her and gripped Luke's hand. 'Did I say let's enjoy it,' she panted. 'I was talking through my hat.'

'You're doing fine,' he soothed. She looked up into his loving eyes and thought how different it all was this time. How wonderful it was to have his love and support. Lynn's birth had been such a sad, painful, lonely one.

'I love you, Luke,' she whispered.

'Still?' he whispered back as another contraction

hit hard. They were much quicker than they'd been with Lynn and much stronger, nevertheless she was shocked when her midwife said cheerfully, 'Devlin, you're nine centimetres dilated. You're ready to deliver. Just push now when I tell you. Your gynae is on the way.'

'So soon,' Devlin panted.

'Well, it is your second. It can happen like that, lucky girl, it will be all over soon.'

The birth itself was a blur, so intense was the pain. Even Luke seemed to fade from her as all her energies were concentrated on this last final effort. It was just her and the baby and her body doing what it had been preparing for, for the last nine months.

'It's a boy, Devlin. It's a boy.' Luke was beside himself with excitement as he squeezed her hand so hard she thought he was going to crush it.

'Is he all right? Is he all right?' Devlin asked as her baby slithered out of her after one last push.

'He's fine, he's fine. He's got five fingers and five toes and a head.' Luke was babbling.

'He's grand, Devlin, everything's perfect.' The midwife laughed as Devlin heard a lusty roar, and her son was placed in her arms minutes later.

Her heart felt as if it would burst as she looked down at the tiny face and felt the tiny hand grasp her little finger. He had a head of jet-black hair and a doty little nose and a perfect mouth.

'Oh Luke,' she whispered. 'Oh Luke, here, hold your son!'

Reverently Luke took the minute bundle and then Devlin did cry, so moved was she at the sight of her big strong husband cradling his firstborn with tears streaming down his face.

It was the most perfect moment of her life. It was incomparable.

Later, back in her room, they held each other tightly. In his small crib, their son slept peacefully.

'This is almost the best day of my life,' Luke said.

'Why, what was the best?' Devlin was surprised.

'Don't you know? The best day of my life was the day you told me you loved me for the first time.' Luke kissed the tip of her nose.

'Oh, Luke.' Devlin could hardly speak.

'Don't start crying again,' he warned.

'I won't.' She gulped.

But she did cry again when Caroline and Maggie arrived the following day, Caroline having driven over from Galway specially to see her.

'Oh girls! Oh girls!' Devlin blubbered.

'He's beautiful.' Maggie bawled. 'And I was right. It was a boy,' she added smugly, despite her tears.

'Oh Devlin, he's a dote,' Caroline sniffled.

'Oh my God!' exclaimed Luke in mock horror as he walked through the door right at that moment and saw the three weeping women.

'Three of them at it. I can't hack this. I surrender.' They laughed.

'Six hours in labour, you lucky wagon,' Maggie said enviously. 'I was ten with Shona.'

'It felt like ten. It was tough at the end.' Devlin grinned, relieved beyond measure that the whole ordeal was over. She was still on a high.

'Luke, take a photo of the three of us, will you?' she asked her proud, beaming husband.

It was a perfect photograph. Devlin held her baby with Caroline on one side of the bed and Maggie on the other, with their arms around her and melon-slice grins on all their faces.

It was the best of times.

THE END

Patricia Scanlan

A Time for Friends

When are the boundaries of friendship pushed too far,
and when is it time to stop flying over oceans for
someone who wouldn't jump over a puddle for you?
There comes a time when Hilary Hammond
has to make that call.

Hilary and Colette O'Mahony have been friends since
childhood, but when irrepressible Jonathan Harpur
breezes into Hilary's life and goes into business
with her, Colette is not best pleased.

After their first encounter Colette thinks he's a
'pushy upstart' while he thinks she's 'a snobby
little diva'. And so the battle lines are drawn
and Hilary is bang in the middle.

But as the years roll by and each of them is faced
with difficult times and tough decisions, one thing
is clear . . . to have a friend you must be a friend.

And that's when Hilary discovers that sometimes
your best friend can be your greatest enemy . . .

Patricia Scanlan
With All My Love

On a crystal clear Mediterranean day, Briony McAllister
sits playing with her four-year-old daughter, Katie,
while she waits for her mother, Valerie, to join them.
Valerie has recently moved to a picturesque town in
southern Spain to finally leave behind her turbulent past
and find a peace that has always eluded her. Briony has
no idea that in a few moments' time her relationship
with her mother will change irrevocably.

As Katie plays, Briony pulls from her bag an old
photo album, found in a box in her mother's
new home. As she begins to study the faded photos,
a letter falls to the ground. It is addressed to her.

My Darling Briony, it begins. As Briony reads the
words with mounting shock, realisation dawns. Her
mother lied to her about what happened with her
beloved grandmother Tessa all those years ago – and
denied Briony that most precious of relationships, the
type of relationship Valerie now enjoys with Katie.

The lives of three generations of women are set to
change forever as the past is revisited and the truth
unfolds through the undelivered letters Tessa wrote to
Briony over the years. Secrets, lies, betrayals and
sacrifices – the complex bonds between mothers,
daughters and granddaughters are intricately
explored as Patricia Scanlan takes us into
the hearts and homes of a family at war.